T0278681

By TESSA HATFIELD

Say It Again

Published by DREAMSPINNER PRESS
www.dreamspinnerpress.com

Say It Again

TESSA HATFIELD

Published by

DREAMSPINNER PRESS

8219 Woodville Hwy #1245
Woodville, FL 32362 USA
www.dreamspinnerpress.com

Say It Again
© 2024 Tessa Hatfield

Cover Art
© 2024 L.C. Chase
http://www.lcchase.com

Trade Paperback ISBN: 978-1-64108-726-1
Digital ISBN: 978-1-64108-725-4
Trade Paperback published August 2024
v. 1.0

For my lava rock.

Author's Note

When a dear friend asked me to stand by her side as she filed a restraining order against a man, I said yes. I awoke early, I walked through metal detectors, I helped carry a ream of papers into a packed courtroom where we were told to take a seat and get comfortable, as we were the last people to testify. I expected us to win that day, and we did. What I didn't expect was for this book to be born.

To the two men who stood with your chins lifted to tell a courtroom of strangers your painfully relatable story, I may never know your names, but I want you to know I laughed with you that day. When your story turned intense and difficult to tell, I held my breath with you. And when you shared the deepest parts of yourself, holding nothing back while a roomful of people speculated, I want you to know I cried with you that day too. This may not be your story—your story is yours and yours alone—but you are the essence. Someone was bound to come along and capture your beauty, your spirit, and your heart, so I went home that day and started writing.

I've always found myself drawn to fiction grounded in imperfect human experience. The stuff that gives us a reason to laugh. To cry. To stay up late holding our breath, hoping for a happily-ever-after.

Acknowledgments

When I told my husband, Chad Hatfield, that I wanted to write this book, he didn't say, "You don't know how to write a book," or "But who would want to read that?" What he did say in that honest, salt-of-the-earth way of his, was "Do it."

You let me dive all in, running on negative sleep, doughnut fumes, and borrowed time from sweetly napping redheaded babies. What a tremendous pillar of faith you are. There's no one else with whom I'd rather weather this journey. Or that journey. Or even that one where we eventually take a vacation again. I lava lava you now and always.

To my agent, Madison Scalera: Girl, what a constant delight you are to work with. There's not a single interaction with you that hasn't left me feeling wildly uplifted, beautifully supported, and confident that Daniel, Aaron, and all future characters are in the most capable hands possible. From the bottom of my little Midwestern heart, I thank you warmly for taking a chance on me.

Speaking of beautifully supporting debut authors, to my brilliant editor, Brenda Chin, you are precisely that: brilliant. It's more than talent that you possess. It's vision, and you're so good at what you do that you make me look good too. I'll continue to osmosis your genius as long as you have me.

Ebony Granger. Where do I start? Would this book be what it is without you? No. Would it have even been written? It's difficult to say, as I can't imagine a world in which I'm not writing and you're not right by my side, telling me to keep writing. I adore you. Thank you for being the world's most comforting friend and possibly the greatest believer this story had. (P.S. I'm sorry Aaron's hair isn't longer.)

Similarly, Nicki LaFoille & Sue Tejada, my lovely critique partners in crime, take yourselves to the bank as you are literal gold, and profoundly invaluable.

I would like to extend an extra special thank-you to the incredible team at Dreamspinner. To my Editor in Chief, Ginnifer Eastwick, you have a way with not only words but, as it seems, a way with just about anything you touch. L.C. Chase, you have a way of taking a humdrum suggestion and making it dazzle. To anyone else who worked their tails off on this manuscript, thank you, thank you, thank you. And I'm sorry about the commas.

Chapter One

THE DANCE floor at the St. Louis School of Dance didn't care if Daniel Greene didn't have his life together. It didn't pass judgment if he showed up late to teach class, dressed in another guy's clothes from the night before, smelling of self-loathing and just a hint of wine slushy. Very *Eau de Walk of Shame.*

These old hardwoods beneath his feet didn't care, because they were his home. No, they were homier than home. They were the homiest. And not even because his actual home was also littered with dust and hair, with the occasional fascinated onlooker peering in through the front window. (Well, but in all fairness, Marvin wasn't an onlooker so much as he was the landlord, and a generally clingy man. It was the whole *Where's the rent?* business. Like, every. Single. Month.)

Twenty long years he'd been dancing, which meant twenty long years he'd been in love. Now, at twenty-five, it was the only thing that kept his quivering Jell-O mold of a nervous system quelled, and it worked just like a miracle tonic for all life's pesky lemons.

Except for when it didn't. Like right now.

Olivia, his best friend, fellow dance instructor, and the peskiest lemon of all, whined as she mooched all up in his space. She mooched so hard that he couldn't crest a delicate arm up to the ceiling all gracefully or properly pirouette without whacking her. "Daniel, you can't say no. You *can't.*"

"I can't? Let me try." The hardwoods creaked as he corkscrewed in a spin to the floor, where he sat with his toes pointed and torso folded in half, snug against his thighs. He smiled, eyes serenely closed. "No."

"You're not thinking about the consequences." Olivia plopped to the floor beside him. "If you don't help me tonight, I'll be forced to tell the rich people they won't have a bartender for their rich party. Do you want that on your conscience? A bunch of sober rich people? They'll bore each other to death talking about cryptocurrency."

Olivia's side "business" of bartending and serving private parties was the definition of amateur. Other than harassing the dance studio's instructors, she hadn't gone to any lengths to hire employees for her LLC, After the Pumpkin. An homage to *Cinderella*, it was supposed to mean something like "after midnight." But all it did was spawn a lot of confusion that ended with Daniel cornered and answering questions like *After what pumpkin?* And *What happens after it?*

It was too late to change it now. The promotional stress balls had been ordered. Why had she designed them to resemble a clock set to a random two thirty instead of, say, pumpkins? Because Olivia was a mess.

"Do you remember what happened last time I helped you?" he asked with a stern eyebrow raised. "What happened to my *dignity*?"

"Oh my God, you have to let that go. It was an honest mistake!"

"My life has never been the same."

"People confuse other people with their Louisianan aunt from the back all the time. You have to admit you have a delicate frame, and you *were* wearing a sun hat. Plus, that guy was really high."

"My life," he said, toying with his necklace as he gazed into the distance, "has never been the same."

"Look at me, Daniel." She leaned forward. "*See* me."

He couldn't help but smirk as he scanned her face. The havoc of it all—the outline of yesterday's winged eyeliner; a gemstone nose ring that had lost the gemstone; black, chin-length hair that looked as if it'd been chopped with those tiny construction paper scissors (because it had been). She was indisputably lovable.

"I know you could use the money," she said, gently tapping his chest. "Because you have none."

His smile died. Her lovableness was suddenly up for dispute.

"You're too cute to be so broke. We both are."

He groaned as he scrubbed a hand over his face. It wasn't like he could deny how broke he was. Or how cute.

He hailed from humble-ish beginnings, far from able to use "summer" as a verb. It turned out his dad was right, and he couldn't make any money as a dance instructor, but he was willing to admit he cared about making money like he was willing to "summer" on the surface of the sun. "We are really broke."

"*Really* broke."

"And so cute."

"*So* fucking cute."

"You don't have anyone else?" He bounced a little. "I thought you finally hired someone. Audrey Something-or-Another?"

"Audrey? You want me to bring that aggressive ostrich to a party? *Indoors*?"

"Why'd you hire her if she's that bad?"

"I didn't know she'd be shattering a plate every four minutes. You know who's never dropped a plate both times he's helped me?" She smiled, all lopsided, as she pointed a finger. "This guy."

Well, had he known that was all it took….

"But that's not all. There's so much that makes you special, Daniel. Starting with your perfect skin."

He rolled his eyes so hard he could swear colors looked different. "You can't just compliment my skin every time you want me to do something—"

"Not only is it sheeny, but it's like it's aglow from within. Must be your smoldering lust for life."

Not that he was falling for it—how silly—but he did risk a glance in the mirror, and okay, perhaps, yes. He did look a bit more *bedewed* than usual.

"Wow." She glided her fingertips down his cheek. "An English meadow on a spring morning. What a waste for you to be holed up inside your house tonight, in the bored arms of your disinterested boyfriend—"

"He's not *that* bad."

"—when you could be out. Spreading your radiance. Your incandescence."

He scrunched his face at the thought of being hauled up in his house. Not that his boyfriend was disinterested. He just wasn't, well, interested. He was more of a safety net than a boyfriend, anyway. Good old safety net Nate. A Safety Nate.

Awkwardly, they'd been sleeping together long enough that it sort of enfranchised into its own relationship. Nate, who didn't really like to go out on dates. Nate, who didn't really see Daniel's potential, but in Safety Nate's defense, it was difficult to hear another person's hopes and dreams over the harrowing screams of one's video game victims.

Was now the time to revel in the joys of dating Safety Nate? Not when he had a favor to try to avoid doing. "But I wouldn't have time to go home and change."

"What's wrong with what you're wearing?"

"*This*? I can't wear this. Look at me, Olivia." He spread his arms and peered down at his outfit, which was a lot of slinky black atop slinkier black. "I am the personification of liquid eyeliner."

She studied his clothing, tipping her head side to side. "Yeah, shoot."

He widened his eyes. "Well, you're clearly not supposed to agree with me! God, you think I look like the personification of liquid fucking eyeliner?"

"Oh, um." She sputtered to recover, shoving a lock of hair behind her ear. "Well, not in a bad way! Hey, it's better than what you wore yesterday? Nude-colored anything just doesn't flatter your complexion."

It'd be impossible for his eyes to get any wider. "So now you think I'm too pale for the pursuit of happiness?"

"*What*? I do not think—! Okay. You have to come tonight, so I'm willing to beg." She threaded her fingers beneath her chin and squeezed them in a tight prayer. "Please, Daniel? Please, best friend of mine? This is me begging."

He grumbled as he splatted onto his back like a pale, broke starfish.

"Pretty please?" Her voice had gotten obscenely high, just like her smile had gotten obscenely hopeful.

He huffed out a sigh. "Dammit."

Chapter Two

DAMMIT. LATER that evening, Daniel followed Olivia up the walkway of an excessive home in the posh but downright arrogant Central West End of St. Louis.

"Well, hello." A shirtless guy with dark statement eyebrows and lavender hair spilled his martini as he answered the door. He shrugged a beach towel over his shoulders and frowned. "Yikes. You guys know it's a pool party, right? You're a little formal."

"We're with After the Pumpkin," Olivia proudly announced. "Eric hired us."

"The what?" The guy cocked his head. "What pumpkin? What happens after it?"

Olivia's eye twitched, but she continued, "Yeah, is Eric here?"

"He's floating around somewhere...." The guy trailed off as his gaze snagged on Daniel's lips. Then torso. Then crotch. "Ooh, he's gonna love you."

Daniel sucked his lower lip, darting his eyes to the side. "Okay?"

"Eric!" the guy squawked. "Your staff is here."

After a loud whump from inside, a drunken cruise ship captain, or presumably Eric, circled the corner and tossed an arm around the other guy. "My whaaa—? Ahh!" His laughter jiggled his body. "I forgot I hired you guys."

"I'm sorry we're a little late," Olivia said. "Hopefully, you still need us?"

"Well, yeah. It's still a party, baby," Eric said with a wink, a shimmy, and a bawdy Mae West inflection that stopped existing after the 1920s. "The more the merrier. Go find the caterers. They'll tell you what they need."

Daniel started to follow Olivia into the kitchen, but Eric snagged him by the elbow and asked under his breath, "Hey, what's your deal?"

He studied the man's tan-in-a-bottle face. "My deal?"

"Yeah, name your price."

Daniel opened his mouth and closed it again as his eyes narrowed to a squint. Had they accidentally wandered onto a spy movie set? "Come again?"

"Your price, boy." Eric worked his hands in agitation like Daniel's answer should've progressed by now. "What is it? How much to take your shirt off and go stand over there with the others?"

He scanned the living room for the shirtless *others* to no avail. "I'm sorry, but the other what?"

"Eric!" someone yelled.

"Coming, my sweet." Eric whirled toward the stairs and pointed a finger back at him. "Think about it. Come find me later. I'll be in the sauna. Not the steam—the infrared."

That storm of confusion fizzled just as quickly as it brewed when Olivia grabbed his hand and yanked him to her side. She giggled and pointed to a recessed living room off the kitchen. "Look."

Above the fireplace hung a portrait of Eric and Lavender Hair Boy. Naked. Fearless. Surrounded by puggles.

A grin twitched his lips. "The dream, though."

She sighed wistfully and rested her head on his shoulder. "The dream."

The party consisted mostly of older men, all puff-bellied, white-bearded, and oily-skinned. They slipped in and out of the pool like seals, only bobbing up to cackle or take a sip of something spritzy from a cocktail glass.

Daniel strolled around, filling waters, gathering empty champagne flutes, doing his best to avoid eye contact so no one would ask him questions he didn't have the answers to. Questions like *Where's the bathroom?* or *Do those meatballs contain pork?* or *What are you doing? Do you know what you're doing, Daniel?*

He did not know what he was doing, as all he'd ever done was dance, then study about dance, then dance some more, but at least he didn't shatter any of the plates that a mother-daughter team of caterers kept stocked with canapés or toothpick-speared meatballs no one ate. (Because they contained pork? Because they didn't?)

"Daniel," Olivia hissed from where she stood behind the bar outside, surrounded by blinking sugar-skull string lights. Her eyes were all wide and insisting as she beckoned him over.

"Yes, ma'am, how can I help you?" He brushed off his apron and checked his pants for grime. "You want a mysterious meatball? Maybe pork? Maybe not? Hey, this party is weird, by the way. Everyone's either twenty or literally mummified—there is no in-between—and I just saw an adult man doing a whip-it. Like, when does the Grateful Dead start playing?"

"I need you to cover for me." Olivia clutched her phone to her chest. "It's Puddles."

"Olivia." Daniel fortified himself with a breath, then firmed his glare. "Let the cat die."

Her mouth fell open as her shocked voice barely escaped. "*Whaaa*? I can't believe you would say that. It's not his time."

"It is his time. That's why the kitty doctor said it was his time."

"Wow, Daniel." She squinted, nodding. "No, *mewow*. Glad to know you and the *kitty doctor* are both cold-hearted thugs—"

"The cat has a brain tumor, and that's like the least of its worries. He's miserable, he wants to go, and you artificially keep him alive with your *medication*."

"Why do you say *medication* like allegedly that's what it is? That's what it is! And he won't let my roommate give it to him, so I have to go."

"No!" A meatball rolled from his tray as he grabbed her arm. "Dude, you can't leave me here."

"I'll be back in half an hour, tops. You'll be fine. But you need to work the bar. That's more important than"—she waved a hand around his person—"whatever you're doing."

He blinked hard. "Oh, now it's 'whatever I'm doing'? When earlier, it was imperative that I come and be incandescent for all."

"You're practically ablaze, you're so glowy. Now, come stand back here." She shuffled him behind the bar by his shoulders. "That's all you have to do."

Panic started to bloom as his eyes darted around the bar for anything that looked recognizable. "But. But I don't know how to make drinks. What if someone asks for a mojito? Aren't there things to be muddled? I don't know how to muddle."

"No one's asking for a mojito," she scoffed. "Well, they might. You should learn how to make those. Sounds refreshing."

"Please don't go—"

"Daniel." Olivia gasped and pointed a shaky finger past his shoulder. "Look."

He flinched but squashed the urge to spin around, because they had *not* wandered onto the set of a spy movie, and there was nothing exciting to see behind him. "You know that doesn't actually work in real life."

But her eyes stayed wide as she continued to gape. "I cannot believe—what is she doing here? She's, like, really famous."

"I'm not turning around so you can ditch me."

"This is insane." Olivia started toward what was surely not anyone famous. "Let's go get her autograph."

Daniel finally whipped around as Olivia's footsteps vanished in the opposite direction. With a sigh at himself and a grimace at her back as she fled, he knelt on the ground to orient himself with the items of the bar.

"Oh, you're so dewy, Daniel," he muttered as he angrily sorted bottles of gin. "You're just aglow. A smoldering lust for life. Come out and spread your radiance. Well, here we are. Not one person has complimented my fucking dewiness!"

"Are we supposed to be complimenting your dewiness?" asked a voice from above. "I'm sorry. I didn't get the memo."

Daniel's anger transformed to shock when he laid eyes on the creature from which that voice hailed. The creature who stood tall like a lighthouse among a sea of mummies with his icy blue irises and dark chocolate hair and ever just a touch of amber honey to his skin.

Daniel straightened in slow motion. Or he *rose*, rather, as if by tractor beam, with his eyes rounded and dick awakened, to gawk at the guy. The guy who was probably used to that sort of thing—people gawking. Paparazzi following him to the important places he went to speak to the important people about what stock did whatever it was that stocks did.

"Sorry, I didn't mean to interrupt. Did you need to finish your conversation?" The elegant stranger combed a hand through his hair, lifting his shirt just enough to display Herculean stomach muscles. "With yourself?"

"Hmm?" Daniel salivated like a St. Bernard, struggling to peel his eyes from his belly. "No, I can help you with your desires." *No! Gawd.* He shook his head. "With your beverage desires, that is. Err, *needs*. Err, order!" Even his organs cringed. "How can I help you?"

The guy's lips curled in amusement. "Well, I could really use a drink if you catch my drift."

"Ahh." He struggled to unglue his gaze from the guy's mouth. "Rough night, huh?"

"A little," said the Adonis. The incisors of his pretty smile bit down on his lower lip in a way that could make a boy suddenly wish he were a tooth. "But I'm not one to complain about things getting rough."

Daniel had a mini stroke, but he made a full recovery. He should really respond to all of these comments like an adult instead of a horny teenaged Neanderthal. "Well, you're in luck, because this is a bar." Then, a little less convincing: "And I am a bartender."

"I can see that." He leaned on his elbow and propped his chin in his hand. "So then, how about you make me anything you please. Bartender."

Pleazzz. The way he said it had to have been intentional. It melted into the space between them, all blood-warm and buttery. It hardly registered that Daniel had also leaned over the bar, but in his defense, beverage options were less important than sudden uncharted fantasies about what it might be like to touch this tall, dark, and foxy person's large hand. Or muscular shoulder. Or the toned chest that peeked from under his deep-V-cut shirt.

Did the Adonis probably think this staring contest was a bit much? Daniel smiled like a rum-drunk idiot. Did it matter?

He inched his hand across the bar a little. He let his pinky wander closer. It wasn't like him to be so emboldened, but he did it. He touched him.

The guy broke their eye contact to glance down at their mingling pinkies.

Then reality slammed into Daniel hard enough to shock his spine straight. "Apologies for that!" he said way too loudly, causing a few heads to whirl around. God, he was sweating. "Allow me to get right on that drink."

Hands on his hips, he spun on his heels to face the opposite direction. It was too bad he didn't think that plan through, because now he was faced with an empty wall and, against it, a single potted pygmy palm.

Instead of doing anything else—like making a drink, any drink— he doubled down and studied the plant like it was something remarkable and not a fucking plant. *Get it together. Get. It. Together. Are you really losing your whole-ass sanity right now?*

"Are you okay?"

"I am." Daniel spun back around without looking at the guy. He could be charming. He could. Give him a damn minute.

He took a breath and surveyed the items of the bar. Neon red cherries, something called sloe gin, and a ceramic dish of either salt, sugar, or cocaine—who could be sure?—all sat around, being intimidating.

"Okay." He nodded and held up a bottle of vodka. "I have *theee* drink for you. See this? Well, my specialty happens to be pouring it into a vessel. Like so." Warm vodka glugged into a plastic cup. "Then, this? I pour it on top." Warm sour mix slopped over the sides.

The Adonis pursed his lips. "That's your *specialty*?"

"Correct."

"What do you call it?"

"Don't ask questions."

"Oh, sorry."

"No, that's the name of the drink—" He dared a dishy smile. "—but apology accepted."

The guy laughed, looking a whole lot like a matador who could tame a bull with a wink, and Daniel's ego moonwalked across the stage.

"Now, do you want me to add the secret ingredient?" He arched an eyebrow, invigorated. "Or are you not feeling that adventurous?"

The matador's icy eyes sparkled with his smile. Now they were getting somewhere. "Can't wait to see this."

Daniel dropped in a cherry. It flumped to the bottom.

"Innovative."

"Hugely." He then sprinkled in a dash of sugar. Or cocaine.

"Mm-hmm."

"Oh, and one more thing. Can't forget this—"

"Yeah, I wonder if we shouldn't stop there?"

Daniel pulled a bucket from the freezer and splashed in two ice cubes with an awkward pair of mini tongs he couldn't quite grasp. He slid the drink across the bar with a wink. "Gives it a little extra something between you and me. Enjoy."

The guy gazed at him, then down at the cocktail. It started sweating too. "So, is bartending your life's passion?"

"Isn't it obvious?"

"I'm Aaron." He extended his hand. "What's your name, handsome?"

Handsome. Daniel bit his lip and took his hand, but before he could answer, "I'm Daniel, and I'm really adventurous in bed," the bottom fell out of the moment when an older guy with ultraplatinum hair squeezed Aaron in a hug from behind.

SAY IT AGAIN 11

Aaron jerked his hand away from Daniel's touch.

"There you are," the guy said in a British accent that sounded like it just crawled out of the River Thames, still sopping wet and covered in muck. He nuzzled into Aaron's neck. "I've been looking for you."

Dressed in black satin capris and loafers with oversized gold emblems, the guy looked like the runner-up in a contest of *Who Can Look the Richest?* The most obnoxious piece of his outfit (a metallic yellow jacket as bright as the surface of the sun and just as painful to stare at) snugged his lanky frame, twisting and swathing, studded with too many buttons to count.

With his fantasy tugged from under him, Daniel had to stifle a scowl at the guy. And the urge to chuck a meatball at his face.

"Come," he said, taking Aaron's hand. "There's someone *dying* to meet you."

That jacket. Daniel needed somewhere to direct his totally justified hatred. *So... yellow.*

"I'll be right there." Aaron wiggled his hand free from Yellow Jacket's. "Give me a second."

"We don't have a second." The guy took his arm. "People are waiting—"

"We do. We do have a second." Aaron peeled him off and flashed his gaze to Daniel. "I just want to enjoy this drink. It was made with such flair."

Daniel's heart did a little squiggle.

"I don't give a shit if it was made with holy water. It's not your job to stand here drinking it. Come *on.*"

Aaron's eyes sharpened on the other guy's. He suddenly looked a touch threatening as he stood taller, peering down at him.

"Um. Apologies, kitten." Yellow Jacket's smile had quickly turned contrite. "People are excited to see you, is all. Can you blame them?"

Daniel could. Daniel could totally blame them all day and night.

"I, for one, *still* get excited to see you." Yellow Jacket closed his eyes and puckered his lips toward Aaron, a cartoon princess waiting for a smooch.

Aaron looked to Daniel. Daniel looked to Aaron. He didn't know what he was expecting, but it wasn't what happened next.

Without breaking their eye contact and wearing a sexy, *sexy* half-grin, Aaron leaned in and pressed his lips to the other man's.

Daniel couldn't help but stare while his scalp, suddenly impossibly hot, started to itch. But watching two people kiss was creepy, so he skirted his gaze to the ground. He chanced a peek after a few moments, when any normal kiss would've stopped being a thing, to find Aaron was still staring. And still kissing.

"Uhh," he said to the ground, smiling politely. "If you'll excuse me? I'll just—I'll be right back." He slid off his apron and scanned the patio for signs of authority that would probably prefer he didn't take a break. When no one looked in-charge enough, he rushed inside, around a corner, and into the chest of a topless dude with a bowl of popcorn.

"*Gugh*," the guy shrieked as it clanged to the floor. "Hey, watch where you're going!"

"Oh no." Daniel dropped to his hands and knees and scrambled to gather the pieces, but they'd scattered everywhere. "I am so sorry."

The guy bounced a little like he was trying to refrain from yelling.

"I can make you some more," he offered. "Just, er—if you show me where it is."

"We worked on this, Stevie," Stevie said to himself in a meditative voice as he exhaled, long and slow. "You're not angry. You're just hungry."

Yikes. Daniel crawled to retrieve kernels from under a table. "I really am sorry."

"Okay, my bad." Stevie lowered to the floor. "I didn't mean to yell or whatever. I'm ravenous I'm so hungry. Do you have any gum?"

"What's that? Gum?" Daniel tapped his pockets. "No, but I saw some mints over there on the counter."

"I can't have mints. I'm fasting."

"Ahh, I do that too. Not on purpose." Daniel collected the last of the popcorn. "I'm just poor."

The guy nodded, but his attention had been captivated by his phone. His thumbs tapped at warp speed over the screen. "That must suck."

"It really does. So hey, can I ask you a question? See that guy over there?" He tried to nonchalantly point to Aaron with his entire hand, which looked like a strange dance move. "What's his deal?"

Stevie didn't look up. "Which one?"

"The one that looks like the statue of David. But Greekier."

He squinted at the group of men surrounding Aaron. "Who?"

"Right *there*." He tried to point with his head, which ended up looking like an even sillier dance move. "The foxy one in the blue V-neck."

Back to the phone. "If he's wearing a shirt, he's an attorney and an asshole."

Daniel frowned as he gazed at Aaron. "Really?"

"Yes. They're all attorneys." The guy inspected his hair with his phone's camera. "And they're all assholes."

"He seemed nice."

"Yeah, I'm sure. That's why I'm about to serve them floor popcorn." He stood and dusted himself off. "Because they're *nice*."

He strolled off, and Daniel tried to send Aaron a telepathic message not to eat the floor popcorn, but he didn't get it. He was too busy shaking hands, flashing teeth, and forgetting about their encounter altogether.

Daniel rolled his head to the side and hummed to himself as one sad little snort escaped from some sad little place from within. Oh to be so entranced by a stranger with a boyfriend. And who did he have to thank for the overactive imagination for thinking someone who looked like that guy would ever be interested in him?

Down the hallway he found the bathroom, where he locked himself inside and met his own big caramel-colored eyes in the mirror. *Someone like him can have whoever he wants.* He dropped his chin to his chest. He was no matador.

AARON TONGUED the corner of his mouth and pressed up to his toes to see where the little guy went. Precious. Extraordinarily precious with the dusky brown curls and the pouty crimson lips that looked like he'd spent the past couple of hours sucking on hard candy.

He was a nervy little thing. Nervy in tongue and yet fluid in movement with those delicate fingers and quicksilver curtseys and shoulder squirms. It sure seemed like he could use some *soothing*. Someone to shush him sweetly with a few whispered exchanges.

It sure seemed like he could use someone to take the lead.

He'd never seen him at one of these parties, which could mean nothing, or it could mean a lot. Maybe he was new to the scene? Maybe he was just a guy trying to make money. Like everyone else.

"Who are you going home with?" Stevie suddenly stood by his side, fake-smiling at the group of men before them. "Tweedle-dee over there looks fun. Oh, but then how could I resist Tweedle-fucking-dum?"

"I came here with Corey," Aaron said, reaching for a handful of popcorn. "I should probably leave with him—"

"No." Stevie smacked his hand away. "Trust me."

Aaron swiped his palms together and scanned the crowd for the little bartender. "Hey, you see where the sexy guy went? Did he leave?"

Stevie grimaced as he extracted a long hair from the popcorn. "There are no sexy guys here."

"No, not one of them."

"Oh, one of us?" Stevie squinted. "There are no new *us* that I know of."

"I don't think he's one of us either. About yea tall." He flattened a palm next to Stevie's ear. "Skinny. Super funny in a clever way, and he's got this…." He trailed off as he gestured vaguely over Stevie's face. "Mouth."

"Oh, the clumsy guy? Like, *real* skinny?" Stevie tipped his chin toward the house. "Check inside. Be mindful as you take corners."

Yeah, it was just about getting inside, which was easier said than done. Aaron smiled graciously as he began his descent into the lion's den, skirting a few tugs on his arms and the beginnings of "conversations." Mostly *Where do you think you're going, young man? And Leaving so soon? No, you don't. Come here. Come here, come here, come here. There's someone* dying to meet you.

Free at last, he snuck inside and checked the sunken living room with the incredible curved sheepskin sectional he would someday own, then checked the kitchen with the extrawide champagne-colored refrigerator he would also be sure to own. Once he had enough money. He swung around a corner and—

"Where do you think you're going?" Corey asked in his royal-pain-in-the-ass British accent, always manifesting at the worst possible time. "You're leaving with me, yes? You ready?"

"I am." He managed a patient smile. "I can't wait. Two minutes to hit the bathroom, and I'll meet you at your car."

Corey's lips curled sheepishly. "My apologies about earlier, love. For losing my patience. Can you forgive me?"

"Absolutely. No worries." He gently squeezed his arm as he stepped past him. "Excuse me—"

"Wrong direction. I believe your bartender is in the bathroom down that hall."

Aaron whirled around, then halted. He preferred to keep the borders of his worlds way more defined. Clients stayed in one world. Cute bartenders stayed in another. But he'd known Corey for years, so for the sake of courtesy, he scrunched his face and smiled as he dropped his head. "That obvious?"

Corey looked a hint sentimental as he melted into a sigh. "Christ, you are so beautiful. What it must be like to be twentysomething and catching your eye. I dread the day someone catches it for good."

Aaron swallowed and forced his smile wider. "I'm all yours tonight."

"Mm-hmm, I'll give you five minutes with him, and the clock is ticking, so better hurry." Corey winked back on his stroll toward the door. "Then you are *all* mine."

"YOU ARE an ass cork," Daniel whispered to himself as he furiously prodded at his curls in the bathroom mirror. "Even if Aaron was interested—which he's not—where's it gonna go? You have a boyfriend. Ass cork."

He rolled his sleeves and picked lint off his pants in a huff. His mom, that earth angel, had always said in her charming Midwestern way that wearing black made him look *terribly underfed, sweetie. Are you sure you're eating?* But in black's defense, everything made him look terribly underfed. Everything also made him look too pale. He had that bright-light-at-the-end-of-a-tunnel kind of skin tone that didn't work with a lot of outfit color choices.

"So I'm near-death pale. *Does it look like I care?*" he asked in an aggressive, mock-British accent. "Yellow Jacket—ha! At least I'm not an asshole. Well." He cut his eyes to the side. "At least I'm not *always* an asshole. God, what's he doing with that guy? He could do so much better. Like me. Me who is not *always* an asshole—"

"Can I come in?" a voice asked from outside the door.

Daniel froze.

"I just need a second of your time."

He recognized that voice. It was Aaron's.

"I wanted to ask you something," Aaron continued. "Can you let me in, please?"

Daniel stood motionless, stuck in a game of Simon Says where a sadistic Simon had told him to freeze and not let the fetching matador into the bathroom.

"*Pleazzz?*" There it was again—a soft, sensual, coaxing way of saying that word that cradled around his earlobe like a warm little hug.

Daniel defrosted, checked his hair once more, and opened the door.

Aaron peeked around the hallway, then stepped inside. His lips curled into a smirk as he leaned back against the door. "Hi."

Dear heavens alive. Icy blue, dark chocolate, and amber honey—it was all so… appetizing. "Hi."

"I'm afraid I don't have much time," Aaron said.

"Oh, are you dying? Or do you just have to get back to the future?"

"I have to leave the party, smart-ass," Aaron chuckled as he dug his phone from his pocket. "Can I have your number? I'd like to take you out on a date."

Daniel gasped as he slapped his hands to his heart. "You want to take me out?"

Aaron nodded down at his phone, swiping it open. "Here, put your number in."

"You want my number?" Daniel's voice had gotten ridiculously high-pitched. He bounced on his heels a bit. "To take me out on a date?"

The way Aaron stared, it was as if that answer were obvious. "Yes."

"*Yes!* Or, no." Sorrow instantly washed over him. "God, I would love to. I would genuinely love to go on a date with you, what with you looking like a literal matador and all."

Confusion twitched Aaron's features, but he recovered with a soft smile. "Thank you?"

"But I have a boyfriend." It came out sounding way more disappointed than it probably should have. It was, in part, that term. They probably shouldn't have had that "boyfriend" discussion while Daniel was high on wisdom-tooth premedication, but live and let live. "And you. You clearly have a—" He struggled to summon the right word. "—*spirited* British person."

Aaron grinned, the sexy one from earlier when he shared a kiss with his spirited British person. "Fuck your boyfriend. Or is that part not very enjoyable?"

Daniel erupted in an accidental laugh, then slapped a hand over his mouth. *Is it that obvious?* "That information is confidential."

"What's his name?" Aaron asked. "Chester?"

"You're going with *Chester* as your first guess?"

"Give me your number. Chester will get over it. He's seen this coming for a long time."

Daniel couldn't help his belly flipping like a two-timing floozy. He chewed his thumbnail. "Chest—er, Nate would, well, yes. He'd get over it. But it would make him sad."

"Aw, sad ol' Nort."

"Nate."

Aaron prowled nearer. "One date is all I'm asking."

Daniel leaned away and braced the sink. "Well, I would, but I have a—"

"A boyfriend? Yeah, you mentioned that." Aaron eased nearer. "But what happens when you're with him later tonight, staring into space like you guys do? Eating leftover clam chowder, you know, like you do."

"Why would we be eating...?" He squinted. "What—?"

"And you can't help but think about me?" Aaron stepped closer still, grinning like a man confident Daniel would be thinking about him. "What then?"

Daniel gulped as he tangoed backward. As Aaron followed. "I don't know."

"Hadn't thought that far?"

"Hadn't had time."

His back hit the wall, and Aaron leaned into him, his hands framing either side of his head. Without a hint of modesty, he said, "Break up with him."

Daniel would've stumbled backward if he had anywhere to go. "*What?*"

"You heard me."

"I did. But." Well. He didn't have a very good response, did he?

"I'd like to take you out. You have a boyfriend. So break up with him."

Then, there they stood. Chests nearly grazing. Breath sizzling. Daniel's back against the wall. Physically and metaphorically.

"Well," Aaron sighed after a moment. He shrugged and pushed himself backward, swiping his hands together. "I tried. I have to go."

Daniel blinked rapidly. Oh. Oh no. No, no, no. He grabbed Aaron's arm as he started to twist away. "Wait—"

Slam. Daniel's body hit the wall. *Thunk.* A painting of a sunflower hit the floor. Aaron cupped his face and crushed their lips together.

His eyes widened, then rolled shut, then widened again as he palmed Aaron's chest, but any protesting nonsense for the sake of playing it a lot cooler than this got buried somewhere deep, somewhere beautiful inside Aaron's expert mouth, in a casket right next to the wherewithal to change a single detail about the moment.

Dearly beloved, what a moment it was.

Aaron demanded as much as he gave, and he ventured a calculated risk as a firm hand gripped Daniel's jaw and another pinned his wrist against the tile. He couldn't move. He didn't want to move. Could he not live here for a night or two? *Pooled* into this near-stranger's arms, letting this near-stranger's tongue transgress his boundaries, which were either asleep at the wheel or drunk in the cheap seats and rooting them on.

Aaron's hands on Daniel's ass, his mouth on his lips—it was all too feral to be happening in the first place. Too fucking wet to lend a passing worry. And despite being nailed against a wall like a secret lover Aaron was running out of time to consume, Daniel somehow felt... treasured? Yes, he would go on that date. Yes, he would gladly give it up before the appetizers arrived. If ever there'd been a time when he'd been handled with such vehemence, with such shocking intuition, whoever it was just got demoted to second place.

The cold tile behind his back began to contrast against the boiling point of magma below his waist, and Aaron chose that moment to sink his teeth into Daniel's neck, steamrolling right over the question *How far do I let this go?* Insisting the only answer was *Someone lock the goddamn door.*

Then, as wild as it started, it slowed just as gradually when Aaron transitioned into these measured, fairy-tale kisses that softly peppered Daniel's temple, across his chin, and down to his chest. He smoothed Daniel's collar, locked their gazes, and said in a husky whisper, "Thank you. That was fun."

Daniel blinked.

Fun. Said matter-of-factly. Said like the last few minutes had simply been on Aaron's to-do list. His fun quota for the night.

"You'll break up with him now?" Aaron asked.

He nodded.

"Cool." Aaron offered his phone and repeated, sans the question mark, "Your number."

"My phone—my telephone. Number. Yes." Daniel cleared his throat and tried to will his face less frazzled. He nearly dropped the phone, he was shaking so much.

"Go ahead and put the name in as *Hard to Get*," Aaron said, peering over his shoulder. "So I know how to find you."

"Seriously?" Daniel gazed up at him hopelessly. "*That* was hard to get?"

Aaron tipped his head side to side. "Somewhat."

"Jesus, what's easy? You: *Nice to meet you. Divorce your husband.* Him: *Done.*"

"Once or twice."

Daniel slapped his arm and typed the name as:

hARd TO gET OvEr (poor chester)

The way Aaron grinned down at his phone, it was as if he'd just scored a new baseball card. "What's your real name, sweetheart?"

"Daniel."

"Daniel what?"

"Greene."

Aaron lifted Daniel's hand to his lips in the old-fashioned gesture of a gentleman and kissed it. "I'll see you soon, Daniel Greene Hard-to-Get-Over-Poor-Chester."

"The Third."

"Just so you know, that was the worst drink I've ever tasted." He swirled a thumb over Daniel's palm, stretching their arms long on his way toward the door. "I'd order ten if it meant I got to watch you make them."

Without another word, the matador was gone.

Chapter Three

"PLACES!" DANIEL clapped from where he stood in the front of the room, holding eye contact with each of his students in the mirror. He attempted to keep his face straight, but these grown adults in leotards, taking their once-a-week modern dance class seriously, were too cute for their own good, and he loved each of them. Percy, with his racquetball goggle glasses, knee brace, and fifty-two-year-old crisis ponytail. Brenda, with her high blood pressure, side boob sweat, and use of the phrase "Lord Jesus" when Daniel made them do primitive squats. He even loved Nadja, a German dog groomer who took smoke breaks during the hour-long dance class.

The music started.

"Five, six, seven, eight!"

Daniel breezed through the choreography, shooting a reassuring smile at the students who struggled, because who cared if they landed the double turn? With respect to the principles of any dance—first position, fifth—technique could never hold a candle to spirit. Technique could never translate *language of the soul*. It was what he strived to unearth in his students: transient freedom from their lives. Without judgment. Without concern for how they looked. Equipped with only their movement. Only their soul.

The song dwindled to a finish, and his students, puffing and panting, bowed their heads.

"Beautiful," he said, emotional with gratitude, probably nearing the misty-eyed look he so frequently had. "I love you all more today than I did yesterday. I'll see you next week."

Each of his students praised and hugged him—the icing on the whole heartwarming, misty-eyed cake—and meandered out the door, happily exhausted.

Olivia took a different approach with her students. More utilitarian. She didn't necessarily arrive on time to her class, which started ten minutes after his, and she didn't piddle around with pleasantries so much as she firmly patted backs, and occasionally butts depending on if she was sleeping with the student.

"So?" She flopped her duffel bag onto the back counter and hopped on top of it, batting her eyelashes down at him as he tried to answer an email from a student on the studio's computer. "You haven't thanked me for leaving you at that party."

His lips twitched. "Thank you, Olivia, for leaving me and creating a stressful environment that I happened to make the best of."

She rolled her hands. "And?"

"And?"

"You need to thank Puddles."

He scrunched his face. "Hmm, do I?"

"Yes. If he wasn't under the weather, there's a chance you never would've met Bathroom Make-Out Attorney Man."

His breath caught a little as his smile split his face. Each time he relived their kiss—every twelve to thirteen seconds—the air around his head suddenly seemed balmier. Like dark chocolate, blue ice, and amber honey. "Okay. Dear Puddles, thank you for refusing to leave this earthly plane. You obviously know something we don't. I hope whatever awaits you on the other side involves whole rotisserie chickens. How's that?"

Olivia held a hand to her heart. "Actually, quite moving. I think this man has changed you for the better. Have we heard from him today?"

"We have." Daniel squealed as he scrambled for his phone under the counter and swiped open his texts. "Get this, you'll never believe it. He said, *Good morning, Daniel.*"

"God," Olivia moaned, fanning herself. "That's so hot. I'm so glad you finally ended it with What's-His-Nuts."

"Nate."

"Doesn't matter. So when are you seeing him next?"

"I don't know yet," Daniel said, chewing a nail. "But I'll tell you this—"

"You're nervous."

"I'm nervous."

"Shocking."

"He's just so foxy. He's the foxiest person I've ever touched in real life and also in the life I fantasize about having. The one where I'm surrounded by, like, twenty men—all named Alejandro—and they're saying things like *You know, I think it's kind of cute that you steal your neighbor's internet because you can't afford your own.* And *Emotional maturity is less important than being able to make really good Netflix recommendations*—where was I going with this?"

"I think what you're trying to say is his foxiness out-foxes your own, but that's where you're wrong. *You're* the foxiest person a lot of people have ever seen in real life and in their Alejandro fantasy lives. I'm sure there's a ton of folks who probably picture you when their partners are going down on them."

"Aw, Olivia." He pinched his lips together. "That's the sweetest shit you've ever said to me."

"And so true. Case in point, how can you have, like, negative 12 percent body fat and still have an ass like that?"

He shrugged. "Genes?"

"Jeans?"

"Yeah, genes."

She studied his lower half. "But you're not wearing any."

He squinted. "What?"

"Daniel, can I see you for a second?" asked the studio owner, Madeline, emerging from her OR.

That's what they all called her office. The Operating Room: a germaphobe's wet dream, an environment as sterile as the aftermath of a vasectomy. And it wasn't like she cleaned it. It was that she never soiled it in the first place. Causing messes wasn't Madeline's bailiwick. One couldn't smudge surfaces or collect dust if all they did was float on air. The woman *floated* on air. She might have been angled bones, hollowed cheeks, and thin lips coated in matte burgundy lipstick, but the way she moved gripped the attention of every person in the room. She was as timeless as the pearl pin that held her bun in place, and Daniel secretly wished to be her when he grew up.

She draped herself in a willowy black scarf and gazed out her office window at the dance floor where Olivia's class commenced. All she needed was a jade cigarette holder and the hazy exposure of a spotlight to illuminate her green eyes and complete her silent film look.

"Your classes are doing so well," she said, her eyes following the pirouetting students. "In fact, they do the best. But you know that."

He burrowed into the validation of her words, all warm and fuzzy. "If they do the best, it's because I learned from the best."

He'd met Madeline when he was eighteen, just starting college, and in desperate need of a part-time job. He'd been dancing his entire life, but until her, he'd never had an opportunity to teach. It felt like she'd taken a chance on him by assigning him one of their most popular time slots, directing him how to control a room, but she'd always insisted she could "see something" in him. It must've been why she supported him in unimaginable ways—surprising him with new dance shoes when his got holes, stocking his refrigerator with pastas and soups she cooked from scratch. She'd ask if he liked lemongrass and then say, "Oh, it's nothing," as she stuffed homemade egg rolls and cans of sparkling water inside his backpack. "I made extra by accident."

She turned to him. "How old are you now?"

"Twenty-five."

"Twenty-five." She nodded. "Peculiar age, isn't it? Try your best you may, but you just don't know what you don't know." She always spoke like that. Part riddling cat and part sexy shaman. "Come to think of it, I was not much older than you when I started this place."

"Yeah, you were twenty-six." Daniel twisted to locate his favorite picture of her where it hung on the wall—she and her husband mid kiss in front of a much newer St. Louis School of Dance sign before years of harsh weather faded its zest.

"Do you like working here?" she asked.

"Is that a real question?" He raised his eyebrows. "I love it. Of course I love it."

"But you've got to be thinking of your future, no? And what you wish to do with it?"

If by *thinking of his future* she meant *worried until he ground his teeth about how he was going to afford his humble lifestyle once he had to start paying back his student loans*, then yes. He'd thought about it. What he'd learned in his bachelor of arts in dance had been invaluable, but what he'd spent to learn it didn't come without loss.

The whole endeavor had cost him in more ways than one, putting him in debt and driving a deeper wedge between him and his dad. His dad, who insisted he "get a real hobby" when he'd started dancing competitively, then "get a real degree" when he'd pursued dance in college. At least Robert Greene was consistent as the current mantra was: "For the love of God, get a real job."

He plunked into a chair and exhaled. "I'm glad you asked, because, yes, I have been thinking a lot about my student loans, and what if I sell a kidney? People live perfectly healthy lives with one kidney—"

"Let me stop you right there. I have something better than organ trafficking. I have a proposition." From her desk drawer, she produced an envelope. "I want you to take this, and I want you to go out to your car when you're ready to leave and read it there."

"What is it?"

"It's a number. I've recently received an offer to buy the studio, the space, everything. And if I'm going to sell my company, I would rather it be to you."

His jaw fell to the floor with a clang that shook the building. Or maybe that was Olivia's class doing a well-timed V-jump. "Wait. Why did it just sound like you said you're selling the studio?"

"Because I am selling the studio."

"No! No, no, no. What? You can't do that—"

"I'm done, Daniel. My husband got offered his dream job in Oregon. After all these years, I'd like to support him the way he's supported me."

"Okay, but what about this place? All your hard work. You can't just leave it behind. Where are you going to dance? You can't *not* dance."

"Sweetness. Even if I wasn't ready to pass the torch, my body is. These old feet can't do what they once could. Who I'd like to see carry that torch is you."

He blinked, eyes wide. "Madeline. This is…. I'm flattered, but I'm not ready to own a business. I don't know anything about running a business."

"Don't you see?" She leaned in a little closer. "You run it already. I've never had someone care so deeply about the students, about their personal lives and if they're progressing. I've never had someone pay such attention to the scheduling or the variation of classes. You even care about the bathrooms."

"The bathrooms?"

"Yes, you roll the washcloths and arrange them all pretty in that basket so the students can feel like they're in a spa."

He chuckled and dropped his head. "I thought it was a nice touch."

"It was. You are the person we call when the computer stops working, or a student has questions about their membership. You are the heart of this place, and I'd rather see it under your care than watch the building get turned into another financial office."

"This is bananas."

"No, it's not. The studio is solvent and growing. You will make back what you spent in no time. The only caveat, of course…." She sighed while her tone sobered. "I would need to know by the end of July."

"The end of *this* July? That's in two hours."

"It's in two months." She grinned, accustomed to his dramatics. "I will help you secure a loan. You can do this."

He smoothed his thumb across the envelope. "So, this is the price you're asking?"

"That is *your* price. I wouldn't offer it to anyone else. It's fair. I promise."

He shook his head as his eyes started to sting. Not that it took much to make him cry. It was sometimes torturous navigating the world with oversized tear ducts. He was about to walk out of here looking like he'd just strolled the greeting card aisle again. "I can't believe you're leaving me. What'll I do? I'll wither to my death without you here."

The gentlest of smiles softened her lips as she palmed his cheek. "I hope that someday soon you'll wake up, look in the mirror, and finally see what everyone else sees."

Speaking of the greeting card aisle….

"You won't wither on your own, Daniel. You'll bloom."

DANIEL SAT in his car and ripped the envelope open. Inside was a folded piece of paper with a number written in blue ink. Under the number:

I hope it didn't make you faint.
If you're still conscious, that's the first step in a much bigger dance.
Love always,
Madeline

Chapter Four

It was later that evening, and Aaron had texted:

Can I take you out tonight? 7ish? Send me your address.

Which Daniel had done in an itchy six seconds. The thing about going on a date with the foxiest person one had ever seen in real life (and their Alejandro fantasy life) was that it was nerve-racking to the point where he had to hang his biggest quandary, Madeline's proposal, on the refrigerator to be dealt with another day.

Expecting a calm head as the hour approached sevenish was overly ambitious, but did he have to feel like such a squirrel on stimulants as he glared at the front door? Demanding that it sound in a knock already? If only he could be more like Aaron with his ultra-suaveness. With his *Hey, break up with your boyfriend, why don't cha? That'd be swell.*

But he wasn't an Aaron. He was a Daniel, a rodent with a meth problem, and if that fucking door didn't make a fucking knocking noise soon, he was going to die all over the place. The authorities would find his body in about a month or two. *Boy perishes from having to wait a few minutes. No, he was not just being dramatic. More at eleven.*

A sudden knock. He gasped and swung the door open, and there stood Aaron, flashing an unfairly kissable smile.

"Hi," Aaron said. Oh what grand timing that a choir of angels crooned somewhere in the distance.

Daniel leaned on the doorknob, a little swoony that he was really here, filling that shirt with all those muscles. It was obscene how many muscle groups looked like they'd been prioritized in whatever workout regimen he must've religiously followed, all well-defined and bulging to life as if to say, *What do you mean, can we bench press your body? Of course we can. Don't make us laugh.*

"Your front door is orange," Aaron said, pointing a thumb at it. "Interesting color choice. Was it like that when you moved in?"

"Mm-hmm, you smell so good." Someday, he'd be a better conversationalist. For now, it appeared he'd just blurt whatever was on his mind. "Won't you come in?"

Aaron's grin tilted in amusement as he stepped inside. "Daniel Greene," he said, taking Daniel's hand and lifting it overhead to twirl him in a little circle. "You look remarkable. Are you ready?"

God yes. Take me. "Ready for what?"

"It's a surprise." Aaron twirled him a second time, making him giggle. "Do you like those?"

"Do I *like* the feeling of complete darkness, having zero control over what's happening?" He mustered excitement for his face as he twirled for his third time. "*So* much."

"Campy little thing," Aaron chuckled, continuing to spin him. "This doesn't make you dizzy?"

"Nope. Used to it." Daniel freed himself to complete a triple turn, landing in a graceful révérence bow. "I have about twenty in me before I start to get dizzy."

Aaron's eyes widened. "What? That's so—do it again."

He obliged, spinning thrice, landing in a deeper bow.

"Is that ballet?" Aaron asked. He almost looked shocked. "You do ballet? Like, just for fun? Or in some professional capacity?"

It was unfortunate that the first sensation to rush through him was embarrassment, but he couldn't help it when Robert Greene's voice was so damn loud—*get a real hobby, get a real degree, for the love of God, please get a real job.*

"Yeah," he said, chewing the inside of his cheek. "I, um, teach dance for a living."

"That's incredible."

He zipped his gaze up to Aaron's.

"Really, *really* incredible to be doing something you love," Aaron said, shaking his head like he was awestruck. "Assuming you love it."

"I do love it." He stood a little taller. "I've never loved anything more."

"Sheesh, it makes sense." Aaron's brow furrowed. "I should've known."

"What makes sense?"

"The way you move, sweetheart." Aaron's icy blue gaze softened or intensified. Or both. "It's dazzling."

Daniel cupped his hands over his mouth, frozen mid rhapsody.

When a few moments passed and he still hadn't spoken, Aaron rolled his lips and said, "Okay, you ready?"

"No." He sighed, dramatically fanning himself. "You can't say things like that to me if you want me to function like an adult human, but I see it's killing you, so go ahead and say it. Just one more time, though."

A smirk teased Aaron's lips. "Call you dazzling one more time?"

"God," Daniel moaned, generously bending his knees as he wiped imaginary sweat from his forehead. He wafted his shirt on his way to the closet. "Let me get a jacket. I need to cover up some of this dazzle. I don't want to stop traffic—"

Then Aaron did that thing. That archetypal breadwinning-spouse thing where he took Daniel's jacket from him and held it up. Daniel worked his arms through in slow motion as he gazed up all doe-eyed at Aaron's archetypal-breadwinning-spouse profile.

Aaron also then proceeded to lead him to his car by the small of his back, where he held the door open—because of course he did—to a sleek little glossy black number. Not that Daniel was a car person. His manual-windowed sedan, which he'd regally nicknamed *Turdingston IV*, just got a fresh coat of duct tape for the bumper.

But this car… this was the type of car around which one might struggle to stay fully clothed.

"Goodness, mister." Daniel itched to touch all the shiny buttons. "I've never been inside a more beautiful car."

"No?" Aaron winked, starting the engine. "Well, you look good sitting there."

"Duh, that's my thing. Everyone knows that's my thing." Daniel leaned back in the seat and grinned. "I pride myself on looking cute in other people's vehicles."

Aaron chuckled as he pulled from the street and into traffic. "You should pride yourself on the way you kiss."

Daniel sucked in a quick breath. The kiss. The kiss, the kiss. It'd consumed his thoughts, his prayers, and his text message trail with Olivia, but Aaron didn't need to know that, so he waved a blasé hand about. "Wait, so remind me which one you were again? It's just, I kissed a lot of guys in the bathroom at that party."

"Oh, I kissed so many guys in the bathroom," said Aaron, mocking Daniel's voice. "When was that? Last night? I cannot possibly remember. It was just *soooo* many."

Daniel pursed his lips to keep from smiling at that impression, which was alarmingly accurate.

"If it helps to narrow it down," Aaron said, back in his own husky voice, as he raised a naturally arched eyebrow, "I was the one you would've let take it a lot further than a kiss."

How utterly true. "How utterly presumptuous."

"Sure, Daniel Greene."

"Sure, Aaron—uh. Aaron…?"

"Silva."

"Ooh, *Sil-vah.*" Daniel winced. "That's gorgeous. Like *silver*, but *vahh.*"

"I guess?"

Daniel Silva. Daniel Alexander Silva—

"Think it'd sound good with your name in front?"

Daniel choked on a cough.

"Kidding." Aaron laughed, holding a hand up. "Kidding. I promise I'm not crazy. That'd be pretty scary."

"Right!" Daniel loudly cleared his throat. Speaking of kisses, he should probably address the other one. The British one. The pesky Yellow Jacket that someone needed to shoo. "So, speaking of the party, Mr. Silva. I believe *you* were the one who kissed more than one person."

Aaron tipped his chin at another driver, who went out of her way to let him cut in front, because mountains moved when he wanted them to. "Isn't that what parties are for?"

"Well." Daniel blinked. He was suddenly flooded with the memories of that one party where he kissed two separate fraternity brothers, both named Jordie. "I guess so, yeah. Unless you're with someone, of course. You're not with him or anything… right?"

Aaron winced as he sped through a yellow light, then chuckled. "Who?"

"The other guy you kissed at the party." *Obviously.* "The British one."

"Ahh. Corey."

"Okay, Corey. So is this someone you're dating? Seeing?" He chewed his lip. "Very serious about?"

Aaron's startled eyes zipped to his. "Am I *dating* Corey?"

Daniel squinted. This conversation seemed disorderly.

"No. No, I'm not *dating* Cor—" He couldn't even get through that sentence without laughing. "Holy shit, no. Can you imagine? Wow, that's funny."

"Yeah, hilarious!" Daniel forced a laugh, then quickly swallowed. "So, then. A friend?"

"A friend? Let's see." Aaron pulled into an empty spot on the street corner next to a brick building with the word Nektär printed on the windows. He slid the car into Park and rubbed his lips as he gazed at the dashboard. "Professionally, I've known Corey four or five years now, and yeah, I might call him a friend even if he is a pain in my ass. But I'm not dating anyone, sweetheart." Blue ice flashed tenderly, full-hearted. "Actually, this is the first real date I've had in a long time."

Daniel slowly nodded his understanding. As someone who'd blurred his fair share of boundaries in the past—usually to the detriment of the friendship or, that one time, his Uber rating when he never called the guy back—it wasn't like he had much room to judge.

"Plus"—Aaron grinned as he fixed his gaze on his lips—"Corey's not really my type."

Daniel got all smiley and flustered. If he had longer hair, he'd have twirled it around his finger. "What's your type, mister? I can't wait to hear. Is it someone who *dazzles*?"

"Redheads."

Daniel frowned.

Aaron chuckled as his pink tongue slid between his pretty teeth. "Joking. I mean, I do like redheads, but you know what I prefer? Ballet dancers." His pink tongue then wet his lips, and oh, who could stay mad? "Sweet, funny, sexy little ballet dancers."

Daniel batted his lashes. "Who dazzle?"

Aaron nodded and crinkled his nose as he began to lean in. "Who fucking dazzle."

Oh hell yes, this was happening. This was happening so hard as Daniel parted his lips, hooded his eyes, and prepared to be kissed—to be *taken*, actually. Like a willing fucking casualty. Just like at the party.

Aaron leaned in until their lips grazed and whispered into his mouth, "I just need to grab my wallet."

Daniel's whimpering protest squeaked like a dog toy as Aaron fished his wallet from his seat back.

"I think you would've let me take it further than a kiss." Aaron's nose nuzzled his. "But isn't it kind of fun to wait?"

Daniel vigorously shook his head. "Yes, of course."

Aaron chuckled and flung his car door open. "Come on. Don't want to be late."

As he popped from the car, Daniel stuck his tongue out at the back of Aaron's head, because he was a grown-up. "So this is the surprise? What is this place?"

"Oh, you've never been here?" Aaron almost looked mischievous as he held the door open. "I'm in utter disbelief."

"Welcome!" said a woman's bubbly voice as they stepped inside, and judging by the walls of cocktail glasses, tinctures, and stainless-steel gadgets, it became very clear what kind of establishment this was. "I'm Kara. Are you perhaps Aaron? The one who booked the private bartending class?"

Daniel blurted out a laugh.

"Yes, and this is Daniel." Aaron shook her hand. "He has a specialty cocktail he'd love for you to taste, just to get your professional opinion."

"Oh, how lovely," Kara said, her eyes brightening even more. She dripped with baubles. The canary-yellow ribbon in her ponytail matched her drop earrings. "I'd be honored to offer feedback. What's the flavor profile?"

"Yeah, Daniel." Aaron rubbed his chin as he twisted to him, a ridiculous smirk on his lips. "What's the flavor profile?"

"The profile?" Daniel sucked his teeth. "Pudgy. With kind of a longish nose."

Kara's smile faltered a bit, but she recovered. "Interesting. What kind of spirits does it take?"

"Oh, I think when making any drink, it's important to use real alcohol. And cocaine."

Kara's head twitched to the side.

"Mm-hmm, and what do you call it again?" Aaron asked.

"Oh, it has a name? What's the name?" Kara asked, perking up again. "Is it perhaps a twist on a classic, or—?"

"Don't ask questions."

Aaron burst into chuckles.

Kara zipped her gaze between them but, to her credit, didn't let it stymie her pep. She twisted an imaginary key near her lips. "Secret recipe—got it. Okay, well, follow me to the back and we'll get started."

Daniel clasped his arms behind his back and trailed after her with Aaron behind him. Midstep, he spun around. "I see you think you're so hilarious—"

Aaron's gaze bounced up from his ass. He suddenly looked a tad startled. Or busted? More importantly, he looked hungry.

Maybe they weren't just fluffy words. Maybe Aaron really was a bit enamored by the way Daniel moved. For the love of offering a tiny feast for this delicious man's eyes, he could lean into it. If there was anything he did well, it was fucking *move*.

He skated his fingertips over his collarbone and exposed his neck as he slinked backward, holding Aaron's gaze, parading his body's seasoned grace.

Aaron rewarded him with a deep breath and a subtle nod as he followed behind on an invisible leash, eyes skidding down Daniel's silhouette. They arrived at the workstation where Kara was relaying something about a jigger, but their hushed world didn't concern cocktail lingo.

Chills pebbled Daniel's shoulder when Aaron brushed it with his as he stepped by, leaning down to whisper in his ear, a smile underscoring the single word: "Dazzling."

AARON MASSAGED his cheeks. His face hurt from laughing at full force for the past hour. It was the kind of nonstop laughter that felt so genuinely rare at almost twenty-eight. Like he and Daniel were two kids at a sleepover and not grown adults at a cocktail class, while their instructor also lost her composure to laughter.

"I'm not going to say it," Daniel said, pointing a finger at Kara and then him. "I'm not! You two are filthy. *Filthy.*"

It was a gin fizz, and Daniel had surely maxed out all the lewd comments any one person could make about whipped egg whites. He was the kid at the sleepover orchestrating the dares. The class-clown type of kid.

"Hey, Aaron." Daniel spooned the last of the egg whites onto his drink. "If this accidentally gets on the wall, would it be called a wal*nut*?"

Aaron covered Daniel's mouth with his hand while Kara chuckled. "I'm sorry, Kara. I'll make it up to you. I'm a really generous tipper."

"Ooh, what do we think, Kara?" Daniel said, pushing at Aaron's arms, doing his best to wiggle free from his grip. "Do we think he'll be generous with more than just the tip—?"

Aaron spun Daniel around and sealed a hand over his mouth from behind as poor Kara's face stayed scrunched and pinkened in laughter. "I'll give you two a minute," she cooed, patting under her eyes as she retreated toward the front of the store. "Enjoy your 'baby batter,' Daniel."

Daniel twisted back over his shoulder, his big, melty, caramel-colored eyes flashing up. He winked as he said, muffled against Aaron's palm, "Delicious."

Breathe. He slowly dropped his hand and couldn't keep his gaze from trickling to Daniel's lips. They were always a touch rouged, but just the light pressure from his hand had stained them deeper. It was the contrast of red flesh against his creamy skin that made them look swollen, but they weren't swollen. They just had that look. Pouty. Puffy. Sexy. He'd be curious to see how they looked after a bit more *impact*.

"Do you want me to make you anything else?" Daniel asked, waving a hand over the littered table. "Gin and tonic? Vodka and tonic? Bourbon and... tonic?"

"You almost had it there."

"How about an extra dry daiquiri?"

"And by daiquiri, you mean martini."

"Yes, I'll make you that. That seems fitting for you."

"Why's that?" Aaron leaned over the counter and watched Daniel pour what were definitely not the ingredients for an extra dry martini into a cocktail shaker. "Why's it seem fitting?"

"Fancy man with the flashy car." Daniel shrugged and added some random lime juice as if he'd learned nothing. "With the flashy *job*."

God, there was a topic that could die before it was born. It wasn't that he wouldn't be willing to talk about it eventually, but it wasn't the only interesting thing about him. It didn't define who he was, like guys wanted to act like it did. He'd watch their eyes sparkle in curiosity as he answered the same questions over and over, driving one of two outcomes: They'd run for the hills. Or they'd urgently want to screw him.

Either way, he was left with the same ending. Adding one more number to his body count had lost its charm a long time ago.

"I wouldn't call it flashy."

"Your car?" Daniel asked, adding a little hip bump to his cocktail shaking. "Or your job?"

"Oh, I know my car's flashy." He grinned as Daniel twirled around, shimmying the shaker like a maraca. "But I don't love talking about my job. Unless there's something you're dying to know, I'd rather not talk about it, if that's okay?"

Daniel stopped shaking to shoot him a curious look. "Is it that stressful?"

"No," he answered without thinking about it. Then he lent it some consideration and corrected, "I guess it can be. Depends on the client." Then he lent it even further consideration and settled on "Honestly, I think I might hate it. But I'm stuck."

"*Hate* it?" Daniel pouted his bottom lip. "Oh no. Why?"

"Err—no." He scrubbed a hand over his face. "Yes. I don't know. I'd rather not spend our time talking about it."

"Sure. Well, how about this? If you could do anything on the planet, what would you do?"

He didn't need to think about it. "Interior design."

Daniel's face lit up. "Shut the French whore!"

"That's not an expression."

"Oh, I bet you'd be incredible at that. Yes, Aaron. *Yes*. You should go for it. You should one hundred and twelve percent go for it. You already have the look. Now you just need the… wallpaper? What do interior designers need to, uh, design interiors?"

He chuckled. "A degree."

"Then you'll get that. Easy peasy. Here, we'll toast to celebrate." Daniel plucked two port wine glasses from the wine rack because "Oh look, how cute" and poured whatever he'd made into them. It looked similar to a margarita, minus the vodka and the peach schnapps and whatever else he'd splashed in on a whim. "Cheers. To having dreams."

Aaron couldn't help but grin. Grin and melt. It was naïve to assume it'd be "easy peasy" with the years it'd take to get established and the massive hit to his savings account, but he'd have a tough time arguing with this kid, who did exactly what he loved for a living. "Cheers."

Daniel sipped the drink. "Oh God," he mumbled as he spat it back into the glass.

"That good?"

"Mm-hmm, *so* good, but hand me yours. The recipe might need some tweaking."

Aaron gladly handed the glass over. "You are adorable."

"Oh, just adorable?" Daniel asked, dumping the drinks in the sink.

"Dazzling."

Daniel winked as he grabbed his gin fizz. "There we go."

"Did you have fun?"

"So much fun." Daniel grinned as he shrugged one delicate shoulder. "How would you like to come back to my place, mister? Keep the fun going."

And there it was. He couldn't help his smile from fading a bit. Did he want to go back to his place and keep the fun going? Of course he did. He wasn't a lunatic. He'd have Daniel's tight little body trembling in seconds, and he'd keep it trembling until some shaky, broken version of his voice begged for mercy.

Then he'd make it tremble some more.

Not to say that Daniel was the type of person to sleep with him and disappear, but usually, when guys said, *Do you want to come back to my place? Keep the fun going?* they meant, *Do you mind if I try you out? Come on, I've never been with someone like you. It's just sex. You're used to it.* He was a novelty—a piece of equipment that didn't serve much purpose outside the bedroom. He wasn't the guy someone like Daniel typically settled down with.

"Or—and hear me out—the back seat of your car." Daniel waggled his eyebrows, then blinked hard like he was orienting himself. "Huh. Yeah, I wonder if I'm not a little tipsy. I'm not usually *that* forward. Unless you're into it. Then I meant to say that."

He swallowed. "I'd like to take things a little slower than that."

Daniel nodded in understanding. "Like we leisurely *walk* to the back seat of your car."

"Okay, so I'm glad we're having this conversation. Here, sit. Uh." While Aaron was twisting around in search of a chair, Daniel hopped onto the counter and sat with his legs crossed, somehow without spilling his drink. Nimble little fellow. "That'll do. I'm going to start by saying I haven't had the best luck with relationships in the past. I think my issues are because I've not been upfront with my needs."

"Oh?" Daniel arched an eyebrow, swinging his legs in kicks. "He says with an air of mystery. Well, do tell. What are your *needs*, sir?"

Here went nothing. "I don't want a hookup, or a friend with benefits, or a one-night anything. I want way more than that. I want a genuine connection with someone, so I'd like to take the intimacy part a lot slower. I'd like to get to know you first."

Daniel's legs stilled as his head slowly cocked to the side. "But you... in the bathroom at the party?"

"I know. I know I came on strong, but in my defense, I had to do something. You were being stubborn about giving me your number."

"Stubborn? You know it took less than five minutes for me to decide to break up with a whole-ass person and make out with you." Daniel circled a hand over Aaron's face. "I wonder in what other ways looking like this has misshaped your worldview."

"Lots of guys play hard to get. It's nothing to be ashamed of."

"Five minutes. Maybe four."

"But anyway, I'm telling you this because I don't want to pressure you." He captured Daniel's hand and held it. "If you're looking for something more casual, that's fine, but you should tell me. Because I know what I want, and I want long-term. I want a real relationship."

Daniel blinked. "Did you just use the words *long-term* and *relationship* in the same sentence?"

"I did."

"Oh my God, stop. Just stop." Daniel huffed an exhale as he employed Aaron's hand to fan himself. "This is too much. I don't think I'm going to make it."

Aaron rolled his eyes but couldn't stifle his smile as he fanned Daniel with both hands.

"I'm a bit dizzy, but keep going. What else? Do you want to go to the farmer's market together?"

Aaron pursed his lips. "I'm afraid to say it, but yeah, that'd be nice. That's where I buy soap, and stuff to make quiches. It'd be great to have a companion."

Daniel moaned as he slung an arm across his forehead. "Long-term relationship *and* he makes quiches. I swear to everything holy, if you mention anything about browsing paint swatches for a DIY home project, I might implode."

Aaron chuckled as he swabbed a hand over his face, but when he met Daniel's gaze, it was sincere. Smirking, likely because he knew how over-the-top he was, but sincere.

"I'm looking for the same things." Daniel nodded, his half-smile kind and present. "I want *more*. I want long-term and a real relationship. It's nice to know I'm not alone."

Aaron's heart had the nerve to wave at him from the sidelines as if to say, *Is this me? Is it my turn? Can you put me in, Coach?* While it was way too soon to put his most irrational organ on the playing field, his smile still shaped all on its own. This was maybe… hopeful. "That's refreshing. *You're* refreshing. You're, I don't know, secure in yourself. Secure and confident."

Daniel's eyes widened. "Secure and confident?"

"Yeah, you don't think so?"

"Oh, Aaron." Daniel stroked his hand. "I've been called a lot of things—dramatic, ridiculous, *dazzling*—but never secure and confident. You go ahead and think that. Sounds better than neurotic and riddled with daddy issues."

Aaron's chuckle transformed into a hum as he nodded.

"We can take it slowly. Then, whenever you decide you're ready, we can go to the farmer's market, if you know what I mean." He winked as he whispered loudly, "Go to the *farmer's market*."

"Yeah, I got it. Come on, sweetheart." He held Daniel's hand as he hopped from the counter. "I take it you're not a big drinker. Let's get your tipsy ass home."

"Am I tipsy? I'm trying to decide—oh, Kara! There you are." Daniel skipped to the front. "Put your number in my phone. We're going out dancing—don't argue with me. You can bring your man, or whoever, and I'll bring this hunk of meat—I know, isn't he gorgeous? I'm sorry I didn't learn anything, but I'm sometimes really bad at listening. I think I might talk too much. Anyway. Wait, what was I saying?"

AFTER THE car ride home, the buzz from the evening had begun to wear thin, and Daniel realized something interesting. At the risk of humble bragging, he'd never before been turned down for sex.

He'd been turned down for walks in the park, road trips to the beach, and requests for minimal emotional commitment, but never sex.

Was he not as hilarious, or smart, or fun as he thought he was? Heavens. Was he not as *cute*? No. They'd sailed right past second base in a random bathroom at a party. Surely he was cute. Right?

He shuffled his feet where he stood on his front porch, toying with his keys. "Are you sure you don't want to come inside? I have wine. I don't know how old it is, and I hate to admit, it's in a box. But do you want to come in for a bit?"

"I should be heading home." Aaron's smile was all full of grace, like the damn Virgin Mary. "Thank you for the offer."

"Are you not that into me?" Daniel licked the corner of his mouth. "Is that it? Because you can tell me—"

"That's laughable." Aaron chuckled and stretched his jaw. "Please don't make me laugh anymore. My face hurts from doing it all night."

Daniel pointed a thumb back at his door. "So, you're into me, but I'm going inside there, and you're going home, and we are not going to the farmer's market tonight."

"That's right."

"Like a couple of normal people living in the same year, and one of them is not a time traveler from the 1800s?"

"One of them is definitely not a time traveler. Just someone who wants to take it slowly."

"Okay," Daniel sighed as he crossed his arms. "Okay, I can allow it. Under one condition."

Aaron's eyebrows knitted together. "*Allow* me to leave? You're tiny. I'm not sure what you think you're gonna do—"

"And here it is: you have to be telling the truth. The reason you don't want to come inside is because you're charmingly old-fashioned. Not because you don't find me—oh, what's the word I'm searching for?" He snapped his fingers a few times. "Ahh. Dazzling."

Aaron's mouth twitched.

"In fact, I wonder if you shouldn't go ahead and tell me I'm dazzling," Daniel struggled to keep a straight face as he scratched the back of his head. "Just to make sure we're on the same page."

Aaron snaked an arm around his waist and yanked his body flush, making him whimper all over the place. His words were all breathy and hinted in tart lemony fizz as he said, "You're dazzling, sweetheart."

Daniel ached a little at the points where he pressed flush against Aaron's body. His hips. His lower belly—flush. Flush and tight. Like he could just fuse into him.

"So dazzling that you're genuinely precious."

Swoon.

"And I want to take things slowly *because* I'm excited about you. You and your dazzling preciousness."

Daniel melted. He swooned again, then totally melted. His voice was a strained mess as he said, "Kiss me. You should kiss me like you did at the party."

Aaron's gaze dipped to his mouth. "How did I kiss you at the party?"

"Like you owned the room." Daniel pressed up to his toes and threaded his arms around Aaron's shoulders. "Like you owned the air you walked on. Like you owned *me*."

Aaron didn't hesitate. He crashed into him in the most thrilling way. Not delicate, because who had time for that shit, but needy with the way he clawed the skin on Daniel's back and pressed their lips together, moaning in these sexy little bursts like he was loving it too.

Loving the ownership.

"You'd feel so good," Daniel whispered into his mouth between rough kisses, "buried deep inside of me."

"Gah." Aaron jerked away, adjusting his pants. He half chuckled, half winced as his face contorted in pain. "That is not nice. You're not nice."

"Me? No." Daniel held an innocent hand over his innocent heart. "I'm *precious*."

"I have to leave." Aaron grinned as he pointed a stern finger at him, trudging backward toward his car like he was afraid to turn his back on him. "I'm leaving right now."

"Oh, does the portal to the 1800s close soon?"

"Shut up and answer your phone when I call you tomorrow. We're dating now."

"Yes, sir, Father Celibacy. You know how they say not all heroes wear capes? Well, not all saints wear robes."

"Goddammit," Aaron chuckled. He looked like he didn't quite know what to do with his face, so he settled on a tight-lipped smirk. "I like you. I like you, Daniel Greene."

Daniel tried to stay cool, but he wholeheartedly wasn't, so he covered his eyes with his hands and giggled. After a moment, he regained enough composure to say, "I like you too."

They shared a sidelong glance that lasted until Aaron vanished inside the shiny black number.

"Mr. Silva." He leaned against a column and waited for his taillights to disappear. "I like you a lot."

Chapter Five

IT WAS the next day, and Daniel was hiding from his boss. He ducked behind the studio's front desk and peeked over the edge. *Shit!* She saw him.

He'd been avoiding Madeline because what was there to say? She needed an answer to the question: are you going to buy the studio? Well, he didn't have one of those. He had a whole lot of fear about being in charge of something so treasured, and was he really going to take out another loan? What if he failed? Just nosedived straight into bankruptcy. Then all the students and all the employees would hate him—he would hate himself.

He scrambled for a towel and started dusting as Madeline floated toward him.

"Hi, Daniel."

"Madeline! Well, what a lovely surprise. When did you get here?"

She peered over her bookish round glasses with her arms crossed and burgundy lips pursed. "What are you doing down there?"

"Me? I'm checking on the printer."

"I see. Something you do often?"

He cleared his throat and patted the printer. "Not typically. But lately, its behavior has been... well, it's been worrisome. I'm concerned about its ink consumption. And hey, no judgment, none of us are perfect. It could just be going through a rough patch, you know? Stress from all the printing, trouble connecting with people and the internet—"

"My office."

"Yes, ma'am." He followed her into the OR with his head hung.

She closed the door behind them. Her emerald gaze burrowed under his skin. "You're avoiding me."

"That is absurdity—"

"Why are you avoiding me?" She folded her hands in her lap. "Is this about buying the studio?"

He rubbed his neck and *eeeeeee*'d.

"Daniel, I made you that offer because you were the first person that came to mind, but if you're uninterested, I more than understand. You don't need to pretend like I don't exist. Just say the word, and we can move on."

"No! I am *so* interested. I love this place, and I would love to call it my own. I just need time to think about how I could make it work and also convince myself I'm not a loser who tricked you into believing in me."

"How would you have done that?"

"My hubris, obviously." He sighed. "It's a blessing and a curse being this magnetic."

"Look, I'm sorry for the pressure. I wish I could give you more time. But I'm going to tell you what I've already told you—you're capable of doing this. Abundantly capable. I trust this place in your hands, with my students, my legacy." She rested her beautiful bony palm on his shoulder. "I trust *you*."

He gave his ever-present anxiety permission to wane. It was her touch. Her faith. If his mentor was leaving, he wouldn't have that touch or that faith to remind him he might have been *capable of doing this*. He scrunched his face and routed his eyes to the floor.

Madeline's gaze jumped to the front door as a curious smile split her face. "Look."

When Daniel spun around, a flower delivery man stood at the entrance, holding a bouquet of long-stemmed midnight calla lilies tied with a white ribbon.

"Those are for you," Madeline said. "I can tell."

He shook his head, eyes glued to the flowers as one of the instructors walked them to the back. "No, they're not—"

"Daniel," the girl said, poking her head into the office. "These are for you."

His hands shook as he reached for them. Up close, they were wildly pigmented and, judging by the beauty and the quality, also wildly expensive. He scrambled to read the card.

Daniel Greene Hard-to-Get-Over-Poor-Chester III,
You're dazzling.

"Who are they from?" Madeline asked.

Daniel fell into his seat, whisked the bouquet to his forehead, and dipped dramatically backward as if he felt faint. "This fucking guy."

"I assumed that much."

"He is so perfect, and I cannot figure him out. I meet him at a party, he comes on hot and heavy—stop me if this is TMI—then we have our first date, and he doesn't even *try* to sleep with me—TMI? Stop me—like, at all. He drops me off, kisses me good night, and goes home. What gives?"

Madeline gave him a funny look. "It's been a while since I've had a first date, but isn't that how it's supposed to go?"

"I suppose if you're a character in the Bible, but I thought we were all sex-positive nowadays. Free love and free the willy. It makes me feel like he's not that interested in me."

"Not interested? Well, the flowers would beg to differ. Don't confuse disinterest with old-fashioned courtship, my love. It sounds like you might just have yourself a gentleman."

"A gentleman?" He squinted and sucked his lower lip between his teeth. "What's the difference between a *gentle*-man and, like, a *rough*-man?"

"The difference is that a gentleman takes his time and does what he does without expectations. A gentleman will put in the effort to make you feel special."

He thoughtfully hmphed. Well, that was... new. Was it possible he needed to reevaluate his standards? Maybe there was a correlation between diving into bed with someone and his history of misconnections with men. "Is it possible I've never met a gentleman?"

Madeline shrugged. "It's probably a dwindling tradition. So maybe hold on to that one."

I intend to. He smiled as he twirled for the door but caught himself. "Oh, and hey, I'm sorry for, you know, checking on the printer. Give me just a little time, and I'll get back to you."

She smiled that people's princess smile of hers. "I believe in you."

He plopped the flowers into someone's leftover plastic gas station cup and found his phone to see it'd been sweetened with a text message from Aaron:

What are you doing tonight? Besides letting me cook you dinner.

Daniel grinned down at the screen.

Going to this fancy place for dinner where I heard the food is so-so, but the chef is really hot. Send me your address.

When his phone pinged with a location, he zoomed in on the map. It pinged with another message.

I'm just a few blocks from your studio.

Good, then I can walk. It will give me more time to figure out how I'm going to thank you for the flowers.

But he'd been dancing for six hours. He could probably use a shower.

Any chance I can get hot and naked at your place? I mean, shower at your place?

Any chance you can speak without innuendo?

Was I doing that? Man, I'm just stiffened with embarrassment. Absolutely rock-hard with shame.

Aaron took a moment, then responded:

Yes, you may take a shower. I hope it relieves all that tight, thick, explosive stress of yours.

Daniel tossed his head back and laughed. Fat chance, but a boy could dream.

DANIEL TRIED not to sashay *everywhere* he walked, but Aaron lived in the type of building that made it impossible not to swish one's hips as they strutted up. It was all the seamless glass and chrome trim, and these grand front doors that took him two tries to heave open. Everyone knew the more mammoth a front door, the fancier the place was.

Once inside the vestibule, he pressed the button for Aaron's apartment and waited to be buzzed in, which happened in seconds, prompting the doorman, Santa Claus's equally jolly brother, to chirp as he directed him to the elevator, "Enjoy your evening, sir. Give my best to Mr. Aaron."

Of course he would give his best to Mr. Aaron. Mr. Aaron could have whatever he wanted. The whole thing felt very romance-in-a-Hallmark-movie with a montage of their laughing faces as the credits scrolled. *What happens when high-powered and distinguished falls for indecisive and broke? Coming this fall.*

The elevator dinged open, and there stood Aaron, wearing a dusty blue cashmere sweater, dark trousers, and his chocolatey brown hair all tousled to one side. It was very Young Elvis the way it fell into his eye, and his smile even pulled a bit higher on one side as he said, "Hi. You made it."

"Hi, mister," Daniel said, a little too breathy, a little too literally weak in the knees. "I just have to tell you that the flowers you sent are the most beautiful flowers I've ever received, and just because they're the only flowers I've ever received, doesn't make them any less beautif...." He trailed off, sniffing the air. "Oh my. What's that smell?"

Aaron twisted back over his shoulder, pointing a thumb behind him. "Oh, does it smell like food? That's my apartment."

"Don't you fucking tease me."

Aaron chuckled. "I told you I was making dinner. Are you hungry?"

He nodded forcefully. The thing about food was that it was expensive. What wasn't expensive were those tiny rectangles of jelly that sometimes came with bagels and such. He kept those in his car just in case he needed a pick-me-up, which did not do wonders to lift one's pride.

"Well, come on. Dinner's almost ready," Aaron said, which was the same as saying, "Well, here's a bunch of literal gold," because the apartment he led them to—aside from being gorgeous—smelled like fresh bread had been baked and butter had been melted, and garlic had been simmering on a stove for a while.

"Oh my heavenly heavens." Daniel's mouth filled with saliva as he tapped his fingertips together and gawked over a pile of rolls in a basket. "What are we doing with these? Can just anyone eat these, or...?"

Aaron pointed to them. "Those? You want one?"

"I want seven."

"Yeah, take as many as you want. And here. The bathroom's this way."

Seven seemed excessive. With six rolls cradled against his chest, he followed Aaron into the bathroom, where the stainless steel shone, and the towels made pretty towel accordions, and the multiple-faucet shower looked like it would accost whoever got in its way (in a good way). Even the lights had a welcoming pinkish hue.

"Wow, your bathroom is just as fancy as you are," Daniel said as he gazed around, chewing on a roll. "And look, you even have a roll warmer."

"Or some of us call it a blow-dryer." Aaron prodded through a drawer. "Okay, here's an extra razor. Hair products in that cabinet, a washcloth. What else do you need?"

"Nothing. All I require is a shower and your cock."

"What?"

"What?" Daniel grinned sweetly. "I said all I require is a shower that's hot."

Aaron's eyes narrowed to a squint. "I'll leave you to your hot shower, then."

"Mm-hmm, you do that."

Oh, the posh shower products. The posh everything. A boy could get used to this kind of treatment with dinner rolls in excess, and hair masques with labels in French, and a bodywash that smelled like a sexy woodworking shop. Why was this man single?

He sped through the shower, toweled himself off, and swiped some styling product through his wet hair. For being so elegant, it was shockingly cozy at Aaron's place. Even Aaron's desire to take things slowly was oddly comforting. With the topic of sex off the table, perhaps there'd be more opportunity to get to know each other.

Wow. He had to blink hard at his reflection. He was officially this many days old when he'd had that revelation for the first time.

He wrapped his waist in a towel and padded into the kitchen, where he'd left his duffel bag. Aaron, busy tossing long-stemmed broccoli with a cream sauce, glanced up, and his gaze snagged on Daniel's naked torso.

They stood in a staring contest for a long several seconds. Well, Aaron was in a staring contest with Daniel's stomach, and Daniel was trying not to eat it up like the seventh dinner roll he secretly wanted. Every day, he moved his body in unimaginable ways. Even if he did have a bit of a featherweight frame, he was still etched with lean, functional muscle. It was probably shocking to see him shirtless for the first time.

"Hey." He snapped his fingers. "Excuse me, sir. Eyes up here."

Aaron's gaze bounced up.

"Do you think this is some sort of a game, Aaron?" He squinted as he held a palm to his chest. "We are supposed to be taking things slowly."

Aaron opened his mouth and closed it again, almost abashed looking.

"You think I'm some kind of a floozy for whom you can just buy flowers, and cook dinner, and treat like a literal prince? Well, I'm not a prince, Aaron." He pointed a finger to his chest and dropped to an indignant whisper. "I'm a Midwesterner."

Aaron dropped his chin and chuckled. "Ahh, my mistake."

"Yeah, it is your mistake, because I don't appreciate"—he reached both arms up to the ceiling and twirled toward the kitchen—"you ogling the way you do. It's obscene."

"God, I'm the worst."

"And, for the love of Zeus, if you could please give me some *space*?" He stopped mid twirl to brush against Aaron's body, then continued in a slinky, snaking walk around him. "I'd feel a lot more comfortable."

"I'm sorry you feel uncomfortable here," Aaron said as Daniel draped himself back over the counter like he was sunbathing. "It's clearly insufferable for you. Do you need to borrow something to wear? Would that help?"

His spine instantly snapped straight at the thought of getting to see the bedroom. "What a gentleman. This way, then."

He followed Aaron into the bedroom, which looked precisely how he'd pictured it with all the clean dove grays and live edge woods and oh, the scent. Geez, the scent. It smelled like vanilla bean, orris butter, and expensive suede. The sheets probably smelled like that. What if he just crawled in for a moment—? No.

They were old-fashioned gentlemen. Or Aaron was an old-fashioned gentleman. Daniel was a Midwestern prince who was trying.

"This is stunning," he said, gazing around, working his arms through a white V-neck that Aaron handed him. "Did you *design* this space?"

"Not just this. All of it. The whole place." Aaron grinned as he unearthed some gray sweatpants from a drawer. "That's *my* dancing. It makes me happy."

"Aww, do you mind if I explore a bit?" He quickly stepped into the sweatpants. "It's just so lovely."

"Of course not. The lamb ragù isn't ready yet."

"Okay, well, that's kind of long and complicated for a safeword, sweetie." He patted Aaron's chest. "We'll work on that."

He started on a meandering stroll around the apartment, gliding his fingertips over a table that looked like petrified wood and a chair that looked like it was from the Ming dynasty. He hadn't really noticed the attention to detail when he arrived, but maybe because it was so uncrowded, as if each piece of furniture had been selected carefully and not acquired through hand-me-downs or left outside by a dumpster like most of Daniel's stuff. It was half Trinidadian yoga studio and half Cubist mansion, if both of those things could coexist inside a cloud. The most stunning part had to be the floor-length windows through which neon city light poured, illuminating a huddle of green houseplants.

Daniel touched the leaves of a few different vines. One plant stood out among the rest: a bonsai tree with an ivory tassel earring dangling from one of its branches. He thumbed the delicate beads. "What's this?"

Aaron looked up from dicing a tomato. "Oh, it's a bonsai tree."

"Yeah, I can see that, but why is it wearing jewelry?"

"The earring was my mom's."

Was.

"I'm training the tree. That one's called a semi-cascade. It was her favorite."

He sucked his lip. "She's passed?"

"She was sick for a long time." Aaron didn't look up from the cutting board. "Growing up, she had a sunroom where she always had, like, two or three bonsai going. They were beautiful. She was beautiful. She would try to teach my brother and me how to prune them, but we were too young to care. I wish I had cared a little more."

Daniel's heart squeezed. He couldn't imagine life without his mom. Even if he only got to see her once a month because he'd moved to the city and she'd stayed in the burbs, it was still nonnegotiable that he could see her whenever he wanted. "You care now." He kept his voice mild and smile sweet. "If you ask me, that counts."

"Thank you." Aaron blinked his striking eyes, the being behind them melting into a warm, golden puddle. "I still think about her. I still miss her."

"Well, you'll always miss her, right? What about your dad?"

Aaron instantly hardened. What had been soft and golden was suddenly bleak and stony. "I don't talk to my dad. Neither does my brother. He's—he's not a good person." Aaron's shoulders shuddered. He cast his gaze down and parted his lips like he had something more to say but remained silent.

Daddy issues, hard same. Daniel wanted to press, but if Aaron was anything like him, talking about his dad caused his mood to shift so sourly it puckered his mouth. It was better to deflect. "How old's your brother?"

"Two years younger than me, so twenty-five. Your age. Andrew. He wants to be a pilot, and you would *love* him. Everyone loves him."

"I'm sure if he's anything like you, he's wonderful."

"Way better than me." Aaron beamed, pride oozing from his pores. "Smarter, funnier, better looking."

"Quick! Give me his number."

"And straighter," Aaron laughed. "I'm sorry to disappoint, but as straight as they come. What about you? Siblings?"

"Nope." He shrugged a shoulder. "Only child."

"Ahh," Aaron said, his head bobbing in nods. "That explains *so* much."

"What does it explain? Why I can't stand it when someone doesn't like me? Or why I think I need the unwavering attention of everyone in the room?"

"Why you became a dancer." Aaron grinned down at the salad he was preparing, but when he glimpsed up, it almost looked like admiration in his expression. "A boy who just needed a stage to feel at home. I've never dated a dancer."

Kind of like how Daniel had never dated someone who liked that he was a dancer so much. It was sort of amazing to have someone appreciate it. He pirouetted his way through the kitchen until he hard-stopped in front of Aaron, leaning on the counter beside him. "I know you're dying to ask it, so go ahead."

Aaron's eyes slid to his. "Ask what?"

"The answer to your burning question is yes." He winked. "I am *that* flexible."

Aaron ran his tongue over his teeth but failed to censor his smile as he swiped his hands together. "The lamb ragù is ready."

"See, that's the thing about safewords. They're supposed to be simple."

"No, here's the thing about safewords." Aaron grinned, a gorgeous and seductive Young Elvis. Without warning, he gripped Daniel's body, spun him around, and caged him against the counter from behind. "You're not going to care about a safeword, sweetheart. You're not even going to remember your own name."

Daniel's smile fizzled into a whimper as Aaron pressed into him.

"But that's okay." Aaron leaned into his ear, tangled one hand into his curls, and whispered, "You can just use mine."

Sacre bleu. Was the room suddenly seesawing?

"Use it. Praise it." Aaron's teeth grazed Daniel's neck as his hand tightened on Daniel's hip bone. "Scream it."

The sound Daniel made was pretty unladylike.

"But like I said...." Aaron grabbed the salad and smacked his ass on his way to the table. "The lamb ragù is ready."

Chapter Six

AARON DIRECTED the kid to the sofa, where he groaned as he splatted to the couch and curled onto his side. He'd eaten an astonishing amount of food, not even for his size, but in a universal, food-competition kind of way.

"I can tell you don't need help cleaning. You've got this." Daniel's words were barely audible through his intense yawn. "But if you did, I could totally help."

"And I can tell by your choice of phrasing that you desperately want to help, Daniel, but I do have this. Relax."

"If you insist." Daniel snuggled into a pillow. "Everything was so delicious, by the way. The broccoli-adjacent things—"

"Broccolini."

"—were cooked to perfection and the ragù. Oh, the ragù was beautiful—no." His lips curled into a ridiculous grin, like whatever about to roll from them was pure genius. "It was ragùtiful."

Aaron snorted—okay, not bad—as he fanned a blanket over his body. Their conversation had bopped around all freeform and giggly with no particular objective. Daniel was easy to talk to. He was even easier to take care of. Maybe because he coasted into Aaron's nurturing nature without a fight, or perhaps he preferred a more passive role. Whatever the reason, something about Daniel begged to be tended like a tarty little emperor, and something inside of Aaron ached to do it.

He tucked the blanket around Daniel's chin, lapping up his sweet, humming reaction like a thirsty dog. He should probably slow way the hell down with the… fondness he was beginning to experience. Not that he was against *fondness*, but for all he knew, Daniel might choose to vanish after a night or two. It seemed like most guys vanished after a night or two, after *going to the farmer's market*. Unless they were clients. He wished those guys would do less lingering and more vanishing.

Aaron leaned over the edge of the sofa. "You want hot chocolate?"

"Why, I'd love some, Norman Rockwell," Daniel responded without opening his eyes. "Sounds scenic."

Aaron tossed his gaze upward but couldn't *not* chuckle as he started for the kitchen.

"I hope you know how difficult it's going to be to get rid of me, as you've thoroughly spoiled me," Daniel called out. "I might as well go ahead and move in."

Aaron smirked as he poured milk into a pot. Of course, he was kidding, but the Fondness couldn't tell and thus grew anyway. "You think we're ready for that?"

"Duh. What's up there?" Daniel pointed to the loft upstairs. "I'll need somewhere to store all my mangling insecurities."

"Up there?" He rubbed his fingers over his mouth as he gazed up at the loft. Man, he hadn't been up there in a while. He grinned at the thought of it.

"Why are you smiling?" Daniel gasped as he shot up from the couch like he wasn't just dying in a food coma. "Aaron. Do you have a sex dungeon?"

"How can it be a dungeon? It's upstairs."

"A sex… sky parlor?"

"Get up. Follow me."

They trekked up the spiral staircase, and Daniel's mouth fell agape when they reached the landing.

Aaron's black baby grand sat in the corner, all shiny and over-the-top. It'd cost a fortune to haul up here and keep it tuned. But it sure did look objectively impressive, sitting atop a white sugar shag rug, surrounded by chic, spongy white chairs.

"Whoa." Daniel looked afraid to touch it as he pinged around, gawking at different angles. "Holy cow. Can you play it?"

That was the typical reaction from clients. Especially if they were stressed or nervous, he'd mix them a drink, usually something more robust than hot chocolate, and take requests (of all sorts). It worked wonders to loosen up newcomers.

"Be silly to own it and not play it." He scooted onto the bench and lifted the cover. "Your wish is my command, sweetheart. Shoot. We'll see if I know it."

"How long have you been playing?" Daniel asked. "Where'd you learn?"

"What's that? Oh." He cleared his throat. He wasn't necessarily used to questions about it. "Since I was four. My mom was a piano teacher."

"She was?" Daniel pressed both hands over his heart. "Oh, and look at you now. Still playing. Doing so well. If she could see you, I'm sure she'd be so proud of you."

Aaron had wondered before if she would be proud of him. Or if she would be shocked at who he'd become. He liked to think she'd find a way to see *him* beneath how he made his living, but he tried not to wonder in earnest.

"Play me something she taught you. Something she loved."

He didn't mean to give Daniel what had to be a vacant stare.

"If you feel comfortable, that is," Daniel hastened to say. "No pressure."

"No, I like it. That's, um, a different request, but nice. Nice to think about." He scratched his cheek and scanned the walls as if they'd help. As if they were printed in music. Something she loved? Something she loved. A smile tugged at his lips. Man, what didn't she love?

He tipped his head to the side and started to stroke the keys. Before she got sick, she loved badminton. She loved cozy mystery novels and the idea of a tearoom, even though she barely tolerated tea. Whatever he was playing began to pick up rhythm, still gentle but bubbly. Like her. She loved her fish tank. She'd make the same guilty face every time she came home with a new impulsive "fish buy."

He softly snorted as his fingertips danced over the keys in a spry little melody that began to take shape. Cool and slick, the keys warmed as he played on.

She loved her sunroom, cinnamon-flavored anything, bluebirds, and bonfires. She loved making fun of that one lady at church who scolded Aaron for being too fidgety. She *loved* him and Andrew. *Loved* lounging around, stroking their hair, substituting the words of songs with their names to make them giggle. She loved her boys. All of them. Even their dad.

Aaron's hands hesitated to continue as something clenched inside his chest. It was as if the melody suddenly didn't feel right, so he added another layer to balance it. Balance was important. Maybe that was it; she thought she could love their dad so much that, eventually, the scales would stabilize. She loved him so much that she didn't leave. Said she couldn't. Said she wouldn't. *I don't have a dime to my name, boys. We won't make it. They'll take you away. I can't let them take you away.*

Whatever he was playing had evolved into something deeper with a blunt blueprint. He clenched his teeth as he played harder, leaning into how complicated it sounded.

The thing was, they all loved their dad. They didn't know any better. It wasn't until Aaron got a little older that he realized they weren't thriving as a family so much, bonded by traditions. A strand of hair fell as he stamped the keys.

I don't have a dime to my name, boys. Money. She couldn't leave because of money. *We won't make it. I can't let them take you away.* So they stayed. They weren't a family, and it wasn't a home. It was a waiting room, and they were all just sort of there. Waiting for change that would never come.

Aaron sucked in a quick breath and slowly exhaled. It was probably a little late to be playing, and his neighbor on the right was a total chode, mostly about visitors but sometimes about noise, so he softened whatever tune that was. His fingertips barely licked the keys as he quelled the song to a finish.

"I'm rusty." He cracked his knuckles and twisted back to Daniel. "I should probably practice—"

Daniel sat stiffened in the chair with his fingertips clenched white in his lap and his eyes wide and reddened. He was... crying?

"Holy hell." Aaron stood so fast he nearly knocked the bench over. "Oh my God, what happened? Why are you crying?"

"Um." Daniel's hands shook as he frantically wiped his cheeks. "I don't know. I'm sorry. I'm so sorry."

"I don't understand." Aaron knelt in front of him and grasped his arms, fighting for his eye contact. "Are you hurt?"

"No," he whispered pitifully. "Th-th-the piano."

"What?" Aaron knitted his eyebrows together and shook his head. "You're crying over the piano?"

"No."

"Then why are you crying?"

"Over the way you played it." Daniel's voice sounded broken and strange. He buried his face in his hands. "Which is so embarrassing— I'm fine. I swear, I'm fine. Give me a minute."

"Aw, kid." He wrapped his arms around him and pulled them up to a stand, where he rubbed his back in slow circles. "Shh, it's okay."

"That was intense and heartbreaking for some reason." Daniel curled into his chest. "And so beautiful, Aaron. Really, *really* beautiful."

He hugged Daniel tighter. He felt so fragile in his arms, almost frail, like he could break, which wasn't true. Daniel wasn't frail, and there was no shame in crying, but it also wasn't a language Aaron knew how to speak. It almost felt like a language no one knew how to speak anymore. Like somewhere along the way, everyone had forgotten how. The Fondness grew until it bulged around the seams.

"*You're* really beautiful." He cradled Daniel's head against his chest and kissed his curls. "You're intense and beautiful. You know that?"

Daniel's words were muffled as he sniffled and said, "I know it doesn't seem like it right now, but I promise I'm normal."

"No, hey. Look at me." He held Daniel's shoulders and ducked down to catch his gaze. He kissed the wet streak of a fallen tear on his cheek. "This is precious. It's so precious. Thank you."

Daniel blinked his pinkened eyes. "Thank me? For what?"

"For letting me see that. How brave." He kissed his lips, whispering every few seconds, "So brave."

Aaron wanted to stand there holding him until his legs gave out, bearing his weight, soaking up the tenderness like a chunk of bread in soup. It was like seeing a beautiful vase in a museum only to discover that the long crack running down the side was what made it so priceless.

After a minute, Daniel broke them apart to swab his shirt over his face as he forced a weak smile. "Well, if ever there was a mood, I sure did ruin it, huh? I should probably take off. Thank you so much for everything. Dinner was so delightful—"

"You didn't ruin it." Aaron's breathing was edgy, and his hands were suddenly on Daniel's body, in his hair, gripping with agency of their own. How was he to soak up the tenderness if the tenderness left? "You didn't ruin anything. Don't leave. Stay. I want you to stay."

Daniel's lips parted and a speck of a tear from his long lashes splashed his cheek as Aaron tilted his head back for him. "Stay as in… the farmer's market?"

He pressed a kiss on Daniel's pouty lips. "Yes." He pressed another. "Or maybe just the parking lot of the farmer's market."

Daniel chuckled. "I mean, do *not* get me wrong. I'm *amped* about whatever the hell that means, but what about taking it slowly? I thought you wanted to take it slowly. Like gentlemen."

Yeah, about that. Aaron couldn't pretend it wouldn't hit deeply if they messed around and Daniel didn't answer his phone tomorrow, but he didn't have it in him to say, *Good point. We should wait.* The kid just cried in front of him. There wasn't much more intimate than that.

"You precious, *precious* thing," he whispered into Daniels mouth, then bent down, caught him by his waist, and slung his little body over his shoulder, making him squeal all raspy and cute. He slapped his ass and started for the stairs. "I only have so much gentleman in me."

DANIEL YELPED when Aaron flung him onto his bed, tossing him down like the sack of sex-fiend potatoes he was. It barely had time to register that it smelled better than expected—orris butter and expensive suede— before he was scrambling back off it to undress Aaron.

"I want you to promise me something," Aaron said as Daniel tried to work his sweater off for him. He should probably not stretch it or rip it to shreds like he wanted. People who could afford cashmere likely frowned upon that kind of thing. "I want you to promise you'll answer your phone tomorrow."

"Boy, what a ridiculous thing to say to me—off! Sorry." He took a breath. "I didn't mean to yell, but you must take this off before I lose my mind."

Aaron chuckled as he gracefully pulled the sweater overhead, which had an annoying undershirt beneath it. "I don't want to be someone you only talk to at one a.m., but never during the day. I'm done being that."

"I'm so into you I could scream. I might. I might actually start screaming."

Aaron unbuckled his belt in slow motion, or it was probably regular motion, but it needed to be about twenty times faster if anyone cared about Daniel's opinion. "And like you said, we'd planned to take it slower than this."

"Don't you love it when plans change? I personally love a good, modified plan."

Aaron stepped out of his jeans to reveal midnight blue boxer briefs that just *worked*. They worked so hard. "But I know what I want. It's not to be someone's occasional hookup."

Daniel had to halt. God, someone had done a number on this man. Someone, maybe more than one person, had genuinely hurt him. Which, *what*? It made no sense, but whoever it was deserved to be cursed with bad sex for a year.

"Jesus, okay." He swatted his hands around the air. "I can't believe I'm about to say this, but stop undressing and listen to me."

Aaron froze.

"You are a spectacular catch, Aaron. Not only are you caring, but you're witty, and talented, and wildly successful—and I'm really trying to name things that have nothing to do with how you look, but I'm only human—you're *stunning* too. I'm shocked you've had the kind of luck you've had with guys, but my only guess is that you've dated assholes who don't deserve your time. Who don't deserve to hear you play the piano."

Aaron's mouth curled into the most sheepish grin possible.

"I wasn't joking when I said you're never getting rid of me. You're lucky I don't put a fucking tracker on you—why are you smiling at that? Don't smile at that." He couldn't help but smile too. "You shouldn't indulge my crazy. It'll only make it worse."

Aaron exhaled a chuckle.

"I'm into you, mister. I'm going to answer your call tomorrow, and the one after that, and the one after that, because I'm so into you. Okay?"

Aaron's shoulders softened a bit with his nod.

"Now, if we're done with the whole *I like you; I like you too* business, come stand right here"—he positioned Aaron by the soft light of the lamp—"so that I might objectify the shit out of you."

He stepped back and chewed his thumbnail as Aaron tugged his shirt overhead, and whatever generic image he'd been using in his mind for Aaron's body tucked its tail and retreated to its cave as the troll it was. Dear Aphrodite, goddess of horny, this man was art.

The V-cut lines just above his hips were even more pronounced than the muscles funneling into them, and then, speaking of muscles, the serrated blades of his rib cage—the ones people often overlooked but gave such depth to a fellow's torso—didn't disappoint. Neither did all that perfect, *perfect* skin. It was apparent he worked for it, but Daniel was the one cashing in. What a blessed day.

"Lie down," Aaron said, unclasping his watch. "Open your mouth."

The hairs on Daniel's arms stood in salute. Oh. He hadn't expected both hot and straightforward, and he stumbled a little at how to respond. "Right now?"

"Lie down on the bed," Aaron calmly repeated, tipping his chin toward the bed. "Open your mouth."

So, right now it was. Daniel failed at *composed and nonchalant* with the air he caught on his leap to the bed, but he made up for it by draping himself sensually over a pillow. Oh, but dammit, he was still wearing pants, so he scrambled to yank those off, then back to the sensual pillow draping.

Aaron chuckled and crawled in after him. "You look good in my bed."

He batted his lashes. "Do I?"

"Uh-huh, all laid out. Easy to read." Aaron didn't hold back his full weight as he edged between Daniel's legs. Heavy. Heavy and broad, like dozens of pounds of weight-trained muscle. "Just a pretty little book."

"Yeah?" He wrapped his legs around Aaron's waist. "I'm an open book?"

"Easy." Aaron nuzzled his nose. "*Easy* to read."

He raked his fingers through Aaron's hair. "How so, mister—?"

Aaron swiftly wedged two enormous fingers into Daniel's mouth, stinging it in salt, nearly brushing the back of his throat. Daniel's eyes rounded, but his moan generated from somewhere within, somewhere guttural, as his underwear instantly slicked.

"Like that, sweetheart," Aaron whispered inches from his face. His aquamarine eyes were even more gorgeous, all half-lidded with lust. "Nod if you're okay."

He nodded, clenching Aaron's shoulders as his fingers pushed a little deeper. Aaron worked his underwear down with the same proficiency as he seemed to do other things: with a magnitude of skill and without breaking their eye contact. He started to stroke, and Daniel's spine arched like a poetic dance in response.

"You know what I thought when I saw you walk into that party?" Aaron paused to lick his hand, then back to the stroking. "I thought, how do I taste him? What do I say so he'll let me put my tongue on his body? Because I was sure you tasted as sweet as you looked."

Daniel had rhythm, but it was nowhere to be found as he writhed like a whimpering worm on a hook under Aaron's body.

"And now?" Aaron continued. "I *know* you do. Which is why I'm going to take you into my mouth. And drain you completely dry."

Daniel... nodded again? Maybe? He did something with his head.

"Every last drop, sweet boy." Aaron continued to stroke him as he tenderly kissed his cheek. As he not-so-tenderly fucked his mouth with his thick fingers. "That sound good?"

It did sound good to Daniel, who suddenly felt like an inexperienced teenager with a first-time encounter, all adrenalized and felt up behind the bleachers. For someone who was sugar by nature with his dinners and his flowers, Aaron sure had some spice to unearth. It was just words. It was just his hand. So why was it also goddamn everything?

"And just like that." Aaron breathed a light chuckle into his ear. "You're close, aren't you?"

Yes, you demon! You steamy, life-giving bed demon! Usually, he'd feel humbled if he couldn't last longer than five minutes, but who could blame him? This was madness. It wasn't his fault he had slipped under a bed demon's control.

He whined when Aaron pulled his fingers from his mouth, suddenly less full, less complete—come back; he wanted them back.

"I like you," Aaron rasped as he gripped his jaw and sealed their lips together in a kiss. A kiss that streaked Daniel's skin in wet licks when it journeyed down his chest and beyond his belly. "I like you a lot."

"You. I like...." Daniel trailed off in some gruff version of his voice. He'd meant to return the sentiment, but he lost all mental ammo when Aaron's tongue and full lips wrapped around him in his fucking entirety. As it turned out, between Aaron's hand and his mouth, his mouth was the bigger half of the wishbone.

A little shaken—or how about flummoxed; undisputedly flummoxed—Daniel pushed up to his elbows and stared down at Aaron, who had the type of mastery one only fantasized about. Skill, heart, fury, it was Goldilocks the way he took it deep and rough yet cautious and smooth. Entire worlds could bloom inside his mouth, where his confidence fused with his appetite to ensure *Every last drop, sweet boy. Every last drop.*

Orris butter, expensive suede, and soaking wet drool all blazed Daniel's senses as he gritted his teeth and twined his fingers into Aaron's chocolate hair. Emotions churned from somewhere deep in his core: adoration for the demon, respect for his prowess, gratitude to be lying here, and anger. Because it was already over.

He growled like a rumbling volcano with a need to erupt as his loose grip on Aaron's hair constricted into a tight fist and his breath swooshed in loud gasps. His limbs galvanized, and his spine bowed from the mattress in a wild arch as if this were some kind of a well-rehearsed ballet and not the most exciting thing to happen to his dick in ages.

Aaron nodded his encouragement, or nodded the best he could, when Daniel urged himself deeper and even offered a hand for him to squeeze—what a fucking gentleman—which Daniel clasped until it turned white and screamed through his teeth until they vibrated and worked his hips, almost blurting *sex demon!* as he finally exploded into Aaron's mouth.

Aaron didn't so much as flinch. He did, however, burn a stunning visual into Daniel's memory—the way his throat bobbed with each swallow; the way his hard jawline danced in the light like cut glass; the way his mouth grew carnal and even more urgent as he guzzled cum like an expert on his quest for *no drop left behind*.

No drop was left behind.

Daniel's muscles stayed taut for what felt like an eternity as he rode the waves of his little buzz until they mollified into the laps of some distant shore. He tried to anchor into the support of the bed, but it was made of kitten-shaped clouds, and his whole body trembled, including the hand he almost poked himself in the eye with as he smeared it over his face.

"You know what I just remembered?" Aaron said, standing and wiping his mouth on the back of his hand. "The hot chocolate. Do you still want it?"

"Put a tracker on you." Daniel genuinely didn't mean to say that. It wasn't an answer. It wasn't even a complete sentence. "I mean, marry me—what? Shh, demon." He held a finger to his lips. "Shh. Let's start over."

Aaron's smile was wide and amused. Like a life-giving bed demon.

"I mean, I'd love to recipra-reciprote-recip—I can't talk—*reciprocate*." Daniel outstretched his arms, which were shaking an embarrassing amount. "My brain doesn't need to work for that. Come. Come forth."

Aaron swatted a hand. "We'll worry about me some other time. The hot chocolate. Yes? No?"

Hot chocolate? How could they be talking about hot chocolate like Aaron hadn't just fucked him up with his mouth and they hadn't just combusted on a rocket ship, never to return? In the end, he managed a quivering thumbs-up, because why not sip hot cocoa in bed like a couple of proper Boy Scouts? Golly gee whiz. It actually sounded swell.

"I'll go make it." Aaron strolled around the bed. He leaned down to tilt Daniel's chin up with a gentle command of his fingertips. "I don't expect it to taste as good as you. You are fucking *dazzling*."

Daniel watched him leave the room through a bit of a daze.

What.

The.

Hell.

Marry me, demon.

AARON'S ROOM smelled like cocoa powder and marshmallows as he lay with Daniel snuggled into the nook of his shoulder. Daniel walked his fingertips up and down his stomach, giggling to himself and whispering an occasional *so good* against his skin. *So good, you beautiful man.*

The Fondness had swelled. It'd ballooned out of control, filling the room with an intoxicating gas that made Aaron feel high on the possibilities of what the future could hold. He loved Daniel in his arms. Loved that he fit so perfectly—a little *jig* to his *saw*. He loved his orange sherbet-y taste and that his curls smelled a little like Aaron's shampoo. A smile tugged at his lips as he dipped his nose into Daniel's hair and inhaled. Almost as if he'd been claimed. *If found, please return to Aaron. This is Aaron's Daniel.*

Daniel rolled onto his belly and gazed up, all blooming pink lips and melted caramel eyes. "Hey, mister."

He shook his head as he picked an eyelash off Daniel's cheek. "Why do you call me that?"

"Mister?" Daniel plopped his chin in his palm and swung his legs in kicks. "I don't know. I think because you have your shit together. Like a mister."

He snorted and smeared a palm over his eye. "I don't know about that."

"You clearly do, Aaron. You've purchased broccolini. At least once."

"I didn't realize that was all it took?"

"Yep." Daniel nodded. "I would do it myself, but I'm not ready for people thinking I have my shit together."

"Oh baby." He petted Daniel's hair. "I don't think you have to worry about anyone thinking that."

Daniel chuckled as he swatted him off. "What's it like having your shit together? Do people expect you to show up on time to appointments? Throw dinner parties with cloth napkins? Do they expect you not to cry in bank lobbies?"

"You've cried in a bank lobby?"

"Of course not." Daniel cut his eyes to the side. "It was a bank office."

"Aw, kid. Come here." He pulled Daniel into him and gripped him in a tight hug. "Goddammit. I'm sorry."

"Oh, well, this is nice," Daniel said, his words muffled against his chest. "But it's okay. I've been a stereotypical hot mess for a while."

"Man, I don't know what I'd do if I saw someone like you crying in a bank." He rested his chin on Daniel's head and searched the walls. "I bet I'd be tempted to give you all my money."

"What bank do you use, and is there a time of day you prefer to handle your banking needs? Asking for a friend."

He smacked Daniel's ass.

"Oh, is that the best we can do?" Daniel asked, furrowing his brow as he squeezed Aaron's biceps. "I would've thought these muscles would be good for something, but just kind of for show, hmm? Shame."

Aaron smirked as he spanked him more forcefully.

Daniel rolled his eyes so hard it looked like he might be possessed. "I see you think I'm made entirely of glass—"

He spanked him one more time at his full strength, which spurred a rewarding little yelp from him.

"Oh, ouch, Mr. Silva, ouch, it hurts." Daniel pouted, the sexy swell of his mouth curling upward. "Don't stop."

Aaron sucked his cheeks. *Trouble.*

"So, speaking of being a hot mess—"

"Well, at least you're hot."

"—I might be crying in a bank soon. Hopefully tears of joy, but we'll see." Daniel shuffled out of his arms to sit up, suddenly beaming. "My boss has offered me a chance to buy the dance studio where I work."

Aaron's eyebrows shot up.

"I've been mulling it over for a few days—" Daniel swallowed. "—and I think I'm going to do it."

"No way! Well, holy hell, kid. That's incredible. Congratulations."

"Yeah?" Daniel winced as he tapped his fingertips together. "You think so?"

"Obviously. I mean, if you want to own a dance studio. You want to own a dance studio?"

"Oh, I would love it. Aaron, I would love, love, *love* to own it. I don't think there's anything I would love more. It'd be a dream come true."

Was Aaron within his right to suddenly feel so proud of him? To pump the Fondness full of even more *fond*?

"But do you honestly think I could do it?" Daniel squeezed his fists beneath his chin and huddled into himself like he was scared of the answer. "As someone who is not a hot mess, do you think I could do it? What if I fail? What if I'm the worst studio owner anyone's ever seen?"

Well, there was no pretending that wasn't valid. Even if another person's leap of faith always seemed so feasible—*Are you kidding me? Do it! Absolutely. It's your dream. What's stopping you?* But if he were in Daniel's shoes, if it were *his* leap of faith up for debate, would he do it?

No.

That was why he'd been stuck in the same relentless pattern since he was nineteen, a prisoner to his fear of change. His fear of loss. There was no job he was qualified to do that would make him the money he made now. Money was a fickle friend with crushing demands, and there was never enough.

But Daniel was different. Not only was he more magnetic and wholeheartedly feisty, but there was something rare and honest about him. Self-effacing, sure, but honest. He was a precious little gemstone that just needed the right tools to make him shine, and if anyone could be shameless enough in their pursuits—the fucking troublemaker—to bear the brunt of owning their own business, it would be him. Not to mention, the way he moved was dazzling and he commanded any room he was in with an unrivaled amount of sass. People would probably gush to hand him their money. Hell, *Aaron* would probably gush to hand Daniel money.

"What kind of an attitude is that?" Aaron wrinkled his brow, firing some bravado behind his words. "This is your dream. You've been given a shot to make your *dream* come true. I have no doubt you'll be the best dance studio owner anyone's ever seen. You won't fail. There's no way. I bet you'll fucking soar."

Daniel launched forward into his arms and clutched him hard enough that Aaron had to hold his breath to keep from grunting. "Thank you, mister. Thank you. I needed to hear that."

He smiled into the crook of Daniel's neck as he hugged him back. "You're welcome, kid."

"Shit, I'm sorry." Daniel chuckled as he wiggled free to wipe his eyes, because that exchange had made him… start to tear up. "It's just a lot to hear someone say something like that to me. I appreciate it so much. I'm fine—er, I'll be fine in a second. Give me a second."

Aaron twitched for something to do with his hands. He didn't want to give him a second. He wanted to yank him back in and coo into his ear until his tears dried, but he forced himself still, because it didn't need to be stopped or shushed. It needed to be honored. It was fascinating how Daniel's emotions seemed to govern him, like with the piano.

"Okay," Daniel said, his face splitting into a soggy grin. "Sorry about that."

Just like with the piano, Aaron couldn't keep his mouth from lifting in a half-smile as he watched in a bit of wide-eyed wonder while the kid *felt*. He *felt* so deeply.

"So," Daniel said, clearing his throat. "I might need to elicit your help with some of the legal stuff."

Aaron had perhaps been a little distracted. He parted his lips to respond but closed them until he'd had a chance to repeat that sentence in his head. "What? What legal stuff?"

"The contract. Do you think you could look over the contract for me? To make sure all looks well with it?"

He blinked. "You want *me* to look over your contract?"

"Well, maybe just skim it? Look, I'm not expecting you to read it word for word. I realize you probably charge a fortune for something like that, and the only currency I have is maybe a back massage. Could I pay you in a really good back massage?"

He couldn't speak, but it wasn't his fault. It was the air in the room. It was like it had evaporated in an instant. "Wh-why would I charge you for something like that?"

"So, does that mean you'll do it for free?" Daniel winced as he lowered his chin and peered up through his lashes. "Oh my God, if you do it for free, I promise I won't ask you for a bunch of pro bono legal shit. I'm not even going to mention my two outstanding parking tickets. And by two, I mean six."

"But why again?" he asked in some rough variation of his voice as he aggressively smoothed his eyebrow, blood swooshing in his ears loud enough to sound like white noise. "Why do you want me to look at the contract?"

Daniel's pouty mouth tilted into a lopsided grin as he crawled across the bed. "Because I trust you, mister."

Aaron didn't shut his eyes when Daniel pressed their lips together. He kept them wide open.

"And because you're the only attorney I know."

Chapter Seven

AARON HAD made it to the kitchen. Coughing and claiming he had something itching his throat, he'd ambled out of bed to chug what would be the first of two large glasses of glacial refrigerator water. Now his temples ached in a brain freeze, but it was nothing compared to his heart, which throbbed through beats like he just threw up. He might throw up.

Daniel thought he was an attorney. He scraped his hands through his hair over and over. An attorney. How? *How*? Because of the party?

Well, no wonder he'd agreed to go out with him. No wonder he'd argued Aaron was a "spectacular catch." He probably wanted to introduce him to his friends. His parents. *This is the successful attorney I'm seeing. Aaron Silva, Esquire.* No wonder Daniel liked him at all.

He shrank into the shadowy corner of the kitchen like a struck animal. He liked him *because* he had no idea who he was. It'd be almost laughable if it wasn't so fucking unfair.

"Are you okay?" Daniel was suddenly standing in the kitchen, eyes alarmed and forehead etched in concern.

Aaron licked his lips. A voice from within wanted to blurt it out. Blurt it out and own it and be done with it. If Daniel wanted to judge him, then Daniel could fucking leave. He could leave, and he could stay gone and fine. Just fine. They'd never talk again.

But that wasn't the most deafening voice demanding his attention. The voice demanding his attention was the one terrified to lose something so precious. It was the voice that said, *If you tell him, he'll hate you. You'll die if he hates you.*

"Aaron," Daniel said, his voice underscored in worry. "Did I say something wrong? Did I overstep with you? You don't have to look over the contract. It was just a thought."

Aaron pushed himself off the wall and stood a little taller but couldn't quite meet Daniel's gaze. If he didn't find a way to be alone and sift through his manic thoughts, he'd be sure to regret whatever poured from his mouth, which had to be so perfectly stated that Daniel wouldn't hate him. *You'll die if he hates you.*

He forced a smile. "I had a really good time with you tonight. A really, *really* good time. Did you enjoy yourself?"

Daniel tilted his head as his eyebrows slanted. "Well, yeah. Tonight was amazing."

Aaron nodded. *Remember that.* "It *was* amazing. But I need to get some sleep, okay? I have an early day tomorrow."

Daniel didn't budge or say anything, probably waiting for a follow-up, an explanation, or an invite that included his presence, but Aaron pinched his lips together on the urge to recant and let the silence dilate between them. The thundering silence.

"Oh," Daniel finally said, his voice a bit shrunken. It looked like so much hurt on his pretty face, and Lord, if he started crying, Aaron's armor would sop into a pathetic puddle on the floor. "I see. So then, I guess I'll take off."

Fuck. "I really did have an incredible time with you."

"Yeah, me too. I'll um, I'll get my things." Daniel wandered around the apartment in bit of a daze, gathering his bag, phone, and shoes. He shed Aaron's sweatpants and T-shirt and slipped back into his dance clothes while Aaron drank more water just to have something to do that didn't involve violently screaming.

He rubbed his eyes as he followed Daniel toward the door. "I'll call you tomorrow."

"Uh-huh," Daniel said, a bit clipped. "Sounds good."

Or maybe he wouldn't call. Maybe this was the most optimal outcome. They'd shared a few amazing nights together, and now they could part ways, and neither of them would get hurt. Daniel couldn't hate him for being very much *not* an attorney if he never knew.

He would just hate him in other normal ways. Hate him for being an asshole. For kicking him out like an unwanted squatter. *He'll hate you. You'll die if he hates you.*

Aaron unclenched his teeth. "Kid, wait—"

"Why do you call me that?" Daniel spun around, his arms crossed over his jacket.

Aaron blinked.

"You wanted to know why I called you *mister*. Why do you call me *kid*? You're not that much older than me."

"I don't know, honestly." He shook his head. "But if you don't like it—"

"I like it." Daniel's eyes widened. He nearly glared in contrast to his words. "Of course I like it. I think it's sweet and I think you're sweet, and I like you too, Aaron."

He was going to throw up.

Daniel pressed up to his toes and quickly pecked his cheek. "I hope you get some rest."

Aaron watched him leave in a haste, passing right by the elevator on his dash to the stairs.

No, he wouldn't get much rest, and no. Daniel didn't like *him*.

Chapter Eight

IT WAS the next day, Aaron hadn't called, and Daniel was *not* freaking out about it. He rubbed warmth into his arms as he hunched over the steering wheel of his car outside of the studio, waiting for it to heat up. He dialed Olivia.

"Let me guess." Her voice chimed over his car speakers. "You're freaking out about it."

"No," he responded, huffing into his cupped hands. "Why would I freak out that he expelled me from his house?"

Her eye roll was almost audible. "He didn't expel you from his house."

"Oh yes, he did. He practically picked me up and *threw* me out. I'm surprised he didn't start playing symphony music as I was getting dressed like they do at the Oscars."

"Literally all he said was that he had to work early."

Daniel rumbled in fake laughter. "An excuse if I've ever heard one. What's next? His invisible dog ate my phone number, and that's why he never called me again?"

"*Never* called you again? It's been less than one day—"

"Let's face it." He sighed, flittering a hand about. "He just wanted to get me into bed."

Olivia barely contained a chuckle. "Which he did, correct?"

"Mm-hmm." He flicked his gaze upward and inspected his nails. "Typical man."

"The bed where he pleased *you*. Blew *your* mind. Almost killed you with his extreme sexiness and asked for nothing in return. That bed?"

"Yep," he said, popping the *p*.

"God, you're right. Sounds awful. You think this was his evil plan from the beginning? With the flowers and the dates and the homecooked meal from scratch. It was all so he could *never* talk to you again?"

He narrowed his eyes to a squint. "Okay, I see what you're doing here—"

"Well, I would hope so. I'm not being subtle."

"—and I don't appreciate it. Lest we forget, he *ejected* me from his house. Basically dropkicked me. You know what? That's it." He threw his hands up. "I'm blocking him."

"Daniel. Has it ever occurred to you—?"

"No," he said, balancing the phone on his console so he could search his dance bag for his lip balm. "Whatever you're about to say, no. I'm pretty self-absorbed."

"Has it ever occurred to you that maybe it had nothing to do with you?"

He found the lip balm, flipping down the visor mirror to apply it. "Did I not just mention the self-absorbed thing?"

"Maybe he really was tired or, I don't know, practicing healthy boundaries."

"The hell do those have to do with this?"

"I'm just saying. Let's not write him off as some asshole when so far—"

After a few seconds of silence, he realized the call had disconnected, and Olivia wasn't just taking her time to formulate an argument. He tried to grab his phone to call her back, but it stumbled from his hands and wedged between the seat and the center console. The worst place for a phone to wedge.

"Well, shit. Hold on," he said, jamming his hand to reach it as it started to ring. When he finally got ahold of it, it seemed he'd already answered the call, and it wasn't Olivia.

His eyes widened as his stomach folded over itself in protest. "No," he breathed. But it was too late.

"Hello?" His dad's voice sounded over the speakers.

Shit, shit, shit. He could hang up and pretend it never happened? It'd been over a month since they'd last spoken, but in his defense, why would he take a phone call that was sure to leave him feeling empty, enraged, and hungry for deep fried chicken he didn't need?

"Dan. Hello?" His dad's voice was its usual *burdened* but with an extra dash of *vexed* to spice things up. "Are you there?"

"Yes," he said, hanging his head. "I'm here."

"Jesus, finally. Where the hell have you been?"

Nowhere special. Probably sitting somewhere with his phone in hand, declining his dad's calls. He rolled his lips. "I've been busy."

"Doing what?"

"Working."

"You mean *dancing*?"

He ground his teeth as he glared at the windshield. "Yeah, can we maybe not do this whole thing tonight? I've got a lot on my mind."

"What whole thing?"

"The thing where you call and make me feel terrible about my life."

"You mean, the thing where I call and offer guidance for your life? And all you do is bitch about it, then shut me out?"

"Telling me to give up dance is not guidance, Robert. It's hurtful."

"No, what's hurtful is my twenty-five-year-old son *dancing* as a career."

Daniel fought a longing to wither up like a forgotten houseplant. It was difficult to describe the sensation he got whenever they had this conversation. If he sat quietly with it for a minute, it felt suspiciously familiar to a craving. The sensible part of him knew he didn't *need* his dad's approval, but the feeble, manic part of him insisted he *wanted* it. Either way, he wasn't getting it, so he ran his tongue over his teeth and said, "Like I said, I don't have the mental capacity for this tonight—"

"You never have the 'mental capacity' for it. That's the problem."

"Don't you have other things to worry about? I'm sure you have a new girlfriend. Hopefully she has a kid, so you can raise one that isn't such an embarrassment."

He'd never met any of his dad's many girlfriends. Never been invited to their house for a potluck. But his emotionally aloof father didn't have the "mental capacity" for conversations that didn't revolve around Daniel's career, which is why he said, "The financial choices you make today will affect your future. I know you're young, but someday you'll thank me. You want to have a normal life someday, right? You want to be able to pay your rent?"

"I love my life, and I pay my rent."

"Always? Is that always the case? Or do *I* have to pay it sometimes?"

One time. *One* time, he'd asked for help—something he'd always regret—and that was because his car's timing belt went out at the worst possible timing. "I paid you back for that."

"That's not the point. You shouldn't be this far behind on retirement. Irresponsible isn't even the word for it, and all so you can, what? Wear a fucking crop top to work?"

Daniel squelched a scream. "I dance because I love it. It makes me happy. It's always made me happy."

"Then dance in your living room, Dan. Don't stake your future on it."

"It's Daniel, and too late. I'm buying it." No. No, rewind and unsay that. He should not tell his father about buying the studio. If he was seeking any approval whatsoever, he was about to get the opposite.

"You're buying…? What?"

His words got snagged on some jagged inner fear. Saying it aloud meant he'd very much have to own it. In more ways than one.

"What are you buying? You can't afford to buy anything."

He invited a long breath in and sat up taller with his exhale. "Madeline is selling the studio. The price is fair. It's my literal dream come true, and so I'm buying it."

An empty silence filled the car, or it could have been his dad disconnecting the call. That might have been the wedge that finally split their relationship's foundation, but either way, it'd been shoddy craftsmanship from the start. He wouldn't let himself do what he wanted to do, which was to begin to hope.

Even if this was maybe the one place hope could grow after all, within the confines of a business proposition was where Robert felt most comfortable. Perhaps the silence meant he was weighing the outcomes in his numbers-over-people managerial style and had discovered the value in owning a dance studio as adored as Madeline's.

Daniel wrung his fingertips together and asked, "Hello? You there?"

"Unfortunately," his dad finally responded with a heaviness he didn't have before. "I cannot believe my ears. Are you absolutely insane?"

"Yeah." He tried to keep his chin lifted enough to nod, but it wobbled like a balloon on a stick. "Figured you might say that."

"Even if you didn't have to take out another loan to buy it, you don't know the first thing about running a business."

"Madeline thinks I do." It was a weak argument, and he knew it. "Madeline says I run it already."

"Lord, how are you still this naïve? I'm sure Madeline would say a lot of things to get out from under a bad investment, and of course she'd prey on someone like *you*."

Someone like you. It stung worse than venom. Someone like him was someone always a little too young to be taken seriously, a little too old to not have his shit together, and a little too naïve to own a business.

Daniel, settle down, you're too anxious. Daniel, stop crying, you're too emotional. You're too amateur. You're too gay; too dramatic; too annoying. Daniel, you're too much.

He hated being too much.

"All I want to do is help you," his dad said, sounding exhausted. "That's all I want, and I'm trying, but you need to listen. I have a real plan. A friend of mine might be willing to hire you at his accounting firm. You can't show up to work in damn yoga pants, but—"

"As always, Robert, great chat."

"Wait—"

A headache the size of a Buick rolled from the crown of his head and down his forehead, crashing behind his eyes, but it was nothing a hot bath, half a box of wine, and a good linoleum floor cry couldn't fix.

A few minutes later, he pulled into his driveway and dragged himself out of the car. With his bag slung over one arm and Aaron's calla lilies in the other, he trudged up his walkway when he heard a plink. He sighed down at his keys on the concrete. Because of course he dropped his fucking keys. He could join them. Just lie down. Give up.

"Shit," a voice hissed from the shadows of his front porch.

Daniel jumped enough to spill the lily water. His heart galloped over itself as he focused through the darkness on the figure of a man crouched on the porch.

"I'm sorry," said the figure, scrambling upright. "I wasn't expecting you to come home—not, like, in a stalker way!"

Which sounded exactly like something a stalker would say. His heart careered faster when the stalker stepped into the light, and then he froze.

Rich chocolatey brown, striking blue ice, and more dusty cashmere, Aaron looked like the first snowfall of the season—it never sticks, that snow. It just covers the streets and grass in beauty for a while.

"Did I scare you?" Aaron asked. "I hope I didn't scare you."

"What are you doing here?" Daniel asked. He couldn't remember the last time he'd been so comforted to see someone. What he really wanted to ask was *How did you know I needed someone here?*

"Um." Aaron blinked down at the small white box he held in his hands. Something looked different about him. Beyond his fidgeting, he looked a bit weary. Even his hair insisted on falling from its style and pawing at one of his eyes. He tried to rake it back into place, but it broke loose again. "I was planning to leave this on your doorstep."

Daniel's eyebrows raised as he zipped his gaze from the box and back to Aaron. "Why? What is it?"

"It's a nothing."

"*A nothing*?" He dipped his head to the side. "Is it *a nothing* for me?"

Aaron pursed his lips like he was embarrassed it was *a nothing* for him, but he nodded.

"Can I see it?"

No. No, apparently not, because Aaron gave him the strangest look, like *Why would you want to see it? How dare you ask me that? Back, swine.* Then he twisted around to literally shield him from whatever he was doing. Daniel pushed up to his toes and tried to peek around his frame as shuffling sounded like maybe he was opening the box, and crinkling followed like maybe he was… eating paper? Who knew? He spun back around and thrust the box into the space between them.

Oh. Well, this was progress. Daniel dropped his things, took the *a nothing*, and pulled on the silver ribbon wrapped around it until it unraveled. He pried open the lid, dug into white spring-fill paper, and wedged his fingers around something heavy, round, and cold. He fished it out and held it up to the streetlight.

It wasn't *a nothing*. It was a something. It was a snow globe. A dancer dressed in a blue-and-gold soldier outfit stood inside, striking a beautiful arabesque.

"And it does this." Aaron twisted a knob on the bottom. Music from *The Nutcracker* began to chime from its tiny speakers.

He gasped, but he didn't even mean to. Kind of how his hand absently hovered near his mouth without his awareness.

"It took me forever to find a male dancer," Aaron said. "You guys are underrepresented in the snow globe market."

The ragged edges of Daniel's headache fizzled in real-time into tolerable softness. "What is this for?"

"I wanted to get you something." Aaron sniffed as he stuffed his hands in his pockets, shrugging at the snow globe. "For your studio. For when you own it."

Daniel's breath caught in his throat, somewhere between his overwhelming affection and the words *Thank you*. If the conversation with his dad had drained him, Aaron's presence had filled him back up.

"Anyway, I hope—"

Daniel hauled Aaron into his chest, colliding with hard muscle and downy cashmere. Aaron's eyes widened, and his shoulders tensed.

"I needed this," Daniel whispered as he lifted to his toes and circled his arms around Aaron's shoulders. "How did you know I needed exactly this?"

Aaron pulled pack to study his face. He was still tense, but his lips twitched into an almost-smirk. "You needed a snow globe?"

"I *needed* a snow globe." He pecked Aaron's cheek. Then the other. Aaron unknotted a little beneath his touch. "I was having a night, and you came. You brought a snow globe. You made it all better."

Aaron swallowed, unspooling even more as he settled his gaze on Daniel's lips.

"You make everything so much better. Kiss me." He pulled Aaron in even closer. Close enough to feel the voltage crackle between them as he breathed Aaron's air. "Kiss me. Like you did at the party."

AARON'S HANDS were on Daniel's skin, and his mouth was on his neck. He was kissing him all rough and unhinged like he'd done at the party, while the kid ground his tight little body against his, moving the way only he could. He was vaguely aware of how inappropriate it might be to kiss a dude so wildly in his yard with the neighbors so close and the occasional passerby out walking their dog, but heaven help him, this might be the last time he got to do it.

He had a plan. The plan was never to see Daniel again.

Never call him. Never answer one of his calls. The plan was to leave a stupid snow globe with a stupid note on his doorstep like the coward he was so he could retreat back to the outskirts of his life. So he could pretend Daniel didn't exist.

What the plan was *not*? This. Kissing him. Kissing him with his whole body while the grass did its magical sparkly dewy thing, and Daniel whispered *Thank you* onto his lips over and over. Kissing him with the note explaining how he wasn't an attorney shoved into his pocket like a grocery receipt, worthless. No one ever returned groceries.

Regardless of the grass and its dreamy glistening, and regardless of Daniel's leg doing that kicked-back-behind-him thing as they kissed—just because this looked like a scene from a music video—he wasn't Daniel's knight in shining armor. He wasn't saving him with snow globes, making *everything so much better. Kiss me, mister. Like you did at the party.* He was making things complicated. He was an imposter.

"Do you want to come inside?" Daniel rasped into his mouth, his hands urgent and clawing Aaron's back.

"Yep," Aaron said. Really? Fucking *yep*? So not only was he an imposter, but he was an imposter who wasn't even trying to do the right thing? Come on. The least he could do was try. "Yep, I do."

God, he was bad at this. He was bad at trying and even worse at honesty, which is why he let Daniel lead him toward the house by his hand. Maybe he'd do the right thing once inside? That was it. He just needed a roof over his head to be a good person.

"I'm so glad you're here," Daniel said, risking a hesitant smile as he pulled Aaron into his living room. "A part of me didn't think I'd hear from you after last night."

If Aaron pretended for a moment that there was no better setup for coming clean than that sentence, it still didn't address the potential that he'd vomit all over the floor if he had to say it aloud. He had a weak stomach. How was vomit fair to Daniel? It wasn't, so he responded, "Ahh."

Terrible. He was a terrible person.

"Is that why you brought me a snow globe?" Daniel slung his bag onto the sofa on his way to the kitchen, flashing back a tiny smile. "Because you felt like it ended weird too?"

"In a way, yeah." Abysmal. He was an abysmal person.

"I know I can be a lot." Daniel refilled the water for the calla lilies, which needed a proper vase. Perhaps he didn't have a proper vase, because he set them on the counter, arranging them around their plastic cup. "A *lot*."

Now that Aaron had a closer inspection, Daniel probably needed a lot of proper things. If he were Daniel's boyfriend, he'd buy him a utility basket to store his mail so it wasn't falling off the counters and a hook to hang his keys so they weren't currently sinking between the couch cushions. He'd do something with all these empty yogurt containers with the spoons still sticking out—get him a trash can?

If he had the chance, he'd take care of Daniel.

"And I know I can come on a bit strong," Daniel said, "but if I ever overstep by demanding legal advice, or threatening to put a tracker on you, or handcuffing you to a radiator so you can never leave—"

"What?"

"What?"

Aaron cocked his head. "That last part?"

"Oh, who could say? The point is, I hope you know you can talk to me. I promise I can be rational."

Aaron sighed and spoke the first honest words he'd spoken all evening. "You did nothing wrong, kid." The least he could do after being a liar-y liar was make sure the contract looked sound, and he happened to know an unlawful amount of attorneys. "Look, uh. I'd love to help you with your contract."

Daniel's face lit up. "Seriously?"

"Of course. Where is it?" He spun around, trying to spot anything that looked like a contract. There were plenty of half-empty glasses of water and slinky black items of clothing. There were also one, two, *three* feather boas? Why?

"Oh, I don't have it yet, but probably by the end of this week."

"That's fine. Give me your parking tickets too. I'll take care of them." And by *take care*, he'd pay them off.

Daniel squealed in an eek as he clapped. "You are the best. Now, what do you want to do tonight?"

"Clean." He nodded with his hands on his hips as his gaze swept the living room. "I want to clean your house so hard. Was it like this the last time I was here?"

"No. I'd had enough sense to shove everything into the bedroom. I figured if you made it that far, it meant you'd be willing to ignore"—he gestured a hand down his body—"the mess."

Aaron snorted as he glanced down at his watch. He had an appointment with a client in thirty minutes, and he'd done enough damage here. He scrubbed a hand over his face. "I actually can't stay, sweetheart. I have plans."

"Cancel them."

He darted his gaze up to Daniel's to find it impish.

"You have plans." Daniel glided toward him in satiny pouty lips and quicksilver. "I want to hang out with you. Fucking cancel them."

This conversation felt familiar. *You have a boyfriend. I want to take you out. Break up with him.*

"Then we can watch a movie or go for a walk—"

"Clean? Could we clean?"

"I'd rather die, but we could listen to music and chill. We could get it on somewhere—literally anywhere; right here is fine—or we could even lie down and have a good cry on the linoleum if you want." Daniel shrugged a shoulder. "But I feel like doing that less."

Aaron chuckled.

"Oh, what about a board game?" Daniel's eyes brightened. "I have Scrabble."

He chewed his lower lip. Would it really be so bad to spend a little more time with him? To let himself enjoy him for one more night? They wouldn't *get it on*, he'd be sure of that. He didn't need to sleep with him on top of deceiving him. But he'd never gotten such a whole-body thrill out of someone's company. If it was going to end anyway, what was the harm in savoring him for a little longer? It took him a moment bouncing on his heels, but eventually he gave in to his smiley sigh.

One more night. The minute he got the contract addressed, he'd bow out of Daniel's life once and for all. One more night was the new plan. Totally a decent plan. The best.

"Let me just…." Aaron trailed off as he sent a *Sry can't make it* text to his client, who was sure to be pissed, but it was only one more night. His smile split his face as he shoved his phone into his pocket. "I love Scrabble."

Several hours later, Scrabble had turned into laughter, had turned into a movie, had turned into more laughter until Aaron felt a little high on it. He sat on the sofa with Daniel's head on his lap, raking his fingers through his sandy curls. He even felt a bit high on the comfortable silence that finally ensued. It was peaceful after all the laughter. Peaceful instead of clunky.

"You know what I was just thinking?" Daniel asked without opening his eyes. "I was thinking about how you've made me dinner and taken me to a fun class thing, and I've done nothing. Should I plan a date for us?"

"Hmm. I'm worried your idea of a date will involve zero food or entertainment and one hundred percent us 'getting it on' somewhere—*literally anywhere; right here is fine*—as you point to a tree stump in the woods."

Daniel's eyes shot open. "Have you been reading my diary?"

Aaron nodded. "And hey, I'm flattered to appear on every page, but honestly, Daniel, no one uses the term *stud muffin* anymore."

Daniel's lips curled into a smirk. "What about *beefcake*?"

"Are you an eighty-year-old Southern woman? Leave the dates up to me." He patted Daniel's chest. "You just worry about looking cute and doing the thing boys like you do."

"Boys like *me*?" Daniel arched an eyebrow. "What do we do?"

He grinned as he twisted one of Daniel's curls around his finger. "Pretend like you don't see the check get dropped off."

Daniel huffed in laughter. "Okay, I can't even be insulted. I'm stealthy as hell at that."

"I'd be disappointed if you weren't."

"So, when's our next date, hmm?" Daniel reached up to dance his fingertips over Aaron's lips. "You taking me out, mister?"

His smile faltered a bit. There for a beat, he'd almost forgotten that *this*—sitting here in his house, talking about the future, growing fonder of him by the minute—wasn't reality. Reality was waiting for him outside like a skilled hitman.

One more date. He could enjoy him for one more date. No harm had ever come from a single date. Maybe he'd wait to deal with the contract until after the one more date, and then he'd leave him alone forever. *That* was the new plan. Brilliant at plans, he was.

He kissed Daniel's fingertips. "I'd love to take you out, kid."

"To your favorite tree stump in the woods?"

He continued kissing, smudging his mark over Daniel's delicate wrist and arm. "To my favorite radiator."

Daniel's face split into an absurd grin. Way too wide. Way too elated. "I'll bring the handcuffs."

Chapter Nine

LATER THAT week, Aaron was struggling to move a federal judge's arm off his chest without waking him. He'd wiggled all the way to the edge of the bed. He was almost there. If he could hold his breath. If he could snake a bit farther. If he could inch one more inch, he'd be the winner in peace-out limbo.

"Where do you think you're going?"

Dammit. Busted. He patted the guy's arm. "I was hoping I could take off a little early."

His client squinted at his watch. "Not going to happen, boy. We have another eleven minutes."

Eleven minutes wasn't anything to be so melancholic over, but Aaron barely stifled a groan as he sank back into the bed.

"Excuse me, young man." His client propped himself up to his elbow and arched a silver eyebrow. Maybe Aaron didn't stifle that groan. "You have somewhere better to be?"

Yes. There were about one thousand better places than right here, and that was on an ordinary evening. Tonight wasn't ordinary. Tonight, he had a special little date with a special little dancer.

Just because it was their last date—one more date—until he got the contract handled didn't mean he couldn't look forward to it. What was so wrong with looking forward to it with every pound of his body until he wanted to scream that he was wasting precious time in this knucklehead's bed?

He glanced at the grandfather clock in the corner of the bedroom. Who put a grandfather clock in their bedroom? It didn't work in the otherwise modern space. If he ever had the privilege of designing a space like this, it'd be a masterpiece. "Nowhere better to be."

His client's expression twisted into a skeptical frown. "Yeah, I'm not feeling the love today, Aaron."

"My apologies." He lightened his tone and feigned a smile. "There's nowhere better than right here."

"Eh." His client scrunched his nose and tipped his head to the side. "Still not entirely convinced. What can you do to convince me?"

Yeah, because it was a lie. They both knew it was a lie. A white-bread generic mockery of a sham. So why make him plod away at niceties? Answer: men and their fucking egos.

Aaron's face may or may not have exposed his annoyance as he rolled on top of his client and whispered, "You're so sexy, baby. God, you're sexy."

Now was a good time to run through his grocery list. He needed avocados, Roma tomatoes, and aluminum foil. He needed garbanzo beans and a red onion. That sounded like a delightful salad.

"And so much fun to play with," he said, withholding a teasing kiss from the guy. "I wish I could stay here all night."

He should get Daniel something from the grocery store. He'd probably twist into a tizzy over a box of chocolates. Aaron could almost hear the squeal, all high-pitched and raspy.

"I think about you when I'm at home sometimes," Aaron said, because that was always a crowd-pleaser. "I find myself hoping you'll call."

"Yeah? You like coming over here?"

"Like? I *love* it." He almost lost his composure on that one. "But how much more do you want to wear me out tonight? You've exhausted me."

The guy chuckled.

"Show some goddamn mercy." His voice dripped with seductive sugar as he swiped his tongue over the guy's lips. "Your Honor."

"Go." The guy swatted at him. "So full of it. Go. Get the hell out of here."

That was his cue. He scrambled off the bed and straight to his clothes before the guy changed his mind.

The judge pushed himself to a seat and fished a joint from his nightstand drawer. He sniffed the length of it, then hovered it over the flame of a lighter. "So, what's your deal lately? You're different."

Aaron checked his phone. Three texts from a fussy client who liked to argue about money, and one from his brother with an article about gay penguins. But only one name made his insides get all warm and slushy:

hARd TO gET OvEr (poor chester)
Hi mister. Thinking about your face and how I want to lick it.

He grinned down at his screen. *Thinking about your face and how I can't wait to see it later. We still on for tonight?*

God, yes. If you stand me up, I'll die. I'll just crawl into an early grave where I'll choke the chicken.

Aaron opened his mouth and closed it again, slowly tilting his head to the side.

Is it "choke the chicken" or "kick the bucket"? said Daniel's follow-up text. *I'm not good with idioms.*

He chuckled. *Split the difference? Kick the chicken? I won't stand you up, kid :)*

His client loudly cleared his throat. Oh shit. The dude had been saying something. Something about Aaron acting differently. "My apologies, sir."

"Doing that a lot today, aren't we?"

"What's that?"

"Apologizing."

"Sorry." He hopped to work his jeans up. "What were you saying? I'm different? Different, how?"

"Always checking your phone. Always in a hurry." The judge took a long drag of the joint, holding his breath at the top of his lungs as he asked, "You got yourself a man or something?"

Aaron didn't mean to burst into what had to sound like startled laughter. He typically tried to keep the two spheres of his life as separate as possible, but something about it was hilarious. It was the word *man.* Of course, Daniel was a man, but he felt more like a needy Tamagotchi someone forgot to feed. One who threatened to crawl into a grave and choke the chicken if stood up. "I wouldn't call him my man."

"What would you call him?" the judge asked on an exhale, marijuana smoke clouding the room.

"Trouble." He grinned as he buttoned his jeans. "And a handful."

"I knew it. Well, let's see him." The guy snagged a pair of reading glasses from the nightstand and extended his hand. "You have a picture of the handful?"

He did, actually. He had one picture they'd taken at Daniel's house; one Daniel had insisted they take with the lens way too close, and their faces squished together to fit inside the frame. For being such a small thing, it was kind of exciting to show it off to someone. To talk about him with another person. *His* Tamagotchi.

It also highlighted the fact that he didn't have any friends beyond this. With his secretive lifestyle, he really only had clients to talk to. While it was somewhat inspiring to be surrounded by so many successful men, it was disheartening at the same time. He'd never know money like they knew it with their dignified degrees and titles. At almost thirty, it was too late for him to start over. He'd never have some dignified title. Some dignified life.

"Well, looky there," the judge said as he peered down through his glasses at the picture. "Adorable, isn't he?"

Aaron melted into a grin. His imagination was behaving a bit like a child, itching to indulge in some fictitious life that didn't exist, as if to say, *But can't we just pretend for a moment? What's the harm in pretending?* Pretending what it'd be like to be boyfriends. Maybe they'd live together. Maybe they'd be the type of couple to take weekend trips to the beach and host summer barbecues with badminton and homemade sangria. Maybe one day, they'd find themselves on one of those beach vacations, and as the ocean rolled over itself in the background, one of them would lean in and say, *You. You are it for me.*

"Yeah, thank you. He's, uh, he's a professional dancer." Aaron sucked his teeth to keep from smiling so big. "He's actually buying the dance studio where he works, so he'll have his own place. It's a big deal. I'm proud of him—"

"So, how much for you both?"

Aaron's smile died as something icy leaked down his spine. He cleared his throat. "Excuse me?"

"For the both of you at once, how much are we talking?"

"We're not." Aaron blinked, widening his eyes in a warning glare. "We're not talking about that."

"Fuck. His mouth." The guy didn't catch Aaron's warning glare because he was too busy ripping the glasses off and zooming in on the photo. "Does he get loud? I bet he gets loud. Shit, I'd probably pay just to watch you hold him down and—"

"Hey!" Aaron snatched the phone back, making the guy flinch. It was probably a tad overblown, the way his anger spiked, but screw it. It suddenly felt like the most natural thing in the world to say to his federal judge of a client, "You absolutely do not talk about him like that. Do you understand me?"

The judge's eyes rounded. After a moment, he mumbled under his breath, "Whoa. Take it easy."

"In fact, forget his face. Forget I mentioned him at all because, like I said, he's a *dancer*."

"Okay." The guy showed his palms. "Holy shit, Aaron. Can you take a breath? I just thought since you do what you do that your boyfriend would—"

Aaron turned his glare to full force, and the guy snapped his mouth shut. His clients weren't his friends. He didn't have any of those.

He scraped a hand through his hair. "I have to go."

"Are you mad?"

He worked his shirt overhead. *Mad* was probably a decent description. *Over it* was probably even more fitting.

"So you are mad. Geez, you're worse than a woman. My wallet." The judge nodded to the dresser. "Bring it to me, won't you?"

Aaron eyed the guy as he swiped the wallet from the dresser. Holding another man's wallet always felt strange. Somehow more intimate than holding his hand.

His client shuffled through cash, taking inventory. He offered it over. "You can have everything in it."

Aaron pricked an eyebrow as his gaze bounced from the guy to the wallet and back. "How high are you?"

"Moderately high?"

"You already paid me."

"I'm very aware of how much money you take from me, young man. So is my accountant. Good thing it's my brother."

Aaron snorted.

"Go ahead. Open it."

He pried it open, and his heart jump-started back to the moment. To what was important. So important that he bit down on his tongue until it hurt as he gazed into the wallet. It sucked to care so deeply about a few cuts of paper. It sucked that *paper* was so intertwined with his self-worth to the point that he refused to say no. He *couldn't* say no.

His body craved money as much as it craved connections with other people.

"Oh, would you look at that?" The guy smirked. "Does he suddenly have time to spare?"

The only issue? In a fight between money and connection, money always won.

"So generous of you," he said with as much spunk as he could manage as he plucked the bills from the wallet and stuffed them into his pocket. "I can stay for a while. What would you like me to do?"

"I don't know, smile? Are you capable of that?"

Aaron was struggling with that at the moment, so he bared his teeth. "How's this?"

"On second thought—" His client pulled a drag from the joint and lounged back in the bed with an arm tucked beneath his head. "—go ahead and keep your beautiful mouth shut."

Fine. Perfect. Talking seemed like the more annoying choice, anyway. He yanked his shirt back off and crawled into the bed, where he stretched long, mirroring the guy.

"Look at you," his client cooed, dragging his gaze over his body. "It never gets old. I ought to buy you something to match those pretty eyes of yours. Would you like that?"

He nodded.

"You may speak."

"Yes, sir. How kind."

"Attaboy. Come here." The judge sucked an extralong drag from the joint, touched their lips together, and exhaled it into Aaron's mouth. Great. Not only was he going to be stuck here a while longer, but he was going to be stuck here and high.

"Now get your ass to work." The guy patted his cheek in light smacks. "I'm not paying you to get high on my weed."

His clients weren't his friends. They were barely even friendly.

A FEW HOURS later, when the buzz had worn off, Aaron stood on Daniel's porch under an old oak tree that shed acorns in little plunks. Things were so wholesome over here. Not that his tiny, horny dancer was wholesome in the traditional sense. Hardly. He cussed like a drunken sailor and probably fucked like one too, but he offered sanctuary. With easy, bright-eyed humor and heartfelt rolling tears, he offered warm waters where Aaron could shed his armor and take a little swim.

"Aaron, is that you?" Daniel's voice sounded behind the door, along with his hurried footsteps. It didn't sound easy with bright-eyed humor. It sounded panicked.

"Yeah," he responded, slanting his brow. "Everything okay—?"

Daniel swung the door open in a fury, his melted caramel eyes huge in distress. "Thank the heavens you're here. I have a crisis—God, you look gorgeous—that I need your help with. It's my dad."

Aaron's eyebrows shot up. "Your dad? What's going on?"

"He's doing something completely uncalled for. He's…." Daniel whimpered and fell into his arms like a corseted damsel in a period film. "He's turning fifty."

Even though he had questions, he squashed those along with the urge to break a smile at the dramatics, because if he'd learned anything so far, it was best just to let him *feel*. He wrapped Daniel in a hug and said, "Oh no. Did you say *fifty*? How could he do that to you?"

"I know, right? And look." Daniel swiped open his phone and handed it over to display a text from an unknown number:

My name is Melissa, and we've yet to meet, but I'm your dad's girlfriend. Throwing him a surprise birthday party tonight at my place. Would mean so much if you could make it.

Ahh. An instant sadness deflated Aaron's shoulders, but maybe it was a sign. He had no right to be standing here taking Daniel out on one more date.

"I'm sorry," Daniel said. "I'm sorry about our date, but I feel like I have to go."

"It's okay." He rallied a smile. "This is more important."

"Do you think we can reschedule whatever you had planned?"

No. He'd cashed in a favor from a client to reserve a private room at a Michelin restaurant complete with a sommelier, an opportunity he likely wouldn't get twice. "Sure. All right, well, I guess have fun. Text me if you need—"

"Oh, you're going."

Aaron blinked.

"Right?" Daniel's eyes widened even more. "Aren't you going with me?"

Aaron opened his mouth to respond, but nothing came forth.

"Aaron, you have to go. I can't go alone. Please? *Please*?" Daniel gripped his hand. "I need someone there. I want *you* there."

He chewed the inside of his cheek. He shouldn't. He *really* shouldn't go and meet Daniel's father. Meeting his father would only complicate things further, but someone tell that to the little swell of weightlessness zipping through his body. The one that sounded an awful lot like the child's imagination, pointing out how it'd be better than Michelin stars and a sommelier. That it'd be so harmless to be the rock that Daniel leaned on for an evening while they played pretend boyfriends. It'd be so... wholesome.

He sparred with himself over *should he, shouldn't he*—a pointless battle in the end because, of course, the answer was always going to be "It'd be an honor to go."

Chapter Ten

LATER THAT evening, Aaron tried to parallel park his car in Melissa's cul-de-sac with his left hand. His right hand, the one he needed, had been confiscated by Daniel, who squeezed it like a stress ball while he bounced his knee and gnawed his nails, his nervous energy making the whole car feel like a hamster on a wheel.

"This is bad." Daniel's lip bled from where he'd bitten it. "This is a bad idea."

"Do you want to turn around?" Aaron shifted his car into Park. "Say the word, and we can leave."

"Should we trade shirts?" Daniel unbuckled his seat belt, then buckled it back in. "What I'm wearing is stupid, and he won't like it. Do you like it? Do you have any gum? My neck hurts, can you tell? I feel like I'm not blinking enough." He blinked a lot. "Like a lizard. Why are we sober?"

"Inhale." Aaron demonstrated. "Exhale."

"I don't want to argue with him." Daniel petted Aaron's hand, his emotional support hand. "Not on his birthday."

"So let me ask you something. Why are we here?"

"*Why* are we here?" Daniel prodded at his curls in the visor mirror, then slammed it shut. "I don't know. Astute observation. Let's leave."

"I think you do know. What'd you tell me on the way here?"

Daniel's eyes glassed over as he gazed out the window as if deep in thought. "I want a connection with him. I want to celebrate his birthday."

"Okay. What else?"

"My relationship with him has been terrible, but it won't ever get better if I don't try." Daniel scrunched his face and shrugged. "Is that silly? Am I wasting my time?"

Aaron wasn't the right person to ask about relationships of any kind, but especially not relationships with one's father. From everything Daniel had told him about his dad, it seemed like a stretch to try to mend their connection over one evening, but it wasn't his job to dissuade him from trying. It was his job to be the pillar on which he leaned. He offered a gentle smile. "It's admirable that you're here trying. And even if it doesn't go as you'd hoped, it wasn't a waste of time."

"God, you're so spiritual-leader-during-cacao-ceremony. Okay, so if shit hits the fan, what's your one job?"

Aaron's instructions had been explicit. "To keep you from 'exploding like an atomic weapon.'"

"And?"

"And to keep you from 'saying something churlish, then storming out in a fit of rage.'"

Daniel rolled his palm. "Even if...?"

"Even if he 'totally fucking deserves churlishness and rage-storming.'"

"Perfect. And you're up for this task?"

"I'll be right there if you need me. Right by your side." He kissed Daniel's hand. "Lean on me."

They walked hand in hand through a series of white townhomes with black shutters until they found Melissa's house number. For how dead it looked from the road, it brimmed with people on the inside—mostly cheery, middle-aged folks who stood around tables of dips and finger foods, exchanging cut-and-paste party comments: *It's starting to warm up out there. Seen any good movies lately? Try the macaroni salad. It is to die for.*

The more time passed, the more Daniel's nerves seemed to lessen until he literally leaned on Aaron with his head on his shoulder while they sipped rum punch, chatted with two different women, both named Debra, and stole giggly glances whenever they could. They were good at this. At being a couple.

A woman with strawberry blond hair and an hourglass waist caught eyes with them from across the kitchen and bounced up like a fizzy soda. She clutched Daniel's hands and squealed in a thick Texan accent, "I'm Melissa, and you must be Daniel! Oh look, how cute. You look just like your daddy."

Daniel's face twitched. "Hmm, do I?"

"I'm so glad I got ahold of you," she continued. "I had to sneak through Robbie's phone for your number. He's going to flip when he sees you. And you brought a date, I see?"

"I did." Daniel interlaced their fingers and gazed up proudly. "This is Aaron."

"Welcome, Aaron." She enthusiastically shook his hand. "You are hotter than a jalapeño's armpit."

"Thank you?"

"He's here," someone whisper-shouted, then shushed the crowd.

Melissa shot them an elated smile as she scurried to the door, perking her hair and breasts along the way.

"I'm nervous," Daniel whispered. "Should we escape out the back door?"

Aaron squeezed his hand. Everyone was so kind; there was no way the evening wouldn't be a thorough success. "I'm right here for you. Whatever you need."

"*Surprise!*"

Daniel's dad jumped as he stepped into the house. He was better-looking than Aaron would've expected for some reason, probably because Daniel described him as *uninteresting*, *troll-like*, and *Satanesque*. They did favor one another. It was in the eyes, maybe. Although where Daniel was petite, his dad was bulky like he lifted weight in excess.

At least he looked warm as he worked his way through the crowd, patting people on the back, shaking their hands, flashing a pair of matching dimples when he smiled. Then he laid eyes on them, and something shifted terribly.

"Oh no," Daniel whispered as his dad rushed through his hellos on his way to get to them, his smile growing more contrived by the second. "We should leave."

Shit, should they? Even though he didn't believe it, he said, "Maybe he's just surprised."

"Okay." Daniel gulped as his dad quickly approached. "Hey, Dad. Happy birthd—"

Robert hauled Daniel through the kitchen by his arm and outside to the patio.

Aaron stood frozen as Robert sealed the glass door shut and twisted around to start what seemed to be a staring contest between the two of them. If they were talking, they did it without moving their mouths much.

He shook out his limbs. Welp, he couldn't very well prevent Daniel from exploding like an atomic weapon through a glass door. Here went nothing. Fortifying himself with a breath, he slowly slid the door open.

"Care to explain what's going on?" Robert asked, his arms staked across his chest as he glared at Daniel. "Do you want something?"

"I don't understand how to answer that." Daniel squinted at him. "I don't *want* anything. I'm here because it's your birthday."

"Dan. You haven't—"

"It's Daniel."

"Fine, Daniel. You rarely answer my calls. You sure as hell don't ever want to see me when I ask, and now you show up here unannounced? You expect me not to be a little startled by that?"

"Unannounced? Do I need to explain how a surprise party works? For it to work, it has to be a *surprise*, but you're right. I'm not sure what I'm doing here either. Come on, Aaron." Daniel charged for the door. "We're leaving."

"Whoa, whoa, whoa." Aaron blocked him. "If you want to leave, we can leave, but let's make sure you're thinking clearly. Remember why you're here. Remember what you said."

Daniel scowled.

"You want to have a connection with him? You don't want to storm off in a fit of rage? Those are your words."

Slowly and reluctantly, Daniel softened his glower. He twisted back around and offered Robert a tepid smile. "You're right. I could make a better effort at keeping in touch with you."

There, that was good. Mature.

"But you make it really fucking challenging when all you do is—"

"Nope." Aaron cleared his throat, nudging him. "Try again."

"Okay." Daniel unclenched his teeth. "Dad, I could make a greater effort to keep in touch with you. For that, I'm sorry."

Robert studied Daniel for a moment as if trying to decide if he believed him. Then he tilted his chin at Aaron, and it felt like a *Thanks*. "Well, I guess. I guess, here we are. You boys want a drink?"

Okay, this seemed promising. "That'd be nice, right, Daniel? We'd love a drink."

"Fine, just…." Robert held up a hand as he started for the house. "Please wait here."

Aaron and Daniel exchanged glances. He didn't want them inside? It was starting to feel like he didn't want them inside. A few moments later, he returned with a bottle of bourbon and three glasses, which he filled and handed out. "Cheers. To... surprises."

Robert emptied his, tossing it back in a rush, so Aaron did the same.

Daniel placed his glass on the corner of the grill without touching it. "So, Melissa seems nice."

Robert wiped his mouth. "What's the matter? You don't like it?"

"Oh, that? Um. I'm not a big whiskey person."

"It's not whiskey, son," Robert said with a frown as he poured refills. "It's aged bourbon, but I think Melissa has some wine coolers in there if you'd prefer that?"

Ouch.

"Well, that has to be more tolerable than this." Daniel shrugged. "May I go inside and get it, or is that also a massive inconvenience?"

"No." Robert glanced around as people began to meander onto the patio. He mumbled under his breath, "You're not drinking a fucking wine cooler here."

"Who cares what it is so long as someone keeps pouring it, right?" Aaron said, extending his hand. "I'm Aaron. Nice to meet you, Mr. Greene."

"Hi," Robert said without making eye contact and tipped back his drink, wincing a little on the finish. That one had been pretty full. "How do you two know each other?"

"Dad, obviously, we're dating." Daniel snuck in an eye roll but played it off as just gazing around the backyard. "Not that you would care."

Robert whipped around to Aaron, confusion clouding his expression. His head shook a little as he scanned him up and down. "Wait, you're...? But you don't look... huh. I wouldn't assume, just by first impression, that you were *like him*."

A reddish tint, either hurt or anger, spread across Daniel's face.

Jesus, man. "If only we could all be more like Daniel," Aaron said because *Fuck you, Mister Greene* would've been crass, "we'd be better people."

"Sure. What do you do for a living, Aaron?"

"He's an attorney," Daniel said, a little snappier. "Do you care about meeting him now?"

Aaron tried not to wince, shifting his attention to his drink.

"No kidding?" Robert said, suddenly engaged. "A professional. Well hallelujah. What do you think of the dancing? You can't tell me you approve of a career in dancing."

Daniel opened his mouth to speak, then clamped it shut, his gaze traveling to his shoes. He took a tiny sip of the bourbon, his jaw tight as he swallowed. Deflecting jabs at him was starting to feel like navigating a minefield, but as messed up as it was, maybe having Attorney Aaron's input would help this asshole gain a new perspective.

"Oh, I wholeheartedly approve of his career. I think his long-term goals will be highly lucrative. Plus, he's got a thirst for it, he's dedicated, and he's not afraid to take risks. I know that's more than I can say. Than most people can say. I'm proud of him."

Robert seemed nonplussed, but Daniel perked up a bit, his little half-smile adorable.

"There's the birthday boy!" a voice boomed from the house, and Robert flinched. A graying man with a protruding gut stepped out holding a beer. "Hey, Greene. Earth to Greene."

Robert scrunched his face for a moment and quickly said under his breath, "My coworker. Be cool." When he spun around, he'd plastered on a wide smile. "Jerry!"

"Hey, I met your new girlfriend. Not the brightest, is she? But smokin' hot."

"Not that smokin' either." Robert winked. "Until I bought the tits."

Geez, when did they get teleported to a scuzzy locker room? Robert and Jerry laughed and pulled each other into a pat-on-the-back man hug.

"She calls you Robbie," Jerry said, rubbernecking a woman in a green dress walking by.

Robert tilted his chin toward the same woman. "*She* can call me whatever she wants."

They both chuckled again, and the picture was suddenly clearer. Daniel's dancing must've not aligned with Robert's image. Rather, his membership to the boys' club.

"This guy." Jerry swung an arm around Robert. "What are you young folk doing hangin' out with this son of a bitch? Don't you know he's old and boring now?"

"I definitely wasn't expecting them," Robert said, finishing off another bourbon. "Jerry, this is my son Dan, er, Dan-yuul. And this is his, uh, friend."

Aaron had to shift his weight around to keep his irritation quelled.

"Son?" Jerry blinked, stunned. "I didn't know you had a son."

Robert scratched his head. "I'm sure I've mentioned it, no?"

"I would've remembered you had a son," Jerry said, extending his hand. "Put 'er there, Dan."

Daniel looked fragile taking the man's hand.

"You a cheap—I mean, *chief* financial officer too? Like your old man?"

"No, he isn't, but let's not—" Robert rubbed the heels of his palms into his eyes as a dark chuckle rumbled in his chest. "Oh, screw it. You want to tell the man what you do, Dan? Maybe he'll buy a damn lesson from you."

Jerry asked, "A lesson?"

"Sure, go right ahead, son." Robert's voice dripped in scorn as he said, "Nothing to be embarrassed about."

Daniel gazed up at his dad for a moment. Then something shifted horribly.

His posture started to crumple like a time-lapse video into a hunched back and drooped skull. The words shook when he said, "Dance. I teach dance."

Jerry's wiry eyebrows shot up obnoxiously. He'd get cut from a movie for overacting. "Well, can't say I was expecting that." He wagged his hips around a little. "What kind of dance?"

"Mostly modern," Daniel sighed. "But I'm trained in all kinds—"

"'Cause the only dance worth a toot is exotic and sorry, boy, but you don't have the jugs for that."

Jerry and Robert burst into laughter, and Aaron adjusted his shoulders. His skin felt tighter. Tighter and warm. Maybe tighter and hot. He tugged on his collar and cleared his throat. "Daniel is extremely talented."

"Oh, just teasing," said Jerry, flapping a hand. "I'm sure you'd have to be to do it for work." His expression flipped into mock seriousness. "But what do you *really* do? You know, to make money?"

When more laughter erupted, Daniel tried to gulp the bourbon like everyone else but spurted in coughs.

"Relax." Robert patted him on the back. "You don't have to drink it. No one's judging. No need to get all theatrical."

Daniel rubbed his chest and tried to stand taller, but he just looked like an abashed child who'd broken the rules. Where was his kick? His anchoring sass?

"We gotta go easy on our little ballerina—ballerino?" Robert asked. "What's the male version of that word?"

Aaron might have been making a strange humming noise, not unlike a pressure cooker, as he stared at the side of Daniel's head. *Kid, look at me. Look at me.* He'd scoop him up and take him home, where he'd kiss and soothe and whisper until it was all better. If that was what he wanted? *Fucking look at me.*

Daniel didn't dare look in his direction, or anyone's, like he was muzzled in shame. His lip bled even more from where he'd bitten.

"Well, we gotta go easy on him," Robert said. "He's a sensitive little guy. He's always been that way. I couldn't take him to the movies; he'd be a mess. It didn't matter what it was. He'd cry when the bad guy got shot."

They chuckled again while Daniel nodded in agreement. *Agreement!* Like he owed them an affirmation. Like he owed them anything.

A strange, thick feeling in Aaron's throat struck him with a need to cough while he squeezed his cocktail glass hard enough to crush it. With the way his blood burned his skin, if he didn't say something, he'd hit something. He cracked his neck and flared his nostrils. He had promised he wouldn't let Daniel ruin the evening, but it seemed Daniel wasn't the one about to ruin anything. He was.

"*Enough!*"

The laughter ceased.

"Enough, *enough*! You know what?" Aaron pinned Robert with his murderous glare and snagged Daniel's hand. "He came here to celebrate your birthday, not to be bullied by a couple of classless men. We're leaving."

"Wait, what?" Robert grabbed Daniel's arm. "Hey, stop."

Aaron jerked Daniel toward the door. "Let's go."

"Hold on a goddamn second." Robert tug-of-warred with Daniel's arm. "Dan, tell this guy to chill out! We're just joking. What the hell is your problem?"

"What's *my* problem?" Aaron spun around, and they all flinched. His blood swished in his ears loud enough to make them itch. "Your son would love to have a relationship with you, but you can't see him. Open your eyes and *see* him. He's brilliant, he's charming, he's the funniest person I've ever met. He's filled with passion and soul, and his heart—God, I can't even describe it. It's so pure and he's so kind. How did *you* raise someone so kind?"

He tried to shake his fists out, but they stayed tightly bound. "For his sake, I hope he never answers another phone call of yours, but he probably will. Because your son is a bigger man than you, Mr. Greene. And my problem is with anyone who makes him feel less than *precious* the way he is."

"Wait. Who are you?" Jerry asked, confused.

Aaron glanced at Daniel, who had turned into a wide-eyed statue. While he was already here beheading His Majesty, he might as well burn down the goddamn kingdom. "I'm his boyfriend."

The statue's eyes bulged even more.

Jerry floundered, "B-boyfr—?"

Aaron whacked the beer from Jerry's hand then kicked it. "Boyfriend! Which is why I won't tolerate another *joke* at his expense. Oh, and before I forget." He pulled a small blue box from his coat and tossed it to Robert. "He got these for you."

Robert fumbled to catch it like a juggling clown.

"Cuff links engraved with today's date." He tucked Daniel beneath his arm. "Happy birthday, asshole. Kind of hope you choke on them."

Robert looked like he might already be choking.

With Daniel in tow, Aaron stormed back through the party like it was about to explode behind him. But even a slow-motion walk as the house burst into flames couldn't make him look chill. *What the hell just happened?* He stopped to swig someone's cocktail from a console table, to which a voice yelled, "But that's mine."

I am a caveman. He slammed it down and charged forward, yanking Daniel's body past an electric-sliding Melissa, between the two Debras, then finally outside.

Because only a caveman would lose their entire MIND. He jerked Daniel down the street. They ran like they were being chased.

I didn't just say any of that to Daniel's dad. He fumbled with his keys. *Because that would be out of line, domineering, and unforgivable.*

They hurried inside the car and slammed the doors.

So, none of that happened.

They stared at one another.

None of that happened.

Daniel asked, "Did that just happen?"

"Fuck!" Aaron scrubbed his face. "I am so sorry. I'm an idiot. I have issues, and if you want me to apologize, I will go back—"

"Did that just...?" Daniel's eyes were wide as he laughed, slamming his hands on the dashboard over and over. Then he shadowboxed the air. "Tell me all of that just happened. You knocked that guy's beer out of his hand. You made us look like badasses back there. Aaron." Daniel covered his mouth with his hand, his face positively aglow. "You told my dad to choke on those cuff links."

"Did I say that?" He searched the walls of the car for answers to his behavior. He could not get more oafish if he tried. "I did. I said that. That doesn't even make any sense. Why would he have them in his mouth?"

Daniel cackled.

"God, I'm the worst." He buried his face in his hands. "My instructions were to defuse *you*, and what do I do instead? I detonate."

"No, no, no. Sweet, *sweet* man. Come here." Daniel shushed him, cradling his face in his palms, lifting it to see him. "Don't apologize. Please don't apologize. I couldn't have asked for more. You stood up for me. You said those remarkable things about me. You did what I couldn't. *You're* the bigger man, Aaron. It's you."

With that, the whole evening got a little softer. With that, they both eased back into their skin. Their roles. Daniel with his buzzing effect, a dragonfly on a pond, unaware of the ripples it made. And Aaron as his pillar. The stillness behind him.

"That's why I went out on a mission one night to find myself a hero," Daniel said. "And what falls into my lap? The most amazing, sexy, heroic guy ever." He delicately kissed the tip of Aaron's nose. "But he was taken, so I settled for you instead."

Aaron exhaled a laugh and melted into the sound of the silence as it stretched between them. As he gazed into big molten-copper eyes.

Daniel licked his lips and grinned. "Boyfriend."

His smile faltered. He'd said that too, hadn't he? The word "boyfriend" thrust into hyperfocus the fact that he was definitely making things more complicated for himself. Of course, this wasn't his victory to celebrate. This wasn't his life to feel so happy about. This was Attorney Aaron's life. Attorney Aaron got to save Daniel from fiftieth birthday parties and got to pretend like he had any control with his clients.

Attorney Aaron got to kiss him so deeply while he future-dreamed about badminton, barbecues, and ocean waves rolling over themselves while one of them leaned in and said, *You. You are it for me.*

"Do you want to come back to my place?" Daniel asked.

Tell him. Tell him, tell him, tell him.

"Come back to my place and stay the night with me." Daniel smudged slow kisses all along his chin and jaw. "Stay the night. Stay as long as you can. You never have to leave if you don't want."

Tell him. Say it.

"You made everything better. Again. You *make* everything better."

Aaron's mind knew better, but his heart screamed and scratched until it bled, begging for his attention, begging for a taste of what it'd feel like to let himself have it. For once, to experience what it was like to be cherished, and to cherish someone else in return.

"I can't wait to show you," Daniel whispered. "Show you how much I appreciate you."

His mind knew better, but his heart pleaded for more time. He just needed more time. What if he had one more night with him? What was the harm in one more night? "I'd love to—"

"Oh, before I forget," Daniel said, his face brightening. "I got the contract."

Aaron froze.

"Remind me to give it to you when we get to my place." Daniel shimmied his shoulders. "It's very official-looking."

But that was the thing about time. Eventually, it ran out.

Aaron's muscles had stiffened, and his swallow hobbled down his throat. "Great. You have your parking tickets too?"

"Yeah, I put them in the folder."

"I'll get it taken care of." Aaron pushed himself to smile. "And I'm so sorry, I actually can't stay tonight. Super duper early morning."

"Oh." Daniel's smile withered a bit. "Well, dang it."

Aaron crushed their lips together and drank in his orange creamsicle taste. "Some other time, okay? Let's get you home."

Chapter Eleven

IT WAS the next day, and Daniel was doing this. He'd crunched the numbers, he'd made a spreadsheet, and he'd printed it. Once something had been printed from a combative library printer, there was no going back. The studio was as good as his.

Well, after he got a loan. And got the contract back from Aaron. And did whatever it was that people had to do for the IRS to never call them.

"I've contacted a few loan companies. Still waiting to hear back, but this?" He pointed to a figure at the bottom of the spreadsheet. "This is what I would owe in two years. Which is a lot but doable?"

Madeline peered through her reading glasses and punched a few figures into a calculator. She offered a clenched half-smile.

"Oh God." He sank into a chair. "I know that look. You don't think it's doable, do you? You feel sorry for me. You think I'm doomed to poverty."

"I didn't say that. I think it'll be tough for a few years."

"Because of my student loans. Because I owe more than you thought."

"That's part of it. Let me work on the price on my end. Maybe I can find some wiggle room—"

"No. Please, no. This is your life's work, and what you've offered me is discounted enough. I shouldn't have brought this to you." He gathered all the papers in a tizzy. "I didn't know who else to talk to, but I shouldn't burden you with this. It's not your responsibility."

"Hey, stop." She pinned the papers down on the desk. "I said I would help you, and this is me helping. Leave it with me, and let me look at everything tonight. Even if we have to get creative, we can do this. *You* can do this."

Could he? Her devoted faith in him was lovely and all, but it highlighted his lack of faith in himself.

She shuffled the papers into a messenger bag. "I've got to run. Paul and I are off to a microwinery for the weekend." Madeline's plans always made his look déclassé by comparison. "I'll see you Monday."

"Okay." He followed her toward the door. "Let me know if your husband changes his mind about adopting me."

"Ciao, Madeline!" Olivia held a bag of chips as she materialized from the back room. "Have so much fun. I'll miss you."

"I was just going to say that—have so much fun, Madeline!" Daniel smiled. "I'll miss you more than her."

"But you'll miss me more," Olivia said, cutting in front of him. "Because I'm your favorite."

"No, you won't." Daniel punched the chip bag. "And no, she isn't."

"Behave." Madeline kissed them both, the double-cheeked French thing, and disappeared around the corner.

"So." Olivia waggled her eyebrows. "How's it going with your fancy boyfriend?"

"Girl, perfect." Daniel ran to perform a striking fouetté sauté in the mirror, which he ended in a deep bow. "He's the perfect man. God's gift to gays."

"Show-off." She joined him on the dance floor, circling him in spins, chips in hand. "Is he that sexy?"

"He's more than sexy." He fouetté turned, balanced and beautiful. "He's honest and tender, and you should have seen him stand up to my dad. That man could take me to a random tree stump in the woods, and I'd be all *Oh, this stump? Enchanté, stump.*"

She high-kicked, flex-footed and clunky.

"And plus"—he grand jeté'd because now he was showing off—"he thinks my emotional instability is adorable."

"I will say," she said as she shimmed across his view of himself in the mirror, "you do pull off emotionally unstable well."

He landed a brilliant aerial cartwheel to abruptly stack his hands on his hips and catch his breath. "You think so?"

"Well?" She tipped her head side to side. "No. But you can't tell an emotionally unstable person the truth about most stuff. I thought you knew that."

"You make it seem like everyone lies to shield me."

"No. No, of course we don't." She crunched a chip. Then tipped her head side to side again. "Well?"

"Anyway. He doesn't know it yet, but he's hanging out with me tonight." He clapped giddily. "Listen to this plan. Firstly, I write a thank-you note from the bottom of my thankful heart. Secondly, I snag a delicious albeit frozen pizza from somewhere. Lastly, I show up at his apartment with the note and the pizza and surprise him. What do you think?"

She blinked. "Okay, and...?"

He cut his eyes to the side. "Okay, and what?"

"Well. That's it? You're not showing up in a trench coat with nothing underneath it?"

"A trench—?" He angled his head. "No one does that in real life. Who owns a literal trench coat to do that with? A pizza and a thank-you note."

"It's just not that sexy."

"It's not supposed to be sexy." He squinted at her as he grabbed his coat from under the counter. "It's supposed to be cutesy."

"You could just use that coat. It's not *trench*, but it'll work. Here, I'll shield you. Take off all your clothes."

"I would just use the restroom if I were getting completely naked, and no. Pizza and a thank-you note."

"It's just...." She shrugged. "Not hot."

"It's not supposed to be hot." He glared as he started toward the door. "Cutesy."

WHEN AARON answered his front door, relief softened his shoulders. "Thank you. Thank you for coming over. I know your time is valuable."

Corey leaned against the doorframe, suited and tied with a popped-collar peacoat cinched tightly around his waist. He was stylish in an overconfident way. No one argued if you had swag when everything you wore looked as if it'd been chosen by a team of professionals to tailor-fit your frame. "It's not often that *you* call me, love. How was I not to rush over like a desperate girlfriend?"

Aaron grinned as broad as he could with all his teeth showing, which did nothing to negate his mood. What he really wanted to do was crawl into his bed and learn how to cry like Daniel. "Come in. It's so good to see you."

"Is it, Aaron?" Corey strolled inside with a suspicious eyebrow raised. "Is it good to see me?"

"Yes. Here, I'll take your coat. How about a drink? What would you like?"

"What is going on?" Corey mumbled under his breath as he unraveled the scarf from his neck. "So long as you're not poisoning me? Vodka. Neat."

Aaron ordered his smile to sit tight as he leaned in and kissed Corey's cheek, taking the coat. "Coming right up."

"I haven't been to your place in quite some time." Corey slid his hands into his pockets and gazed around the apartment. "Lovely what you've done with it. I see I'm paying you too much."

Aaron snorted as he poured two vodkas. It wasn't nearly enough.

"You still have the piano?"

"I do." He glanced up at the loft as he handed him the drink. "You want to hear me play? I'll play anything you'd like."

"I want you to tell me what the hell I'm doing here," Corey said, his tone a bit lower. He could be intimidating when he wanted. It was all the swag. "I highly doubt it's because you wish to play me the piano. You do nothing for free."

Aaron scrunched his face, scratching the back of his head. "I need a favor."

"Oh Christ." Corey rolled his eyes. "What have you done?"

"It's not for me."

"Then who's it for?"

"It's for a really special guy I need to do right by." He hadn't necessarily planned to tell Corey that, but surely there was a human soul inside there that could be warmed by a display of vulnerability. "I've not been good to him. I've lied to him, and I'm going to hurt him—" He tried to keep his chin lifted, but it was no use. "I owe him."

Corey studied him cautiously. "What does it have to do with me?"

"This"—Aaron snagged the contract from the table—"is a bill of sale. Can you look it over and make sure it's sound?"

Corey's eyes scanned it for a second; then he shook his head. "Oh, these things are standard. I'm sure it's fine—"

"Please? I trust you. I wouldn't trust anyone else with it."

"Aaron," Corey groaned. "I *just* left work—"

"Please?" Not that he had much pride to begin with, but he squashed what little tried to bubble up. "For me?"

Corey's cool gray gaze settled on his, a bit annoyed, a bit intrigued. "I don't do anything for free either, love."

He swallowed. It wasn't like he didn't see that coming, but God, if ever there was a night he didn't feel like getting on his knees. "I will happily pay you."

"I don't want money."

"I—" Aaron snapped his mouth shut as he dropped his chin. Over the past couple of weeks, he'd let himself seep into the cracks of a world where friends did things because they were friends, and he had a special someone and an ordinary life.

"Done." His stomach twisted, but he lifted his drink. This *was* his ordinary life. "Anything you want."

Corey smirked as he clinked their glasses and peered down at the contract on the table. "Mr. Daniel Greene, huh?"

Hearing his name sort of felt like someone had tightened a belt around his heart.

"Someone you're seeing, then?"

Aaron sucked his teeth hard enough to sting. "Someone I *was* seeing."

"Thank God." Corey tossed back the vodka. "I fully dread the day someone steals you away for a life of monogamy. I know it's bound to happen, but please not yet. What will I do with myself?"

He swigged his own drink. "Spend time with your wife?"

Corey grinned, batting his lashes. "Oh, but if I start doing that, what will become of her boyfriend?"

Aaron dragged a hand down his face. His ordinary life.

"You can start right here." Corey pointed to his shoulders as he plopped into a seat at the table. "*So* much tension. Must be all the extra work I've been doing lately."

He exhaled as he rolled his sleeves and began kneading Corey's shoulders.

"Christ, that is to die for," Corey moaned, stretching his neck a little. "Don't ever change, darling. You've genuinely met your calling."

Aaron's gaze traveled around the apartment, snagging on the paintings he'd selected and the finishes. All of the intimate touches that made the place so stunning. "You think so?"

"You're bloody gorgeous, Aaron, and you fuck like a stud horse." He tapped the empty vodka glass. "Go fetch me another of these—well, not so fast." He'd snagged Aaron's elbow. "Kiss me, love. Like only you can."

Kiss me, mister. Like you did at the party.

It wasn't normally so bad kissing clients, and specifically kissing Corey was somewhat pleasant. He tasted nice—a bit spicy like cardamon or clove—and for being so bossy, he was shockingly gentle. Aaron closed his eyes and got it done, struggling to feel an ounce of *fondness*, but it was eerily quiet inside his body. Either that or he couldn't really hear his body anymore.

"Off you go." Corey winked as he gave him a little shove toward the kitchen. "When you come back, it's straight to your knees."

THIRTY MINUTES later, with the pizza in hand and having changed into something a little hotter because Olivia had gotten into his head—except not a trench coat with nothing underneath it because people didn't actually own those—Daniel strolled up to Aaron's building.

Was it a teensy bit risky showing up unannounced? Always. But it was also a language Aaron spoke, as evidenced by the whole snow globe delivery. Not to mention, tonight might be *the night*. The night they finally made it to home base.

Because home base was the ultimate base—or was that third base? From which base did one start? Furthermore, how many bases were there? It didn't matter. Whichever one was the most desirable—third base?—they might be sliding to that tonight. Yeah, he should probably avoid sports-ball metaphors about sex.

He was standing in the apartment building's vestibule contemplating searching for a last-minute trench coat when a blond guy leaving the building caught eyes with him and held the door. "Pardon. Coming in?"

He bounced for a beat. Aaron found him plenty sexy without a trench coat. "Why yes. Thank you—"

"You look so familiar."

Daniel halted on his way through the door.

"Right?" the guy asked. He did have a distinctive British accent. "Don't I know you?"

He studied the guy. A bit older. Silvery blond hair. Uniquely dressed, fashion-forward even, with these dark, hooded eyes and this polar-white smile, just a little too perfect to put a person at ease in its presence. He was missing the gold everything, but it was definitely him.

Yellow Jacket.

"The party last month," Yellow Jacket said, pointing as he followed him inside. "You were the bartender, no? The one that Aaron…. Are you here to see him?"

He didn't know why he suddenly felt a bit disjointed. "Yeah."

"Well, he's upstairs. I'm Corey Hutton, by the way." Yellow Jacket extended his hand. "I didn't catch your name, love."

"Oh, sorry." Daniel shook his head clear and finally took his hand, suddenly grateful he was wearing clothing beneath his coat. "I'm Daniel Greene. Nice to meet—"

"No." Corey's eyes brightened. "It's impossible. You're not *the* Daniel Greene? The lad who's purchasing one St. Louis School of Dance?"

His eyebrows dipped a bit. "Yeah."

"Well, what are the odds? I just reviewed your contract upstairs." Corey tipped his chin upward. "Looks good, love."

Daniel slowly dropped his head to one side. Upstairs. Upstairs in Aaron's apartment? He couldn't keep the memory of the kiss they'd shared in front of him from bombarding his higher reasoning. Just because Cory had been upstairs just now didn't mean anything beyond… whatever it meant. But why? "Why would you be looking at the contract? Do you work for Aaron?"

Corey gave him a funny look. "Pardon?"

"At Aaron's law firm. Do you guys work together or something?"

Corey blinked. It almost looked like he couldn't quite settle on an expression with his gray eyes narrowing a bit and, at the same time, twinkling, like at any moment, he might burst into laughter. To muddle matters more, he licked his lips and said, "Christ, you are pretty, aren't you?"

Normally, it'd be the kind of thing to make Daniel moon, regardless of who said it, but his smile lapsed a touch.

"Very young," Corey said with his gaze plunging the length of his body. "Very fit. I can see why he did it."

Daniel's system, wired to overreact, couldn't help but ignite in fight or flight. His breath sounded behind his words as he asked, "Why he did what?"

Corey grinned—arctic white and uncomfortable—as he slipped a step closer, his hand suddenly on Daniel's shoulder. "Why he lied."

He sputtered for a half a minute. Questions, important questions, paraded around his head, but it was like he couldn't wrangle any of them. "What'd he lie about?"

"Hmm, what did he lie about?" Corey stroked his chin as he gazed around the lobby. "Well, I do not work for him, love. Quite the opposite. See, my friends and I pass him around like a spit bucket at a wine tasting. Does that answer your question?"

Daniel shook his head, but only fractionally. Did it? It didn't. Or did it?

Corey's brows slanted as he patted Daniel's chest. "Aaron is not a lawyer."

"Well—what? Yes, he is—err. He—"

"He's not a lawyer." Corey's gaze sharpened on his, his words pinpointed and clear. "But he charges by the hour like one."

Chapter Twelve

A FEW MINUTES later, Daniel stood outside Aaron's apartment in a puttering daze. He couldn't talk. He couldn't form words. He barely remembered the elevator ride, his manic thoughts pinging around the walls of his skull like a gymnast on a trampoline.

"Leaving? No? Suit yourself," Corey had said as he held the door for him, then winked as he slipped through. "See you around, Daniel Greene. Cheers."

Cheers.

His mind replayed the night he met Aaron over and over. The kiss he'd shared with Corey. To the way Corey had spoken to him—*I don't care if it's made from holy water, it's not your job to stand here and drink it.* Now he stood at Aaron's door with a defrosting pizza. *My friends and I pass him around like a spit bucket at a wine tasting.*

Cheers.

He quietly knocked on the door.

"What'd you forget?" Aaron answered with a toothbrush poking from his mouth. Maybe he hadn't meant to say that, or maybe the expression Daniel wore was that alarming, but a shade of color evaporated from Aaron's face. "Daniel."

What'd *who* forget? Daniel chewed his lower lip, his voice barely there. "Expecting someone else?"

"No. Uh, what a nice surprise. Come in." Aaron rushed to the sink to rinse his mouth. "And you brought a pizza? How thoughtful. Here, let me take it."

Like a spit bucket at a wine tasting. He scanned the apartment as Aaron took the pizza from his arms. One chair at the dining room table was twisted askew like someone had just sat there. Probably reviewing his contract, which lay scattered around the table next to two half-empty tumblers. He tried to keep his voice steady as he said, "What kind of law do you practice?"

Aaron was punching numbers on the oven display in a haste. "What's that?"

"Law. I asked what kind of law you practice." He cleared his throat, rubbing an arm. "I don't think you mentioned it."

Aaron's back was turned to him, but his shoulders bunched around his ears and his breathing had changed. Quickened.

"You do practice law. Right?"

He didn't turn around. He didn't speak.

"Aaron. Look at me."

When he finally twisted around, his skin had paled even more. He almost looked sick, like he might throw up at any moment. He tossed the pizza onto a counter, his voice deep and uneven. "No. I don't practice law."

"So, what do you do?"

"Please sit, Daniel."

"I don't want to sit."

Hands bracing the sink and head drooping, Aaron sucked in a sharp breath. "What I do is offer people my companionship. In return, they pay me for my time."

Like a spit bucket at a wine tasting. It wasn't that it hit him like a tidal wave. A tidal wave usually had more warning. This was more like an undertow, strong and slick, sucking the *truths* about his world from beneath him in an instant.

"You're—" The words stuck in his throat began to trickle out cold and thick. Even as he asked it, there was no way the answer could be yes. "You're a prostitute?"

Aaron's blue ice flashed to his. He nodded. "But I prefer escort."

The swelter in his body pooled in his ears. He suddenly didn't know what to do with his limbs, which twitched enough to start throbbing.

"Daniel. I'm so sorry."

"I can't believe you—you lied to me."

"I know." Aaron rushed to him, hesitating to reach for him. "I'm sorry. If you want to hate me, you're entitled to hate me, but—"

"I don't hate you." Daniel scrunched his brow, eyes widening. "I would never. I *could* never hate someone for what they do with their body. It's your body, and you get to do whatever you want with it, but how dare you not tell me. How dare you lie to me this entire time."

"I didn't lie! Okay, yes, I did, but not the entire time."

"What? What does that even mean?"

"I thought you knew at the party. I swear I thought you knew."

"How would I know that?"

"Because!" Aaron's arms shot out to the sides. "Everyone at that party was either an escort or someone paying for an escort. Why'd you think I was an attorney?"

"Why?" He shrugged with his whole body. "Well. The guy."

"What *guy*?"

"You know, the—" He flittered a hand about, but his brain was a hazy mess, the party an even hazier mess. Something about a yellow jacket. Something about floor popcorn. *If he's wearing a shirt, he's an attorney and an asshole.* A bunch of older men lounged about his memories, surrounded by their beautiful young companions. A game of shirts versus skins with the only part worth remembering being the special kiss with the special boy. "Guy."

"Look, I would never intentionally hurt you." Aaron's voice was so earnest. So pained. "I had planned to tell you in a note and leave it for you to find. Then I just...." He trailed off, gesticulating in the air with his hands.

"What?" he asked. "You just *what*?"

Aaron gazed up through his lashes. "I couldn't."

Daniel raised his eyebrows.

"I know how it sounds. I know it wasn't fair, but I couldn't because, well, I *couldn't*, and so I let you think I was an attorney because if you were going to be gone the second you found out anyway, then at least I got to see you for a little while longer."

His body was betraying him, because that shouldn't have sounded romantic, and yet a part of him wanted to melt, so he wrenched his arms. "You more than let me think it. The contract? The tickets?"

Aaron bared his palms. "I said I'd get it taken care of, and I did. I took care of everything."

"*You* didn't take care of shit." Daniel jabbed a finger toward his chest. "You had Yellow Jacket do it."

Aaron's confused eyes zigzagged around. "Wait, *what*?"

"Ugh!" Daniel punched his arms by his side. "I broke up with my boyfriend for you."

"Are you serious?" Aaron's eyes rounded. "How magical of a relationship could it have been if all it took was five minutes in a bathroom to break you guys up?"

"Enjoy the pizza." Daniel patted around his jacket in a tizzy for the thank-you card, then slung it onto the table. He whirled for the door. "I also wrote you that for being so fucking wonderful."

"Wait. Stop. No, no, no." Aaron rushed to the door and blocked it. "Don't leave. I'll answer all your questions if you'll just stay. Please stay. I like you! Kid, I like you so much. I'll do anything you want, but please don't go—"

Daniel whipped his hand away as Aaron tried to grab it, glaring at full force. "*Don't* fucking touch me."

It'd be impossible for Aaron to look more hurt. He hugged himself. "Sorry."

"Move."

Aaron stepped aside, and Daniel didn't hesitate. He stormed down the hallway without a glance back.

Chapter Thirteen

IT'D BEEN an entire week since Daniel discovered the news about Aaron, and he was still having frequent and dramatic meltdowns about it. He itched for the studio's last student to leave so he could commence another. (Meltdown number nineteen? Twenty-two? Three hundred?)

The second they left, he sprawled across a bench in the window with one arm draped over his forehead and the other limp to the floor like a *CSI* dumpster body, and moaned at full volume. He summoned his most pitiful voice and said, "I don't think I can carry on."

"Is that permission to kill you?" Olivia asked from behind the counter, where she stood sweeping the floor. "Man, that'd be great. Then you'd stop talking about it."

"Yes," he sighed. "Do it. You can use the broom. Or I think Madeline has a nail file back there. Just make it quick."

"It's been seven freaking days, Daniel. If it's driving you that nuts, just respond to him."

"Yeah, let me get right on that. Did I mention he's a hooker?" He lifted his head and shouted, "A hooker, Olivia!"

"I know, and I just have so many questions. I'll name them in no particular order." She stopped sweeping to begin ticking off fingers. "One, how much does he charge? Two, will he break up payment between credit cards—scratch that. Do you think he'll accept a very heartfelt IOU? And three, I'm not saying the 'back door' isn't 'open for business.'" She was using way too many air quotes. "But does he, by chance, do 'front' or 'side door' stuff?"

His gaze wandered. "What would be considered the 'side door'?"

"Lastly, how does one sign up? Is there an app or something?"

Daniel shot upright to fire a menacing glare. "Oh, I'm glad this is so fun for you."

"It is."

"Because it's not freaking fair." He summoned his whiniest voice. The one he used for police officers pulling him over or the bank teller in charge of canceling overdraft fees. "There is finally a gorgeous guy who I genuinely like, and he's a fucking *gigolo*?"

The weight of the word "gigolo" hung in the air like a sex-working balloon while he and Olivia found themselves in an unofficial staring contest over it. Which didn't last long. All it took was for him to silently mouth "gigolo" once more for Olivia to erupt into laughter.

His own laughter followed, ridiculous and real until his stomach muscles hurt. What else was he to do? Cry? This whole thing was too absurd for tears. Even for him.

When his phone buzzed with a text, he gasped and sprang to his feet. "Aaron."

The laughter halted.

I get that you're officially done with me. His voice shook and his heart splintered all over as he read Aaron's text. *This is the last time I'll reach out. It was wonderful getting to know you, Daniel Greene. From the bottom of my heart, I'm so sorry I hurt you.*

Olivia pressed a hand over her heart as her lips pinched together and her eyes saddened with sympathy.

"I know," Daniel sighed. "You don't need to say it."

"He's just so—"

"Sweet? Kind? Incredible?" He squeezed the bridge of his nose. "I said you don't need to say it."

"I don't see why you're not even going to try," Olivia said. "I've never seen you pine so dramatically over a boy."

He scoffed. "I'm not pining."

"You are *piiiiiining* over that boy, and hey, I'd be pining too. First, he saves you from that dumpster fire of a relationship you were in—"

"It wasn't *that* bad."

"—with a magical bathroom kiss. Then he saves you from your dildo of a dad, all while making you adore every minute you spend with him to the point that you're all swimmy around the studio and the students think you're high on edibles."

"Wait, did someone say that?"

"And did he not almost kill you in bed with his extreme sexiness?"

"Oh God. Don't make me think of that. He's all *Every last drop, sweet boy. That sound good?* And I'm like, yes, sir, Lucifer. Welcome to my orgasm."

"Exactly. And now you cannot stop thinking about him."

"But—"

"But he's an escort. Okay, trust me, baby, you've dated worse. Shall we review some of the dudes you've dated? Would a little trip down memory lane help?"

He blinked, suddenly twitching with an urge to flee the premises. "That's really unnecessary."

"Remember the guy with the rock candy fetish?"

He scrunched his face. "Yeah. That hurt my teeth."

"Remember the guy who said you have the kind of face that 'probably won't age well'?"

"I do." He plopped back down. "What a bitch."

"You remember the professional hockey player—"

"Okay, I think you've made your point—"

"—who pretended you didn't exist when you ran into him at that taco truck?"

He glared. "In his defense, he was with his teammates."

"Oh, the same two teammates that wanted to run a train on you?"

"Jesus, Olivia! Language!"

"And what does your 'boyfriend' do?" More air quotes. "He just gives them your number."

He hung his head.

"And God help me, Daniel, you kept seeing him after that."

He opened his mouth and closed it again. "Mmkay, but you don't think that was maybe a little flattering?" he asked in an octave too high, crinkling his nose. "Just a little? No?"

Her expression didn't look like she thought it was a little flattering. "Look, it's obvious you're way into Aaron, and he's way into you. So far, he actually treats you well."

"Treats me well?" He widened his eyes. "Lest we forget, he *lied* to me."

"Okay, yes, Daniel." She flopped her arms by her sides. "He did. Welcome to the world where sometimes people lie. Even really good people."

"I don't." He blinked hard. "I don't lie."

"You lie constantly. Mostly to yourself about what you need. He lied because he wanted to keep seeing you, and because he knew you'd do this." She swirled a finger around his chest. "Daniel-spiral it into a whole thing. At least he didn't cheat on you with his first cousin like that investment banker. Remember him?"

"Okay, I get it! I have so-so taste in men."

"You have horrible taste in men. And you date these men who look great on paper—even if they treat you *horribly*—because deep down, you're seeking someone's approval." She slowed her words and repeated, "You're seeking someone's approval. What does that sound like to you?"

He let his gaze zigzag around the room.

"You're going to make me say it? Fine." She took a breath and nodded as if in solidarity, like whatever she was about to say, they'd get through together. "You date your dad."

He gasped so loudly he swallowed the gnat that'd been buzzing around the studio for a few days.

"Shh, it's okay. You're okay." She was suddenly so close to his face as he wheezed. How'd she get there so fast? "It could be worse. It's not that bad."

He jerked his head back as not to hack directly into her eyeballs. Very, *very* close.

"Aaron is not your dad, and that freaks you out."

He coughed harder, suddenly freaking out worse.

"No! I mean, dammit. Let me rephrase that. Aaron may not look good on paper, but he's not a horrible man, and you actually like him. Think about it. You've never dated someone you've liked."

"*What?*" He patted his chest as he tried to roughly clear his airway. "Of course that's not true—"

"Could it be for the first time, maybe ever, you're scared?" She gripped his face in her palms and tugged it close. Very, *very* close. "You can't get hurt if you never date anyone worth liking."

He finally gulped—hopefully gnats had a little protein—while his shoulders softened. For being so clodhopping in her explanation, that might have had some merit.

"Give Aaron the same grace you would give a horrible man."

Now surely that wasn't a piece of advice he needed to hear. Was it?

"What if you just talked to him? What if you guys could figure something out that works for you both?"

"That's like, two decently sized *if*s."

"But what harm could it do to try?"

"To *try* and date a sex worker? You're asking me to change my entire personality. Have you ever met me? I get paranoid pulling into an automatic car wash because I feel like my tire's never aligned on the track, and my windshield wipers are going to go swishing out of control because I don't know how to turn them off, then finally, the big brush is going to come crashing through my window and impale me."

She nodded as she petted his arm. "We lose millions of people a year that way."

"I'd be too nervous, Olivia."

"Too nervous about what?"

"That every time he left, it would be to fall in love with someone else."

"I see." To her credit, it was genuine empathy shining in her eyes as she offered the tiniest of shrugs and said, "But that's always the risk you take when you finally find someone worth liking."

He blinked. Even if it was terrifying, he couldn't deny that Aaron was someone worth liking.

"You bitch." He stood and staggered forward, falling into her arms for a hug. "Thank you."

DANIEL RESPONDED to Aaron with a single text message:

Come over if you want to talk.

He hadn't expected Aaron to show up at his house in half an hour, looking handsome as ever. He'd actually hoped to have a few moments to ground himself, but here they were, sitting at Daniel's kitchenette table, *not* talking. The silence was getting a bit unnerving, but he was waiting for the perfect words. The ones that would convey how agonized he'd been the past week, how challenging it would be for him to try to date someone like Aaron, and how blistering his anxiety could get if he let it. The words would soon pour from his lips like poetic water down a fall. He took a massive inhale and, with an uneven sigh, said… more nothing.

"So." Aaron leaned his elbows onto his knees. The silence sounded strange with his deep voice finally breaking it. "You were really angry when you left, so thank you for agreeing to meet with me."

Daniel gulped. Why did it feel like he was going to have to talk?

"But you mentioned you might want to talk?"

There it was. "Yeah, but that was before I had to do it. Now I'd rather die."

Aaron's eyebrows shot up. "You'd rather *die* than talk to me?"

"Not fully die. Die just enough to get out of this conversation."

Aaron chewed his lip. "So you don't want to talk?"

"Sorry. It's really not about you. It's about me. I don't know if you've noticed, but I'm kind of a fretful person. I fret about stuff."

Aaron looked like he was suddenly holding back a smile. "I hadn't noticed."

"Well, it's true, and I'm wondering if learning more about what you *do*—" He stopped to peer around his house as he dropped to a whisper. "—might help to ease some of my fretting around it."

"Isn't it just us here?" Aaron whispered back, also gazing around. "I'm not sure we have to whisper."

"So here goes nothing." He drummed the table. "How long have you been doing *the thing*?"

"Eight years."

"*Jesus*—sorry." He squeezed his eyes shut and inhaled. "I didn't mean to yell. That's a touch startling, as it's a slight eternity, but now that I have that fantastic piece of information, we can move on. So these clients of yours, you see them often? How often would you say you see clients?"

"Uh, well, it depends. I have my regulars I might see once a week, then I have others I might only see—"

Daniel flung himself out of the chair to cover Aaron's mouth with his hand. He shook his head. "No, I've changed my mind. I don't want to know that. Not ready for that."

Aaron nodded, his eyes a bit startled.

Daniel yanked his hand away and shook it out. "Okay, so what about age? How old are they typically?"

"Age? Again, it depends, but it probably ranges from—"

"No!" Daniel slapped his hand back over Aaron's mouth, then ripped it away. "I don't want to know that either. Feels... *no*. How about, is it always sexual? Do you do other stuff? Dinners or something?"

"Well—"

"Stop! Just stop talking, Aaron. That's *definitely* something I don't want to know."

Aaron's expression pinched in confusion.

"Okay, so," Daniel said, starting to pace, "what about location? Do these guys come to your place? Or do you go to theirs?"

"Usually, they—"

"Dammit, Aaron!"

Aaron's blinking doubled.

"The party." Back to the pacing. "Is that something you do frequently? How often are you working parties like that?"

Aaron hesitated, then continued slowly, "So, most of the time—"

"Oh my God, read the room! Why on earth would I want to know that?"

Aaron scratched the back of his head as he licked his lips and whispered, "I'm sorry, kid. I'm not sure what we're doing here."

"We're talking! Clearly. Final question. So what happens if you start to fall for one of them? For one of your clients."

"Start to f—? Wait." Aaron halted, eyeing him. "Before I continue, do you want me to answer?"

Daniel squinted. What the hell kind of question was that? "Duh."

"Sweetheart, you have to understand something. I've been doing this a long time. I have boundaries in place. I don't stay the night with clients. I don't do overnight trips. I've never developed feelings for one of them. That'd be ridiculous."

"But what if it does happen?" He bounced a little. "Boundaries slip sometimes. What if it does?"

"Look at me." Aaron leaned over his knees again and held his gaze. "You. You, you, *you*, Daniel Greene, of all people, have nothing to worry about."

He had a way of saying things, didn't he? It wasn't that it was perfect. It was that it felt unforced, reassuring. It felt real. Words like that could be life-changing in the right context.

Daniel sat down, then stood up too fast, because he had something to declare. But what? What would he declare? He sat down again because he'd gotten dizzy on the stand. Then he stood back up. Since there was nothing to declare, he sat down, only to stand again. Aaron's eyes moved like the puck on a high striker at a carnival, following his posture as it continued to ping up and down and back again.

Decisions were not his specialty. It wasn't that he was bad at them. It was that he was *so* bad. So, so fucking bad. Since he was a little kid, he'd struggled to get the two sides of his brain to agree on whether a decision was worth the calculated risk or doomed to fail. For someone so palsy-walsy with failure, he sure feared it.

"I'm tired." He finally collapsed into the seat with a sigh and squashed the urge to breakdance out of the room. "I'm tired of being this person who overthinks everything to death. What if we just tried?"

"Tried… to date?"

"Tried to be together." He pursed his lips and shrugged. "Tried on a trial basis to be together."

Aaron's eyes danced as the corners of his mouth curled. "Yeah?"

"Yes." *That's always the risk you take when you finally find someone worth liking.* "I want to try."

Aaron grinned, hesitantly reaching for him. "I think it's a great—"

"But I don't want to talk about it!" He flailed his arms in the air, which, at least poor Aaron was quick at ducking. "About what you do. At least until I can wrap my head around it. Does that work for you?"

"Sure. Sure, no problem." It looked like Aaron was trying to decide which angle might be best to get a little closer without getting whacked. "We don't have to talk about it."

"And you have to promise you'll tell me!" Daniel's flapping had probably gotten predictable by that point, because Aaron was able to grasp his hands and pin them to his lap. "If you start to have feelings for a client, you have to tell me. You *have* to."

"Kid." Aaron squeezed his hands when they tried to jolt into action. "Nothing like that is going to happen."

He clutched Aaron's hands back, hard enough for his knuckles to turn white. "Please. Promise I'll be the first to know. Do me that kindness."

Aaron slow-blinked as if attending a feral feline, carefully lifting one of Daniel's hands to his mouth for a kiss. "I promise."

Someone worth liking. He crashed into Aaron's chest, letting his bones go limp in his arms, the weight of the evening and the decision pooling heavy beneath his skin as Aaron rubbed his back in slow circles. It was like his nerves got to slip back into their cocoons until the next crisis.

"I'll be so good to you," Aaron whispered, pulling them up to a stand where he swayed them back and forth. "So, *so* good to you. I'll take care of you. Has anyone ever taken care of you?"

No. He couldn't quite fathom what that meant, so he said, because it was what people said in the movies, "I can take care of myself." Then because that didn't feel wholly true, he followed up with, "Well, most of the time. At least some of the time. When the occasion calls for it."

"Oh, of course you can, sweetheart. Of course, you just…." Aaron trailed off as his gaze started to scan the house. "Not in every way. Do you mind if I take a peek at the bedroom?"

"The bedroom?" He trailed behind as Aaron darted toward the bedroom. "Why?"

"Hmm? No reason," Aaron said, prying open the door and flicking on the light. "Oh Jesus."

Daniel examined the room. "What?"

"Oh Jesus God on earth." Aaron spun in a delirious circle, whisper-repeating under his breath, "Worse. Worse than I expected."

"Well, I told you my plan. Get you to like me, then reveal the messy."

"You precious little thing, look at me." Aaron cupped his face and pulled him close enough for their noses to nearly touch. "This is not messy. This is how most horror movies start."

Daniel chuckled.

"I'm going to clean it." Aaron zoomed toward the kitchen. "It'll just take me a sec—"

"Are you insane?" Daniel hooked his fingers into Aaron's jeans and pulled him back. "I'd literally rather watch it all burn than spend tonight cleaning it."

"That…." Aaron trailed off again as he cut his eyes to the side, slowly twisting back around. "Might be your only option."

"I want to spend time with you, mister. How am I supposed to do that if you're off fairy-godmothering my room?"

"I want to spend time with you too, kid. But if you don't let me clean your house, I am going to lose my entire mind. My *entire* mind. Do you understand?"

Sort of. Not about cleaning—how charming. But about other stuff. Normal stuff, like dancing or eating. Or that one time when all he wanted to do was drive that person's golf cart, and they insisted he was "too excited to not be trying to steal it."

He reluctantly nodded, and sometime later, Aaron had moved mountains with what little supplies he'd been given. He'd scrubbed dishes, filled trash bags, and assigned homes for things like books, charging cables, and body butters. He'd angled furniture toward focal points and rearranged shelves. They'd even gotten past their first mild disagreement, which was about separating light clothes from dark—the urban legend of laundry—only to land in another gently heated discussion about furniture polish. Aaron couldn't understand why Daniel didn't own any, and when he tried to explain how it was because he would never buy something so ludicrous, Aaron made it. *Made* it from olive oil and lemon essential oil.

The whole thing was very demigod-turns-domestic and beyond sexy, and if he wasn't so exhausted, he'd properly thank him. But he was exhausted, so he flopped atop his fresh bedsheets and rolled himself up like a piglet in a blanket.

Aaron blew out a candle he had lit, transforming the room from lemony heaven to a birthday wish come true. "Sorry, it's so late. I'm going to take off, okay? Let you get some sleep."

"Oh no." He pawed at Aaron's arm, half-delirious. "You don't have to leave."

Aaron grinned as he sat on the corner of the bed. "Aww. Exhausting watching me do all that work, wasn't it?"

"Yeah, you wouldn't think it would be."

"Because you didn't do anything?"

"Because I didn't do anything—" He interrupted himself with a yawn and wiped his watery eyes. "But here we are."

Aaron snorted and twirled one of his curls around his finger. "Hey, what are you doing tomorrow? I'd love to take you out. Something low-key and relaxing. Just us."

Daniel hummed as he snuggled into the covers. Was this what it was like having someone take care of him? Not only was it physical—the house; his body—but it was like Aaron was meeting him where he was emotionally. "I'm hanging out with my boyfriend. Just us."

Aaron took a breath. When he spoke again, his tone was a bit different. Almost tense. "I'm glad you texted. I was worried.... I'm just glad you texted."

He shook his head and patted Aaron's chest. He couldn't even reach for the fury he'd felt a week ago. The well of anger had bled dry, replaced with hope. "Olivia said I should stop dating my dad."

Aaron's head twitched to the side.

"Err, no." He scrunched his face and swabbed a hand over it. "What I meant was, uh, you're not my dad. You're better and I shouldn't keep dating my dad because he's horrible."

"Yeah, how about you get some rest, sweetheart." Aaron kissed his forehead. "We'll unpack that later when you have more energy."

"Sounds super," Daniel said, his eyes drifting closed and his thoughts swirling together. "But you should kiss me before you go."

"Mm-hmm, and how do you want to be kissed?"

"Duh." Daniel grinned, his eyes still shut as he puckered his lips. "Kiss me like you did at the—"

The kiss from the party immortalized. Again. Thrilling and yet caring. Mild and yet not at all. Demanding tongue that said, *Lie on the bed and open your mouth*, and a delicate touch that said, *You. You, you, you, Daniel Greene, of all people, have nothing to worry about.*

"Get some sleep," Aaron whispered through a gentle smile. He clicked the lamp off and wound the dancer snow globe on the dresser.

Someone worth liking.

"I'll call you tomorrow." Aaron stood at the door, his comforting voice lingering in the air like birthday candle smoke. "Good night, kid."

"Good night, mister." He closed his eyes while the soft clinks of *The Nutcracker* serenaded him to sleep.

Chapter Fourteen

NESTLED SOMEWHERE on the list of things that made Daniel nervous were boats. It was the next day, and he followed behind Aaron as they made their way down a dock toward a shiny cabin cruiser named *Nauti Rhonda III*. One might wonder what happened to *Nauti Rhonda I* and *II*. One might fear they sank. Perhaps attacked by something monstrous from the choppy, ominous waters below.

"You okay?" Aaron said, coaxing him by the hand as they stepped onto the shaky deck. "Almost there. You're doing great."

The boat shifted and swayed as if to prove Aaron wrong about him doing great, but they reached the stern, where a touching scene unfolded, nearly taking his breath away. Someone had strewn blankets around cozy seating and uncorked a bottle of malbec on a table with two stemless glasses and a lit candle between them. A setting sun in the backdrop glistened over the lake in individual ripples.

"How did you...?" He cupped his hands over his heart. "Did you rent this? It's stunning."

"No, a friend of mine owns it. He's always told me I could use it whenever, but I've never taken him up on it. You know why?"

"BUIs?"

"Because I've never operated a boat in my life. I don't know what I'm doing. Like, at all." Aaron laughed.

Daniel did not.

So they never left the dock. They never even started the engine. They snuggled into the blankets and one another, drinking wine and joking about how people should not lend boats to people who didn't know how to work them.

The water lapped at the wood around them in a serenade of warbles and swishes, and the sun dipped lower until darkness fell. When the mosquitoes grew too handsy, they meandered to the sleep quarters downstairs, where Daniel huddled into Aaron's chest atop a bed surrounded by purple ambient lighting.

"We shouldn't get too comfortable," Aaron said, massaging Daniel's neck. "We have dinner reservations."

Daniel nuzzled farther into the nook between Aaron's chest and shoulder, reveling in his little hum. "Fuck your reservations."

"Daniel," Aaron gasped. "I can't believe you would say that. They're *our* reservations."

"I'm not going anywhere. I live here now."

"You do? Okay, I'll live here with you." Aaron squeezed him tighter. "But we have to get rid of that dresser."

He lifted his head to see where Aaron pointed. "Why? Looks fine to me."

"Exactly. *Fine* is not a good look. Like that valance—fine. That chair needs something downy; a pillow or something. And gray to cool it down in here."

"God, I'd hate to hear what you think about my place."

"Oh, I try not to think about your place."

Daniel snorted. "What do you mean? It's all rearranged, and it's still perfectly clean."

"No, it's not."

"No," Daniel sighed, recalling the dishes that had started to pile up and the clothing on his floor. "It's not."

Aaron chuckled. "I actually don't mind that you're a tiny, messy monster."

"Duh." He rolled his eyes. "Because you're obsessed with me."

"It's not an obsession." Aaron kissed his forehead. "It's a weakness."

"Is that what you tell yourself when you're making a doll from my hair?"

"And it's not a doll." Aaron slid his fingers through Daniel's hair. "It's a mini replica, and it's finally taking shape. Just a few more strands—"

He chuckled as he swatted Aaron off, rolling over on his belly to let his eyes get their fill of Aaron's face. No one should be allowed to have a face like that. It was genetically unfair. He touched his fingertips to a small white line on Aaron's upper lip. "What's this scar from?"

Aaron's pink tongue poked out to feel it. "When I was fourteen, I got into a fight."

"You did? With whom?"

"With my dad."

Daniel's eyebrows raised and his smile vanished. "Not a physical fight? Right? Are you serious?"

Aaron chuckled as he nodded. "Yeah, guess I'm good at fighting with dads, huh?"

Daniel couldn't find it in him to smile as he rubbed Aaron's arm. Say what you will about Robert Greene, he would never get physical. "What was it about?"

"Money." Aaron blinked at the walls. "Er, not directly, but I'd asked him for money because I needed new shoes for soccer, and he got mad. We started fighting. He hit me."

Daniel's hand snapped to his heart as he widened his eyes. "What do you mean, he *hit* you over soccer shoes?"

"That's what it was about." Aaron shrugged as he smeared a fingertip over the scar. "I had braces. Busted my lip wide open. I had to get three stitches."

Daniel shook his head. His breathing was suddenly a bit hitched.

"But he felt bad," Aaron continued, like they were having a conversation about a broken vase and not three stitches in his face. "Because he gave me forty dollars when I got home, and the shoes didn't cost that much."

The blood in Daniel's heart ran cold enough for him to shiver.

Aaron toyed with a loose thread in the comforter. "He'd buy us stuff when he felt bad for doing something. Or give us cash. I guess it was usually cash."

"Who's *us*?" Daniel tried to level his voice, but it squeaked as his eyes began to sting. "You and your brother?"

"Me and my mom. And my brother, yeah. Less him, though, which thank God. I suppose because he was younger."

"He hit all—?" His composure was wavering as terribly as his voice. "He hit all of you guys?"

"Only when he got mad. Not all the time. Not, like, every day or anything—woah, hey!" Aaron's eyes widened as scrambled to cup Daniel's face. "You're crying? Don't cry, kid. I didn't mean to upset you."

"Oh dammit," he hissed, wiping his face on a blanket. "I'm sorry. I'm so sorry."

"Shh, no, don't apologize. It's okay." Aaron yanked him into his chest, where he petted his hair over and over. "It's okay, shh. You're okay."

Daniel rolled his eyes at himself as he bounced a bit, trying to wrangle his emotions. No, it wasn't okay. He was terrible at being a solace to others because he *felt* it. Whatever they were saying. Whatever pain they were going through. Even in movies or stories he'd hear—it was all so visceral, and he couldn't keep it separate from himself. It was one of the worst things about him, and it was just as bad as it'd ever been. "But I'm supposed to be consoling you, not the other way around."

"Well, in a way you are." Aaron sweetly combed his fingers through his hair. "In *your* way. Have you always been like that?"

"Like what? Like a human water faucet?"

Aaron chuckled.

"Yes. My mom's the same way. We can't control it. We *try*. But when the single parent in the commercial finally gets their online degree, or the bodywash brings the family together, we lose all composure."

Aaron took a breath and hesitated, sorting through his words maybe. When he spoke again, it was with this low whisper, like they were sharing a big secret. "Can I tell you something without you thinking I'm weird?"

Daniel nodded, curled against his chest.

"I think I might *really* like that about you."

He lifted his eyebrows and cleared his throat. "You *like* that I'm a human water faucet?"

"I like that you show people your heart. It's enormous, your heart." Aaron kissed his curls. "And it's courageous to live your life that way."

Well, did Aaron want him to cry again? He'd never had someone *like* it. It'd always been too much for everyone. Especially men. He rolled back to his stomach and smoothed a fingertip over Aaron's lip. "Well, I think your scar makes you look tough."

Aaron captured his fingertips and kissed them. "Yeah?"

"Oh yeah. Tough and rugged. Classic man-raids-tombs-because-of-his-sexy-vendetta-against-artifacts, or whatever."

"Is that supposed to be an *Indiana Jones* reference? He's an archeologist. Why would he have a vendetta against artifacts—?"

"Shh, the point is"—Daniel crawled on top of him and straddled his waist—"it only enhances your beauty."

Aaron skated his hands up and down his thighs, his gaze sweeping down his body. "Does it?"

"You're a survivor." He framed Aaron's head with his elbows and hammocked his chin on his hands. "There's nothing more inspiring than that."

Aaron bunched Daniel's shirt into a fist and pulled him down into a kiss. A kiss that began an ambitious journey to becoming more than just a kiss.

"But Aaron," he said as he drew back, grinning, "what about your reservations?"

"They're *our* reservations—"

"You would miss them?"

"No. Yes." Aaron's hips had begun to roll up into him, barely detectable like it could've been the water beneath the boat. "I don't know. I want to take you out."

"But you want to get me naked more?"

"Yes," he chuckled. "Okay? Yes."

"You can say it."

Aaron rolled harder, his voice a bit husky as he said, "I want to get you naked."

"Why?" He pouted his lips, dodging when Aaron tried to kiss them. "Surely you have a reason?"

"Because I want to watch your face and watch your mouth telling me how good I feel. Telling me not to stop."

Daniel narrowed the space between them to smile against Aaron's mouth, sliding a palm over the bulge in his pants. "Keep going." He yelped when Aaron flipped him to his back.

"Telling me you want me harder and harder." Aaron drove into him. Speaking of harder…. "Until you can't say it anymore. Until you've just come all the way undone in my arms. I can't wait."

Daniel nodded feverishly. God, where did he sign up? Was there an app or something? "Then don't. Get me naked. Get me so naked, mister—"

The lights flipped on the same time someone yelled, "What the *hell*?"

Daniel's heart slammed in his chest as he and Aaron scrambled out of bed to stare up at a house of a man with bulging biceps who clutched the hand of a younger guy tight and said, "Who the hell are you?"

"Uh." Aaron yanked Daniel behind him. "This is my friend's boat."

"The fuck it is." The guy's eyes somehow got wider. "This is *my* boat."

"No, I-I swear. His name's Justin. Justin Whittemore."

Muscle man's eyebrows kneaded. "How do you know Justin?"

"Through, um, work."

"That's my husband."

"Oh shit," Aaron said, like they were about to get pulverized.

"Oh shit," Daniel said, certain they were about to get pulverized.

Then Aaron turned to him with the saddest expression possible and whispered, "Forgive me."

Daniel couldn't get more confused. "What?"

"Gauge, right?" Aaron asked, spinning back around.

"Yeah," Gauge answered with a skeptical squint. "Who's asking?"

"Aaron Silva."

Suddenly Gauge softened. He even smiled a little. "You're Justin's Aaron?"

Justin's Aaron? Daniel wrung his fingers. He might be getting seasick.

"You're married?" the younger guy asked, wiggling his hand free from Gauge's.

Gauge whipped around to the other guy, alarm hazing his expression. "Uh. I was gonna tell you."

"When?"

"Tonight. I was gonna tell you tonight. We have an open kind of thing."

"An open kind of thing?" The guy's skin splotched in red as he whirled for the stairs. "Son of a—again! Again with this shit."

Gauge grabbed at his hand. "Aiden, hold on—"

Aiden slapped Gauge's bare arm hard enough for everyone to flinch. "Forget my face, asshole, and lose my number." He stomped up the stairs.

A stilted silence clung to the air like an old odor.

"Oh, and go all the way to hell," Aiden yelled down.

More silence.

"Oh, and take your husband with you!"

Is he actually gonna leave, or…?

"Dammit," Gauge whispered, shoving his hands in his pockets and stamping his foot. "I've been working on that dude all night. God, I probably spent a hundred bucks on drinks. And he's all 'Are you trying to get me drunk?' No, not at all. Why would I want to speed things along when I could sit here all night long, listening to you talk about how many fucking followers you have?"

"I am so sorry about this," Aaron said, ushering Daniel forward. "We'll leave right now."

"No, stay." Gauge's chuckle was morose as he extended his hand. "It's not like *I'll* need the damn boat tonight. Nice to meet you, Aaron. Never quite understood why Justin needed to pay for it, but that's been made crystal clear. You look like a *GQ* cover."

Aaron shot Daniel a tense glance over his shoulder as he took Gauge's hand.

"And you are?" Gauge asked, reaching his hand toward him next.

Immediately leaving. Daniel smiled. *Right this second.* "Excuse me," he whispered and wriggled past them. "I need some air."

"Okay, let's get you that." Aaron followed him toward the stairs. "And maybe some more wine—"

Gauge snagged Aaron's shoulder and held him back, whispering something in his ear. Then he turned to Daniel. "Hey, you don't mind if I borrow this guy for a sec, do you?"

Aaron looked a bit shell-shocked, like he didn't know what to say. "Oh, now's probably not a good—"

"Just a little chat. It won't take long. Please?" Gauge grinned sweetly up at Daniel as if it'd help facilitate his approval. Sweet but shameless. "*Please*? He'll meet you upstairs."

Suddenly both of them were staring up at him, awaiting his blessing. *Of course you may proposition my boyfriend for sex! How terrific!*

"Pffft, totally." His tone didn't match his words, making him sound a little unstable, so he delivered a wimpy thumbs-up to convince them he wasn't. "By all means, sirs. Good sirs." Still unwell. "And by that, I mean, take your time." It wasn't getting better. He scurried up the stairs.

Once on deck, he heaved a gust of air and started pacing to offset some of the seasickness. What was he doing? Honestly. What the hell did he think he was doing? He didn't have the neural network necessary to handle open husbands and *GQ*-escort boyfriends and *Nauti Rhonda III*—whatever happened to the goddamn first and second! He needed a sedative.

And this wasn't Aaron's friend's boat. This was Aaron's *client's* boat. Aaron probably knew the tweak to get the shower to work, and which towels were for fancy nautical use and which ones were for other purposes. *Cleanup* purposes.

Queasy and parched, he balled his fingers into fists. He could run away? Swim?

"Hell yeah. I'll give you a call." Gauge's voice carried up the stairs with his footsteps until Aaron shushed him. He asked quieter, "What? What's wrong—oh, him? Sorry."

When they arrived at the top, Daniel stood with his hands perched on his hips, smiling way too much.

Gauge shot Aaron a look. One that said, *Better luck next time* as he hopped onto the dock, whistling as he strolled away.

"Kid," Aaron sighed. "I am so sorry you had to see that. I wouldn't have even entertained talking to him, but since it's his boat, I felt obligated—"

"Can you take me home?" asked Daniel, still a ball of sunshiny smiles. "I'd like to go home."

Aaron's forehead crinkled. "Home? But what about dinner?"

"I'm not hungry."

"Because you're… upset?"

"Upset? Me?" He slapped both hands on his chest and laughed. "No! I'm fiiiiine."

Aaron swallowed.

"I just wonder," he said, laughing harder, his heart starting to whirl through beats, "if there shouldn't be a shared calendar for these things. To eliminate confusion. Do you think Aiden would appreciate a shared calendar? Aiden with all the followers?"

"Daniel—"

"This isn't going to work out." Daniel whished his hands around the air. "It's not going to work out, because I can't handle it. I can't even breathe. Oh my God." He tested his breath, but it was ragged and seizing his chest. "I c-can't breathe."

He couldn't. Or if he could, he definitely wasn't. He wasn't breathing.

"Whoa, whoa, whoa." Aaron's eyes widened in alarm. "Hey— whoa. Sit for a second."

"I can't," he panted as he scrambled for the dock. "Because I have to go." *Three. Two. One.*

"Wait, *what*? Shit." Aaron darted for his things. "Hold on."

He couldn't hold on. *Three. Two. One.* He had to leave and be alone so he could panic without Aaron seeing him and then he'd just die alone because to live was to panic and he didn't want anyone seeing him! He sped down the dock with the opposite of a plan because he had no car either. *Three. Two. One.* He only had the sound of blood in his ears, pumping loud enough to muffle the sound of Aaron yelling at his back as he staggered through steps, failing to catch his breath.

Then everything got dark. Not because he'd fainted like he originally thought but because he'd been gripped into a hug. A strong hug with strong arms as Aaron crushed him into his chest. It was almost enough to steal what breath he did have, but it didn't. For some reason, it started to steady him.

"In," Aaron whispered with his lips pressed against his ear, his chest slowly expanding with air. "Out."

Daniel whimpered.

"In." It was so simple, and yet working like the sedative he needed. "Out."

He hummed, trying to match Aaron's breathing. His was still a little faster, but it was getting there.

"In, kid. Out."

"Shit," Daniel finally said after a minute or two, still hugging him. "Shit, I'm sorry. You probably think I'm nuts—"

"Don't apologize." Aaron shook his head. "It's not your fault, and you're not nuts. I think you just need food. Let's go to dinner, mmkay?"

Daniel scraped his teeth over his lower lip as he released the hug to gaze up at blue ice. He parted his lips to speak.

"No," Aaron said, cutting him off, reading his mind. "No, we're not overthinking this. We're going to dinner. Come on. Everything's fine."

Everything wasn't fine. Daniel wasn't built for someone who slept with other men for a living. That wasn't him.

"If you give me a chance," Aaron said, "I'll be so good to you. I'll treat you how you deserve to be treated. I'll help you deal with it. I'll help you breathe. Weren't you okay just now?"

"Yeah, but—"

"I made a mistake. You have to let me make one mistake. I shouldn't have brought you here. I don't know what I was thinking, but I can do better."

"You need to be with someone who can handle it."

"*You* can handle it. You were doing great. Come on." Aaron tried to lead him toward the car, like getting him to dinner would change the root issue. "Dinner."

"Can I ask something without it sounding too presumptuous?" Daniel resisted, standing firm on the dock. "You say you want a relationship. If escor—*the thing* impacts that, then the obvious solution would be to quit. Is there a reason you don't quit?"

After a long minute of hesitating, Aaron finally said, "Yeah. I can't."

"You *can't*? Why do you feel like you can't?"

"Why do I...?" Aaron trailed off as he pushed a hand through his hair, then let it flop by his side. "I don't have an education. I don't have any skills. I don't know a trade. This is all I've done since I was nineteen, and because I've never done anything else, I have zero work experience."

Daniel's heart squeezed a little. Well, when he said it like that, it did sound a bit thorny. Hell, it was thorny out there for someone who *did* have all those things.

"And I know from your perspective, it would seem like an easy fix. Just quit. Do something else." An intensity burned behind Aaron's words. "But I've had to fight for everything I have, and it's taken years to get where I am. To have a steady stream of clients who value me. A steady income. There's nothing I could do to make what I make now."

Well, that couldn't be true, could it?

Aaron must've sensed his resistance, because he said, "I'm telling you, kid. *Nothing*. Not even close."

"That much, huh?" Daniel chuckled at his feet. He shut down the part of his brain that wanted to suggest he might be in the wrong business.

"You like me," Aaron pleaded. "I know you do. You have from the beginning, and not because you thought I was an attorney. You like *me*. Beyond how I make money."

He dissolved into Aaron's gaze. No one had ever pursued him so fervently. It was marvelous. *He* was marvelous. What a catch he was, and one who deserved the normalcy he seemed to crave. Daniel just wasn't the free-loving 1960s beatnik cut out for that job. He was more of an egg-protecting, dedicated penguin cut out for monogamy.

"You could see yourself with me." Aaron's fingers grazed his hand. "Tell me you can't. Say that, and I'll walk away."

Of course he could. And at the same time, he couldn't.

"Mister." He palmed Aaron's cheek. "I think we tried."

Chapter Fifteen

DANIEL STEPPED onto his stoop as Aaron trailed slowly behind him. The car ride had been glum as could be, and nothing he said was making it better.

"You know how they say comedy is just tragedy plus time?" He risked a smile as he twisted to face Aaron. "Well, tonight is going to be one funny story someday." All his levity efforts were landing on slumped shoulders and a crestfallen frown. "The sunset was beautiful, right? And the boat. Oh my goodness. So gorgeous. I might have to rethink my stance on boats."

Aaron nodded, silent.

"Thank you for everything." He pursed his lips. "I mean it. Thank you for getting my contract taken care of, and the parking tickets. Thank you for being an incredible human being. You are going to find the perfect person someday. I feel it."

Aaron kept his gaze lowered. "I'm sure you are too."

Daniel's heart pricked as he pushed up to his toes and gripped Aaron to him. Aaron's arms wrapped around him, and there they stood in the gray area between *But I tried* and *Did I try hard enough?* It was like he was as frightened to hold on as he was to let go.

"Okay, mister." But he let go. "I'll see you around?"

"See you around."

"Just—" He snagged Aaron's hand as he tried to leave. It felt wrong to let him leave quite yet. It was like something was missing. "One more hug?"

Aaron wrapped him up for the second time, and there it was. That would do the trick.

What was unfortunate was that he'd never get to smell this again. Never experience the potent combination that made his scent so unique. If this was the last time, then he was going to make it count. He buried his face in Aaron's neck and inhaled orris butter and expensive suede, then released his breath. Out poured an accidental moan.

Aaron jerked back a touch to peer down at him, probably to make certain he was okay.

"Oh," Daniel whispered, clearing his throat. "Sorry about that. Don't know what that was."

Aaron studied him, his beautiful face unfairly drenched in moonlight.

"Okay, then." He pressed up to his toes and pecked Aaron's cheek. "Good night."

Aaron squeezed his hand. "Good night, kid. I'll see you around—"

"Wait." He yanked Aaron back. "Nothing. I just think it'd be fine to kiss. Don't you?"

What the actual hell? Had he been possessed by the ghost of terrible decision-making past? How was it *fine* to *kiss*?

"Like, one last time," he continued, just to make sure his logic was as ridiculous as it sounded, and it was. "A kiss goodbye, if you want. Europeans do it."

Aaron angled his head to the side. It was dark, but the confusion was clearly scribbled across his face.

"But actually, if you don't want to—"

Aaron held his hips and kissed him. How... cute. Cute and closed mouth. Cute and chaste. It wasn't the type of kiss Daniel had grown accustomed to from Aaron, but that was perfectly fine. A good-night kiss was supposed to be as harmless as a baked potato without the butter and just as bland. They didn't need to make it any deeper than that.

"How nice," Daniel said, stepping back and offering a little wave. "Now that it's out of our systems, we can finally get some sleep. Good night, mister."

Aaron hesitated for a moment, all tall and noble like an armored knight in an oil painting, while the moonlight did that unwarranted glowy thing to his skin. "Good night, kid—"

Daniel jerked Aaron in and crushed their mouths together. He took liberties, too, snaking his hands over his chest, writhing in tight to his body, tasting his mouth in excess because this was spring break in Cancun and not a front-porch breakup.

"Accident," Daniel suddenly said, flittering his hands about. "I obviously didn't mean—nope. Accident. Go. Good night."

A smirk lifted one corner of Aaron's mouth.

"I'm serious." Daniel pushed at his chest. "Go." Then he fisted Aaron's shirt and tugged him back to kiss him, because he was not a balanced human.

Aaron stumbled forth beautifully. A knight with a white flag of surrender.

"I can't just stand here kissing you all night," Daniel hissed against Aaron's lips and kissed him deeper. "That is not what we're doing."

Aaron matched his crass amount of tongue.

"Are you listening to me?" He scraped his fingers through Aaron's hair and down his back. Europeans probably did that kind of thing too? "I said it's *not* what we're doing."

"So, am I leaving?" Aaron sounded out of breath and confused.

"Yes, duh." His words were muffled by Aaron's lips. "I'd clearly like you to go."

"It's not really that clear—"

"Go!" He shoved Aaron away.

Aaron grunted when he staggered backward, his back hitting the railing. At least he was smiling, even if he was a bit flustered. "Damn, all right. I'm leaving."

Daniel thrashed his arms in the air and nodded like it was about to be outlawed. "Finally!"

They both stood frozen for a beat, breathing sharply. Aaron took one step toward his car.

"Where the fuck are you going?" Daniel crashed into him.

If he was going to be an unbalanced human, he might as well be the kind of unbalanced human that threw caution to the wind, and if this was going to be his decision, then it might as well be the kind of decision he made with his whole body on hyperdrive.

He *consumed* Aaron with everything he had as orris butter, expensive suede, and the neighbor's honeysuckle all crowded his senses. He spun around and struggled to unlock his door—stupid door with its stupid sticky key—the gorgeous stallion of a man behind him not helping. With his hands tracing all over Daniel's body and his mouth glued to his neck with unspeakable skill, it was enough to make a guy scream.

Aaron's tongue lashed around his ear, and maybe he did scream, because the lock finally gave up in fear that Daniel would destroy it with his bare hands.

He flung the door open, and there was a moment when time seemed to freeze. Well, not freeze so much as it patiently waited for them to catch up, to get into position—Daniel's legs hopped around Aaron's waist; Aaron's hands cradling him in the tightest, juiciest kiss—as someone slammed the door closed but no one turned on lights and so they both rammed into a runner table, then an armchair, trying not to laugh as that interrupted the kissing and the kissing was already out of proportion.

It was Daniel's fault. He was done with civilized. He wanted it rough and mindless, like a drunk sorority girl—all needy tongue and no tact. Aaron seemed to be fine with rough and mindless, because he pounded Daniel into the doorframe of the bedroom. "Shit! Sorry."

Okay, maybe that was an accident. Just like the something that fell from somewhere with a clunk and rolled across the floor. Daniel managed to flick on a lamp as he chuckled against Aaron's lips, his chuckle transforming into a squeal when he hurtled through the air, landing on his back in the bed.

"How is your room"—Aaron hurried his shirt off in a chaotic heave that got stuck over his face—"this messed-up already?"

"Shh, ignore that." Daniel slid from the bed like a Slinky and hit his knees. He worked Aaron's belt loose and his jeans down his legs.

"I don't underst...." Aaron trailed off, twisting to gaze around the room. "Like. I *just* cleaned it."

Daniel took his time with the underwear. Wouldn't want to hurt what he was working hard to see. So hard. Deliciously hard. "Look at you."

"Did you have a party after I left or something?"

"Watch me."

Aaron's gaze zipped down to him as a hand gently twisted into his curls.

"You like the way I move, mister? You need to watch me." He stroked Aaron, a bit mesmerized as he tasted the tip. "Watch me fucking *dazzle*."

Aaron looked just how Daniel would've pictured, fully naked: flawless. He was perfectly sized for his frame and centerfoldworthy with the muscles that cut their way around his stomach, stretching all that honeyed skin tight. The messy room must've lost its place on the list of Aaron's concerns, because blue ice never left Daniel as he invited Aaron into his mouth. Sweet and soft, sweet and soft, sweet and soft. Slow, slow, slow. For a while.

Until it wasn't.

He had a technique. It was a whole thing that brought the boys to the yard, and Aaron suddenly wobbled on his feet, his hands sort of hovering in the air like he didn't know what to do with them as he grunted, "Holy."

Yes, sir. Holy. Holy mackerel. Holy hell. Holy head. Daniel didn't need vocal encouragement to lavishly apply himself, but it didn't hurt that Aaron was falling apart under his command. It was kind of cute that his body jerked the way it did as he struggled to stay upright, supporting his weight on the bedframe, cursing under his breath.

It also didn't hurt that he tasted just like he smelled: expensive.

Rich velveteen suede and lush orris butter. Fuck, Daniel would swallow with pleasure. He hadn't really eaten much today....

"Holy—stop!"

"Holy *stop*?" Daniel asked, swiping his tongue over his lips as Aaron laughed and stumbled away. "That's a new one."

"Jesus." Aaron's breath bucked his chest. "You want it to end before it starts?"

"I think I would enjoy anything *it* did."

"Your mouth." Aaron lifted him from the floor and sat him on the bed to cup his face and smear a thumb over his bottom lip. "I was wondering."

"Mm-hmm." Daniel nodded; then he shook his head. "No, that doesn't make sense."

"Sorry," Aaron chuckled and dragged a hand down his face, his wild gaze heavy on Daniel's lips. "I was wondering how it'd look afterward."

"Oh?" Daniel batted his lashes and pouted his lips. "How does it look?"

He was expecting an answer like hot, sexy, bangable, but Aaron leaned in and kissed him long and tender. He whispered, "Precious. You're so precious."

That was the difference, wasn't it? Some guys saw black and white. Hot or not. Sexy or not. Bangable or not. Aaron looked at him and saw shades of precious.

He melted back onto the bed while Aaron undressed him, then riffled through the nightstand drawer like he was taking inventory of its contents. "Condoms in here? Lube?"

A part of him knew better. It knew sleeping with Aaron was only going to muddle things further. It was taking an already complicated maze and redefining the layout halfway through.

"You're so flexible." Aaron pretzeled Daniel's leg around himself. "Look. You're like Gumby."

He chuckled, scrunching his nose. "Can we maybe pick someone hotter than Gumby?"

"No." Aaron grinned. "I've always had a thing for Gumby."

It was taking a complicated maze and lighting that shit on fire.

"Hey, I want you to know something." Aaron was suddenly close to his face. "I want you to know how excited I am to be here. How excited I am that you want me here."

Daniel pushed a strand of chocolate hair away from Aaron's eye. It was taking an already complicated maze and maybe never finding his way out.

"But I don't have any expectations for tomorrow."

Daniel raised his eyebrows.

"If tonight's the last time I see you, then tonight's the last time I see you." Aaron raked both hands through Daniel's hair and held his face stable. "But I'm going to enjoy the hell out of it."

Daniel's breath caught in the back of his throat. He couldn't tell if it was something he needed to hear or if it just jumbled things more. But maybe it was for the best. If tonight was the last time he saw him, then tonight was the last time he saw him. Either way, he should also enjoy the hell out of it.

"Look at me," Aaron said. He wet a finger with his mouth, then wedged it between Daniel's legs and slowly pushed it inside him.

He couldn't stifle the gasp or the way he gripped on to Aaron's shoulders.

"Into my eyes, kid," Aaron whispered. He grinned a little as he pushed a second finger inside him. "Nowhere else."

It was easy following his command. It was easy getting lost in the depths of blue ice. So heated to be so frosty. Like the bottom of an iceberg or the center of a flame, either one delivering a burn if touched.

Aaron grinned fully now. Attentive. Mischievous. "Oh, you're mine now."

God, yes.

Then it was happening. It was happening in the condom Aaron ripped open with his teeth and lube he drizzled in excess. It was happening in sharp whips of tingling tenderness and wide eyes and even wider gasps, and damn, he was tight, but he was *alive* with adrenaline, and Aaron was so… controlled.

"Now, see, I had a hunch." Aaron smiled as he gripped the flesh on his hips, slowly pushing himself deeper, one disciplined inch at a time. "I had a hunch you might feel the way you feel."

Daniel wrapped his legs around Aaron's waist, a little dizzy, a little lost in frosty blue. "How do I feel, mister?"

"Oh, you don't know?" Aaron's eyebrows furrowed. "I'd think you'd lead with that. 'My name's Daniel, and I feel perfect.'"

Daniel rolled his eyes to hide all the swooning.

Aaron leaned down until his lips touched his ear. He whispered, "Perfect."

He shook his head, but he was as giddy as could be with Aaron's face buried in his neck, insisting that he was "Dazzling. Inside and out, you're dazzling."

He might as well have been on drugs with all the starry-eyed chemicals beginning to surge into his system. One or two (or seventy) might have penetrated his emotional center, but it wasn't like it was hard to do. He wasn't good at this. At containing his emotions at all, but at keeping them in a safe compartment where they didn't run rampant over his decisions.

"So good." Aaron buried himself a bit deeper, coaxing a whimper from Daniel's mouth. "So, *so* good. You are my new favorite place to be."

Even if they were just words, it didn't matter. They were words no one had ever said to him, and he suddenly didn't care if there were a million reasons for them to remain unspoken. He'd carved out plenty of places in his heart for men who didn't deserve it, but this sweet, nurturing jewel of a man did. He deserved an entire corner in Daniel's heart. It could be Aaron's corner, and no one would be allowed inside but him.

"Kiss me." Daniel rocked his hips harder as he touched their foreheads together and inhaled Aaron's expensive skin. "Kiss me—"

"Like I did—"

"At the party."

The kiss from the party transformed into the night Daniel met his match as an electric current clutched the moment, and Aaron bored into his body with a shocking amount of intuition.

How Daniel liked it—mostly rough. *When* he needed the rhythm to slow while he wrangled his breath. *What* he needed to hear hissed into his ear as he clawed at flawless honeyed skin: "My new favorite place to be."

Daniel wholeheartedly agreed as he surrendered into the moment with one hand pinned to the mattress above his head and the other gripping Aaron's jaw, because he didn't want to see anything other than blue ice with its swirls of white topaz and the tenderness behind it all.

"If you stop, I'll kill you," someone suddenly threatened. Daniel realized it was him.

"Aww." Aaron smiled, all cocky. "That it, sweetheart?"

Yeah. That was it. Aaron knew that was it, which is why he didn't stop. Which was why he muscled through thrusts, rasping into Daniel's ear, "You tiny fucking thing. Take it."

Then Aaron more than fucked him.

"Take it."

He more than had him.

"Take it."

He ruined him.

Daniel had never been ruined so good. He'd never had a man pierce his soul with a few words, a few flicks of his tongue, and with such flawless certainty. He'd never had a man make him come.

Not like this. Not hard and heavy, sensational and coarse-grained without so much as a single stroke to himself.

His voice crackled from his throat while he suspended disbelief long enough to trust his eyes as hot streams of white spilled from him, over and over, coaxed stunningly from his body in bright bursts that obeyed Aaron's thrusting hips and speckled both their abdomens as a reward.

Aaron jolted still to breathe or maybe stare while Daniel trembled all over, giggling through an attempt to rub his eyes.

"Goodness," Aaron said, out of breath. "Do you do that often? Look at me. You do that often?"

Daniel shook his head, loopy and light-headed. "I don't even know what just happened."

"Don't tell me I'm the first." Aaron shook him a little. "If you tell me I'm the first, I can't be responsible for my ego."

"You're the first." *And the last. A radiator and a pair of handcuffs.*

"Oh my God, it hurts." Aaron collapsed on top of him. "My ego *hurts* it's so swollen. What a little unicorn. So hot." He slowly pushed up to his hands. "You probably need a minute. I'll give you a min—"

"Nuh-uh, keep going." He sounded strangely confident, like a porn star on poppers and not someone barely clinging to lucidity. "Whatever you want. Take as long as you need. But keep going."

It was the kind of moment that was sure to become a memory, all saturated in dreamy colors and soft-focused around the edges. He cradled Aaron's head in his neck and took him gracefully. Skillfully even. He'd do anything Aaron needed.

He'd arch his spine and moan through his teeth. He'd grip the sheets and whimper while Aaron unleashed into him. He'd part his lips and swallow his own cum because Aaron had said *Drink* and shoved dripping fingertips inside his mouth, down his throat. *Every last drop, sweet boy. Every last drop.*

He'd gaze up at him, completely blitzed with his eyes wide and his heart battering through beats, and he'd say somewhere between a whisper and a growl, "You are a fucking god."

And Aaron would come inside of him within seconds.

THE ONLY sound in the room was the slow revolution of the ceiling fan. Daniel lay twisted in a tangled heap of arms and legs atop Aaron's chest as he breathed in the neighbor's honeysuckle, an easy rhythm in sweet succession of inhales.

He'd be sore tomorrow, but he couldn't locate a single bone that cared. He smiled against Aaron's skin, almost vibrating in the lingering high from their little joyride. "Aaron," he whispered. "Are you asleep?"

Aaron drifted his fingertips down his arm. His voice was deep and underscored with fatigue as he said, "No, sweetheart. Just thinking."

"About what?"

Aaron sighed, "My life."

"What about it?"

"I don't know." He tossed an arm over his face and shook his head. "Nothing. Never mind. I think I'm just tired. Would it be okay if I stayed here tonight? Or I can leave. No worries."

Something in Daniel's heart sputtered. He shook his head and squeezed Aaron tighter. "No, don't leave. I don't want you to leave."

Aaron pecked his forehead. "Thank you."

"In fact…." Daniel took a gulp and mustered all of his courage. "I want breakfasts."

"Yeah?" Aaron rubbed his arm. "We can do breakfast."

"No, *breakfasts*. Plural. I want more than one."

Aaron angled his head to see him a bit better.

"And I want lunches too. I want dinners and dates." He bravely pushed himself up to a seat. "I want you to meet my friends and Madeline. I want you to meet my mom. I want all of it."

Aaron's eyes brightened, and his smile got spectacularly sappy. Underneath his handsome, steel-clad exterior was a creature with such a tremendous soft spot that Daniel ached to touch it. To soothe him. To stitch up his painful past with a patchwork of affirmations. *You're good enough. You did nothing wrong. You're safe with me. I'll take care of you too.*

The potential for something epic here had to outweigh the chance his entire heart would thoroughly break one day. And even if it didn't, that was a problem for future Daniel.

He shifted to wriggle onto Aaron's lap and loop his arms around his neck. An hour later, he could still feel him inside like the wind could feel all the thrown caution. He closed his eyes and whispered onto Aaron's lips, "I want all of it with you."

Chapter Sixteen

A FEW WEEKS later, Aaron stood in a hotel room with his arms crossed, trying to keep his irritation from bubbling over into a screaming match. He was supposed to have met Daniel at the studio five minutes ago, and his new client—well, new *and* former client—had turned out to be a nightmare.

"Come on," the nightmare said. "Just take it and go. It's a lot of money. A *lot*."

"I'm not arguing that it's not a lot," Aaron said, cracking his neck. "I'm saying it's not what we agreed on."

"Are you kidding me right now?" The guy slung an arm toward the bed, where an envelope stuffed with bills lay. "That's an insane amount of money. Not to mention, I bought you an entire meal, *and* this is probably the nicest hotel room in the city."

No, it wasn't. Not even close. Usually Aaron got the money up front—*always get the money upfront*—but he'd failed to do it because sometimes he was human, and sometimes being human meant he leaned too far on the goodwill of others. Plus, this guy had been referred by a solid client, which should've had some merit but didn't.

"The price is the price," he said, checking the time on his phone. Daniel had made plans to attend an outdoor concert. He was supposed to be meeting Olivia. Aaron was going to disappoint them both. "You don't like it? You never have to see me again."

"Look, man." The guy shrugged, his arms thwacking heavy by his sides. "I don't have that kind of money right now."

What a liar. What a cheap and backbiting liar. There was nothing worse than men like this. A couple of hours ago, he'd been stumbling over his words, praising Aaron's looks, begging just to touch him. Now that their time together had dwindled to an end, suddenly it was an *insane amount of money* that he just didn't have. "That's not my problem."

"I don't know what you want me to do. I'm telling you, I. Don't. Have. It," the guy said, punctuating his words with claps. "Please just take what I do have and leave."

"It doesn't work like that."

"Fine." The guy arched an indignant eyebrow. "Do I need to call security?"

Aaron's laugh was loud. "Uh-huh, and what'll you tell them?"

"That you won't leave!"

"That the escort you hired wants the money you agreed to pay him? You tell them that. Or tell the cops. Whatever."

The guy's cheeks ruddled in an angry pink as he crossed his arms and pouted. He mumbled under his breath, "Maybe I'd pay it if it'd been worth it."

Aaron tossed his gaze at the ceiling and plopped onto the bed. He didn't have time to squat in a hotel room, waiting for this guy to grow some dignity, but he'd be dammed if he moved another inch without his money. He rechecked his phone, his stomach churning a bit at the time. He shot Daniel a quick *I'll be there soon!* "The price is the price."

"Get out." The guy thrust a finger toward the door. "Now."

Aaron propped himself on his elbow and smiled. "Hand me the remote, won't you?"

"GOOD AFTERNOON, this message is for a Mr. Daniel Greene. Hi, my name is Bill Oren with Missouri Loan Express. I'm sorry to inform you we were unable to approve your small business loan application. Give me a call back with any questions you might have."

Daniel sucked his lip as he punched his phone into his pocket. It was like the studio was slipping through his fingers. Maybe he'd been naïve to think he was capable of buying it, let alone running it.

His phone pinged with another text from Aaron:

I'm sorry I'm running late, sweetheart! So excited to see you!

Well, if ever there was a reason to smile. The state of his finances and overall life might have been a flaming trash pile, but at least his love life was sensational. And by sensational, it was *sen-fucking-sational.*

Aaron had gone out of his way to make sure of it. It was giggly park walks, and scooping Daniel up between classes, taking him back to his apartment for fancy espresso drinks made with love and quickies over the kitchen counter, made with lots of noise. It was browsing shops on the Loop where Aaron bought him little gifts: bags of gummy candy, a new scarf, and a dangly silver earring shaped like a ballet slipper that twinkled in the light.

They'd avoided speaking about the Thing, and Aaron artfully directed their conversations if it ever got too close. He also made sure to be very available on a whim as if to say, *Look, dating me is so normal. Isn't dating me normal?* No. And yes. It might have been the most normally abnormal thing he'd ever done, and so far, his anxiety had taken a back seat to allow it.

"Where's your fancy boyfriend?" Olivia asked, stepping from the back room, hauling on a pair of knee-high black boots. "Isn't he supposed to be here? The concert's already started."

"He's running late, but he'll be—" Daniel had started to stuff his phone in his pocket when it dinged again. "Oh, wait."

You guys go ahead and walk down! I'll meet you there soon! Promise!

They'd had this night planned for a week. It didn't feel like Aaron to miss an opportunity to meet Olivia and do something so quaint and Midwestern, like attending an outdoor concert on the Arch's riverbank. He was all about quaint and Midwestern.

Is everything okay?

Of course!! Can't wait to see you!!

So many exclamation points. About four too many for a text from Aaron to seem like everything was okay. Daniel's stomach twisted, but he ignored it, because his anxiety was doing the back-seat thing and sitting in the back seat was good for his anxiety.

Twenty minutes later, he and Olivia arrived at the Arch's riverbank, where families with little ones huddled around brightly lit funnel cake booths, and cackling men, punished red by the sun, guzzled beer under a white tent. They pushed their way toward the stage, settling on a place to stand next to a pod of glow-stick-jewelry people, who he tried to telepathically message to offer him a bracelet.

After a half an hour or so, he texted Aaron:

Still coming?

To which Aaron responded:

Absolutely!!

Another forty-five minutes and Aaron wrote:

What time does the concert end?

Daniel hated to jam Olivia's groove as she was dancing with her whole heart in a way that looked like she might be turned on and also swatting mosquitoes, but something was not right. It wasn't even about Aaron being late. It was *why* Aaron was late.

"Hey, I've got an idea." Olivia twirled around a few times. "You should put me on your shoulders."

"Look at me." He wafted a hand down his body and started to type out a response. "What about this frangible mien says *airlifting* to you? We would both need hospitalization."

Another text from Aaron:

Sorry to do this. I'll meet you guys at your house a little later.

It was *why* Aaron now wasn't coming at all. That was the sticky part, of course, because of the answer: he was with someone else.

The image of the person Daniel's brain supplied happened to be handsome, rich, and impossibly eligible. They also had a fancy electric car and even fancier tech company CEO title, and Aaron couldn't help but be into them.

Daniel bit his teeth together while his anxiety did a full sweep of his body. How could it manifest? A touch of queasiness? Check. Intrusive thoughts? Check. Elevated heart rate? Not quite, but the night was young.

"What is wrong with you?" Olivia asked. "Why aren't you dancing? Dance."

He showed her the text trail from Aaron.

"Oh." She tongued the corner of her mouth. "Well, that's a bummer. He didn't say why?"

"It's a Saturday night, and the man's a sex worker. He's probably at his grandma's house, right?"

"Well, let's not jump to conclusions."

"That is not something I've done. Just because he's with a Swedish billionaire named Sven who's currently flying him to the moon on the literal rocket he owns doesn't mean I've jumped anywhere conclusion-wise."

She rubbed his arm. "It feels a little specific not to be a conclusion."

"Ugh." He dropped his head back and groaned. "Let's just go home."

"No, hey. We're not going home. We never go out, and the night is young. *We're* young. Let's do something crazy! Sow our wild oats."

"All my oats are too tired for sowing. I'd rather go to sleep." He slumped his shoulders and pooched his lower lip. "So I can not think about him for eight hours."

"Screw that! Hey, look at me." Olivia gripped his shoulders and forced his eye contact. "You know what we should do tonight?"

"Cry on the linoleum."

"We should do psilocybin."

He studied her face for a long time, then squinted. "Am I supposed to know what that is?"

"Mushrooms."

"Mushrooms?"

"Mushrooms." Her spirit fingers said it all. "The magical edition."

He stopped blinking to gawk at her. "Are you absolutely out of your mind?"

"Not yet." She winked. "But I could be." Another wink with an added conspiring whisper: "Psilocybin."

"I don't... what? No. No, that's ludicrous."

"That's exactly why we should do it!" She held his shoulders again. "I mean, no offense, but your boyfriend is with Rocket Sven and this music has me feeling awfully saucy. What's holding us back?"

"Well, for one, they're illegal contraband. And for two, where would we even find them?"

"Where?" She scoffed. "Oh, please. Don't make me laugh. I know a dude. A mushroom dude."

His mouth twitched at the confidence. Like a Guido with new hair gel. "Oh, you know a dude, huh?"

"That's right." So much winking happening. "A mushroom dude."

Daniel eyed her for a long moment. He started to speak but hesitated. Barring a few hits from a joint in college that made his heart feel like it had been relocated to his head, he'd never done a drug. "You're serious right now? Well. What are they like?"

"The mushroom dude?" Olivia shrugged. "He's nice. He has a porn star goatee that I personally think he'd look better without, but other than that—"

"No, what are the mushrooms like? I mean, are they... safe?"

"Oh, are *they* safe." Olivia nodded, a slicked-up Guido. "Probably."

DANIEL STARED down at his coffee table, where shriveled, illegal contraband had been poured out and scattered around like they were garden-variety risotto ingredients and not highly hallucinogenic.

"I can't believe I'm doing this."

"You know, I second that," Olivia responded. "I also can't believe you're doing it."

"So, what do we do?" He ferociously chewed a thumbnail. "Does one cut them up? Like, with scissors?"

Olivia tipped her head back and forth but said nothing.

"Does one brew a tea with them?"

No response from Olivia.

"Does one answer me while I'm talking?"

She shrugged all puny. Her confidence had diminished terribly. "I feel like we should just eat them whole."

"Wait." He gripped her arm. "Have you never done the mushrooms before?"

She gave him the strangest look, kind of like a person who had never done the mushrooms before.

"Olivia!" He widened his eyes. "This cannot be happening. You led me to believe you were the magic mushroom expert."

"Okay, but in my defense, you probably wouldn't have agreed if you didn't think I was the magic mushroom expert. If it helps, I've always wanted to be a mushroom expert."

His eyes rounded more. "Why would that help?"

"I'll get us some water." She pointed back on her way to the kitchen. "When I come back, we'll meet the mushrooms. We'll greet them. Everything will be fine. Don't worry about a thing."

He bounced his knees as he stared down at them. "Girl, I don't know about this—"

"Picture it like a belly dance, Daniel. A belly dance for your brain."

"Oh, a belly dance?" His dipped his head. "Well, I do love that."

"See?" she asked from the kitchen, filling two glasses of water. "And wouldn't your brain love to take a belly dance break from all your worries? From Aaron? And Sven?"

The studio came crashing into the forefront of his mind, followed closely by Sven and his literal (and figurative) rocket. "Yeah, it would."

Olivia beamed as she offered him a water and a mushroom. "Cheers. To belly dancing."

AT SOME point, Daniel and Olivia had reassembled on the floor. It wasn't that the couch was bad. Nothing was *bad*, but the floor had room to spare, and just because it was scattered with dust and random unpopped kernels of popcorn didn't mean it wasn't a lovely place to belly dance. Which he did with flourish from where he lay on his back beneath the coffee table with his shirt rolled up to his chest because it was making Olivia giggle.

"You're *so* good at that," she said, her eyes wide with awe. "You are the best belly dancer on this floor."

"And you are *really* beautiful," he said, rolling over to face her. "You're the best friend on this floor."

"Daniel, that is so sweet." She pressed a hand to her heart and puckered her face. "Let me know if you want to make out a little later."

"Will do." He rolled to his back and flicked the underside of the coffee table a few times to make sure it was sturdy. It was. "You know who else is beautiful?"

"Mm-hmm. Nutella."

He melted into a longing smile. "Aaron. Aaron is so beautiful."

"Oh sweet butter sculpture of Jesus," she groaned, fanning herself. "That man. I've only seen that one picture of him, but he looks like he was handcrafted by the gods from granite and unicorn sperm."

"Unicorn...." He squinted. "Sperm."

"And Nutella.

"Ahh, okay. Now that I think about it, yep. I could see that," said Daniel, who definitely couldn't.

"I told you to give him a chance, and look at you now. God, I adore being right. Now you guys are all *You're the wind beneath my wings. Let's have babies together.*"

"The condoms protect us from an unwanted pregnancy."

"I better be the maid of honor. Don't deny me that."

"Okay, but if I make you maid of honor"—he rotated to face her again, pointing sternly—"you have to promise not to bang the best man."

"Who's the best man?"

"Probably Aaron's brother."

Olivia rolled her eyes. "I'm not going to bang Aaron's...." She trailed off, a frown pouting her lips. "Why not?"

"Okay, fine. But you have to give me all the slutty details." He began ticking off fingers. "I'll need the size of things, the quality, and how quickly things get *sturdy* when those things are excited."

"Slutty details are part of my responsibility as maid of honor. I take it seriously. Speaking of Aaron." She jumping-jacked her arms and legs a few times as if she were trying to make a snow angel on the area rug. "How are you dealing with the whole escort thing?"

He poked the tip of a popcorn kernel with his finger. "Phenomenally."

"Really?"

"No! Have you ever met me?"

"A lot."

"I am *so* into him." He curled into himself and moaned. "I want to crawl inside his skin and live there."

"Sounds murder-y."

"You want to know a secret?"

"Is it detailed and slutty?"

"He doesn't know this—" He swiped his tongue over his teeth to make sure they were still there. They were, which was how he was able to say, "But my long-term goal is to just wait it out. He can't do what he does forever, right? Eventually he'll have to quit."

Olivia pressed her lips together and popped them loudly, over and over. Daniel tried to join but couldn't get his as loud.

"Why?" she asked between pops. "Why would he have to quit?"

"Because he'll get too old. I'm pretty sure you can't escort once you turn thirty. Isn't that the rule?"

"What? First of all, that's ageism. And second of all, I don't think you could be wronger. There's probably fifty-year-old escorts out there making a killing."

"Oh, I would so bang a fifty-year-old Aaron. God, think about the salt-and-pepper hair and the un-ironic use of the phrases *Vacation home on Lake Tahoe*, or *Let's get up early and go hiking*, or *We're considering boarding school for the labradoodle*." He narrowed his eyes to a squint. "But would I *pay* to bang a fifty-year-old Aaron?"

"Yes?"

"Yes."

"Let's do it."

"Let's. But first, and hear me out, what if I give him an ultimatum someday? People do that in the movies all the time. Like, it's either those jive turkeys, or it's me."

"Daniel." Olivia's tone lowered, and her eyes widened. "What turkeys?"

"I like your attitude." He nodded his approval. "*What* turkeys is right—"

A knock sounded at the front door. They both scrambled to their feet in a process that hurt as they each thwacked different body parts on the coffee table, then stood wild-eyed in his living room like a couple of busted burglars.

"Someone's already in here!" he shouted and then slapped a hand over his mouth.

They screeched in laughter until the knock sounded again, making them startle.

"Hello?" Another gentle knock. "Daniel, it's me."

"Who the hell is *me*?" Olivia whispered.

"Yeah." Daniel deepened his voice and puffed his chest at the door. "Who the hell is *you*?"

"It's Aaron."

Oh. Oh, Aaron was here. Of course he was here. He'd said he was coming over—no big deal.

"Kid," Aaron said, his voice closer to the door, "I tried calling. I know you're probably upset with me. If I were you, I'd be upset with me too."

So why did his being here feel so… enormous?

"I am so sorry. I get that you're mad, but can you please open the door? Please?"

Daniel's heart was going to fracture his rib cage, it was suddenly beating so intensely. He tried to smooth his outfit, and hopefully the way he probably looked like a frazzled mad scientist with a bona fide Igor, but Olivia's hair refused to comply with any grooming. It also didn't help that the door creaked like an eerie castle as Daniel opened it.

"There you are. Sweetheart, I am so sorry. My night has been…." Aaron's concerned expression gradually transformed into confusion as his gaze zipped back and forth between them. He licked his lips, his eyes narrowing to a squint. "Are you guys okay?"

"We're belly dancing," Daniel said, and because that probably made no sense, he followed up with, "Not with our bellies."

"You are a lot of man," Olivia said, her eyes all pupil as she scanned Aaron from top to bottom. "A lot. Maybe more than I can handle right now."

"Are we... high?" Aaron cocked his head. "Is that what's going on? We're high right now?"

"Yes," Daniel said. "It's technically called psilo-something. But on the streets, we refer to them as—"

"Mushrooms?" Aaron's eyebrows shot up. "You two are on magic mushrooms?"

Daniel tossed his hands up. "Well, how does everyone know what that is but me?"

"So, Aaron." Olivia grinned as she gently squeezed one of Aaron's biceps. "Daniel mentioned your brother might be the best man in the wedding?"

Aaron's gaze danced between the two of them for a long several seconds. Then he softened into a sigh as he swiped a palm over his face. "This has been the worst night, and I was afraid it was about to get even worse, but it won't. Because you two are...." He trailed off, erupting into chuckles. "God, thank you. I needed this."

DANIEL LAID his head on one of Aaron's thighs while Olivia lay across the other. The drugs had worn thin, but they were both still giddy as could be. It was probably because Aaron was running his fingers through their hair, which was a glorious sensation. Almost as glorious as the smile he wore as he did it.

"Oh, granite-unicorn-spermy-Aaron." Olivia sighed. "You are the best."

"Yeah, you mentioned that," Aaron said. "But thank you again."

"We just like you," Daniel said. "We really like you, and you smell good."

"Again, thank you." Aaron was so serene. A beautiful anesthesiologist with a couple of blitzed-out patients. "I like you guys too."

"Do we smell good?"

"You guys smell fantastic."

For the second time, Aaron explained to Olivia the reasons why he couldn't let her pierce his ear while Daniel watched. Well, while he watched Aaron. He was so graceful with the way he spoke. So kind. He carefully reached up and touched Aaron's lower lip with his fingertips while he spoke, sparking Fiji-ocean eyes to lock with his.

Look at you. Daniel could feel his woozy smile growing even more. *Everything. You are* everything *to me.*

That was the first time he'd had such a definitive thought, and it felt final in a way. Did Aaron know? Did he know just how marvelously everything he was? Oh, someone should tell him. Someone should just say, *Aaron, you're everything to me.* Daniel would do it, but he was far too chicken to say something like that.

Aaron lightly kissed his fingertips, causing a coil of nerves to blaze hot at the base of his spine. He bounced a little. He should really say something. Like, now. What was wrong with now? Nothing. Now was great. Aaron deserved to know, so he should say something. Now. Nownownownow.

A grin teased one corner of Aaron's mouth.

Now! Daniel chewed his lower lip. He could say that. *Aaron, you're everything to me.* Only a chicken wouldn't be able to say something so simple, and he wasn't a chicken. He wasn't a stupid fucking clucking chicken.

Aaron silently worded, *You're precious.*

"But I don't *want* to be a chicken!"

The room fell silent.

Aaron blinked at him for a beat, his face a combination of concerned and amused. "Like a rotisserie chicken? Or one that lays eggs? I don't want that for you either, baby."

"Daniel." Olivia rolled over to scowl at him. "I don't know everything there is to know about mushrooms, but they for sure cannot turn you into a chicken."

"I—dammit. Firstly, you don't know anything about mushrooms, Olivia, and secondly—" He pushed himself up to a seat, drank in a gasp of air, and pulled Aaron close until their foreheads touched. "I need you to listen to me, sir. I really, *really* like you."

Aaron pursed his lips, but his grin persisted. "Uh-huh, you feelin' good, sweetheart? You're on drugs. Let's lie back down."

"No."

"No, you're not on drugs? Or no, you don't wanna lie down?"

"I do want to lie down, and you should join me, as that sounds delightful. But I need to explain something first."

"All right." Aaron calmly nodded. "Explain."

"If I may just request a moment of silence from you both." Daniel leaned back and nibbled his nail, scanning the room for any visual guide that might help him explain it better, when he spotted the two root beer bottles on the corner of the coffee table. "Oh, here we go. See, this is me. And this one—isn't it cute that we match, by the way?—is you." He pushed the bottles together until they clinked. "And here we are together."

Aaron's brow pinched as he nodded. "Hmph. Tell me more."

"Well, so, not only are we cuter together—so cute—but as you can clearly see, we're *better* together. Aaron. We are so better together."

That was about as genius and triumphant as an explanation could get, so imagine his shock when Aaron had to cover his mouth with his hand to keep his laughter somewhat contained. Daniel scratched his head as he blinked down at the root beer bottles. Wait. Was he forgetting something?

"Oh, this is so great. Did I already say thank you for being on mushrooms? Thank you, thank you. And you're right, sweetheart. Two root beers are way better than one root beer. Swell job on the visual aid too." He gave a thumbs-up. "That really brought it home."

"What I'm trying to say." Daniel's mouth suddenly itched as he scooted in closer toward Aaron, his heart river dancing into his throat. "Okay. What I'm trying to say is—sorry. Give me a minute."

Aaron chuckled, swabbing a hand over his face. "Uh-huh?"

"Nothing. I mean, it is something. But." He drummed on his lips to cue the tiny dancer to knock it off. "Nothing."

Aaron gave in to a yawn. "Is it nothing? Or is it something?"

"It's just—"

"It's just what, kid?"

"I'm in love with you."

Aaron's eyebrows rose, and his mouth dropped open. Olivia huffed in a breath and shot up to mirror him.

"I think I'm, like, *in love*, in love with you. Like bananas in love with you."

Aaron blinked in response. No words. No facial clues as to what he was thinking. Then, without moving a muscle, he said, "Oh. Shit."

Olivia gasped. "Oh shit."

Daniel gulped. *Oh shit.*

Other than that brief delivery, Aaron was frozen in time. An eternity passed as Daniel sat there, tapping his fingertips together. It was definitely long enough for the sun to swallow the earth, but that didn't happen like he'd hoped. He parted his lips to speak with no clear summary of what might roll out.

"Shh, for a second." Aaron held up a hand. His forehead wrinkled. "Is this the mushrooms talking?"

"Yes. I mean, no! Okay, yes, I said it just now because of the mushrooms, maybe, but there is this gravitational tugging of you and me together, and you are this robust presence in my life that I've never had before and don't want to have with anyone else, because there's no way it could be as good as you and me and us, and you are quite honestly everything—you're *everything* to me." He gasped his first breath in a minute. "And I thought you should know."

Aaron gripped him by the waist and hauled him onto his lap. Not gentle and controlled but fumbling and raw. He straddled Daniel's knees around him and jolted their bodies close and tight. "Say it again."

He tried to hide the fact that he was out of breath and disoriented. He studied Aaron's face for clarification, but it looked just as thunderstruck. "Say....? All of that again?"

Aaron shook his head. "The first part."

"Oh." He swallowed. "Say I love you?"

Aaron nodded. Something behind his eyes was so intense, it was almost punishing to stare at. "Again."

"I love you."

"Again."

"I love you."

Aaron sucked a breath through his teeth as he touched Daniel's face all over. He swept his fingertips down his temples, then cheekbones. He thumbed his chin and rubbed his neck. It was almost like he had to do it. "I wish you could see the way your mouth moves. I wish you could see how you look when you say it. Say it."

Daniel's eyes stung because of course they did, but he stayed present, gripping Aaron's face, smiling against his lips. He whispered, "I'm in love with you."

"You should not stop." Aaron's fingers twisted his shirt, clawing until it was inching up his back. His voice was a deep hook. "Don't stop."

"You like it?"

"Daniel." Aaron nodded. "It's the best thing I've ever heard."

He winced when Aaron thrust them even tighter, tight enough to hurt, but God, bring it on. Give him this man's skin against his. If his nervous system was going to go down in a wonder of flames because he was wholeheartedly in love with a sex worker, then he might as well pour the champagne and eat the damn cake.

"I love you," Daniel said in between these wild, *wild* kisses, breathing only when he had to. Let Aaron's mouth be a journey where no corner was left untasted. "Aaron Silva. I love you."

Aaron was suddenly growling, pushing up into him all rock-hard, and Daniel was panting, struggling to unbutton dumb buttons. He was seconds away from destroying this gorgeous shirt, ripping it open with his teeth, when—

"I'm so sorry to interrupt," Olivia whispered from where she sat curled against the arm of the sofa.

"*Geez!*" Aaron leaped all the way out of his skin, half scrambling up the back of the couch as Daniel whipped his head around.

"Would it be cool with you guys," Olivia asked with her phone angled toward them, "if I recorded a little of this?"

Daniel erupted into laughter while Aaron kneaded his temples and whispered, "I forgot she was here."

"That's exactly right." Olivia grinned to herself as she nestled into her seat and presumably pressed Record. "I'm not even here."

"Okay, no one's recording shit. You, phone down. And you." Aaron pointed up at Daniel, leveling him with a smirky look. "You're a minx, and I don't know what you've done to me, but I feel like I'm on drugs. You need to get off my lap before you make things worse."

Daniel giggled and rolled off him while Aaron adjusted his jeans, muttering a jumble of disputes under his breath.

"I think it's time we get you two dummies to bed. Go get ready. I'll take the couch."

He and Olivia exchanged pouts. "But—"

"It's 2:00 a.m." Aaron had an effective parental side-eye. "Bed. Go."

"Well, yes sir, mister, sir," Daniel said with a wink as he pulled Olivia from the couch. "Can't argue with that."

"Yeah, meow to the authority, Aaron," Olivia said as Daniel guided her toward the bedroom. "Would you say your brother is very authoritative, or…?"

"Good night, Olivia," Aaron chuckled. "I can see why you two are friends."

Daniel held Aaron's gaze, walking backward on his way to the room just to keep him in view for a bit longer. His boyfriend. His beautiful boyfriend who he loved, who he was *in love with*. Like, bananas. He waited for Olivia to collapse into the bed, then poked his head out of his room and whispered, "Hey, good night, mister. I just wanted you to know that I meant what I said. Every word."

Aaron looked a bit frayed, his smile almost forced. He cleared his throat. "I know, yeah. Good night, kid. Get some sleep."

Oh. Daniel tried not to let his expression teeter as he waved a little wave and crawled into the bed. Blame it on the mushrooms, but he hadn't noticed until just then.

Aaron never said it back.

Chapter Seventeen

IT WAS a week later, and Aaron was bustling around his house, trying to clean before Daniel arrived. He'd gotten him an apology gift and baked him apology bread. He had a lot to be sorry for. Not only had he missed the concert and ruined their evening, but then he'd sat paralyzed like he'd been stunned still while Daniel spilled the contents of his heart.

Love. It might have been a mushroom-induced spillage, but that was what he'd said to him. That was what he felt for him.

His brain had pulsed with white-hot electricity, pleading for him to say it back. It was so easy for some people. For some people, people like Daniel, it poured from them all unfussy and whole-souled. For him, it was impossible.

The last time he'd said it, he'd been a child. The last time he'd said it, it'd landed on cold blue eyes, hatefully clouded, the exact color of his own. Blue eyes that were already gone, but he'd said it anyway. He'd said it, and then his dad left.

This was different. Of course it was different, because unlike then, he had resources now. He had utility and foresight and a complete fucking bag of tricks.

He had money.

He wasn't a child anymore—he was a protector. Which was why he had a plan. A plan to protect the precious things around him.

A knock sounded at the door. He opened it to find Daniel grinning, his pouty lips wrapped around a red twist of licorice. He held his phone near his mouth while a woman on the other end—his mom?—spoke about a new carwash that had opened. He mouthed, *Hi, mister*.

Aaron sighed, half smiling, fully delirious. He might have been unable to say those three words, but he could show them. It was part of the plan.

"Okay, Mama, I have to go. I just got to Aaron's," Daniel interrupted her, then said to him, "What smells so good in here? Are you baking things? Mama, Aaron bakes things."

"Oh my gaaaash, does he?" Daniel's mom said in a charming Wisconsin accent. "What time will you guys be here tonight? Oh, I'm so excited. You haven't brought a boy home since that one guy—what was his name? Peter something?"

"Oh, who can remember that far back?" Daniel flapped a palm. "So, anyway—"

"C'mon, Danny, you know. Wasn't he a shrink or something? He did not treat you right. Remember when he said you were too touchy-feely?"

"So, anyway, Mom!" Daniel hard-blinked, and Aaron chuckled. "We'll leave here in about an hour."

"Butchie is going to be so excited to see you. He has a new hotel for his trains he's been dying to show someone."

"Aww." Daniel's shoulders melted as he smiled, a palm pressed to his chest. "Tell Butchie I say hi."

The way Daniel spoke about his stepdad was with genuine reverence.

"Butchie!" his mom yelled into the phone.

Daniel held the phone at a safer distance.

"Danny says hi!"

He held it farther.

"Oh honey, you've made my day. Tell Aaron to bring his appetite."

Aaron's heart rate spiked a bit when Daniel winked at him. He was doing this. He was meeting Daniel's mom. It was thrilling and scary, but he nodded his encouragement. This was a layer that would be excellent for the plan.

"See you soon. And hey, if we could not call me the *name*? That'd be swell—"

"Bye, my little Flapjack Dancake. Love you."

Daniel ended the call and held a finger to Aaron's lips. "Let's not comment. I've tried to train her, but it's useless. God, is it bread?" Daniel sniffed the air as he charged past him and into the kitchen. "Are you baking bread?"

"Banana bread."

"Aaron." He spun around, face aglow. He was still in his dance gear—satiny black capris and an oversized striped sailor's shirt tied in a knot on the side, exposing his stomach. "That's the best kind of bread. Is it ready?"

"Not yet. Here." Aaron guided him toward the sofa and unwedged a tan shoebox from beside the sofa. "I wanted to talk to you about some stuff before we leave, but first, I got you something."

"You got me a gift?"

"Nothing big. An apology." He rolled his lips. "For missing the concert with you and Olivia."

Daniel's eyes flashed to his. They hadn't spoken about the reason *why*, and hopefully Daniel still preferred it that way. Just like they hadn't spoken about the other thing. The thing Daniel had said. The thing Aaron had not said back.

"You've apologized a hundred times. Forgiven. Forgotten. You didn't have to get me anyth—" Daniel froze when he lifted the lid on the box.

"What do you think?" he asked when Daniel didn't budge. "You like 'em?"

Daniel's expression stayed stunned as he lifted one of the shoes out by its long, coiled strap. "Wait. You got me high heels?"

He shrugged. "Just a little something to wear around the bedroom. And the kitchen."

"Aaron." Daniel shook his head and blinked. "You bought me a thousand-dollar pair of heels to, quote, 'wear around the bedroom'?"

"And the kitchen." Aaron nodded toward the kitchen. "Put 'em on and bend over to check on the banana—wait, how do you know how much they are?"

"Everyone knows how much they are. They're, like, famous." Daniel flopped onto his back, strapped on one of the red-bottomed stilettos, and extended his leg into the air. He bubbled in goofy laughter. "This is…. I've never owned heels. I don't know how to walk in them."

"I don't think you'll be doing much walking."

"Is this your kink? Have we just unlocked a new kink?"

"This? Nah, this is just something to wear around the—"

"The bedroom." Daniel admired the shoe, his tongue sliding between his teeth as he twisted his leg side to side. "Got it."

And the kitchen. "Okay, then there's one more thing. Here, sit up." Aaron took his hands and pulled him up. "I need you to have an open mind for this one."

"Ooh, another not-kink kink?"

He squeezed Daniel's hands and gazed directly into his eyes. This was it. The plan. The plan that was going to reconcile him being a dysfunctional mess. "I want to buy the studio for you."

Daniel cocked his head, his eyes pinging around. "Excuse me?"

"I've thought a lot about it, and it'd be an honor to buy it for you."

Daniel's eyebrows shot up.

"I have money saved, and you need money, and you are so important to me, and I want to help. What do you say?"

Daniel blinked for a long time. "That's sweet and all, but you're joking, right?"

Aaron cut his eyes to the side. Of course he wasn't joking. There was nothing funny about it.

"You're serious." Daniel widened his eyes. "No. Aaron. Obviously, no."

"Well. Okay, I don't have to pay for the whole thing. What if I just pay for a portion of it? Like, three-quarters or something. How about that?"

"Pay for three-quarters of my business? That's absurd."

"How's that absurd? Then how about half?" But Daniel's expression tightened further at that. "Geeze, okay. Um, rent? What if I take over your rent and utilities and maybe your cell phone if you're open to it—"

"Aaron." Daniel's expression had transformed into a glare. "This isn't a discussion we're having."

"But why not?"

"Because it's weird as hell."

"How's it weird to want to help you? What if I just paid for—?"

"And what if I talked to you about interior design?" Daniel hitched an eyebrow. "If you're looking for something to do with all your money, then let's talk about that."

Aaron snapped his teeth shut.

"Interior design is something you adore." Daniel flapped a hand around the apartment. "But instead of pursuing that, you want to do what again? Help me buy my studio? Pay for my cell phone? How does that make any sense?"

"That's different. This is your dream, and I can help you make it happen."

"But what about *your* dreams?" Daniel pressed a finger into his chest. "If you want to invest in something, invest in *you*."

Daniel didn't understand. He didn't get that Aaron investing in the studio *was* investing in his dreams. This was so much more important than anything else he did. He might not have been able to say it, but he could show Daniel how he felt about him. If love was money, then he'd give and give until it was enough. *You want it? It's yours. Anything you want is yours.* If love was money, then he'd make so much that no one would ever leave again.

"Look." Aaron squeezed his hands. "You don't have to answer today—"

"I think I just did answer."

"—but I'd like you to think about it." He forced his face calm when what it really wanted to do was scowl. It shouldn't have been this difficult to give someone money. "I'm offering you a solution, kid. The least you could do is think about it."

"Then the least you could do is have a conversation about interior design with me. A real one."

Aaron didn't regret much, but he might have regretted ever telling him about the interior design.

"Because the least *you* could do is admit you'd be fantastic at it. You could admit you'd wholeheartedly love it."

"No offense"—he swirled a finger in front of Daniel's face—"but do you know what this is?"

"Manipulation?" Daniel smacked his finger away. "Duh, Aaron. Why do you think I'm doing it?"

"It's a false sense of hope. I'm not going into interior design. Like I said, there is nothing I can do to make what I make now."

"Would that be the end of the world?"

"Yes."

"Why?"

Why? He shrugged, searching the walls for a way to explain it. The bigger question was *why* were they so not on the same page? Wasn't it obvious *why*? Wasn't it a universal experience? If he didn't have money, he'd have zero control. If he didn't have money, what would he have to offer?

"It just is."

Daniel folded his arms. "But you're making assumptions. You're assuming you won't make as much. What if you did—?"

"False." He covered Daniel's mouth with his palm. "False sense of hope."

Daniel's eyes got all squinty, fiery even as he peeled Aaron's hand away from his mouth to start sucking on one of his fingers. Which… yes. It took all of three seconds for Aaron's dick to twitch alive.

That was until Daniel bit it.

"Gah!" Aaron ripped his hand away and shook it out. His first reaction was to haul Daniel over his lap and spank him. "Get over here, you little—"

"My little what, Aaron?" Daniel wriggled from his grip. "My little desire to see you doing something you'd love?"

He held up the bitten finger. It also happened to be the middle one. "Apologize to me. I accept oral apologies."

"Oh, I'm not sorry." Daniel snagged the other heel from the box, plopped into an armchair, and strapped it up. "I'm not sorry for wanting you to have your dream job, but if you don't want to talk about how wonderful your future could be? That's fine. Let's talk about other stuff."

When Daniel stood, Aaron stood, and for some reason, they stared each other down like two cowboys in a spaghetti western.

Daniel tipped his head. "Like how I've never noticed how short you are."

Aaron tried not to smile. He plunged his gaze down Daniel's body. "Yeah, you know you're still shorter than me—"

"*Itty bitty.*" Daniel strolled around him in a slinky, sultry circle, clicking the heels on the wood. "I almost didn't even see you there."

Aaron couldn't keep his mouth from flinching as he rolled his eyes. "You know you wearing heels doesn't suddenly change my height?"

"Should I probably drive tonight?" Daniel dragged a single fingernail around Aaron's midline, scratching the fabric of his shirt. "Can you even see over the steering wheel?"

"That's a genuinely ridiculous thing to say."

"What's the weather like down there?"

"Wouldn't know, sweetheart. Because I'm six-fucking-two—"

"Cloudy with a chance of Napoleon Syndrome?"

Aaron tried to snatch Daniel's waist, but he swiveled away like a sexy Gumby ninja.

"How do I put this nicely? I prefer *top-shelf* guys." Daniel pressed their backs flush and slowly descended with his spine arched, dragging his body down Aaron's. "Sorry but must be *this* tall to ride."

Daniel yelped when Aaron seized him and flung his little body onto the couch. What a troublemaker. He was all long lines of slender muscle and blue veins under ivory skin with this pouty, fuckable, pillow-perfect mouth that just begged to be roughed up. It was everything about him. The looks. The sass. The delicate frame. It brought out the animal in Aaron.

"You," he said, breathy, pinning Daniel to the couch, working the buttons undone on the satiny capris. "You're so goddamn ridiculous."

"Aww, you want to fuck me in the heels?"

Aaron nodded, leaning in to devour him in a kiss. "I want to fuck you in the heels—"

"Here's the deal with that." Daniel jammed a stiletto into his shoulder and pushed him back.

Aaron gasped, his mouth hanging open as he blinked down at it wide-eyed. How'd he even do that? It was more impressive than anything. It was a superpower to be so flexible.

"You and I are going to have a conversation about interior design. We are going to talk timeline and logistics. We are going to see what it would take."

What a little shit. Aaron couldn't help but growl as he smoothed a hand down Daniel's leg.

"Yes?" Daniel held his gaze as he reached to stroke him over his jeans. "Do we have a deal?"

Of course, he'd gotten played, but he was also so hard his mouth was starting to water. "Deal."

"You swear?"

"I swear."

"Good boy." Daniel wrapped his legs around his waist and yanked him into him. "Now, don't stop until I'm shaking."

AARON FOLLOWED Daniel up the walkway of his childhood home in quaint St. Charles, Missouri. Its A-frame and shades of avocado and institutional green screamed the peasant blouses and pet rocks of the 1970s.

Pink tea roses bloomed on either side of a wooden porch, where a tattered swing, once painted French vanilla, squeaked each time the wind blew. A wreath of blue ceramic birds hung on the door, and the faded doormat below their feet read "Welcome. I hope you brought chocolate."

His palms were sweating. It was so official, meeting Daniel's mom. Meeting Mr. Greene hadn't been half this amount of pressure, because Daniel didn't seem to value anything the guy said, but meeting his mom? Geez, the gravity. It was the proverbial rope in gym class.

Daniel tapped on the door a few times, then opened it, the aroma of garlic, toasted cheese, and something nutty hitting them. Daniel was sweet to hold his hand the way he did, even though it was sweating as he led him into the kitchen where semisheer curtains veiled the windows, "Brown Eyed Girl" played on a Bluetooth speaker, and mismatched ceramic jars lined the counters, each reading *Cookies* in different fonts.

"Hi, Mama," Daniel said, his smile at full tilt.

Daniel's mom spun around from the oven and gasped. "Honey! I didn't hear you come in."

She clutched bagged shredded cheese with one hand, her chest with the other, and she barely reached Daniel's shoulder in height. They had the same hair, the same eyes, except hers were shielded by tortoiseshell glasses. She pushed up on her toes and gripped him into a hug.

"Oh my goodness, when was the last time you ate?" She sandwiched Daniel's torso with her hands. "Oh, honey. This is not good."

"Mom, I've literally been the same weight for like twelve years. This is Aaron."

Here we go. He offered his hand. "Such a pleasure to meet you. You go by Barbara?"

"Jiminy Crickets, look at you." From where she stood, she looked like a toddler begging to be picked up with her arms outstretched.

He leaned down so she could hug him too.

"Dancake," she shrieked in Aaron's ear, still hugging him. "You couldn't find someone just the least bit attractive?" She released him to chuckle at herself, a very Daniel thing to do. "Well, I can see why you're smitten with this one. Like a more handsome JKF Junior, aren't ya, Aaron?"

"You're kind."

"And call me Barbie."

He matched her bright-eyed smile and softened a little. How approachable. How engaging. Like her son.

"JFK Jr. is one of those names I've heard, but I have no idea who they are," Daniel said. "Is it an Olympic swimmer? Why do I feel like that's a swimmer?"

"Oh, don't worry about it, sweetie." Then she leaned in toward Daniel and whispered from the side of her mouth, "All you need to know is he was a very steamy human—so Aaron! Glad you're here. Pour yourselves some wine. Butchie won't drink the moscato with me."

"That's 'cause it tastes like weasel piss," a voice boomed from the stairwell.

"Butchie," Daniel squealed and ran to throw his arms around a lanky, homespun man with squinty eyes and a ballcap twisted backward. He wore a plaid shirt and jeans that sagged, held up by a weathered brown belt that looked like it'd seen some things.

Butchie lifted Daniel off the floor in a hug and smiled at Aaron over his shoulder. "So, this is him," he said in an old-western-movie accent. "Nice to meet you, son. I'm Butch."

"Aaron. And it's an honor. I've heard wonderful things about you both."

"Whatever you heard." Butch peeked over his shoulder, his voice lowering to a whisper. "I was young, and I needed the money." His eyes squinted even more when he chuckled.

Joke or not, Aaron laughed at how hard he could relate.

"That your car outside?" Butch said. "That ain't the F-type?"

"Yes, sir. The R-coupe."

Butch's eyebrows shot up. "Supercharged? What's the acceleration?"

"Nothin' to sixty, three-point-five."

"Is this English?" Daniel asked.

"Wheweee, that car is bad." Butch slapped Daniel on the back, sending him staggering forward a few steps. "We're outta beer. Should we take a little ride? I could drive if you don't want to." That whole request was performed with a sprightly little shoulder dance Aaron would pay money to see again.

"Butchie, no," Barbie yelled, her head inside the oven as she tested a casserole with a thermometer. "You do not ask people if you can drive their vehicles."

"Oh, I don't mind," Aaron hastened to say. "I let Daniel drive it all the time."

"See," Butch hollered back at her. "He doesn't care if it gets destroyed. He lets *Daniel* drive it."

Daniel scoffed. "You total one Mini Cooper, and all of a sudden, you're *an endangerment*."

"Beer run." Butch kissed Barbie on the cheek. "We'll be back, woman."

"Beer run." Aaron kissed Daniel on the cheek. Was he smiling like a goof? He was totally smiling like a goof, but this experience was already singular. Special. He kissed him again. "We'll be back, kid."

DANIEL SANK into a chair as they left through the front door, laughing about some inside foreign-engine-related humor, no doubt. He fogged his wineglass with his smile.

"Lord have mercy, Danny." His mom ruffled his hair. "What a looker."

"Is he?" He fawned, dipping back dramatically in his chair. "I haven't noticed."

"Oh, is that right? Well, you sure seem extra sparkly for *not noticing*."

Daniel sighed and tried not to gaze so adoringly at the front door. The love they'd just made left him feeling a bit out of control of his body, like a part of it was off on a beer run somewhere. Plus, he could still feel him every time he readjusted in his seat. Quite the distraction, indeed.

"Think you'll make it ten whole minutes without him?"

"No, I think I might die." He fanned himself. "Should I call him?"

"Dancake." She chuckled as she refilled his wine. "You might be in trouble, sweet pea."

Because he's a hooker? Or because I would commit first-degree arson for him?

"Are you boys being safe? Using protection?" And it started. The stern eyebrow furl and all. "Trust me, honey, chlamydia sounds like no big deal until it's sophomore year of college and pantyhose are all the rage—"

"Mom, I will pirouette right off this roof."

"Okay." She held up her palms. "Chill out. But you like who he is? He's good to you?"

"*Like* him?" He groaned. "Mama, I'm so bubbleheaded, irresponsibly, head-over-Christian-Louboutin-heels in love with that man, I feel like I might explode all over this kitchen."

She gazed at him for a tick. Then it all happened in slow motion. First, she cupped her hands over her mouth. Then her forehead started to crinkle.

"Oh no," he said. "Oh, hey, nooo. It's okay."

But he knew that look. He was king of that look. She was about to cry.

"No, no, no, Mama." He shot up for a paper towel, but the opportunity to blot it away had passed. Behind the glare of her glasses, big tears spilled over onto her cheeks. "Oh shit."

"Danny," she said, wiping at her eyes. "Language."

"Well, I didn't mean to make you cry."

"I'm not crying." Her nose was all red and splotchy. "It's just, oh, I don't think I've ever heard you say that. It's so snug and magical. Like a queer little Christmas movie."

"Mom, stop," he chuckled, wafting at his eyes because of course it was making him tear up. It was a taste of what Aaron probably felt anytime they spoke of anything with an emotional undercurrent. Heaven forbid they ever watch a queer little Christmas movie together. "If you don't stop, then I'm going to start, and they can't come back to both of us crying."

"You're right." She ripped off her glasses to blow her nose into the paper towel loud as an elephant. "Did I mess up my makeup?"

Yes. The whole situation, amiss to begin with, now looked dire.

"Don't you worry." He patted her hand, then scurried off to the bathroom and returned with her makeup bag. "Dancake to the rescue."

"So," she said as he wiped her under eyes clean. "Have you told him? You know? Told him how bubbleheaded you feel?"

"I have." His smile faded as he rubbed his lips together. "Let me ask you something. Do you think I should be worried that he didn't say it back?"

"Oh, he didn't? *Hmph*. Well, why do you think that is?"

He shrugged as he began to redraw her eyeliner, only better because he took the liberty of adding a pointy cat-eye tip. "Maybe because he doesn't feel that way about me."

"Danny. Don't get in your head about it. People experience life in different strides. If Aaron hasn't said it yet, I'm sure he has a reason."

Because Aaron didn't feel that way about him…?

"And the reason doesn't necessarily mean because he doesn't feel that way about you."

Daniel snorted as he patted highlighter along her cheekbone.

"Butchie took a while to say it back."

"Really?" He squinted. "But he's bonkers about you."

"He took a while to say it." She nodded. "Get out of your head. Enjoy the heck out of that boy. Gosh, I sure would." Then in a quiet mumble, "JFK Junior."

"Speaking of Butchie." He patted the finishing touches of a cream blush on the apples of her cheeks and held up a compact mirror. "He's a lucky man."

"Oh Lordy." Her face lit up as she twisted her head side to side. "Well, look at me. I'm ready for the Miss America. What should my talent be?"

"Hmm. Baked ziti?"

"Oh shit." She ran to check the oven.

"Mama." He smiled, as cheeky as possible. "Language."

"Dear Santa." Butchie busted through the front door, the presence of a thunderstorm. "I know what I want for Christmas. It's that car, baby." He spun Daniel's mom around from the stove and kissed her. "Who's this she-devil?"

She giggled and swatted at him.

Aaron stepped out from behind Butchie, a six-pack of beer tucked beneath his arm, wearing the widest, most adorable smile. "That was a blast. A *blast*. He's hysterical. They both are and thank you." He kissed Daniel. "Thank you for bringing me here. You have no idea how much this means to me."

Garlic bread, a platter of pasta, a bowl of bagged salad mix, and two different kinds of iced tea weighed down the dining room table.

His mom filled their plates with enough food to get them a little high. They ate and laughed with their whole bodies while Butchie told stories of his days as a bass player in a rock band and his former life as a hand on a Montana cattle ranch. He talked about his and Barbie's dreams of visiting the Catskills and why model trains were a good investment of one's time—building something from nothing healed the soul.

His mom asked them questions about where they went out in the city, and "Ooh, what kinda food they got down there?" How were people dressing now during the fancy nightlife scene, and would they be too embarrassed to take her and Butchie to a drag show as she "Sure would love to see one in real life. All those glitzy wigs and fairy-tale gowns."

When the question arose, "What do you do for work, Aaron?" Aaron flashed Daniel a smirk and responded, "Interior design."

They'd discussed this one in the car ride here. It'd probably be best to keep that little secret to themselves, and speaking *interior design* aloud was the first step to imagining it.

"He's a natural," Daniel said, gazing into Aaron's eyes, squeezing his hand beneath the table. "He's going to open his own firm someday, and it's going to be *wildly* successful. You just wait and see."

Aaron tugged his hand to his lips for a kiss.

AARON LEANED forward in the car and waved back at Daniel's mom and stepdad where they stood holding one another on the porch. He'd never seen a relationship modeled so well. It was almost baffling. "Butchie and Barbie, huh?"

"I know," Daniel said. "How ridiculous is that?"

"Ridiculous. And adorable. They could not get more adorable if they tried, and they don't have to try. How do we end up like that?"

"Deliriously happy? I don't know. Until you, my plan was to blow a lot of frogs and see how things went."

"Kiss." He grazed Daniel's cheek with the back of his hand. "*Kiss* a lot of frogs."

"Yeah." Daniel nuzzled into his hand. "I did that too."

The song in the background as they drove down the interstate, slow and dreamy with these faint, sultry lyrics, was the perfect mood for a perfect night, and it was heartwarming to watch Daniel flirt with sleep from where he'd curled himself in the seat like he was just so comfortable. For someone as high-strung as he was, he could sleep wherever. On the couch. Inside Aaron's arms. On top of him. It'd been invigorating being his bed—the person on whom he'd sleep—even with the occasional drool puddle. It all felt so... real.

Aaron waved a hand in front of Daniel's face. Out. He'd mentioned needing to stay at his house tonight, something about different dance shoes, but screw it. They'd figure it out later. He smiled as he whizzed past Daniel's exit. *Oops. Sorry, sweetheart. Wasn't paying attention. Looks like you're coming home with me.*

Daniel didn't *need* to go home. He had everything he *needed* at Aaron's apartment. He had a toothbrush and a couple of shirts. What he didn't have, they could just buy. Or maybe they could designate a drawer for him. Hell, they could designate an entire dresser. That'd be cool. If Daniel had a dresser, maybe Aaron's bedroom would start to smell like orange creamsicle. Eventually, maybe his living room would start to smell like it. His whole apartment? God, his whole apartment. That could be a real possibility. Very real. So real.

"MOVE IN WITH ME!"

Daniel jolted awake as Aaron's eyes widened. What the hell was that? Someone answer the question—*What the hell was that? That* had come spewing out of his mouth just now. Forcefully.

Daniel's voice was thick with sleep as he asked, "What?"

"Nothing. Shhhhh, go back to sleep, sweetheart. You're dreaming."

"No, I'm not. You just yelled at me to move in with you."

"I did not yell." He held up a palm. "It was a statement."

"An aggressive statement—"

"OKAY, BUT WHAT IF YOU DID?" He'd meant to say it calmer that time, but he seemed to have one volume for whatever he was saying. Which, *what* was he even saying?

Daniel's expression was layered with confusion, alarm (likely from all the aggressive statement-making,) and then something else. Maybe excitement?

"I just…." Aaron trailed off as he pushed a hand through his hair, struggling to string together a decent argument. He was not very good at this. "I like you around, kid. I want you around me as much as possible because you make me smile and you make me happy and having you at my place means I can take care of you, and it means you'll be around. You'll be there when I wake up, and you'll be there when I fall asleep, and I know it's soon, but I can't think of anything better. I can't think of anything better than you being around all the time. Move in with me."

Daniel's lips parted, but he said nothing.

"And honestly, I don't even mind that you can't clean. Like, you physically cannot do it—as evidenced by the state of your apartment—but I swear, I don't care. If you moved in, we could just hire someone to help us clean, because you do have a skill of creating messes. Especially for being so tiny. It's almost like how I would imagine an angry toddler leaves a room. You're so cute, but you're an angry toddler tornado—"

"Okay, if I let you keep talking, you're going to ruin what would otherwise be a touching moment." Daniel unhooked his seat belt and crawled across the console to smudge kisses all over Aaron's face while the car dinged in protest.

"You're kissing me." An odd warmth radiated through Aaron's fingertips as he cradled Daniel's head. He almost sounded out of breath as he asked, "Why are you kissing me? Is that a yes?"

Daniel smiled against his ear. "Yes."

"Really?" He rounded his eyes, trying to gaze at Daniel but follow the road. "You don't think it's too soon?"

"I don't really care if it's too soon." Daniel gripped his face and twisted it, sealing their lips in a kiss. "Yes, mister. Yes, yes, yes."

Aaron chuckled as he tried to kiss him back with one eye on the road. "Hey, someone's got to drive, sweetheart."

Daniel slid his cold hands beneath Aaron's shirt, and Aaron about flinched out of his seat. He should've been used to it. They were always freezing. Daniel's mouth, however, was never freezing. It was hot and wet on Aaron's stomach as he kissed his way around, cooing against his skin, unbuttoning his jeans.

"Okay, I love where this is going." He glanced up in the rearview mirror to check the headlights behind them and make sure they didn't look police-ish. "But can it wait until we get home?"

"No. It can't. Because I am so excited I'm already going to die anyway. I might as well go out doing something I love." Daniel licked his navel, then popped up to whisper all pouty, "Not to mention, look at my man. He's so tightly wound. He's so tight that he's literally yelling at me."

Aaron chuckled. "It was a statement."

"An aggressive statement. Guess who can help you unwind?" Daniel's breath sizzled between his teeth as he slid his hand inside Aaron's jeans. "Your new roommate."

Aaron cut his eyes to the side. For someone so cautious, he sure was troublesome.

"You wanna play house, mister?" Daniel asked, stroking him. "That what you want?"

He nodded, surrendering to the trouble. He wanted every experience with this troublesome creature, so he lounged back in the seat while the risk broadened, pressurizing the car in an achy sexual tension.

"You want me to dance for you?" Daniel purred like his very own pet kitten. "Rub your shoulders? My big, strong man. Wait for you to get home from the gym? On my knees?"

Aaron lifted his hips and lowered his jeans to expose himself more, swelling thicker against Daniel's grip.

"Any part of my body? Yours." Daniel stopped to lick his hand. "Any time you want it? Done. How does that sound?"

Aaron's voice was hoarse. "It sounds good—"

Daniel yanked his hair by the roots.

"Fuck!" A car horn blared as Aaron jerked the car back into his lane.

"Just good?"

"Damn, kid." Aaron swallowed, his throat dry as he glanced around at the other cars. Good thing it was dark. "Perfect. It sounds perfect."

"Oh, it will be." Daniel stroked a little faster, a little firmer. A lot masterful. "Because I know what you like, and I know how you like it. Don't I?"

"Yes."

"Yes, what?"

"Yes, you know what I like."

"And?"

"How I like it."

"That's right. I can even wear the heels if you want? Or how about one of your ties?" Daniel clicked his teeth next to Aaron's face. "Wrapped around my wrists, strapping me to your bed. Like it did last Sunday."

Aaron clenched his jaw and smirked, last Sunday's memories flooding back to him.

"Guess what else?" Daniel licked the side of his face and hummed, "I can make you come harder than anyone else."

Aaron didn't need to think about it to know it was true. Harder. Hotter. With his entire nervous system at full throttle.

"Wanna see me prove it?" Daniel didn't even give him time to answer before he jerked Aaron's hair again.

Aaron winced, but he didn't let the car swerve. He growled through a chuckle. "You're asking for it, kid."

"Well, I'm trying to ask for it, but someone I know's all *Let's wait till we get home. Someone has to drive.* Blah, blah."

He turned to find Daniel's eyes ablaze with challenge. He matched his crooked smile. *Trouble.*

"I asked you a question." Daniel stroked, rewet his hand, then stroked some more. "I'd appreciate an answer."

"Do I want you to prove you can make me come hard?" Aaron, stiff as steel, tossed an arm around the headrest and leaned back again. "Yeah. I do."

"Oops, someone's forgotten their manners. You didn't say please."

He licked his lips, trying to squash his grin. "Pretty fucking please. Dancake."

"Here's how this is going to go," Daniel said, punctuating his words with little pokes in Aaron's chest. "You have two jobs, you delicious filet mignon of a person. One is to drive. Can you guess what the second is?"

"Not kill us?"

"Close. Come down my throat."

Aaron's laugh was strangled. "How's that close?"

"And I mean *alllll* the way down my throat. Think you can manage?"

Aaron sucked on his lower lip and nodded.

"You're such a good boy. Oh, and one more thing."

"There's more?"

"Permission granted to have your way with my mouth. There is no such thing as too hard, and there is definitely no such thing as too deep."

"Goddammit." Aaron dragged a hand down his face, his lower half starting to ache. "I'm not gonna last long."

"Perfect." Daniel crinkled his nose. "Because I'm fucking starving. Feed me."

Headlights.

Daniel's full lips encircled him.

White lines.

Daniel lured him deep into his mouth.

Exit 241. Silver guard rail.

Daniel swallowed him, and the road waned from his priorities.

The thing about boys who sucked cock like they needed it to live, those were the ones to watch out for. Because those were the ones who could look like the portrait of pious when they said things like *Have your way with my mouth.* They were the ones whose sweetness—with their pretty eyes and tempting skin—made it hard not to crave them like sugar.

Well, Daniel's skin was more than sweet; it was orange ice cream, his eyes the molten caramel on top. But the way he sucked cock? It was like he'd die if he couldn't. Could anyone blame Aaron for yelling at him to move in? Yelling while offering to buy his studio? Yelling while imagining drawers and dressers filled with his things? It was like his heart had been pried open. His wallet sure as shit had been pried open. Now he knew how his clients felt.

The headlights drifted into the background. So did the white lines, exit 241, and his respect for the speed limit. He twisted his fingers into soft brown curls, revved the gas, and hastened Daniel's pace for him. Daniel moaned, all muffled and sexy, and worked his mouth faster like he loved it, like nothing turned him on more. This sexy little demon could put him out of business. Could steal his clients, one by one, and drive him out of business. It wouldn't take him five minutes.

Daniel suddenly popped him from his mouth like a lollipop.

"Hey," Aaron whined. "No—"

"What did I say?" Daniel was in his ear again.

"About what? Which part?" Aaron started to stroke himself, but Daniel smacked his hand. "Guh. Rude."

"I said to have your way with my mouth."

"I am. I love your mouth. Now get back down." He grunted as he fake-forced Daniel's head back toward his lap, making him chuckle.

"I'm not getting back down anywhere. I'm over you holding back."

"Sweetheart." He rounded his eyes a bit. "I'm not *holding back.* I'm driving."

"You hold back all the time. You talk this big Aaron game—*oh, I'm Aaron. I'm so rough and fun*—then you treat me like I might break."

He chuckled. "I've never once said *I'm Aaron. I'm so rough and fun.*"

"Over. It. And that's really too bad." Daniel started to stroke him again, his voice creeping to a whisper like he had a big secret to tell. "Because I would love to finish what I've started, but I can't so long as you're holding back."

Aaron ground his hips against his grip.

"Because there is an animal inside you, Mr. Silva." Daniel tongued the shell of his ear. "And I wish someone would let you off your leash. Can you imagine how good it would feel?"

Their gazes locked. He knew better than to ask, because the answer was sure to turn him on beyond the point of no return. "How good would what feel?"

"To just lose all control. Unshackle your fire." He said it with this smile. "Fucking *own* me."

This demure, guiltless, dripping-with-good smile, and his teeth grazed his lower lip, and the AC burned Aaron's wet skin, and the air smelled like them both, and he could suddenly taste the aching sexual tension pressurizing the car. If Daniel wanted fire, he was about to get fire.

Aaron clenched his teeth and swerved the car to the shoulder. Daniel squealed like a kid on a roller coaster, clutching the assist handle while the rumble strips vibrated enough to cause something to beep. Aaron jolted the car into Park.

"You little fucking insane person," Aaron said, his words labored as he crushed Daniel's lips to his until it was painful. He shoved Daniel's head back into his lap. "You're in trouble now."

Daniel sucked. Harder. Aaron gripped his hair. Harder. They both danced around blurred boundaries of give and take, and in and out, and commanded and commanding, only who was in control? It sure as hell wasn't Aaron. No. Or else he wouldn't be dizzy and unleashed on the side of the road, primally fucking his beautiful boyfriend's throat.

Have your way with my mouth. Aaron clawed the steering wheel, his white-knuckled grip skidding skin on leather. *There is no such thing as too deep.*

Daniel's mouth dripped, pooling wet heat while the sounds he made filled the car in whimpery huffs and hums. Aaron swirled his tongue around his finger and thrust it down the back of Daniel's jeans because just one finger could make those mild noises turn fanatical. And they did.

Taillights whizzed past their car, and Aaron wanted to care that one of them might be a cop. He wanted to care that the way he rammed into Daniel's mouth, with the kid's full lips pressed flush with his torso each time, might be too far, but he didn't care. So he slid another finger inside him and watched him writhe, drunk on a power trip.

What was it about flooding this perfect creature's mouth that felt so similar to power? Like his body was a plaything. A pretty toy. A possession. Aaron scratched the leather seat with his nails. A possession. He squirmed. It was quite possible he was deranged, and *possession* was an overstatement, but then again—*Imagine how good it would feel. To fucking own me.*

A shock throbbed throughout his system and pried a roar from his lips.

To fucking own me.

His cry of release zinged off the car walls.

Own me.

He came alllllll the way down Daniel's throat. Exactly like he was told.

Daniel's spine bowed gracefully even as he gulped the pulses of liquid with the same eagerness he used to coax it from him. Like he was dying of thirst. Like Aaron had the only thing he wanted to drink.

He held Daniel captive another minute, maybe two. Long enough for the residual shudders of pleasure to finish twitching his muscles.

Daniel's mouth stayed open and flawless, his tongue rolling in a sweet little tempo, his jaw doing the same.

Aaron fell to the mercy of raspy laughter and finally collapsed into his seat, where he tried to assemble the council of his mind, but they were out to lunch. Or all passed out whiskey-drunk. Daniel grazed his way back up, and when he saw him, it was like Aaron could bathe in the way he looked. His lips, red and swollen, even more striking than usual, matched his cheeks, flushed hot with color. He looked full of want and eager to please. He looked consumed with emotion. He looked in love.

Aaron kissed him, but what Aaron really needed to do was get him home and worship him head to toe. "You." He grazed his thumb over Daniel's lower teeth just to feel something sharp against his buzzing fingertips. "So you don't need to breathe?"

Daniel cleared his throat, his smile proud. "There are more important things."

Aaron chuckled and tried to settle his stupid breath. "That wasn't too rough for you?"

"Hell no." Daniel bit his thumb. "I can still talk, can't I?"

"What about me? Am I talking? What am I saying?"

"You were saying how amazing I am."

"You are." Aaron touched their foreheads together. "You are amazing, and I think you might've been *made* for me. Made with me in mind."

"Aw." Daniel thumbed his cheek. "How narcissistic."

Aaron laughed, all high in his head.

"I love you," Daniel said, his little half-smile adorable.

Aaron stiffened, his throat seizing shut.

Three simple words hung in the air like forbidden fruit, but he couldn't pluck them from their branch. Even though they were right there. Even though three plucks were all it would take—one *I*, one *L*, one *Y*—he couldn't do it. He *couldn't*.

"Hey," Daniel asked, his forehead rutted with concern. "You okay?"

Aaron cast his gaze downward and shook his head while he drew a circle, a little too roughly, in the palm of Daniel's hand.

If love was money, then he'd fix this. He'd make enough to keep people around and always keep them safe. He'd make enough to say, *Anything you want, it's yours*. He'd make so much that no one would leave, and Daniel couldn't leave, and *please don't leave*. Not yet.

Stay. Just a little while longer.

"Aaron," Daniel said. "What's wrong?"

"Listen, I'm nuts about you, but I can't say that. I don't know, I'm messed up or something, but um. Let me work on it. I'll work on it, I'll do that, and it'll come with time." He couldn't make his words sound promising. They sounded as shaky as his sigh. "Goddammit. Give me time, okay? Please? Just a little time. I'm so sorry—"

"Shh, of course." Daniel tenderly stroked his hair. "Of course, take your time. There's no rush. What was that…?" He snapped his fingers like he was trying to recall a word. "Oh! My mom said, 'People experience life in different strides.'"

He nodded, biting his lower lip hard enough to puncture it. "I like it when you say it. I like it a lot, but I want you to know that you don't have to."

"*I* don't have to say it?" Daniel tilted his head. He looked like he couldn't get more confused, which was fair. It was confusing. He smoothed a thumb over Aaron's lip until he stopped biting. "Well, I don't mind. What if I say it enough for both of us?"

"Really?"

"Oh, easy." Then Daniel said, "I love you."

Aaron drank in the sound of it. "Say it again."

"I love you."

"Again. With my name."

"I love you, Aaron Silva."

He pulled Daniel into him, buried his face in his curls, and breathed. "What a night. Let's go home."

"My place or yours?"

"Ours." It was a single word, but he meant it. He might not have been able to voice it, but he could show it. He could give him a home. He could help him secure the studio. He could provide for him a future.

"Ours." Daniel laid his head on his shoulder and hummed. "I like it. That sounds, I don't know. It sounds… real."

Chapter Eighteen

"GOOD MORNING, this message is for a Mr. Daniel Greene. Hi, my name is Bill Oren with Missouri Loan Express. I'm sorry to inform you we were unable to approve your small business loan application. Give me a call back with any questions."

Daniel quickly stuffed his phone into his pocket and plastered on a smile so Aaron wouldn't wonder why he was frowning and threaten to drown him in a pile of cash. Two weeks had passed since he'd moved into Aaron's apartment. Aside from all the constant questions about his loan situation and the refusal to accept any form of payment toward anything ever, living with him had been phenomenal.

Aaron pointed to an avocado. "That one."

Daniel plucked an avocado from the heap. Even a run-of-the-mill grocery store trip was oddly lovely, regardless of Aaron transforming into the produce military.

"No, not *that* one," Aaron said, then mumbled under his breath, "Obviously."

Daniel chose another.

"Well, not *that* one either—"

"Aaron." They'd been at this for five minutes. He might just squeeze one until it guacamole'd everywhere. "They all look the fucking same."

"Well, they're not the *faaacking same-uh*," Aaron mocked in a Southern California accent—which was a stretch; his vocal fry wasn't that extreme—and nudged him out of the way. "And you have to pick them right, by color and squish. You maybe want a 15 percent squishiness. See? Feel this. You feel the squishy? That's a good squishy."

He yanked Aaron into a hug, because what choice did he have? It wasn't like there was any explaining how nerdy that sounded.

Aaron glanced around, squeezed his ass, then whispered in his ear, "Do we need lube while we're here?"

"What? They sell that *here*?" Daniel gasped as he spun in a circle. "Where?"

"Over there next to the cucumbers."

Daniel's entire body lit up. "Shut all the way up! Really?"

"No."

They moseyed through the store, ate half a bag of chips, made out in the aisle that had the lube because lube was hot to think about, then gawked at the lobsters in a tank. Well, Daniel gawked. Aaron seemed unfazed that there were literal lobsters. In a tank.

"Hi, buddy," Daniel whispered, bending down to make eye contact with one of them. "Oh, I feel bad. He has no idea what's coming."

"Have you heard back from that last loan officer?" Aaron asked, handing him a bag of peeled shrimp.

"Aaron." He widened his eyes, whipping the shrimp behind his back. "In front of *him*? They're, like, cousins."

Aaron chuckled as he followed him down an aisle with sauces. "Have you heard back or no?"

Daniel glanced over his shoulder to make sure the lobster didn't see, then tossed the shrimp into the cart. "There are two I haven't heard from, but it doesn't mean—"

"Two?" Aaron blinked up from where he'd been reading a cocktail sauce label. "I thought there were three."

"There were three. Now there are two."

"Daniel," Aaron groaned.

"What? It doesn't mean I'm getting denied."

"Yes, it does. Look at me. *Look* at me." Aaron grabbed his hands and forced his eye contact. "This has gotten ridiculous. You need money. I have money. You're letting your pride get in the way of your dreams. There's no reason why you shouldn't already own that studio. Come on. Let me help you."

The temptation tugged at the seams of his resolve. But even if he was running out of time, hope, and options, he couldn't accept Aaron's money. He *couldn't*. "I'll figure it out."

"Madeline is leaving soon. Meaning she's going to have to take the original offer. You realize that, right? Have you thought about what happens if you don't get it by then?"

"Thank you for your concern—"

"Then you'll have missed out on this thing you've always wanted, and you might even be out of a job."

"So generous." He kissed the tip of Aaron's nose, ignoring the huffy eyebrow lift. "But I'll figure it out. Now, if you'll excuse me? I need to find out what a caper is once and for all."

"A caper is a—"

"I know you are *not* about to spoil the surprise."

"Fine. Meet me by the cheeses when you're done. Call me if you need me."

"Wait." Daniel spun around. "Did you just say to call you if I need you?"

Aaron cut his eyes to the side, which meant he probably hadn't even realized it. For being so young, he had a full-blown coddling mother hen of a personality. It was adorable, and Daniel couldn't help but make so much fun of him for it.

"Do tell, Aaron. What would warrant my *needing* you in a grocery store?"

Aaron scrunched his nose, his shoulders bunching. "I don't know. Never mind. Let's not make a whole thing about it."

"Aw. You afraid I'll get lost, mister? Kidnapped?" Daniel tried not to sound so curvy-blond-on-a-subway-grate, but he couldn't help himself. "I'll be super careful in the big bad grocery store. I'll be back before the streetlights come on." And extra breathy as he said, "Daddy."

Aaron's mouth twitched as he glanced around and whispered, "Stop it."

"Did you say the cheeses?" Daniel moaned through his teeth as he slid a finger down his neck. "That's so far. I'll miss you, Daddy."

Aaron spun the cart around. "Okay, I'm walking away."

"I'll miss you so hard." He blew a puffy-lipped kiss.

"Bye, Daniel."

"So, *so* hard."

Before Aaron turned the corner, he whispered back, "Save it for later."

Daniel couldn't find the capers, so they probably didn't exist, and it was a worldwide ruse to make him feel foolish. When he meandered to the cheeses, there stood Aaron being drooled over by a girl who twirled her ponytail around her fingers and giggled too loudly at whatever mediocre dairy joke he likely made (*Have you tried that one? It's really Gouda*). The unfortunate result when hot people made jokes? Hot people growing up thinking they're also funny.

When Aaron saw him, he cinched him by the waist and kissed his cheek.

"Oh." The girl's eyes darted between the two of them, her cheeks flushing the same rosy pink of her blouse. "Thank you for the advice. I'm going to go with the Drunken Goat."

"Good choice," Aaron said as she scurried away, shifting his attention to a wedge of cheese.

"She was cute." Daniel rested his chin on the back of Aaron's shoulder. "Have you ever been with a girl?"

"Yes."

He whipped Aaron around by his shoulders. "You have?"

"Well, yeah. Not a lot."

"What's not a lot? Like, one?"

"Probably more like four. Maybe five."

"Holy shit."

"Shh." Aaron glanced around the store. "I don't know. It was high school."

"You nailed five high school girls!"

"Daniel, shh!" Aaron waved at a glaring old woman.

"Well, how was it? What do you say to a girl in bed? 'Hey, cool boobs' or something?"

"I can't think of a worse thing to say to a girl in bed, and it was fine. Fun, I guess. They're just soft, is all." Aaron's eyes dripped the length of Daniel's body and settled on his lips. "I prefer *hard* if that makes sense."

"No, that makes no sense." He leaned over the cart and giggled like the Drunken Goat girl. "Please, mister, do break it down for me."

The mister, suddenly distracted by his phone, did not break it down for him but responded to a text instead.

Daniel flopped his body over the handle of the shopping cart and sighed with his total lung capacity. When Aaron didn't acknowledge him, he moaned. Then again. "I love having meaningful conversations with my boyfriend."

Aaron tapped away on his phone. "'Hey, cool boobs' is not a meaningful conversation."

"Okay, then what about this—how'd you get into escorting?"

Aaron's eyes zoomed up.

"When did you start doing it?"

"You want to talk about it?" Aaron asked, his attention hooked as he worked his phone into his pocket. "Here? In a grocery store."

Daniel bit the inside of his cheek and shrugged. He was maybe already regretting it, but he'd started something.

"What is happening? Is this a good sign?" Aaron's smile was cautious, but his tone had strayed halfway to excitement. "Are you maybe getting more approving of it?"

"You can settle all the way down, sir."

"Sorry." Aaron held up his palms, but the smile was growing. "I'm just proud of you. Can I not be a smidgen proud?"

Daniel sighed, tapping his foot as loud as he could.

"Okay, so how'd I get started? When I was nineteen, in college, I met this boy out one night."

"Name?"

"Chase Garland. A little older than me. Exciting, super charming, wild as *hell*. And he lived this lifestyle that no one could figure out how. Like, he'd buy everyone dinner, he spent really big, especially on shoes and suits. And every time I tried to ask what he did for a living, he'd say something like 'Nosey isn't cute on you,' then buy me a shot." Aaron bounced on his heels, lost in a reminiscent chuckle. "We hit it off. He liked me."

"Okay, so boy meets boy. What'd he look like?"

"What'd he look like? Sexy." Aaron gazed off into the distance at a colorful bell pepper display, which couldn't help but mimic a romantic sunset with the orange, yellow, and red. Not cool. "Way sexy. Hair color about like yours, eye color about the same too. About your height. Only he had some, you know, pigment to his skin. Not as ivory."

Oh, good for him! Daniel fought the urge to chuck a grape at Aaron's face. It wasn't that he was jealous of Tan Chase. He just wished he didn't exist at all. There was a difference. "So, you guys were a thing?"

"We weren't *not* a thing, I guess." Aaron waved the thought away. "But nothing serious. So, one day, we're hanging out, doing something stupid. Oh! We'd made a fort in his living room and were goofing off in it—think we were kinda stoned—when he gets a text. He looks over at me with a smile and says, 'Hey, Silva, wanna make a quick couple hundred bucks?'"

Daniel pictured Chase, the nonpasty version of himself, as twiddling his paper-thin mustache with lots of maniacal cackling as he asked that question.

"And all I had to do for a couple hundred dollars was—"

"Nope." Daniel spun on his heels and darted toward the exit. "If you need me, I'll be in the car." He balked, goose bumps covering his arms. "Don't say I didn't try."

LATER THAT evening, Aaron was mother-henning around as Daniel sat curled in an armchair, holding his hands over his eyes. "What are you doing back there?"

"Stop asking questions," Aaron called out from somewhere behind him, clanking around. "Meddlesome. Meddlesome is what you are."

Daniel huffed and kicked his legs over the arm of the chair, sinking farther.

"Okay, it's ready."

"It is?" he asked, twisting around to see. "Can I look—?" He grunted when Aaron scooped him out of the chair and tossed him over his shoulder. His arms dangled limply toward the floor as Aaron hauled him down the hallway. He sighed, "I don't know why you do this."

"This? Because I like how burly it makes me feel." Aaron smacked his ass and said with bravado as he thrust an arm toward the sky, "I am big strong man with tiny chosen mate."

He snorted. "But tiny chosen mate can walk."

"Shh, tiny mate. Look what I've done for you." Aaron pushed open the bathroom door and gently lowered him to his feet. "Big strong man has made you fire."

Daniel gasped, his hands snapping to cover his mouth. The bathroom had been transformed into an unbelievably spectacular venue for romance with a bathtub filled to the brim with iridescent bubbles, bath bombs that fizzed like geysers, and glittering candles balanced on about every flat surface.

"When did you?" He could hardly speak, lifting his arms so Aaron could tug his shirt overhead. "Why did you?"

"Because I wanted to." Aaron kissed his cheek. "Because I like to make you smile, tiny mate. Get in."

This man. He shook his head in disbelief as he stepped into the bubbles and settled in. This man was dreamy. So damn dreamy that he even knelt beside the tub and lathered a loofah in the most balanced air of humble and dignified to ever exist. He frothed Daniel's arms and back while they held each other's gaze. While the silence broadened. While Daniel searched his mind, struggling to identify ways in which he might ever compare to how dreamy this man was.

"What are you thinking?" Aaron asked after a moment, rinsing his back with scoopfuls of water. "You seem deep in thought."

Daniel fortified himself with a breath. "You should tell me the story from earlier."

Aaron's surprised gaze flashed to his. "From earlier at the grocery store?"

"Yes. Tell me."

"Why?"

"Because it's something I don't know yet." He folded his hands over the side of the tub and rested his cheek. "I want to know what makes you *you*. I want to know everything there is to know about you."

"Yeah?" Aaron grinned a little as he readjusted in his seat. "Okay, so I was in college."

"For what? For interior design?"

"Yeah." Aaron rubbed his eye. "And I met Chase."

It was quite the task, but Daniel kept his nose wrinkle shockingly brief. "Do we still talk to Wild Chase?"

"No. No, he moved, and we lost touch. Anyway, we're in the fort, and he asks if I want to make a quick couple of hundred bucks. I'm not sure what to think when he follows up with, 'I kid you not, Silva, all you have to do is let this guy kiss you.'"

Daniel squinted, pulling his knees to his chest. "Kiss you?"

"Uh-huh. Kiss me." Aaron smirked. "Kiss me while he did his *thing*."

"His thing?"

"His thing."

Daniel bit his lower lip. "People pay money for that?"

"You'd be shocked. So anyway, I said yes because that's a lot of money when you're nineteen, and kissing isn't that big of a deal, right?"

"Kissing is no deal at all. If it were, I'd be screwed."

"Right. So that experience, which was my first, was eye-opening. Because there I was in this nice hotel room with this nice guy who was trying to hand me money for having kissed me, and I can't take it. I can't take his money."

"Really? Why not?"

"I felt guilty. I felt crazy guilty for some reason. So we talked for a long time. He was a good guy. I'll never forget what he said. He shoved the cash plus a fifty-dollar tip in my pocket and said, 'I know you don't believe it, but trust me. You're worth it.'"

Hmph. Daniel grazed his fingertips down Aaron's arm. "Well of course you are. You didn't believe you were worth it?"

"See, that's the thing." Aaron's gaze wandered around the bathroom. "No. Er, well, not to start. It took me a long time to wrap my head around it. Firstly, to wrap my head around that kind of wealth. Money was always a fight in my house, and there was never enough. And secondly, to wrap my head around the fact that someone would give it to me so freely. For doing what? For showing up?"

"Do you not know what you look like, sweetie?"

"Well, so I learned pretty quickly that I had... we'll call it a talent for it. That guy referred me to another guy, who referred me to another guy, then another, and so on. I started getting popular. Really popular. Here I was, a nineteen-year-old kid who came from absolute squalor with suddenly so much cash I didn't even know what to do with it all. For the first time in my life, I felt powerful. I felt unstoppable."

"So what happened? You dropped out of school to pursue it?"

"Hell no. Don't get me wrong. It was a rush, but it wasn't like I ever saw myself doing it seriously. Certainly not for any real amount of time. I knew what I wanted to do. I had a plan." Aaron's long eyelashes flicked downward. "But then my mom got sick. She'd been in remission, and it came back with a vengeance."

Daniel interlaced their fingers, his heart squeezing at the shift in Aaron's tone.

"My dad had already split. She was barely making ends meet without him. She didn't have money for the medication or for one of those scarves for when she lost her hair. She didn't have money to support Andrew; he was still in high school at the time. She didn't have money for anything that would've just made her life that much more comfortable, and there I was." Aaron's voice had gotten shaky. "Fucking *drowning* in cash."

Daniel gripped his chest.

"Escorting was suddenly a no-brainer. If I dropped out of school, it meant I could take care of her during the day because I was working mostly nights. It meant I could take care of Andrew—drop him off at school, make sure he was fed—so she didn't have to worry about him either. I could make sure she wasn't alone, because above all, she didn't deserve to have to do it alone."

Daniel wiped at his tears.

"I got smarter too. Clever, more tactful. I told myself *the rate is the rate*. I told my clients *the rate is the rate*, then I charged what I fucking wanted to charge, and it wasn't a couple hundred dollars either. By the time she passed, we had the best care for her, everything she needed to make it as comfortable as possible. I just… I never really looked back after that."

"Oh my God. That's. That's so." Daniel sniffled and smeared his hands over his face. "I had no idea. That's *noble*. It's noble, Aaron."

"No-ble." Aaron seemed to dissect the word. He shook his head. "No, not really, but that's a nice thing to say—"

Daniel tugged Aaron into a hug, drenching his shirt in bathwater as Aaron whimpered from how firmly he gripped. "I'm so sorry I didn't ask sooner. I should've asked sooner."

"No." Aaron exhaled, his arms slowly wrapping around him. "No, you shouldn't have. S'okay."

"You're the salt of the earth, you know that?" He released him to run his hands through his hair over and over, kissing him sweetly. "You're everything to me."

It was all so clear. Crystal clear just how everything he was. The dreamiest, everything of a person. His big strong man. His mister. He deserved so much more than *Escorting was suddenly a no-brainer*. He deserved a reset button on his life and one that would erase his pain and reorient his future. He deserved to do something he loved.

If interior design was what he wanted, then interior design was what he would get.

"The salt of the earth," Daniel whispered. "I'm going to make sure you realize your worth."

Chapter Nineteen

LATER THAT week, Aaron knocked on the door of a cabin rental near the lake. It didn't have a sketchy overtone, but it was a tad secluded. At least the car he parked beside was exorbitant. Cars like that were a decent predictor. A person who cared that much about appearances was less likely to do something reckless.

"Hello," said the guy who answered the door. Not his client, judging by the tall, athletic frame. Judging by the face. Geez, the face. He had this deep cocoa skin, sky-high cheekbones, and brown eyes that sparkled when he smiled. "You must be Aaron."

Another escort perhaps? Which meant there was a wealthy hobgoblin inside, surrounding himself with paid company.

"I am, yes. Sorry." He shook his head clear. He'd been staring at the guy for a beat too long. "I'm looking for a Marco… Becker, maybe? I think that's his last name."

"Beckett." The guy extended his hand. "That's me."

Aaron blinked. No way. *This* was his client? He'd never had such a handsome client. Like, ever. Well, there had to have been something crucially wrong with him. He was an awful person. The Pontius Pilate of the Midwest.

"Won't you come in?" Marco's voice was silky and calm. Not like a typical nervy first-timer. "May I take your coat? Would you like something to drink? I have sparkling water or an interesting pinot if you'd prefer?"

Handsome and polite? He'd never had handsome *and* polite. "I'm fine, thanks." Aaron shed his coat while Marco complimented its "exquisiteness."

"You're just how I imagined by the way Terry described you. Albeit taller." He flashed a brilliant smile as he secured the coat on a hanger. "You're a showstopper."

Their mutual connection, Terry, a longtime client of Aaron's, worked with Marco, although he'd failed to describe Marco in any detail whatsoever. All he'd said was, "You'll like him. He's filthy rich."

"Please have a seat," Marco said, gesturing to the table. It had the undertone of an interview as they sat across from one another, Marco leading yet approachable with one ankle crossed over his knee. A bit casual. A bit business. "So, tell me a little about yourself, Aaron."

Then there was that interview-y question, but Aaron's standard speech didn't require brainpower or heart; he could recite it in his sleep. "I'm open-minded and laid-back, meaning you won't shock me with whatever you might ask. I can be dominant, subservient, or both, but above all, I want you to know you're safe with me. You've already been brave by inviting me here. Let's keep that momentum. I draw very few hard lines, so dig deep. Be bold. Tell me how I can best serve you, sir. It'd be my pleasure."

"Oh." Marco's brow wrinkled. "No, I was wondering more about your conversational skills. How are you with current events? Can you hold a conversation about wine? Sports? Etcetera."

"Wine?" That was a new one. "Yeah, I can talk wine. I know enough to hold my own. Sports, about the same. I probably need to brush up. You want to talk sports before we... proceed?"

"Well, not right now." Marco chewed his lower lip, squinting at the walls. "What about economics—no, that can get hairy. Too political. Speaking of politics, how are you at redirecting a conversation?"

"Pretty good. I'm sorry." Aaron cleared his throat, tapping a timeout-T with his hands. "I promise I'm normally more composed than this, but you're so far from my typical clientele. I hope I'm not shooting myself in the foot here, but what are you doing calling me?"

Marco blinked. "Come again?"

"You don't need to pay anyone. You could walk into any club or open any app and have your pick."

"Well, firstly, thank you." Marco snorted, and even that was somehow charming. "That's generous coming from a man who people spend money just to be around."

Aaron could feel his cheeks heating a bit, which was an odd sensation in front of a client.

"But I don't need you for intimacy. Well, I should clarify. I don't need you for sex. I'm hoping for at least some intimacy. Terry didn't tell you any of this?"

He shook his head. Apparently, Terry was a vault for information.

"I work a lot, and I travel for work. I don't have time to date—rather, I don't have time to prioritize another person...." He trailed off as he checked one of his two phones and tapped out what appeared to be an email. "I need a companion because I need to appear trustworthy and loyal during a deal I'll be working on the next few weeks. I'm not looking for sex. Sex is ever-present, and I have men for that...." He trailed off again as his eyes scanned the screen. His phone chimed as he sent it, and then the smile was back. "My apologies. Where was I? I need a business partner."

Aaron scanned his face. "What kind of a business partner?"

"A personal assistant, more or less. Someone who can wear many hats, stand in as my spouse for dinners and functions, then support me with administrative duties. Essentially, be available as I wish. This is what I'm willing to offer per week." From the end of the table, Marco plucked a check that'd been filled out with the name left blank. "But there will be options for more depending on my needs."

Aaron's hands were a touch unsteady as he reached for it. What was the old saying? Something about it being too good to be true. "What's the catch?"

"I'm not sure I understand the question."

"It seems"—Aaron gesticulated his hands around—"I don't know, almost too easy for me. For anyone."

"Well, it won't be *easy*. It could be some long hours." Marco crossed his arms and squinted. "Terry made it sound like you offer a range of services."

"Oh, I do." Aaron needed to snap out of his head and to the present moment where a handsome man was offering him money for doing nothing. For dinners and emails. "I'm absolutely interested. I take all payment up front."

"I'm willing to pay half up front and half at the end of each week."

Aaron's eyes widened as he gazed down at the check. "So this?"

"Is half."

"Tell me what you need from me, partner." Finally, his self-preservation was kicking into gear. "I promise I won't let you down."

Marco chuckled as he scrolled through one of the phones. "Well, let's get to know each other first. Make sure it'd be a good fit. Do you have a suit?"

"Of course."

"If we find we align after this meeting, I'll need you starting tomorrow. I've made reservations at this hotel, or the restaurant downstairs, rather. I can send you the details of how we met, what you do for work, and so forth."

Aaron peered down at Marco's phone at a map marked by a hotel. He knew it. It was beautiful, but a hike, which meant he'd get home exceedingly late. "What do I do for work?"

"You do some freelance copyediting, but mostly you stay at home and take care of the house. You're very good at gardening. You want us to get chickens, but the HOA is being a pain about it."

Aaron chuckled. Easy. So easy. "Which is unfair. We deserve chickens."

"If it works out, you'll need to bring an overnight bag." Marco's attention had been stolen by the other phone. "For appearances."

His smile wavered a touch. "Oh, I don't stay the night. That is a service I don't offer."

"Yes, you'll need to stay the night," Marco said in this definite, matter-of-fact tone as he responded to a notification. "I won't risk my colleagues seeing my partner leave at some odd hour. Trustworthy and loyal, remember? Not sketchy and sneaking off in the middle of the night."

Aaron hadn't spent the night with a client since he was very young. He had to draw the line somewhere, and staying the night, sleeping in the same bed only to wake up feeling like some contrived couple, it was a bit too intimate for his comfort level. Not to mention, how was he to explain that to his actual live-in boyfriend?

He tongued his cheek as he stared down at the check. If it was just a few nights, he could make an exception. Especially if there was no sex involved. No sex. Just money.

"No problem." He slapped on a smile. "Now, tell me how I can make sure we align."

IT WAS the next day, and Daniel sat on the couch perfecting a PowerPoint presentation about interior design, his legs draped over Aaron, who was barking at the television. Things like "Oh come on." And "Pass it. Pass it, man!"

Why? was the Universal question. *Why* were they watching basketball? They never watched basketball. "So why are we watching this again?"

"You don't have to watch it." Aaron scratched the back of his head. "I need to stay current."

"I think my issue," Daniel said, pointing a vague finger toward the screen, "is I don't understand why everyone's so upset."

Aaron massaged one of his legs. "What do you mean?"

"Everyone looks mad. Like that man, for example. That man is legitimately livid."

"That guy? Well, yeah, baby. That's the coach. He's livid because they're losing."

"Well, it's unfortunate not a single soul is smiling at them."

"At whom?"

"The sexy basketball players." Daniel shimmied his shoulders and flashed a grin at Aaron. "They're all ginormous and shiny. If I were there, I'd be smiling at them."

Aaron snorted. "Oh, would you now? What would you say to them as you *smiled*?"

"I'd say, 'I'm sorry everyone's mad at you, sexy ginormous basketball player. I'm sorry you missed the basket and your chance to load the bases or whatever. I'm also sorry—'"

"The what?" Aaron swiveled his head to him, his expression brightening in curiosity. "What'd you just say?"

Daniel cut his eyes to the side. Did he not have that right? It didn't sound right. Damn sports-balls. "Oh. Nothing."

A slow smile curled Aaron's lips. "Oh, you mean the *bases*, bases. Sorry, I thought you were talking about something else. Yeah, he missed his chance to load those. The basketball bases."

"Okay, whew." He chuckled as he swatted a hand. "The way you were looking at me, I thought I had that wrong."

"Precious. God, don't change. Never change."

"Hey," he yelled when Aaron yanked the laptop from beneath his typing fingertips. "Excuse me? I was working on something—"

"Come here." Aaron patted his lap, holding the laptop out of reach. "You can sit right here and work."

"No, I cannot sit on your lap and work. Give it."

"Nuh-uh." Aaron held it higher. "Finders keepers, Daniel."

"More like pilfering larceny, Aaron."

"Come take it from me." Aaron broke into a wide grin. "I dare you."

Daniel chuckle-growled, but just as he started to crawl toward him, Aaron's phone pinged from the coffee table with a text, and suddenly he was lunging forward to retrieve it so quickly that he practically threw the laptop at Daniel.

"Whoa." Daniel fumbled to grasp it. "Everything okay?"

Aaron's eyes scanned the screen for a long moment; then he blew out his breath like he'd been holding it for a while. "Okay, kid. I need you to hear me out on something."

Daniel curled his legs into himself and listened as Aaron began to explain an "opportunity" he'd been given. It was an "opportunity" that involved dinners, business meetings, and a man named Marco. It was an "opportunity" that he described in fantastically vague and nonthreatening language, using terms like "temporary scenario," "mostly platonic," and an "unfathomable amount of money for what it is."

Which was what again? What the hell was it? When Aaron was finished, he looked totally drained. Probably because he assumed Daniel was going to panic, but it wasn't panic muddling his brain so much as it was confusion.

"Do you have any questions?" Aaron asked. "Anything at all?"

Daniel licked his lips, zigzagging his gaze around the apartment. "I guess I don't understand why you're telling me this. It's not usually something we talk about. Are you afraid you'll start developing feelings for him?"

"What? No." Aaron gripped his hands. "I'm telling you this because I won't be home tonight. And there'll be a few more occasions where I won't be able to come home."

"Oh." Ahh, there was the panic, puckering behind his breath. "Oh, but I thought you said—"

"I know what I said, but this is different. I need you to trust me." Aaron squeezed his fingers. "You trust me, right? You trust I have our best interest in mind?"

He did trust him. He wholeheartedly trusted Aaron. But he'd established that boundary for a reason. Regardless of how good the intentions, one couldn't expect their heart to care. Sleeping with this Marco guy as in actually *sleeping* with him felt very heart-forward indeed. The heart carved its own path for better or worse.

"I promise, it's not going to be that bad, and apparently he's only in town for a few weeks. You won't even notice I'm gone."

That was the kind of thing people said when everyone around them would definitely notice they were gone. Specifically, when they lived together.

"I am going to make this up to you." Aaron cupped his face in his palms. "I'm going to make sure you feel supported and taken care of. I'm going to make sure you want for nothing."

"Why do you keep saying that? *Want for nothing.* What does that even mean? What do I want? I've never asked you for anything."

"You don't need to ask. That's the thing. I'll take care of you. I *desire* to take care of you. You know what else I desire?" Aaron cautiously kissed his hand, peering up through his lashes. "To take you out dancing this weekend."

Ooh, no he did not. Daniel shook his head and narrowed his eyes but had to pinch his lips together to keep from smiling. "That is low, sir. You think you can just take me out dancing whenever you need a solution?"

"What's so wrong with wanting to show you off, huh?" Aaron whispered, hesitantly leaning in to kiss his neck. Daniel smothered the urge to gush. "You're so precious. I want to show the world."

Well, dammit. He was only human, so he exposed his neck further as Aaron kissed his way to that one place near his collarbone that made his flesh pebble in goose bumps. Call him scheming, but now would be a good time to hoist the only leverage he had. "Fine. But it's dancing *and* the interior design conversation."

Aaron halted, pulling back to eye him.

"Remember that promise you made?"

Aaron groaned as he stretched his neck. "I'm not going to say it, because I don't think I have to."

"That there's nothing you can do to make what you make now?" His eyes rolled closed with his nod. "Trust me, it's been said."

"So long as you know."

"Oh, I know. And I disagree."

"Absolutely we can have that conversation, sweetheart." Aaron wrinkled his nose. Ever the good sport. "Can*not* wait."

As Daniel stared back at Aaron, his smirk eventually dissolved. He sucked in a breath and dropped his gaze to the sofa. "You remember what we agreed, right? If you start to develop feelings—"

"Not going to happen, kid."

"If you start to develop feelings for one of them, I'm the first person to know."

"I have feelings for you." Aaron lifted his chin. "You and only you. Say the thing."

"I love you."

"Say it again."

"I love you."

"Again. With my name."

"I love you, Aaron Silva."

Aaron huddled their foreheads together and grinned. "You won't even notice I'm gone."

Chapter Twenty

"HI. I'M trying to reach Mr. Daniel Greene. This is Will McCoy, your personal loan operator with Summit One Loans. I regret to inform you that we were unable to approve your application at this time. Again, Will McCoy. Reach out with any questions."

It was nine days later, and Daniel had noticed he was gone. It was in the coffee that wasn't brewed in the morning and the cold side of the bed at night. It was in the lack of sex, because when Aaron was home, he was too tired. No blue ice as the first thing he saw when he woke and last thing he pictured before he fell asleep. Well, that wasn't true. Aaron was still the last thing he pictured before he fell asleep, but it wasn't like he could even tell him that. He wasn't there.

But today, none of that mattered. None of that mattered, because he'd been really good so far about not having a meltdown—everything was fantastic!—not to mention, today they were having the interior design conversation.

Aaron had chosen a restaurant that was white-tableclothed, sterling-wared, and way too swanky for both of them to be sitting on one side of the table, hovering over Daniel's first-edition laptop. A coffee shop would've been better, but at least Aaron was his for the entire night.

If only he weren't so fucking droopy.

"Hey." He whacked Aaron in the arm when he yawned for the second time in two minutes. "Are you paying attention?"

"Yes." Aaron rubbed his eyes and blinked at Daniel's computer screen, where a breathtaking PowerPoint presentation had been executed. It'd taken him over three hours. He was going with *breathtaking* as the modifier. "What am I looking at?"

"These are all of the interior design programs in the city. Look." He pointed to the screen. "The community college even has one"—he jazz fingered for emphasis—"and hello affordability."

"Where is our waiter?" Aaron leaned back in his chair and scoped the restaurant. "I ordered champagne."

"What? When did you do that?"

"When you were off fixing your makeup."

"First of all, it's not makeup, it's under-eye highlighter."

"It looks sexy." Aaron pressed his face into Daniel's cheek and grinned. "You're dazzling."

"And second of all...." He nudged Aaron away, even though he couldn't help but smile at that silly *dazzling* business. "I'm only wearing it because we're going dancing later. We're still dancing after this, right?"

"I missed you while you were gone doing your under-eye makeup," Aaron whispered onto his neck, stretching his arm across Daniel's chair. "I always miss you—"

"Your champagne, sir," said a waiter, materializing with a bottle of something that looked French-made and uneconomical.

"Perfect." For doing what he did, Aaron was usually more reserved in public than this, but it was like his exhaustion had lowered his inhibitions. "We'll get some appetizers too. What do you want, kid? Oh, just send 'em all. We'll get every appetizer on the menu."

"What? No—!" He'd tried, but Aaron covered his mouth with his hand.

"He's fine." Aaron grinned at the waiter. "One of each. No big deal."

The waiter skidded off and Aaron finally uncovered his mouth. To Daniel's *look*, he yanked his chair in, scooting him closer. Up close, his eyes were a bit red-rimmed and glassy like he'd been awake forty-eight hours.

"Are you going to look at my presentation?" he asked, picking an eyelash off Aaron's cheek. "I made a whole damn presentation."

"Of course I'm going to look at it." Aaron handed him a glass of champagne and snagged the other, clinking them together. "But does it have to be this second? I just miss you, and I want to enjoy an evening out with my boyfriend where I don't have to worry about"—he tipped his head toward the computer—"this stuff. Is that too much to ask?"

Daniel pursed his lips. "This *stuff*?"

"I didn't mean it, ya know, dismissively, or whatever. My bad. I just want to enjoy a night with you where you're happy to be with me and not trying to change me."

"Trying to…." Daniel trailed off, his eyes rounding. He wasn't doing that, was he? He was trying to open Aaron's eyes about his options, his worth, but he wasn't trying to change *him*.

Unless trying to change what he did was trying to change *him*. That possibility stung a little. Like the way Robert Greene insisted Daniel need a different career. A better one. One that was respectable.

"I'm sorry," Aaron said, kneading the bridge of his nose. "I didn't mean that. I'm just tired, but you haven't done anything wrong. I promised I would look at it. Let's look at it."

"Why are you so tired?"

"Because I don't think Marco sleeps. He works so late and gets up so early. It's nonstop, and I work with him. I admire him. He's a freaking machine, but I just wasn't expecting—" Aaron suddenly startled at whatever Daniel's face was doing. "Shit. But let's not talk about him. I didn't mean to talk about him. Are you okay?"

That was a solid question. Was he okay? Insisting they didn't talk about it, squashing even his own thoughts before they formed, might have been a long-term plan with a few splinters in the foundation. Not that he would have a meltdown about it—everything was fantastic!—but learning that Aaron admired this person he'd been spending so much time with. Learning he was a *freaking machine* was an added layer he didn't quite know how to shed.

"Yes, I'm okay." He gulped, squashing the thoughts before they could form. "Everything's fantastic."

"I'm batting one thousand here, aren't I?" Aaron's smile was weak, and his long eyelashes looked like a jungle with all the rubbing he'd been doing. "Okay, we'll eat, we'll drink, you'll show me this presentation, then we'll go out dancing. Sound good?"

He let his gaze sweep Aaron's pretty face, smoothing a hand through his hair. Aaron nestled into his palm, his eyes softening shut. "We don't have to go dancing."

"Really?" Aaron perked up a bit. "We can go home and cuddle?"

Daniel uncorked his dramatic eyeroll, just to make it clear that no dancing and cuddling in lieu of other, way more fun bed-related activities wasn't his first choice. "Yes, we can go home and cuddle—"

"Aaron." A specimen of a man suddenly stood by their table, wearing a terrified expression.

The color emptied from Aaron's face. He stood in a big enough fluster to clink glasses, splashing champagne on the table.

Tall, lean, tailored and absolutely striking, the guy had this polished-beyond-fairness look. He said quietly through his teeth, "I need you to not be here right now. My colleague is in the restroom."

"Shitshitshit," Aaron said, grabbing their jackets. "Okay, kid. Come on. Wait, my check—"

"Go. I'll cover your check."

"What?" Daniel asked, as Aaron hauled him out of the chair by his arm. "Who are you?"

"My apologies to you both," the guy said to him, flashing him a rueful smile. Even amidst the chaos, something about him was so calm and commanding. "I'll make sure your time with him is covered as well."

"My boyfriend," Aaron coughed under his breath, shaking his head at the guy.

"Oh." The guy turned to Daniel once again, his eyebrows lifted, shock written all over his face. "Then I'm ultra sorry to ruin your evening. Thank you for your grace. I can only imagine the caliber of character you must possess."

What the hell? Who spoke like that? Daniel didn't have time to respond before Aaron was pushing him toward the exit, murmuring, "I'll explain later," over and over.

"Well, hold on—wait. My laptop."

"Dammit," Aaron hissed as they pushed through the doors. "Wait right here. Don't move."

The moment was too disorienting for questions, so Daniel followed his instructions, shuffling onto the street. For better or worse, he had clear view of the table where they'd just been evicted, where the stakes felt sky-high as Aaron jogged back to rescue the laptop.

He didn't make it.

A woman in a cream business suit on her way from the bathroom touched his arm. He spun around and smiled. He also smiled at the striking guy who stood from his table in the corner to join them.

Daniel could've kicked himself. *He* should've gone back to get the laptop. Not Aaron.

Aaron who was suddenly so casual-looking. Aaron who circled an arm around Striking Guy's waist and kissed his cheek. Striking Guy grinned sheepishly, dropping his head, shrugging while the woman in the cream suit seemed to fawn over them.

Who wouldn't fawn over them? They looked perfect together. *Perfect*. Both tall and elegant. Two put-together A-list actors in a movie where Daniel was an extra, standing on the cold sidewalk looking in. He could look but not touch.

Aaron waved the laptop in the air and tipped his head toward the door, like *Man, wish I could stay, but I have soooo much work to do.* He and Striking Guy exchanged wistful smiles as he left. *Wish I could stay. At least I'll get to see you later.*

Once outside, Aaron's smile vanished as he locked eyes with him, risking a quick glance at the window. "Walk," he whispered. "They can still see. Walk to the car ahead of me."

Daniel didn't budge, but he didn't know why. "Who's that guy?"

"That's Marco," Aaron whispered. "Walk, please."

"What?" Daniel's eyes widened as disbelief cluttered his intellect. "*That's* Marco? *That's* who you've been spending all of your time with? And staying the night with?"

Aaron's gaze sharpened a touch. He suddenly dashed past him until he reached the end of the window, shielded by brick. Then he gestured hurriedly for him to follow, but Daniel shook his head.

"Well, no wonder you don't want to come home." His breath was starting to swell, but was it anger? No. Desperation? "He's so charming. *The caliber of character you must possess.* So well-spoken. He's stunning, Aaron. You didn't mention he was stunning."

"Daniel," Aaron hissed. "I'm asking you to please walk. Get over here."

Daniel's gulp was about as dry as it could get as he gazed into the restaurant. If that was Marco, then *that* was everything he wasn't. In a few ill-starred seconds, he'd discovered his personal antithesis: prestigious, smart, composed, and elegant. But probably most importantly, rich. "What do you admire about him?"

"What?"

"That's what you said. That you admire him. What does that mean? What do you admire so much?"

"Fucking walk!"

Daniel stared helplessly at Aaron, his insecurities, the dreadful creatures they were, starting to scratch at him with their claws. "No."

"What?"

"Come get me."

Aaron looked like he didn't know what to do, his eyes huge and his mouth opening and closing the way it was.

Daniel swayed side to side, stealing glances at Marco. He and the woman in the cream suit had an unobstructed view of him if they wanted it. He hoisted his chin. "If you don't have feelings for him then it doesn't matter if you lose him as a client. So if you want me, come get me."

"I can't even believe—you are putting me in an impossible situation right now," Aaron whisper-shouted. "Get. The fuck. Over here."

Daniel was a little out of control of his body, his head shaking all on its own the way it was and his heartbeat rapid enough to throb the back of his throat. He'd never wanted distance from Aaron before. Distance meant he wasn't going anywhere with him. Certainly not home and certainly not to cuddle. Distance meant that maybe everything was not fantastic.

He bounced on his heels until he'd summoned the nerve to split in the opposite direction.

"Daniel!"

Distance meant he was going dancing.

THE MUSIC sucked. The air in the club sucked too. Like stale and dingy house vodka and cigarette smoke leftover from the 1990s. Daniel tried to dance. He tried to shut his eyes and let his body get lost in a parade of bass, but the guys. Ugh, the guys. Every few minutes, someone would fondle his stomach, face, or hips. One guy even tried to haul him into a "kiss." Which was more like a wet assault to his cheek. No one would bother him if Aaron were here. Probably because they'd be all over Aaron instead.

Whatever. He shoved his way toward the bar. He needed a drink.

Unfortunately, the bar, a stupid-busy horseshoe-shaped cluster, was the kind of place where he wasn't nearly tall enough to be noticed. If Aaron were here, they'd get a drink right away. If Aaron and Marco were here together, people would line up for the chance to buy them a cocktail, wait their turn for an autograph from the two A-listers. They'd kiss for the cameras, and Aaron would flip it: *We have to promote the movie, sweetheart. You know, the one where you're an extra?*

Daniel smeared his hands over his face hard enough for it to sting.

"Daniel Greene," someone said from beside him in a deep British accent.

Daniel snapped his arms by his sides and focused his vision. No, it wasn't just anyone with a British accent, polar-white smile, and fanned peacoat that he wore like a cape, and why would it be? So not only was he clashing with Aaron and involuntarily sober, but now he was standing next to Yellow Jacket. And involuntarily sober.

"Don't you look lovely," Corey said, making a show of examining Daniel's backside. "How's the studio purchase coming?"

"Fine," he lied, crossing his arms. It wasn't that he didn't trust him; he didn't have a reason to not trust him. It was that he really didn't fucking trust him.

"Where's your man? He here?" Corey gazed around the club. "Or did that bomb terribly after you found out he's a whore?"

"Hey." Daniel rounded his eyes and glared. "Don't call him that."

"Oh, is he not indeed a whore?" Corey tilted his head to the side. "Thought that was old news."

"Well, no." He scratched his head. "No. He's an escort—it's like, different—and he's not here."

"He's not?" Corey asked, head still tilted. "Well, then someone needs to buy you a drink, pretty boy. What would you like? Anything you wish."

Daniel didn't necessarily want a drink from *him*, but what was that thing about beggars and choosers? It might be his only chance. To his reluctant nod, Corey whistled over his head at someone.

A waiter bounced up in a miniature leather outfit that hugged his bones. "Hi, Mr. Hutton." His voice was light and breathy as he thrust his chest forward and exposed his neck, ignoring Daniel's existence altogether. "Did you need something?"

"Hi, kitten." Corey's gaze skated down the guy's outfit. "You get cuter every time I see you. Show me. Do a little spin."

The waiter twirled around a few times—terrible form—as Corey rummaged through his wallet. He plucked a few bills and handed them over. "Get young Daniel Greene here whatever he'd like, and you keep the change."

The guy bit his lip and smiled uncontrollably at Corey. Then it was almost comical how swiftly the smile died when he turned to Daniel. With less breathiness and more stank-eye, he rolled his palm and said, "What do you want?"

"Oh, uh. Vodka soda?"

"Shocking," the guy mumbled, then grinned over his shoulder at Corey. "I'll be right back, Mr. Hutton. Don't go anywhere."

"Do not get me wrong," Corey said in a low voice as he leaned over a high-top table and winked at the waiter slinking away. "I'll absolutely be rearranging his insides later, but between you and me, I prefer a bit more of a challenge than that."

Daniel flicked his gaze upward. "It's because you have money."

Corey drew back to peer at him. "Pardon?"

"The only reason he's all over you is because you look like you have money." He couldn't help it. Something about Yellow Jacket wanted to unearth the spice in him. "You should take what you can get."

Corey smiled, his chin resting in his palm. "Well, thank God men like him exist. Men like Aaron."

Daniel blinked down at the floor. What was he doing? He shouldn't be here having a sass-off with a near stranger. He should be at home sorting out whatever he was feeling with Aaron.

"Does talking about him make you uncomfortable?" Corey asked.

"Of course not."

"Then what is it, love? What's wrong? Don't tell me there's trouble in paradise."

Daniel tugged on his earlobe.

"You two young lovers in a quarrel? Can't imagine what it's possibly about."

"No." Was it a lie? Or were two sides of the coin somehow both true: He'd backed Aaron into a corner by asking him to *come get him.* At the same time, Aaron hadn't come to get him.

"It wasn't a quarrel," he said. "I needed a minute of space is all."

The waiter returned with their drinks. It was impressive how he side-eyed Daniel at the same time he giggled for Corey.

"Cheers, darling." Corey clinked their glasses together. "May you find some fellow out there in the crowd and let some steam off down his throat."

Wow. Daniel had to blink hard. And he thought *he* was crude. "I thought we just established I'm in a relationship."

Corey shot him a bizarre look. "Well, yeah, but a relationship where you get to be with other men, I would assume."

Daniel swigged half his drink.

"You do get to be with other men, correct?" Corey asked, raising one eyebrow.

"I don't want to be with anyone else." It was nothing to be embarrassed by, but his shoulders were trying to round protectively. He cleared his throat and squared them. "I only want to be with him."

"You only want to be with…." Corey trailed off, staring for a long beat. "Wow, this man has figured it out, hasn't he? He's a whole lot sharper than I gave him credit for."

Daniel finished his drink and winced, wiping his mouth on the back of his hand. "What's that supposed to mean?"

"So, let me ask you a question." Corey leaned over the table and furrowed his brow like he'd never had a more fascinating discussion. "What do you do?"

"What do I *do*? Like, for work? I dance—"

"No, not for work. While he's out enjoying life. Fancy dinners, expensive hotels, parties, and shopping sprees. The list goes on." Corey tapped a finger on the table in front of him. "What do you do?"

"Well." Daniel swallowed. His words were suddenly oddly jumbled. "I don't know. I guess I wait for him to come home, and then—"

"I'm sorry?" Corey asked with squinted eyes and an ear tilted toward him as if to be sure he heard him correctly. "I'm sorry, but you 'wait for him'? Is that what you said?"

Daniel blinked. He'd also frozen in place. That was what he'd said, but when he replayed it, it sounded… sad.

"Oh, darling." Corey rumbled in chuckles. "So while he's out doing as he wishes, hopscotching the city. While he's out fucking anyone he wants?" He paused for effect. "You wait."

Daniel stammered around an argument, but it was like he was a different extra on a different set that'd been directed to please remain still. No talking. "H-he's not. It's not like that—"

"Countless men, every single week, yours truly included." Corey pointed a finger toward his chest. "And you, Daniel Greene, *wait* for him."

His inner voice was screaming, but he couldn't make it make sense, and his tongue had been shocked still. *No talking.*

"What does he do when he finally gets home?" Corey cocked his head, his lips twisting into a crooked smirk. "Does he get to fuck you next?"

Daniel was suddenly drowning in the music. In the bass and the garbled screams from inside his head. *No talking. You're just an extra.*

"And to be so pretty." Corey grazed his fingers down Daniel's cheek. "That's the part that hurts me. You're too pretty to be so loyal to someone who isn't loyal back. Who can't be."

Daniel clenched his teeth tight to keep them from chattering.

"If you want my opinion?" Corey gently rubbed his arm and lowered his voice. "Whatever hope you're holding on to, let it go. He won't ever be loyal to you, love."

It was happening. *Three. Two. One.* He hated it. Who he was. Too much. He was too much. *Three. Two. One.* Why couldn't he have thicker skin? If he was going to panic, he needed to find a way to be alone. *Three. Two. One.* His heart was lumbering too loud to think, and his legs were cemented in place. He nearly tipped the stool over, but he did it. He stood.

"Taking off so soon?" Corey was grinning, polar white and uncomfortable. "Well, please give Aaron my love, won't you? Tell him I can't wait to see him next week."

HE HAS figured it out, hasn't he? Daniel's body was flooded with a slow-burning rage that seared a little hotter the longer he stood at his front door. He couldn't tell who he was angry toward. Corey for being right. Aaron for having *figured it out*. Or himself. Because what a fucking fool.

While he's out enjoying life. You, Daniel Greene, wait for him.

Of course he'd been holding on to hope. Of course everything wasn't fantastic. The question that rankled as much as it daunted: Was it time to let go?

He pushed open the door of their apartment, and Aaron shot up from where he'd been hunched over the kitchen island. If he looked tired before, he was absolutely fried now.

They both stared the other down in a clenched standstill, until Aaron finally broke the silence, his voice thick and stressed. "I've been calling you nonstop. Where have you been?"

He won't ever be loyal to you, love. Daniel started toward the bedroom. "I don't want to talk right now—"

"No." Aaron blocked his path. "It doesn't work like that. I've been sitting here worried half to death because you storm off, then refuse to answer your phone. Where the hell have you been?"

Daniel raked a hand through his hair and stepped around him. "Out."

"Out?" Aaron paced in front of him again. "That's not an answer."

He hoisted his chin and sharpened his gaze, laser focusing on blue ice. *You, Daniel Greene, wait for him.* "So let me get this straight. You get to go do whatever you want, and I'm just supposed to do what? Sit here waiting for you all night?"

Aaron narrowed his eyes. "You're *supposed* to answer your phone when I call over and over. You're my boyfriend. Since when do we treat each other that way?"

Daniel twitched. He needed to be alone. Space. He needed space. "I'm telling you, I don't think we should talk right now. I don't trust myself not to say something—"

"Well, I do think we should talk." Aaron stepped in front of his path again. "First you pull that shit at the restaurant, and then you go *out*? What's gotten into you?"

The words were already there, burning his throat. If he didn't get alone and find some way to decompress, he was going to vomit them out everywhere.

"Say something," Aaron said.

"Quit."

Aaron studied his face for a long several seconds.

"I want you to quit escorting for me. Tonight. Right now."

"What?" Aaron's shocked voice was barely there. "Daniel. How's that's a fair request?"

"Excuse me, fair?" His blood was starting to swelter. "It's not *fair*? I think what's not fair is continuing to screw other men when it's clearly killing me."

"Oh, it's *killing* you? Really?"

"Yes."

"Are you sure that's not just you being wildly overdramatic as usual? You don't even see it, Daniel. I go out of my way to shield you from it. To make sure you're okay."

"Well, I'm not okay! And you won't even consider doing anything else because you're so obsessed with money. You're *obsessed*."

"Okay, yeah, kid. You caught me." Aaron flopped his arms by his sides. "I care about money. But someone has to. Who do you think pays the bills around here?"

"Hey." He jammed a finger toward Aaron's chest. "I was paying my bills just fine before you."

"No, sweetheart. You were not even eating before me. Take a look around." Aaron spread his arms and spun in a half circle. "Are *you* going to pay for it? With what? With all your dance studio money? Oh, wait."

"Ugh!" Daniel screeched through his teeth as white-hot rage pulsed through his veins. If Aaron wasn't going to let him be alone, then Aaron was going to have to deal with the extinction of his logical mind. "You know, you're right. I should really make more money. I know, what if *I* get paid to bang dudes?"

Aaron expression transformed into a hollow glare.

"Oh, you wouldn't like that? Why not? It's good enough for you. It's the *only* thing you're capable of doing, right?" Daniel shrugged. "Yeah, I think I'll give it a shot."

A muscle in Aaron's jaw danced.

"In fact, I bet I have guys in my phone who would pay for it right now. Should we find out?" Of course, he sounded deranged, but he was too far gone down a spiraling black hole not to dig his phone from his pocket and start scrolling through contacts. He twisted the screen toward Aaron and pointed to a name. "I went on one date with this guy. One date and he sent me text after text for three whole months that I never responded to. I bet he'd pay."

Aaron shook his head. "Not cute."

Daniel scrolled farther. "Oh, this guy *definitely* would. God, this guy would murder his own twin brother to get with me."

"That's enough."

"And what's funny—" Daniel laughed. "—the twin would do the same. Can you imagine? Holy déjà vu."

"I said. Enough."

"Ooh, but see this one." He growled. "This one right here has a painfully sexy Italian accent—"

"Stop."

"Stop here? Okay." Daniel winked and pressed Call, switching to speakerphone. "The Italian it is."

"My, my, my," a man answered after a few rings, his words heavily accented. "Well, isn't this a pleasant surprise."

"Aww," Daniel said with a smile at Aaron. "Miss me?"

The guy's deep laughter cut through the kitchen. "Every damn day. To what do I owe the pleasure?"

"I'm glad you asked," he said, holding Aaron's gaze. "I'm thinking of starting a little side hustle. Curious if you'd be interested."

"What kind of a side hustle?"

"Hmm. Let's put it this way. It involves you and that beautiful uncut cock—"

Aaron snatched the phone, ended the call, and stuffed it into his back pocket.

"What's wrong, Aaron? Does that not feel so good?"

Aaron stared at him, wide-eyed. "No, it didn't *feel good*. In fact, it felt manipulative, intentional, and cruel!"

"Give me my phone."

"The difference between you and me is I don't *try* to hurt you."

"Yet you still do. Every single day. And you can't even tell me you love me?" Tears tried to sting his eyes, but for once he had more anger than sorrow coursing through his body, and it wasn't about to let them fall. "You can't say that to me? Just once?"

Aaron's lips parted as his face crumbled in pain.

"Say it to me."

"I—" Aaron's eyes darted around the room in panic as if the words he needed were written on the walls. He hunched his shoulders and rounded his spine, like he could suddenly throw up. "I-I-I can't. I need more time."

"Time's up." He charged Aaron's pocket. "Give me my phone."

"All I do for you. Every day. I'm so fucking good to you." Aaron dodged his grasps, fighting him off. "I take care of you."

"Keep it." Daniel stormed off toward the bedroom, calling back over his shoulder, "And you take better care of your clients than me."

Aaron trailed closely behind. "What is that supposed to mean?"

"It means—" Daniel whipped around, and Aaron nearly ran into his chest. They hadn't been this close since he got home, and he could almost feel the heat on Aaron's skin as they both labored for breath, standing way too near and way too still not to feel *it*.

It—whatever *it* was—ignited between them almost dangerously. Like a calm pool of gasoline inching toward a molten inferno.

"What?" Aaron hissed, bending his head to grip his gaze. "It means what? That whatever I do to help you goes unappreciated? Because you're an ungrateful fucking brat?"

Daniel heard his own teeth scrape together. "Just like whatever I do to help you also goes unappreciated. Because you're a materialistic cash king."

"I'm sorry you're a starving artist, sweetheart, and wealth makes you uncomfortable."

"I'm sorry you have to make your living by the grace of more successful men. That must be a hard pill to *swallow*."

Aaron's placid expression contrasted against his wild eyes in a way that made him look unrecognizable. "It's not. By comparison, you make me feel pretty good about my living."

"Oh? Because of how 'starving artist' mine is?"

"Because I could buy that studio out from under you. Tomorrow if I wanted."

Fresh fury washed over Daniel.

"I should buy it. Then you could just work for me." Aaron crowded into him farther. "Would *that* be a hard pill to swallow?"

He shook his head while they pierced one another with their gazes. This man. How dare this man stand here breathing Daniel's air. How could he say that? *How*? Surely he didn't fucking mean it, because it'd be absurd, not to mention unforgivable, but then this entire night had been absurd. Not to mention unforgivable.

He moistened his lips and Aaron's gaze plunged to his mouth. Even with his features seared to memory, he'd never seen Aaron look quite like this—compulsive, unbalanced, electrically charged. Angry? That was it. He'd never seen him angry.

"Come closer," Daniel said. There had to have been something broken inside of him to ask that. To *want* it.

Aaron hesitated, but then he did it. He leaned in closer. There had to have been something broken inside of him to oblige.

"Closer."

Aaron shifted his weight. He bowed his head deep enough that the heat from his breath misted Daniel's face and Daniel could reach him with his tongue if he wanted to.

At least the two broken pieces fit together. They each whimpered when Daniel brushed Aaron's lips with his, the gasoline a crawl away from the inferno.

Daniel peered up through his lashes and whispered into Aaron's mouth, "Fuck you. Kiss me."

Chapter Twenty-One

WAS IT pain or was it pleasure? It was funny how the two commingled. Like no matter how diligently everyone tried to keep them separated, they always ended up conspiring together. Or maybe the distinction was perception.

Pain needed a host who cared. Pleasure just needed a host.

Daniel's lips hurt where Aaron was overpowering them, the same as his skin where Aaron clawed at it, but he was also so hard he couldn't stand it. He was a host who didn't care.

The kiss was enough to get him drunk. Which was maybe why he kept stumbling. Or perhaps that was because Aaron was leading him backward toward the bedroom in the world's most volatile tango, ramming them against an armchair, then a dining room table, painting the walls with their sweat and fingertips. Neither one of them knew this dance.

"I can't believe you called some guy in front of me." Aaron's hands were in Daniel's hair, and his voice was a smoky growl. "How could you do that? You don't do that!"

"How could you not come get me?" Daniel sank his teeth into perfect honeyed skin, denting it in little half-moons as he tore Aaron's shirt down his arms. "You chose him over me. You chose Marco over me."

"I didn't choose Marco." Aaron yanked so firmly on the buttons of Daniel's pants that he nearly crashed to his knees. Then he willingly crashed to his knees because, well, he wanted to! "And I would never use another guy to hurt you."

Daniel unstrapped Aaron's belt in a maniacal whirlwind of tugs. "Well, if that ain't the teapot callin' the kettle whore-ish."

"Shut up, Daniel." Aaron's eyes were wide, and he looked like he didn't know what to do with his hands. "God, shut your mouth. *Please.*"

"Shut me up, Aaron." He yanked Aaron's pants down. "I'm so over talking to you that I'm considering selective mutism—"

Aaron jerked Daniel's head back by his hair and shoved the length of himself inside Daniel's mouth. The muscles of his stomach glistened like cuts of wet lattice in the city light spilling through the windows.

"Deeper than that," Aaron said after a moment, which was going to be a challenge, but Daniel was prepared to literally die than admit that, so he made it happen.

"I didn't realize this was amateur hour." Aaron was smiling now, which was both stunning and infuriating. "Make the noises I like. And eyes up here, sweetheart."

He met Aaron's eyes, he made the noises he liked, and he resisted the enormous temptation to bite down, but it paid off. Three minutes later, Aaron was struggling to keep his knees from buckling.

"Okay," Aaron muttered. "Shit. Okay, hold on—"

"And that's my cue," Daniel said, having freed Aaron to swipe his hands together and smack his lips. "I was hoping you might last long enough to have any kind of fun whatsoever, but you're right. This is amateur hour."

Aaron muttered curse words under his breath as he yanked Daniel up to a stand and tossed him onto the bed like he was one of those photorealistic sex dolls. He wished he was a sex doll as he propped himself on his elbows, gnawed a thumbnail, and twitched with his whole body. It would make this far less confusing.

Was this hate sex? He didn't hate Aaron, even though he sort of wanted to fight him. Or did he want to bang him? Did he want to fight-bang him? Whatever he wanted to do, Aaron needed to hurry up instead of taking one million years to weed through his drawer for a condom, then another two million to get it torn open. Then he did finally tear it open only to fucking drop it.

"Is this your first time putting on a condom?" Daniel yelled, wide-eyed, making Aaron jump. "Get on top of me. Like, yesterday."

Aaron blinked. After a few moments, his brows knitted together as his face morphed into a cocky smile. "Wow. Look at how badly you want me. Why do you think that is?"

Daniel rolled his eyes so hard he could swear he accessed another dimension. "I don't know, Aaron. Because I have unaddressed mental health issues?"

"You wanna know what I think?"

"No."

"I think—"

"Cool. So you'll be telling me anyway."

"I think I turn you on in a way no one else can even touch." Aaron crawled on top of him, and Daniel instinctively spread his legs because they just fit so perfectly that way. "I think it's everything. The way I look. The way I fuck—"

"The way you annoy me?"

"The way I own you, Daniel Greene."

Pain lashed through Daniel's limbs and his eyes shot open when Aaron pushed a finger inside him. He tried to breathe, but he should've known he'd be far too tense.

"Oh, sweetheart." Aaron's forehead creased, but a smirk tilted his lips. "I thought you could handle at least that much. Can you not?"

Daniel glared. "I can handle anything," he said through gritted teeth, because he must really have mental health issues. "Anything."

"Are you sure?" Aaron asked in that deliberately silky version of his voice as he nuzzled Daniel's neck and pressed another ginormous finger inside him. "There's no shame in taking a minute. You need a minute?"

Daniel's voice fractured into some high-pitched version of itself.

"We can take our time," Aaron whispered, his breath rhythmic in Daniel's ear as his body started to roll on top of him. "Let's take our time."

"I don't need time. I need you to get on with it."

"Just like I don't *need* to fucking break you," Aaron said through a clenched smile. "I just kind of want to."

He growled. Partially because Aaron stretched his fingers inside him and partially because that was the kind of thing that warranted a growl. "You won't. You can't."

"Are we certain about that?"

"Yes."

"Okay." Aaron's expression was amused as he gently kissed his lips. "You be sure to remember that, sweetheart."

Daniel's self-assured smirk dwindled a touch. "I'm sorry?"

"Remember how you said that." Aaron smiled, his voice pure, graveled sin. "When you can't fucking walk tomorrow."

Daniel's eyes leaped open. He gasped, suddenly flipped to all fours, suddenly fisting the sheets like they might help ground him in a moment that had lost its place in reality. Was this his hate-sex? It didn't necessarily feel like hate as Aaron pushed inside him, somehow unhurried, yet deep as could be and absolutely consuming.

"Such a fucking brat," Aaron said, holding his hips as Daniel stretched his body long to take it. He was going to take it. He was going to go down in history for taking it. "A perfect, precious brat."

Daniel collapsed his face onto the mattress when Aaron clenched his waist tighter, bucking into him a little more intensely.

"You want to call other guys in front of me?" Aaron lowered his mouth to Daniel's ear. "So I can hear them drool over you?"

"It worked, didn't it—?"

Aaron's fingers—one, two, three—filled Daniel's mouth as Aaron slammed into him hard enough for the bed to thud against the wall. He hadn't tasted that sting of salt since their first night together, but now that he was here swallowing it, he could feel himself starting to leak all over the sheets. He moaned as he took him, as Aaron filled him to capacity. The holes of his body. Over and over. On repeat.

"Is that all you got?" he managed to grumble between Aaron's fingers. Should he get those mental health issues addressed?

Aaron hooked an arm around his chest and lifted him to kneel on the bed. His voice was a deep hook as he said, "What did you say to me?"

"You fucking heard me." It didn't matter. The evening was a mess. Their relationship might have been a mess too, and if they were both going to burn hot in a husk of fury, they might as well go ham. Not to mention, Aaron already thought he was a brat. Why not act like one? He reached back and patted Aaron's cheek. "Back to work, sunshine. I'll stop by the ATM later."

He grunted when Aaron twisted his cheekbone into his lips and purred against his cheek, "Yeah? You need it harder?"

"Well, unless you're tired already, sweetie?"

Aaron chuckled and licked his hand, starting to stroke him. "You might be insane. Tell me not to stop."

He leaned back against Aaron's body while their chests rose and fell in matching cadence. As much as he couldn't believe it, he could absolutely believe it, because he heard himself say it. "Don't stop."

Aaron grinned against his ear. "Say my name."

"Aaron."

"Again." Aaron kissed his neck, stroking him harder. "Like it's the only name that matters."

"Don't stop, *Aaron*," he said in some throaty version of his voice.

"You perfect precious brat." Aaron thrashed him back over the bed. "Now loud enough that the neighbors call the cops."

That was easy, because Aaron bottomed out inside his body. He was so good at what he did. He was good with the way he pinned Daniel's wrists behind his back and the way he read his body. He was good with the words he spoke and his hungry, unhinged grasp on dominance like some kind of a mob boss in a movie.

Daniel bowed his chest to the mattress and surrendered again and again. Over and over. He'd turned into a whimpering mess, drooling, clutching the sheets hard enough to sprain a finger, screaming Aaron's name into tangled bedding like it was the only name that mattered. He probably did it loud enough for the neighbors to call the cops.

Then the urgency, the temper, the sweet hate-not-hate peaked, and Daniel found himself skirting an edge without warning. He clawed at Aaron's hand, his voice trembling. "I'm about to—"

"I know," Aaron said, like the confident professional he was. He flipped Daniel onto his back, tugged his legs off the bedside, and fell to his knees before him.

Daniel propped himself up on his elbows, his eyes rolling closed and his head falling back. He couldn't even moan as Aaron took him into his mouth. Not really. It was more of a gasp mixed with a prayer, and it caught somewhere in between his throat and the word "You."

He gripped Aaron's hair to ground himself in a moment that was far too intense, and so good he might die, and so saturated with the weight of the whole night that his IQ dropped to his shoe size. He fell over that cliff with all the cells in his body stiffened as violent quakes of pleasure ripped through him, one right after the other.

You. I hate you.

The room twirled around itself in a dizzying dance of angles and corners as he collapsed back onto the bed. Everything hurt. And stung. And throbbed with the kind of pleasure that'd be visceral enough to make him laugh, if only he could move.

You. I love you.

His eyelashes were a sweaty jungle as he fixed his gaze on Aaron. Aaron, who hadn't met him on this side of the husk of fury yet. Things were so calm over here. On this side, he wasn't combative or angry. He was limp and boneless. Over here, he was himself again.

But Aaron would be meeting him soon because of how wildly he stroked himself, wincing through his teeth, staggering to keep himself lifted.

"Right here," Daniel whispered, softly arching his spine, merging into a canvas with the sheets so that Aaron could paint them both in ribbons of white. "My face. My body. Wherever you want."

He stayed motionless and let Aaron choose. It splattered his belly, chest, and neck as Aaron emptied himself in this stunning display of veins, muscles, and wild blue ice.

Then he was different too. They were both different, reuniting on the other side of the hate.

Aaron's touch was so strange after the past hour, so delicate as he cleaned Daniel with a soft towel and sprawled long in the bed beside him to thumb his cheekbone and silently hold his gaze. He wasn't shaking nearly as much as Daniel, whose fingertips quivered as he tried to smooth the crease in Aaron's brow.

They blinked at each other through a mist of uncertainty. A mist of new meaning. Things might have been calm on this side of hate, but they were also less defined.

"Aaron," he whispered, his voice barely there. "I'm so sorry for what I said to you—"

"No, I am." Aaron licked his lips. "I'm the one who should be sorry. Will you, um. Will you say—?"

"I love you."

Aaron swallowed, barely nodding. In the dim room, scarcely lit from the city, it almost looked like his eyes were beginning to glisten. Which was impossible. Daniel had never seen Aaron cry. Not even close.

"You deserve to hear it," Aaron whispered, his voice wobbly. "You deserve so much more—"

"No, no, no, no, it's okay. Shh, it's okay." He tugged Aaron into him, where he cradled him against his chest, rocking them gently back and forth. "You're fine. Everything's fine."

From the beginning, he'd leaned into Aaron's guidance. What they would do. How they'd amend whatever was wrong. But for once, Aaron seemed as lost as him, so he continued to hold him. Like Aaron had held him dozens of times.

"Let's get some sleep, okay?" he said, brushing his fingers through chocolate brown hair. "We'll deal with tonight some other day."

Aaron nodded against his chest.

"It's okay, I can fix it." He kissed Aaron's forehead. "I'll fix it. I'll be better. I can be better."

He didn't know how. He didn't know how he was going to fix it or how he was going to alter his entire nervous system so that he might suddenly become someone who was unaffected and nonburdensome. But he also couldn't handle losing Aaron. That'd be like losing a piece of his soul. Losing his mister. His tomorrow, and the next day, and the next. That'd be like losing his everything.

"I'll learn how to deal with it. I promise. You get some sleep."

Chapter Twenty-Two

IT WAS four days later, and Aaron was so nervous that it felt like he'd swallowed a colony of bees as he sat across the table from Daniel in the best restaurant he could book on somewhat short notice.

They hadn't spoken much about *the night*. The one where they almost annihilated their relationship and then their bodies with ruthless words and some of the best sex of his life, which had been... confusing. It wasn't even that his sweet, nervy boyfriend had transformed into a hissing baby badger, but it was like that night had unearthed a pivotal truth he'd somehow managed to deny.

Daniel wasn't happy. Daniel needed more.

"Aaron." Daniel snapped his fingers, then twirled a palm around. "What is going on with you? Why are you being so weird?"

That was an excellent question. It'd been business as usual after *the night*, barring the eggshells Daniel seemed to be walking on around him. He'd been extra affectionate and smiley and hadn't even given him the side-eye when he had to stay one of those nights with Marco.

"Weird?" he asked, wiping his palms on his pants. "How am I weird?"

"Well, for one, it's 5:22 and we're at dinner." Daniel shrugged a delicate shoulder, spreading his palms around the restaurant. "What in the geriatric buffet are we doing here so early?"

Making them come to the restaurant so early might have been a detail he'd overlooked, but in his defense, Daniel wasn't happy. Daniel needed more. The sooner he could give him *more*, the sooner he'd be happy. Aaron had come so close to losing him. He needed to cement their relationship with a promise.

"Is it because of what I said last night?" Daniel asked.

"What'd you say last night?" He took a sip of his champagne, scanning the restaurant for the waiter, who should've been here by now.

"When I told you to come inside of me deep enough to get me pregnant."

Aaron spat his champagne back into his glass. Goddammit. He hunched over the table, champagne dribbling down his chin. "The stuff that comes out of your mouth sometimes? You need a muzzle."

"And you need to put a baby inside me." Daniel was grinning too ridiculously for it to not be contagious as a waiter approached the table.

No. Not just any waiter. *The* waiter.

"It's one little baby, Aaron," Daniel said, his voice sexy. "Don't be so selfish—"

He kicked Daniel's shin under the table.

"You ordered dessert, sir?" the waiter asked Daniel, standing over him with one hand positioned behind his back and a white cloth napkin draped over one arm.

"No, I did not," Daniel said, his smile scrunching his nose as he peered up at the guy. "But I should. Looks yummy."

"I think you did order that dessert," Aaron said, the colony of bees at full buzz as the waiter placed the plate in front of them.

"No, I really didn't." Daniel twisted around to flag the guy, but he'd vanished. As planned. "Where'd he go? And when would I have ordered dessert? I swear, this isn't mine."

"Kid, look at it." Aaron swallowed, bouncing in his seat. "It is yours."

Daniel finally looked at the dessert. He stared, rather, unmoving. It'd worked out better than expected. It'd worked out beautifully. A thick chocolate mousse dusted with cocoa powder atop a cookie crust sat in the middle of a white dish. From the center of the mousse, a sugar-encrusted sprig of rosemary jutted out like a tiny tree branch. Hanging from the branch?

A ring.

Daniel blinked. Eyes rounded and mouth wide open, he blinked. Of course he was shocked. They'd never spoken about marriage. But they'd never come so close to breaking up either. Something wasn't working— Daniel wasn't happy. Daniel needed more. Aaron had to give him more. He had to give him a promise.

His insides wound around themselves tightly enough to make his limbs tremble as he stood from the table and fell to one knee in front of him. He whispered, "Kid. Look at me. I have something important I need to ask."

Daniel finally blinked up from the ring to meet his gaze.

Around the restaurant, forks were clinked down on plates and shushes exchanged between couples. Even the pianist playing in the background stopped to provide them with silence. Aaron had always heard moments like this happened in slow motion, but that was an understatement. It was so slow that he had time to scan his entire body for an ounce of hesitation only to come up with *Ask him. Do it now.*

He dug into his pocket and unfolded a crinkly piece of paper with his smudged handwriting. His voice shook as he cleared his throat and said, "Daniel. You make things make sense in a way I've never had. With you inside my house, it feels like a home. With you in my life, it feels like I'm finally growing roots. You are technicolored and dazzling. You're *precious*."

Daniel's hands snapped to cover his face.

"You're it for me, kid. You're *so* it. You can take this as a promise." He stuffed the paper back into his pocket to grip one of Daniel's hands. The memory of him standing outside of a restaurant flashed across his mind—*Come get me*. He'd looked so shattered. "I choose you. I absolutely choose you. Please hang in there with me."

He didn't know when it would be. Someday. Someday when he had enough, when he'd saved enough, when he *was* enough, he'd able to quit. Until then, all he could do was promise.

"I promise to take care of you. To keep you safe. I promise to *always* choose you."

Daniel's tears streaked down his cheeks. It wasn't clear if he understood the secret meaning at first, but then he nodded. It was barely there.

Aaron's smile washed over him. But *barely there* counted. The ring—he needed the ring.

He stretched his neck long to see the dessert, which was slightly out of reach. When he tried to carefully fetch the plate, the ring, having been obediently balanced on the rosemary sprig the entire damn time, plunked into the mousse the second he touched it.

"Oh shit," he whispered. "Dammit, did that just—? Well, son of a...."

He was at a disadvantage where he knelt on the floor, because he couldn't see what he was doing, which seemed to be burying it farther into the mousse the harder he tried to fish it out. His cheeks were getting hot, probably because every person in the restaurant seemed to be waiting on him.

Daniel clenched his teeth into a shaky smile. He tapped his fingertips together and cleared his throat. "Do you, uh. Do you need help, or—?"

"No." His whisper sounded frantic, and he was definitely sweating. "I'm sorry. This is not—hang on." He'd been trying to save the dessert, but it was far less important than not making a complete fool of himself, so he destroyed it as he seized the ring.

Once silver and glossy, the poor thing was now globbed in brown. Aaron tried to suck chocolate off his fingers, probably smearing it onto his face as he searched the table for a napkin. He couldn't very well slide this mess onto Daniel's finger. He widened his eyes as the answer dawned on him. Then he stuffed the entire thing into his mouth.

Daniel looked like he couldn't take it any longer. He burst into laughter, loud like an air horn as Aaron held up a shaky finger and worked the ring around in his mouth. A rumble of giggles began to fill the restaurant until most everyone was laughing too.

Aaron spat the ring out in his palm to inspect it, but because of wet fingers, slippery metal, and the fact that somewhere along the way he'd pissed off the gods, he dropped it.

The crowd grew loud with gasps and *Oh no!*s and *What happened? Was that the ring?*

He'd never be able to replicate the perfect storm of physics to make such a thing possible as the ring chinked on the floor a few times and then started to roll. It was a fast little sucker—faster than outstretched arms could catch, faster than what should've been possible. It also seemed determined to ruin his night, because it traveled five table lengths, then pinged off the shoe of the only man in the room who was not paying attention.

"Tom!" The man's date hurled her napkin at him and pointed at his foot like it was on fire. "Get it. The ring. Get the ring. Pay attention!"

Tom hmmed as he lifted his sole, glanced around the floor, then stepped on it.

"Oh for the love of God, it's under your shoe, Tom! Your damn shoe."

Aaron buried his face in his hands, but he didn't need to participate, because everyone else was yelling at Tom for him.

Tom, a very apologetic cartoon turtle of a man with a shiny bald dome, black-rimmed glasses, and his head kind of sunk in the bulk of his body, heaved for breath as he first rushed the ring to a guy tying his shoe and not proposing to anyone, then finally to Aaron, the other person kneeling.

This was the most explicit torture he'd ever experienced, but he thanked Tom through pursed lips even though he'd really rather find an oven to lay his head inside. And he still had to propose. Not that Daniel was going to be able to see him through his tears or breathe through his laughter. Hopefully he could hear him?

"Okay, um, here we go. Dear Daniel—shit. No." He finally broke into agonized laughter of his own. "Okay, I just, I wanted to ask, if you will, like—shit. Don't say *like*. And I'm gonna stop cussing."

Daniel palmed his cheek and whispered, "Oh please let someone be recording this."

Aaron inhaled a gust of air and blew it out slowly through his mouth. This person was the lens through which he saw his future, the subject of every other thought he had, and his brightest reason for waking up hopeful. His tiny dancer. His light. His Daniel.

Wriggling his posture straight, he held the ring up. Then he finally said with that moment's version of normalcy, "Daniel Alexander Greene, will you marry me?"

Daniel wiped his eyes as his chuckling finally quelled.

"I'll take care of you," Aaron whispered as he linked their fingers. "Whatever you need. Marry me, kid."

Daniel's permasmile set up camp as he swabbed the last tear away. "Yes."

The restaurant erupted into a thousand whoops and applauses, and Aaron slid the band on his hand.

"Aaron Leonardo Silva." Daniel cupped his face as the surrounding sounds ebbed into dim white background noise. They were the only two people in the room when he pressed a single kiss on Aaron's lips and said, "You are it for me too."

DANIEL WAS a giddy, babbling mess as he tossed his arms over Aaron's shoulders, swaying them side to side to music that wasn't playing in their moody kitchen, lit only by the clocks on the appliances. He was positively drunk on dopamine (and one and a half pear martinis), gazing down at the ring on his finger and up into beautiful blue ice.

"Fiancé," he whispered, and goose bumps rushed down his arms. "Aaron. We're *fiancés*."

"Fiancés." Aaron smiled and twirled him around, then pulled him back in. "Husbands-to-be."

"You sure?" He buried his face in Aaron's neck and breathed. "You sure you want to marry me?"

"Yes. If I knew what I know now, I would've asked you the first day I met you."

Daniel grinned and wiggled his fingers over Aaron's shoulder to see the ring. "I admire that level of decisiveness."

"Right? That'd be the story we'd tell the grandchildren. Sit down, little Perry. Let me tell you the story—"

"Perry?"

"—of how I knew your grandpa was the one. It all started when he made me the world's worst cocktail at a party. How bad was it, you ask? It was unfit for human consumption—"

"It wasn't *that* bad."

"Absolutely gut-churning. So naturally, I finished it, then demanded he give me his number. He technically had a 'boyfriend' at the time, so I did have to steal him, which took forever—"

"Five minutes. Maybe four."

"Why yes, little Perry. That's an excellent observation. I *would* compare it to a highly skilled heist. But I pulled it off."

Daniel chuckled, rearing back to see Aaron's face. "How'd you do that?"

"How'd I heist him? Game, obviously." Aaron shrugged. "So much game."

"Game, really?" Daniel cocked his head. "Are you sure it wasn't because he could see the outline of your dick through your pants?" He yelped when Aaron gripped his waist and slung him in a circle, his feet catching wind.

"Whatever it takes," Aaron said, settling him back to the floor. "I gotcha now, kid. You're about to be so married to me."

He melted into Aaron's arms. The past couple of weeks had been a roller coaster, and it felt like they were finally nearing the end. *I choose you. I'll always choose you. Please hang in there with me.*

"Please hang in there" insisted there was an ending worth hanging in there for. Tomorrow, maybe he'd broach the subject of a timeline. Tonight, he'd just enjoy being engaged. Tonight, he'd just enjoy the hell out of his fiancé.

"You want to take a bath with me?" he asked. "Or a shower or something? All this excitement has taken a toll. I feel like I need to decompress, but I don't want to leave your arms."

Aaron's phone vibrated as he pressed up to his toes to peer at it over Daniel's shoulder, squinting at the bright screen through the darkness. He patted Daniel's ass. "No, you go ahead."

"You sure you don't want to join?" He stretched his neck as he filled a glass of water from the sink. "And I know what you're thinking. Just because we're engaged now doesn't mean we suddenly need to start *taking baths* together. What's next? We sit on a log somewhere, brewing our own kombucha? It's actually really tricky with two people in a bathtub, and they always make it look so easy in the movies—" He halted when he spun around to find Aaron frowning down at his phone. "Everything okay?"

Aaron peeled his gaze away from the screen and offered him a lukewarm smile. "Sorry. What now? You want kombucha?"

Daniel glanced down at Aaron's screen, but then his brain reminded him that he was safe with a still frame image of Aaron on bended knee, saying, *I choose you. I'll always choose you. Please hang in there with me.*

"No." He pecked Aaron's cheek, then winked on his way to the bathroom. "Drinking kombucha in a bathtub is somehow more ridiculous than drinking it on a log."

He filled the tub and eased inside, his muscles unkinking as water crowded them. Engaged. They were engaged. He chuckled to himself, biting his thumbnail while fluttering the finger his new accessory hugged. In all the embarrassing amount of time he'd spent picturing his future husband, he'd never pictured someone so desperately swoon-worthy. Someone he couldn't get enough time with.

He snapped a picture of his ring, sent it to a few people, and had nearly drifted off to sleep when the sound of the front door startled him.

A few minutes later, he'd toweled himself off and padded into the kitchen. Their apartment had a way of feeling a bit like an institution at times. It was all the dove gray and sterilized steel. It was worse when Aaron wasn't home. Which… Aaron wasn't home?

"Aaron?" he asked the shadowy apartment, meandering into the bedroom. He wasn't there either. He was seconds from calling him when he spotted a note on the pillow:

Didn't want to disturb your bath. Sorry, I had to leave. Get some rest. I'll be back soon.

He blinked down at the note, his attention divided between it and the texts that began to pour in.

No WAY?!! CONGRATULATIONS!!!

Dawwww! So happy for you two!

Congrats, sweet Daniel! Can't wait to meet Aaron. I'm sure he's wonderful.

He tried to recall the same snapshot from moments ago—*I choose you. I'll always choose you. Please hang in there with me*—but as he gazed at their empty bed, the only image his mind could conjure looked like this. Him tucked in alone at night. Him wondering when Aaron would be home. Him grasping on to the hope that there was an ending worth hanging in there for.

A single streak of moonlight laced in through the window as he crawled into the bed, twisted the ring off, and held it up. Something was engraved on the inside, but he couldn't see it. He could never just see what was written. Even with it in front of his face.

I choose you. I'll always choose you.

He held the ring against his heart, curled away from the moon, and closed his eyes.

"FORGIVE ME." It was Aaron's deep whisper coaxing him from sleep.

It had the hazy impression of a dream, but it wasn't. Daniel blinked his eyes open to find the streak of moonlight had transformed into tones of orange, gold, and pink. Or maybe that was the flowers.

"Please forgive me." Aaron was in bed behind him, holding a plastic-wrapped bouquet of gas-station roses in front of his face. "Please."

Daniel rubbed his eyes, his vision blurry with sleep as Aaron edged the flowers to the nightstand. "What time is it?"

"It's early, but I brought you a coffee and a cinnamon danish thing. Or would you rather go out to breakfast? We can go out to that beignet place you like—"

"You should've told me to my face. You should've told me you were leaving. It was unfair to leave it in a note."

Aaron swallowed behind him, inching their bodies flush. "I know." His whisper sounded weak and sheepish. "I'm sorry. I didn't want to hurt you, but of course I still hurt you."

Daniel inhaled long and slow. "How long does hanging in there with you mean?"

Aaron didn't respond for a while. "What do you mean?"

"That's what you said last night. You said to hang in there with you. How long do you think that'll be?"

Aaron huffed out a gush of air. "Well. I didn't mean it would happen right away. We still need to get our ducks in a row, but let me finish things up with Marco, then I promise we can talk about it. He's the only guy I'm seeing right now anyway—"

"Client."

Aaron blinked behind him, his long eyelashes scraping the pillowcase. "What?"

"He's the only *client* you're seeing right now. You call them clients. I've never heard you call them anything else."

Aaron swallowed. "Correct. Client. He's the only one I'm seeing."

A heaviness troubled his chest. Some emotion he couldn't quite name. Almost like he'd never felt it before. It wasn't anxiety. It was bulkier than anxiety. Duller. Achier. Like a slow and patient hum.

"Whoa." Aaron held Daniel's hand up in the light. "You took your ring off?"

"Hmm?" Daniel dragged a hand down his face. "Oh, yeah. I was trying to—"

"Do I need to read into that?"

It was probably best not to think about that question too deeply, so he shook his head as he searched the sheets until he found it under his pillow.

Aaron took it from him and gently pushed it back onto his finger. He spent a while twisting it around, warming the metal. When he spoke again, his voice was deep and despondent. "I'll tell you what, kid. If you need an out, take it off."

Daniel tried to peer back over his shoulder. "Take what off?"

"The ring."

Daniel's brow crinkled as he searched his words for clarification. "What?"

"I don't know, baby," Aaron sighed, airing warmth onto his neck. "I don't want you to have second thoughts, so I want to give you an out—I mean, don't fucking *take* it—but an option if worse comes to worst."

With that, the foundation of the entire proposal got a bit shaky. One didn't typically say *yes* with a built-in stopgap for when "worse came to worst." But their relationship had never been typical. Daniel's tongue wandered over his teeth. "Like a gesture?"

"Like a gesture. If you need it to be over between us, you take the ring off, and that's how I'll know not to fight it. I'll let you go with no questions asked." Aaron kissed his shoulder. "And it won't be your fault. It'll be mine."

Daniel swallowed, the heaviness in his chest humming away in the background.

"But please don't," Aaron said. "Talk to me first. I'll help you breathe. I'll help you through it. You have to hang in there with me."

As much as he hated it, there might have been a tiny part of him that softened in relief.

"Daniel." Aaron shook him. "You want to hang in there with me, right? You want to marry me, don't you?"

He nodded. "I do."

Chapter Twenty-Three

ONE WEEK later, Aaron sat on the floor in Marco's rental, massaging his calves while he typed away on his laptop. He'd settled into his role with Marco, which was unusual at best. In private he was a personal assistant. In public he was a boyfriend. Then there were times like this where Marco was comfortable enough to state his needs explicitly.

"Just touch me," Marco had said. "I need to be touched. Touch me anywhere, I don't care."

It was times like this when he was more of a pet.

"Do you need anything before I go?" he said, working his hands under Marco's pant legs.

"Yeah." Marco rolled his head around his neck. "I need you to *not* go."

He was a difficult person to read, but it almost seemed like he'd been more affectionate the past few days. Either that, or the gray area between boyfriend, PA, and pet was starting to mess with his mind.

"I wish I could stay," he said, because that was what he always said, even if it was a bit off-putting to white-lie to Marco. The man had his respect, but at the end of the day, it wasn't about truth so much as it was about making his clients feel desirable. "There's nowhere better than right here."

Marco gave him a sidelong glance, then back to the typing. "Are you pleased with how our arrangement has turned out?"

"Of course." That part he meant. Their time together had been a lot of work. Literal work—composing emails and reviewing contracts for errors—but it'd been a welcome change of pace. Plus, Marco's deal had gone through, and Aaron had helped. He was part of something bigger than him. They even had a celebratory whiskey tasting with the clients tomorrow night, which was one way to end on a high note. "You've been the best client I've ever had by a long shot."

"Come." Marco snapped the laptop shut and patted the sofa next to him. "Come sit."

Aaron stood and brushed his pants off, then settled in next to him.

Marco twisted to face him, resting an elbow on the back of the sofa, and sighed as he rubbed an eye. "I'm due a vacation. I haven't taken one in three years."

Aaron snorted. "Shocker."

Marco chuckled, which was a nice change of pace after the stress he'd been through. "I think you could use one too. A sandy beach, a drink in your hand. You've been working so hard. How would you like to come with me?"

Aaron licked his lips. "What's that now?"

Marco's expression was a bit amused. He reached out and brushed a few fingers through Aaron's hair, which was such an unusually intimate gesture for their dynamic that he almost flinched. "Antigua, maybe. St. Bart's. I'd pay for the whole thing, of course, and I'd compensate you for your time. You could just relax."

Aaron sucked in a tight breath. A vacation. Even if no-vacationing-with-clients wasn't one of his rules, he struggled to imagine any kind of trip without a curly-headed little dancer beside him, bitching about the wind being too windy or whatever.

Marco's brow kneaded together. "You hesitate."

"No, I...." He didn't have an argument. He was hesitating. "Overnight trips aren't typically something I do."

"Overnight stays weren't something you did either. And look. You survived."

He chuckled. "True. But if I might just be honest for a second?"

"Please."

"My partner. You met him briefly at the restaurant. He'd probably struggle with that. With a trip."

"Ahh." Marco nodded. "The partner. Well, for what it's worth, he seems very... young. Young people don't always have the best gauge on what's most important."

Aaron squinted. "Which is?"

"Security, of course. Making sure the choices you make improve your future. Now, I want you to please take what I'm about to say seriously." Again with the hair touching, only he'd scooted in closer. "Can you do that for me?"

He glanced up at Marco's hand in his hair. He nodded.

"I'd like to continue seeing you, Aaron. I'd like to see you once a month, give or take. You come to me in Santa Monica, or I come to you."

Something about this was so different. Uncharted. "Oh. Uh. Let me think about—"

"I'd be willing to increase your rate by 20 percent."

Aaron's eyes widened, and his heart tripped over a beat.

"Which is a whole lot of money, Aaron, as you know. You could do big things if you invested it properly. I could help you." Marco gently cupped his face—first one hand, then the other. "But one thing is for certain. You should come on this trip with me. You won't regret it. I'll make it worth your time."

Then the strangest thing happened. Marco kissed him.

For the first time, other than a cheek peck in front of the clients, Marco kissed him, and Aaron allowed it. Why would he not? *This* was his job. His job wasn't sending emails, hobnobbing with strangers, and securing deals. His job was to be a patient and enthused lover. He'd always dreamed about a client like this—someone polite, generous, and attractive. He should've been turned on as the kiss progressed deeper with Marco's jaw working and his tongue mingling with his.

He should've been having fun, but he wasn't.

For the first time maybe ever, doing this, doing his *job*… he felt sick.

THE NEXT night, Daniel clutched a pillow in bed while a true-crime documentary flashed images of some guy killing another guy with a tire iron. It wasn't great for his nervous system, but he was locked in. What was also not great for his nervous system was the thud that thudded somewhere in the apartment. The living room?

"Aaron?" he asked, eyes wide as he grabbed the remote control. Why wouldn't he grab his phone? Or Aaron's baseball bat in the closet? If a psychopath with a tire iron was on their way to bludgeon things, all he'd be able to do was turn up the volume while he got murdered. "Aaron. Is that you?"

Another thud, followed by Aaron's loud whisper-cursing. Daniel's breath rushed into his body as he fell back into the bed.

Aaron suddenly stood in the doorway. Well, *stood* was a stretch. He swayed, held on to the doorframe, and grinned, all silly and blitzed. "Hey, cutie."

"Oh God." Daniel flicked his gaze upward. "You're drunk."

Aaron twisted around the room as if someone was standing behind him and pointed a finger at himself. "Me?"

"I'm surprised you came home." Daniel sat up and sipped his ginger ale, mustering all his sass. "You and your boyfriend have a little too much fun?"

"Okay, I see what you're trying to do, and oh, no, no." Aaron wagged a finger at him. He slid his jacket off and slung it across the room like he was on stage at a strip club. "I don't have a boyfriend. *I* have a fiaaaaancé. And God, look at you. I can't wait to marry you."

Drunk Aaron was an overly sentimental and gushy fellow. Daniel had to restrain his grin.

"Then, when I'm at a restaurant, someone'll say, 'Hey, can I use this chair?'" Aaron crawled into the bed and laid his head in Daniel's lap, smiling goofily. "And I'll say, 'No. I'm saving that for my *husband.*'"

Daniel combed his fingers through Aaron's hair. "It's the little things."

"Oh! And we can have Spoon-Sex Sundays."

"You want a designated day for spoon sex?"

The big spoon beamed. "All married couples have a designated day for spoon sex, silly."

"No. They don't."

"Remind me tomorrow—" He interrupted himself with a yawn. "There's something I need to talk to you about, kid."

"What is it, handsome?" He thumbed Aaron's lower lip. "You want Missionary Mondays?"

"Oh, missionary's good. Yeah, I can watch your face." Aaron's words slurred, and his eyelids collapsed. "But no. Isss about Marco."

Daniel cocked his head. That didn't sound promising. "What about Marco? I thought he was leaving. Is he not leaving? Talk to me now."

"He is leaving. But he wants to take me on a vacation before he goes home. A charter plane. St. Bart's."

Daniel's eyebrows shot up. "A charter plane?"

"Tomorrow night."

"Tomorrow?" They shot higher as he blinked, wide-eyed, his stomach revolting in a somersault. "What? Why so soon?"

"He's gotta gets backs to work."

"But." Daniel rubbed his forehead. No. No, no, no. "Do you want to go?"

"Do I *want* to?" Aaron nodded weakly and nestled into his lap, his words streaming together. "S'good money. He's right, and we need money for, ya know... future self. You're young, Daniel. Young people don't know about security. Ssssecurity's what's important."

It seemed so much worse than any regular time Aaron could've spent with a client. It seemed fucking *catastrophic* to have Aaron gone on a beach vacation with Marco. "But I thought you said you guys were platonic? If you're platonic, why does he want to take a vacation together?"

Aaron didn't respond.

"Hey." Daniel shook him, but his breathing had already progressed to a faint snore.

He stared down at sleeping Aaron for a long time, curling his fingers through his hair, his wedding band glinting in the blue light from the TV. So hanging in there looked like this now too? Chartered planes? Vacations to St. Bart's? All it took was the perfect client, and suddenly Aaron's boundaries were slipping. He was staying the night. He was going on trips. All the things he'd sworn he'd never do.

Daniel wiggled out from under Aaron, tugged his shoes off, rolled him onto his side, and covered him with the blanket. Squatting by the bed, he smoothed Aaron's eyebrow where he creased it in his sleep. "This doesn't feel right."

Aaron twitched.

"This isn't right. Please don't go. Don't go on a trip with him." He gently kissed Aaron's lips. He tasted a little like himself, a little like whiskey, and a little like someone else's cologne. Probably Marco's. Which was enough to hurt all over. "It'll break my heart."

Chapter Twenty-Four

"HELLO, THIS message is for Daniel Greene. This is Deidra Boynton with Value One Loans. I'm sorry, sir, but your loan application has been disapproved. We apologize we couldn't align at this time, but please do consider us for your future needs. Have a great day."

It was the next afternoon, and Daniel had woken to another loan rejection, Aaron gone, and a text that said, *Sorry I fell asleep last night. Had to run out. Didn't want to wake you. Be back in a couple hours.*

He'd gotten a sub for his class so he could be home when Aaron got back, but it was like he didn't know what to do with himself, so he paced around the apartment, drinking coffee he didn't need. He always gravitated toward the plants by the window. It was the liveliest place in the apartment and, somehow, the most peaceful. Maybe it was the bonsai tree. Aaron hadn't worked on it much lately, such that it'd started to deviate from its shape, but it was still beautiful. Daniel smoothed the beaded earring between his fingers.

He happened to glance past the bonsai at the street below just as a shiny black Porsche rumbled up to one of the meters. For some reason it reminded him of Aaron. Maybe because Aaron loved cars. Maybe because everything reminded him of Aaron.

He'd almost turned away when the most elegant of men emerged from the driver's side. The sight of him made Daniel's teeth snap closed. Marco.

Then, from the passenger side, stepping out with a sheepish smile, Aaron.

It was like he couldn't even gasp. His heart climbed into his throat and sealed it shut as Marco jogged around to join Aaron. There they stood on the street together. Laughing.

They looked powerful—same height, same style, same dignified air, full of pride and admiration for the other. The two A-list actors.

Daniel had been haphazardly hiding behind the fishtail palm tree, but he stepped out. It wasn't like they seemed to mind who saw. He pressed his forehead onto the cold glass of the window as Marco reached into the back seat of his car to reveal a thin, burnt orange box. He handed it to Aaron.

Daniel and Marco likely both held their breaths in anticipation as Aaron unwrapped it.

Did he love it? The silky white dinner scarf he fanned out and slid around his neck. The one that made his face light up. It looked expensive. It looked like something Daniel would never be able to afford. Marco pulled Aaron into a hug as Daniel hugged himself.

Then Marco pulled Aaron into a kiss.

Something cold and viscous, like an egg yolk, oozed the length of Daniel's spine. Aaron had lied. He'd said they didn't do that. He'd lied.

His fingernails raked down the window as if he could stop it. He should've turned away. He should've fixed his gaze on anything else or forced his eyes shut, but he couldn't, and so he stared as his beautiful boyfriend softened into another kiss with another man. But not just any man. The perfect man.

To the people walking by, just another couple in love stood holding one another, talking about where they'd get takeout later and should they heat up the hot tub? Did he remember to call the landscaper? Magnolias, they'd decided. Magnolias would look nice.

Daniel's breath fogged the window.

I choose you. I'll always choose you. Please hang in there with me.

Aaron and Marco finally parted ways, stretching their arms long just as a loud crash echoed throughout the apartment.

"No!" Daniel plunged to the floor.

The coffee mug he'd been holding, the one Butchie had gotten for him on a trip to Destin, lay shattered in a hundred sky-blue pieces. It had said "Home Is Where the Caffeine Is" next to a sea turtle in glasses riding a bike. It made no sense, and it was one of his most beloved possessions.

He slumped to his knees. When he tried to sweep up the pieces, he cut himself. "Shit!"

"Oh, hi." Aaron strolled in, concern knitting his brow as he checked his watch. At least he'd stuffed his fancy new scarf into his coat pocket, even if the tassels stuck out like a secret desperate to escape. "What are you doing here? Don't you have class right now?"

"I got a sub." Daniel charged to the sink.

"Oh my God, you're bleeding," Aaron said, following him. "What happened?"

Daniel wrapped a paper towel around his finger. "Nothing."

"Let me see it." Aaron reached for him.

He twisted away. "It's fine."

"What'd you do?" Aaron tugged at his arm. "Just let me see it."

"I said it's fucking fine!"

"Whoa." Aaron held both hands up. "Are you… okay?"

"No." He swallowed over and over until he couldn't anymore. He shifted his weight around. He'd been here before. *Come get me.* "I saw you with Marco." He tipped his chin at the window, his voice a shattered mess. "Down there just now. I saw you guys together."

"What? How…?" Aaron trailed off as he turned to the window. He scanned the starburst of coffee and ceramic on the floor. Then his eyes rolled closed and his face clenched as he squeezed the bridge of his nose. "Okay, I can explain—"

"You said you guys didn't do that. You lied to me. Why'd you lie to me?"

"Look, I didn't lie. It only recently started getting, um. But we haven't. We haven't *done* anything. We've only kissed."

"Yet. You haven't done anything *yet.*"

"Well." Aaron licked his lips, arms folded, fingers tapping on his biceps. "Fuck. Okay, yes. But Daniel, I'm an escort. What is it you think I do?"

Daniel slowly swayed his gaze around their home. He was surrounded by beautiful things, Aaron included. And for the first time, the sight of the place, the presence of Aaron—it was all genuinely tiresome. He ran his tongue over his teeth, then bit it until it hurt. "I don't want you to go on this trip with him."

Aaron started to speak, but it fizzled into a sigh. "Okay, this is good we're talking about this. Here. Have a seat."

"I don't want you to go."

"Okay, or don't." Aaron pulled out a chair at the table and plopped into it, folding his hands. "Listen to me. I don't think you understand how much money it is—"

"I don't care how much money it is."

"But we have a wedding to consider, and the studio and rent—"

"I don't care. I don't fucking care. God!" He dug the heels of his palms into his skull. "I am so *sick* of thinking about money. Aren't you sick of thinking about money?"

Aaron blinked at him for a long time, like the question had been lost in translation. Like the question was so perplexing that he couldn't even summon an answer. He finally said, in a confused whisper, "But we don't have a choice. We have to think about it."

Then it hit him. He stilled from head to toe, because if he didn't ground himself, he would stagger backward at how hard it hit.

This entire time, he'd been worried about Marco. Worried that Marco would sweep Aaron off his feet with the confidence, the looks, and the prestige. But Aaron wasn't going to fall in love with Marco, because he was already in love.

Daniel wasn't competing with Marco for Aaron's attention. He was competing with money.

"Baby, I promise I don't have feelings for him," Aaron said. "I swear it. You are it. I'm marrying you."

The thing about competing with money was: it was a race he was *never* going to win.

"Don't you believe me?" Aaron asked. "Don't you trust me?"

Daniel's wide exhale sank his arms heavy by his sides. "Of course. Of course I do."

Aaron eyed him watchfully. "You do?"

"Yes." If tears were standing by, there'd be no fighting them. "You should leave on this trip if that's what you need to do. But I need to leave too."

Aaron's face didn't budge a muscle. Not one twitch. "What does that mean?"

Daniel sipped in air to keep from crumbling. In a tiny voice that sounded like it squeaked from another room, he said, "Leave, Aaron. Leave us. Leave you."

The way Aaron stood from the table, he almost looked dizzy. "Okay, so. Uh. Look, why don't you take a spa day while I'm gone, hmm? You'll have the whole apartment to yourself. That'll be nice. Then, when I get back, we'll focus on the wedding. That sound good?"

Daniel slowly dipped his head to the side and studied Aaron. Aaron who wasn't convinced, but in his defense, he hadn't said it all that convincingly. "Mister." He shook his head. "There is no 'when you get back.' When you get back, I will not be here."

Aaron froze.

"I will be gone. Do you understand?"

"Uh-huh. I understand ultimatums are how people get hurt. We talked about this." Aaron pointed to his engagement band. "If you wanted it to be over, you'd take it off. That was the deal."

Daniel smoothed a thumb over the ring. "I'm not going to take it off, because I want you to fight for me."

"I am fighting!" Aaron's eyes were so wild and intense as he slung an arm out to the side. "Fuck, can you not see that I'm working to build a life for us? We need money to live. This is the only way I know how to make money. I can't take care of you or Andrew if I—"

"Andrew?" Daniel's brow knitted as he searched Aaron's face. "Andrew your brother?"

Aaron blinked for a moment like he was orienting himself. Like he hadn't meant to say that.

"Oh, sweet man." Daniel held his hands to his heart, his voice tangled with sympathy. "It's so noble that you did what you did for him. And your mom. And me. It's noble the way you tend to everyone around you. You make these huge sacrifices, and you ask for nothing in return."

Aaron shook his head as if to deny it or maybe clear it of whatever fog it was in.

"But I don't need that. I don't need you to take care of me. You understand, right?"

Aaron rushed to him and cradled his face, tipping it back. "Baby, listen to me. You know how much I admire your spirit. I think it's courageous to dream, but we cannot survive on dreams alone. We just, we *can't*."

Daniel parted his lips when Aaron's gaze fell to them. Then Aaron's phone pinged from his pocket. After a moment, he broke his gaze away and checked his phone, then sighed. "I have to get ready."

At Daniel's nod, Aaron pressed their lips together for a sweet second. The smile he wore was stilted but lovely as he backed away toward the bathroom, stretching out their arms as long as he could until they had to drop.

"You should kiss me better than that."

Aaron twisted around.

"You should kiss me." A breath. "Like you did at the party."

Aaron didn't overthink or hesitate, which was such a profoundly admirable trait of his. He narrowed the space between them and yanked Daniel in by the waist, their bodies tense yet snug. At home. He kissed him. He kissed him genuinely and with so much depth. Until the clock ran out, until the last moment he could, until Daniel's eyes burned with tears, he kissed him with everything he had.

"There it is," Daniel whispered once their lips unlocked. He touched Aaron's face and pressed their foreheads together. "That's a kiss."

Aaron blinked a lot as he scratched his temple. "Hey, uh. Don't, um. Everything's going to be okay. Right?"

"Yes." Daniel nodded, warm tears streaking his vision. "Go get ready. I'm gonna take off too."

Aaron chewed his thumbnail as he reeled away a few steps. It was like he couldn't decide where to look, his gaze swinging from Daniel to the bathroom and back to him. "I'll call you every chance I get. We'll sort this out. We always do. Okay?"

I hope he's good to you.

"Daniel," Aaron said when he didn't answer, fidgeting by the bathroom. "Okay?"

But I know he will be. Daniel wiped his face and nodded. *He already is.* "Goodbye, Aaron."

Chapter Twenty-Five

YOU SHOULD kiss me better than that.

Aaron was running late. He should've been ready five minutes ago. He'd tried to hurry through the shower, but Jesus, if he didn't catch himself staring into space, too distracted to rinse properly. Distracted by *I will be gone. Do you understand?* Distracted by *You should kiss me better than that. Kiss me like you did at the party.*

Midshower, he'd dripped water all over the apartment floor to check if Daniel was already gone, which he was. Fine. No big deal. He'd said he was leaving. *I will be gone. Do you understand?* He'd then sent Daniel a text asking to please let him know when he got to wherever he was going safely. That was a typical thing he might text, and even if Daniel usually replied with an eye roll emoji, he still replied.

Better than that. Like you did at the party.

He cut the water and scrubbed a towel through his hair. He'd started to sift through his shirts in the closet when his phone dinged from the bathroom. A text ding. He darted for it, but it wasn't an eye roll emoji from Daniel.

Marco:

Are you ready for some sunshine? Be there in five.

"Shit," he whispered and cradled the phone between his ear and shoulder as he called Daniel.

It forwarded to voicemail, which was fine. No big deal. He probably had class, which was why he had to "take off too." *I will be gone. Do you understand?*

"Hey, kid," he said when the beep sounded. "I was, uh, just thinking about the wedding. I was wondering what you thought about a morning ceremony with breakfast foods. Something bright and airy. White dahlias, maybe. A coffee station with a barista. Sounds mellow, right?" He paused, waiting. For what? For an answer? For something less pathetic to come to mind? "I just. Call me back, Daniel. Please."

You should kiss me better than that. Like you did at the party.

God, he needed to pull himself together. They'd made an agreement. They'd made it together when they were both of sound mind, and just because it was somewhat unconventional didn't mean it wasn't clear. If Daniel needed an out, he'd take the ring off. He hadn't taken the ring off. That was the agreement.

Aaron buttoned up a shirt and stepped into a pair of jeans, then swiped some styling paste through his hair just in time for the buzzer to his apartment to sound. He jogged to the front door and Marco's voice chimed over the speaker, "It's me."

Better than that. Like you did at the party.

Something a bit like a growl hissed past his lips as he buzzed Marco up. Geez, he needed to get out of his head and into the present moment. He bounced a few times, shaking his arms out. The man on his way up to his apartment deserved him at his best, not consumed by a few lines on repeat. *Like you did at the party.*

He growled again, hopping higher. Then a knock sounded at the front door, and he halted. He couldn't move with his stomach twisted into a gnarly knot and his feet rooted in place. Maybe he could play it off as nerves. Who didn't get nervous on luxury charter jets?

Better than that. Like you did at the party.

He finally glued on a politician's plastic smile on election day and answered.

"Hi," Marco said, fully suited and tied, a crisply woven version of everything Aaron wanted to be. "What a sight for sore eyes you are."

Fuck! He was drowning. He was drowning under the weight of how fake he was while his phone shouted at him from his pocket, begging him to check it. One tiny eye roll emoji. "You too," he said because he was the fakest person ever. "Come in."

"Wow." Marco strolled in, gazing around the apartment. "Aaron, your place. Marvelous."

While Marco was distracted, Aaron took the opportunity to check his phone. Nothing. "Thank you. Sorry, I'm running late. I'm almost ready. Let me just get my things—"

"There is no rush. We have time." Marco gently snagged his arm. "We have time for all kinds of things. Come here. I've been dreaming of getting to kiss you for four whole days straight."

You should kiss me better than that.

"Uhm-hmm. Sure. Would love to."

After a moment Marco said, "Hey, Aaron."

He zipped his gaze up. He hadn't realized he'd been nodding at his feet, making any kind of kiss impossible. "Oh. Wow. Sorry."

Marco gave him a peculiar look. "Are you okay?"

"Yes. I just—uh. I think I need some water. Haven't had much today. 'Scuse me." He darted off toward the kitchen sink.

"Sure you don't need something stronger than water?" Marco asked with his hands in his pockets and a somewhat amused smile as Aaron chugged half a glass. "Do you get nervous on flights or something?"

He shook his head, wiping his mouth on the back of his hand. Apparently, he got nauseous on flights, because the thought of getting on a plane with Marco made the ping of nausea that'd been curdling in his stomach peak, but he braced his hands on the sink.

All he needed to do was fake it. He'd done it a thousand times. Fake it for four days. It wouldn't be that hard. What was so hard about being fake as shit?

I will be gone. He collapsed his elbows to the sink and rubbed his eyes. Fake it. *Do you understand?* He'd always faked it. He'd faked his way through countless nights and dragging days. *Better than that.* He'd faked enthusiasm and enjoyment. Every time he'd been with a new man. *Like you did at the party.* Every single one.

Except for Daniel.

He was drowning. Either that or he was beginning to burn alive. Something inside of him was definitely growing hotter, trying to blow his entire world up. But it was a world that'd been peeling away anyway, layer by layer, chip by chip, fake smile by fake smile. *Better than that.* It was a world that had started to change with one night. *You should kiss me.* With one kiss. *Like you did at the party.*

"Marco," he said, his voice shaking. "I'm so sorry, but I can't—"

"Oh," Marco suddenly said, his eyebrows lifted as he stared down at something on the counter. "Yikes. Well, no wonder you're edgy, sweetness."

"I—wait. What?"

Marco's gaze flashed up to his. Then back down at the counter. He looked like he didn't quite know what to do as he slowly pointed a finger at whatever he was looking at. "Apologies for reading it. It caught my eye, is all."

Aaron circled the counter, uneasiness seizing his grasp on his emotions. He followed Marco's gaze, and it was like one of those scenes in a movie when the loud music crunched to a halt. The same as his breath crunched from his chest. Why hadn't it caught *his* eye? He'd walked right by it.

Tucked under a potted plant was a handwritten note. Beside it, Daniel's ring.

He rushed to it, nearly spilling the plant over as he ripped it away and read every word. And every word again.

"Hey. Look at me," Marco said after a beat. "Can you look at me for a minute?"

He scanned the words of the letter again.

"Aaron."

When he finally peeled his eyes from the letter, it was because Marco had lifted his chin.

"My apologies if this is insensitive, but the timing feels serendipitous. This is something that needs to be said." Marco's gaze was so calm. So soothing. "I like you. No, I more than like you. I'm nuts about you. And quite honestly, I think you're into me too. I think you have been for a while."

Aaron tried to glance down at the letter, tracing his thumb over the pen strokes, but Marco lifted his chin again.

"You have no idea the kind of life I can provide you," Marco said in that mercifully sincere way of his. "You'd never have to work another day in your life so long as you had me."

No one had ever said that to him. What a sanctuary.

"Hey, think about it this way." Marco freed the letter from Aaron's grip and tossed it on the counter, then held his face in his warm palms. "Now this trip can be the beginning of *our* future together. A future where I will take extraordinary care of you, Aaron. It'd be my pleasure."

A sanctuary. A surrender. And to come from someone so unsparing and kind.

"Come on. Get your things. Let's go." Marco held his gaze and kissed his cheek in pillowy softness. Then the other. "What do you have to lose?"

"Everything." He didn't need to think about it. He didn't need to squander a second longer in whatever hesitation had led him here. He gently pushed Marco's hands away. "I'm sorry. I'm so sorry to waste your time. Your money. Your effort. All of it. I respect you so much. But I will lose *everything* if I go with you."

Marco's tongue worked over his teeth. It was impossible to tell if he was angry or hurt. Maybe both. After a few moments, he asked, "Are you serious? You're really not coming?"

"I won't lose him." He shook his head, already searching for his keys. What was startling was that he wholeheartedly meant it as he said it—"I'd rather be penniless."

DEAR AARON,

In my heart, I've known all along that you deserve to be who you are, not just who I want you to be. Just like I've known all along I deserve to be who I am too. The part I wish I could change? It's that you being you, and me being me, means our time together has to end.

I don't regret one second of our time together, mister. I will always remember you. I will always wonder if you're happy. I will always love you.
Daniel

Chapter Twenty-Six

DANIEL HAD parked outside of the studio just to be near something he loved. His phone rang with an unknown number. Fucking telemarketers. He waited for the call to run its course. Then it rang again. Only Aaron that time.

There was that feeling. The one that made him slump over the steering wheel with shoulders rounded and knuckles clenched white. The one that insisted he was making the right choice by leaving. He hadn't cried a single tear since he left the ring behind. That had to mean something. If it wasn't the right choice, then he would've been a blubbering mess. His eyes were exhausted, but they were dry.

He pressed his lips together as hard as it took for him to keep from answering as Aaron's beautiful picture illuminated his screen. "I *can't*. I can't hear your voice, I can't beg you to stay, I can't talk to you knowing he's there too. I'm so sorry." He swung the car door open, and it almost felt symbolic when he slammed it shut. "But it's over."

Most of the studio lights had been cut for the night, except for a few, and surprisingly the front door was still unlocked. He tugged it open only to startle Madeline from her graceful crescent moon shape as she held the barre, one leg extended to the side.

She spun around and pink bloomed across her cheeks. She'd been dancing in the dark alone.

"Lovely," he said, offering a tiny wave. "As always. So lovely. Don't let me stop you."

"I don't know why," she said, crossing her ankles, a sweet smile splitting her face, "but I had a feeling I might see you here."

"Yeah?" He sighed. "Well, it is home."

She shrugged a shoulder. "Join me?"

Dancing. Putting heart into motion. Nothing compared. Nothing nourished him or moved him or kept his Jell-O mold of a nervous system quelled. The old hardwoods beneath his feet didn't mind if he showed up full of regret, unsure of himself, and dressed in another guy's clothes from the night before. Just how it didn't care if he showed up battered and heartbroken, yet somehow alive on the other side. It only cared that he showed up.

Their movements weren't coordinated or matching, but they flowed. No music. Just harmony. She smiled and caught his gaze and they both bowed in an homage to the old hardwoods. In an homage to the principles themselves. A goodbye to a special studio that had held space for them over so many remarkable days. So many dances.

He gazed around the walls. "Are you going to miss this place?"

"With every bone of my body."

"Same." He nodded, his eyes watering a touch. "I'm so sorr—" He cleared his throat when it cracked. "Sorry I couldn't make it work."

"No." She held her hand to his cheek, ever the gentlest of touches. "No apologies. Another door will open. Another page will turn. Dancing is your true love, and the thing about true love? It evolves, but it never dies. It'll find a way to live through you."

He pressed his palm over hers, grinning as he let his eyes soften shut for the briefest of moments. "How so very dazzling."

Then she said, "There's something different about you."

He blinked his eyes open to find her brows pinched in. "There is? Like what?"

"I don't know." Her gaze swept over his face. "But it's beautiful. Like a young man who trusts himself."

She had no idea how deeply it hit, and it took everything he had to simply clasp his hands in gratitude instead of pulling her into him and demanding she stay. She nodded at the walls as she floated toward the front door. "I'll give you a few minutes alone with it. Take care of yourself, Daniel."

Take care of himself.

He smoothed his hand over the barre and drank it in. Dance studios smelled like sequence. And sequence smelled like thrill. Like bright lights and the high of the performance. He arced an arm toward the ceiling and pulled his gentle grip over the barre until it ran out.

His phone rang again with the same number from earlier as he gingerly sat on a stool behind the counter. He tilted his head down at it for a minute.

"Hello?" His voice sounded bizarre, cutting through the chilly darkness.

"Hi, I'm looking for a Mr. Daniel Greene."

He wet his lips. "Speaking."

"Hi, Mr. Greene, this is Todd with Capital Equity. I'm contacting you about your recent loan application. Is this a good time?"

Even though he'd likely crumble at more bad news, he said, "As good as any."

"Great. Sorry it's so late, but I wanted to catch you before the weekend."

So he could ruin it. Everyone wanted to ruin his weekend.

"Congratulations, sir. Your application has been approved. Is there a good time for you to drop by next week and fill out some paperwork?"

Daniel tried to stand from the stool in a hurry, and like a baby bird flying for the first time, plummeted straight to the ground.

WHEN THE elevator dinged open, Aaron stumbled into a run and sped out the front door of his apartment building. He'd called Olivia twice in the past ten minutes and he'd called Daniel countless times. There weren't that many places he could be. He could be at Olivia's or the studio. He could be at his mom's. He was probably at his mom's, in which case, he'd need his car.

Aaron hung a hard left at the street corner and sprinted toward the parking garage, when a ring from his phone skidded him to a halt.

The glimmer of hope that sparkled was way too zealous, because of course it wasn't Daniel. But it was the next best thing. He answered in a tizzy, out of breath, "Olivia."

"Hi," she said over wildly loud background music. "Is there a reason why y'all are blowin' my damn phone up?"

"Do you know where Daniel is?"

"Uh, you know I have a life outside of Daniel, right?"

"Sure, sure, sure." He couldn't picture such a thing. "Do you know where he is?"

Clanging sounded. "What?"

"Daniel," he said louder. "Do you know where he is?"

"I can't hear you."

"Dan—! Can you get somewhere quieter?"

"Ugh, hold on." A full minute later, a door creaked, and it was suddenly much calmer on the other end. "Okay. What now?"

"Where are you?"

"Your brother's house."

He flicked his gaze upward as she snickered.

"Should I tell him to keep it down?" More snickering. "He's just struggling to contain himself. Must be all the rhapsody."

"Hilarious."

"Oh, I'm just kidding, silly willy," she said, and he could almost see the hand swat as she chuckled at herself. "You silly willy man. I'm at a rave."

"What?" He squinted. "What year is it? Who goes—? Never mind. Do you know where Daniel is?"

"At the studio. You're not with him? Thought you'd be helping him celebrate."

"Celebrate?" His heart lurched a bit. "What's he celebrating?"

"The loan for the studio, silly. You silly willy."

Aaron opened his mouth and started to speak, but nothing came out. Instead, a soft smile lifted his lips. "He got the loan?" *Well, congratulations, kid.*

"Yeah, how do you not know that? And why aren't you with him? I couldn't really hear him when he was talking about you. I figured you were there."

"I'm about to be there." He nodded at a lamppost. "I'm not going to let him go. I can't. I'd rather be broke."

She didn't respond for a long time. Then she finally said, "Okay. You guys really are a couple of weirdos. You're lucky you're both so hot—"

He was already ending the call. Already sprinting down the street.

Ten minutes later, he staggered to a stop outside of the studio. He'd only ever picked Daniel up from the sidewalk. He'd never been inside. It was mostly dark in there as he hooded his hands around his eyes and peered in.

He checked the handle, and to his shock, the door was open. A ding sounded as he pulled it open, and Daniel's voice called from somewhere in the back, "Madeline? That you? Hold on, I'll be right there."

Aaron's heart rate spiked as he stepped inside. It was an old building with partially exposed brick that'd been painted black and white. It had that feel some old buildings had. Like it'd been designed with care and constructed with love. It was so Daniel in that way.

The lights flicked on, and Daniel came ambling from the back. Not chipper. But not sullen either. He halted when he laid eyes on Aaron, his hint of a smile instantly dying.

They stood in a harsh stare-off that Aaron struggled to soften all on his own. He wasn't typically the soft one. All he could do was try. "Hi."

Daniel's face twitched, but he didn't respond.

"So, this is the studio, huh?" He squatted down to angle his head at the hardwoods. "Maple? Nice."

Daniel didn't speak.

"Original molding too. You need a mirror right there—make it look bigger—and a print on that overhang. Something with color to contrast that wall. Ballet slippers? Or is that too on-the-nose?"

Daniel blinked. "What are you doing here, Aaron?"

"What am I doing here?" he repeated, sucking his lip. "I came here to congratulate you on the studio. I'm so unbelievably proud of you."

Daniel's gaze pinged around the walls, but he remained quiet. Quiet and icy.

"And I'm here to say that I never should've considered going on that trip." He exhaled. "I knew you weren't going to be okay with it, and I shouldn't have put you through that. I'm sorry."

There was something so cold about Daniel as he crossed his arms and rubbed his nose, looking anywhere but at Aaron.

"I told Marco I didn't want to see him anymore." He stepped a little closer. "I'll tell all my clients I don't want to see them. You never have to worry about—"

"I took it off."

Aaron froze.

"I took the ring off."

He could suddenly feel the weight of Daniel's ring in his pocket.

"You said that if I took it off, you would let me walk away. You wouldn't fight it. That's what *you* said."

"I know. I know what I said, but that was before."

"Before what?"

"Before I quit. I'm quitting."

Daniel chuckled, sounding a bit delirious. "I can't ask you to do that for me."

"No, you can!" Aaron rushed to him. "You have every right. You're my fiancé. You can ask anything of me—"

"No, I can't. I *never* should've asked you to do that for me. That doesn't work."

"Listen to me, baby." He started to reach for Daniel's shoulders but stopped himself. "I want to quit. Not for you—okay, that's a lie. It's totally for you, but it's for me too. I don't want to do it anymore. I haven't wanted to do it for a long time. I think I was just scared."

Daniel squinted. "Scared of what?"

"Scared of failing." He shook his head and shrugged. "Or maybe of succeeding, I don't know. Of everything. Of change, of life, of never having enough. Of never being enough."

Daniel sniffed, his melted caramel eyes all enormous and full of pain. It was almost like his frigid walls were trying to fracture, but he waved his arms around and patched them up. "No. Listen. You're emotional right now. If you quit for me, you'll resent me someday."

"No, I won't. I swear, I swear, I won't."

"Yes, you will." Daniel squeezed his eyes shut as he wiped a palm across the forehead. "I know it doesn't seem like it this second, but you will. That's how it works."

"Kid, if I don't fight for you, I'll resent myself."

Daniel startled.

"If I won't fight for you," Aaron whispered, "then I never deserved you."

"Aaron."

"I have your ring, baby." He dug into his pocket in a hurry and scooped the ring out. "I have it right here. This is *your* ring."

Daniel's gazed journeyed down to the ring.

"You know when I bought this ring for you, I had to write down the inscription for the jeweler because I couldn't say it. I tried, and I couldn't do it. And even that was a challenge." His chuckle was a little darker than intended. "I'm sure they thought I was broken. I might be, but I always meant it. From the beginning, I meant it."

Daniel blinked up at him. "Meant what?"

Aaron's heart started to patter a bit faster. "The inscription. On your ring."

It seemed like Daniel was lost in time for a bit; then revelation softened his features. "I forgot about that."

"Have you never read it?" Aaron's eyes widened. "You never saw the inscription?"

"You said not to take it off. I never took it off."

Aaron bit the inside of his cheek as he peered down at the ring in his fingers. A lump had lodged in his airway, or maybe it was bile on its way up. Either way, it was bitter, and he might choke if he continued.

He *had* to continue.

"So what if I read it to you?" he asked, because stalling for time was more manageable than saying it, and his hands had started to shake. "Give me just a second." He swallowed the lump, hard like chalk and just as dry. "Here—here we go. It—it says—"

It was more than muscular and more than his nerves. It was like his bones trembled.

"It says—" It wasn't a memory that bubbled up so much as a feeling, although the images that flashed spun in cryptic revolutions like an old-timey movie. Mostly of his dad's shirt where it stretched when he tripped trying to grab it, his hands and knees skidding on gravel.

"It says—" It said all kinds of things. It said, *I'm sorry* and *What did I do wrong?* It said *Please don't leave.*

"It says—" It said awful things. Things like *Be more.* Be more and more and more until someday, he'd have so much that his dad would be sorry he left.

"I—" It said things that weren't true. Things that weren't real. Things like *He'll hate you. He'll leave you.* He'd have so much one day that no one would ever leave him again.

He fell to his knees because standing was too much, just like the saliva that flooded his mouth was too watery, but he swallowed. He swallowed that and the lump and the cold blue eyes that matched his own and all of it. None of it was real. What was real was right here, and he wouldn't choke. He didn't need to be more for Daniel to stay. What was real was right here.

When he found his words again for the first time in twelve years, he found them patiently waiting for this moment. This second. When no other words would do.

"I love you."

Chapter Twenty-Seven

DANIEL CRUMPLED to his knees too. To meet him where he was on the old hardwoods that didn't judge how tattered they were as he gripped Aaron's face, locking their gazes long enough and in enough silence for it to feel vibrational. Like he could *see* the space between them, defying physics. Like the molecules couldn't compete with how close they needed to be, so they just disappeared.

"May I see it?" he whispered. "The ring. May I see it?"

Aaron stared for a moment longer, then blinked himself into motion. The metal, warm and heavy in his palm, felt different as he held it up, twisting it around in the light.

I love you. That was all the tiny inscription said. Written simply in a basic block font, it wasn't fancy or wordy. *I love you.* It looked naked, even. Like something was missing.

But nothing was missing.

He smoothed a thumb over the tiny words as his vision blurred with tears. To Aaron, writing those three words inside a ring was like writing the rights to his soul. To Aaron, they were the most complicated three words to ever exist, and saying them meant more to him than most people could imagine. And yet he'd gone out of his way to make sure they were written. That they were at least spoken somewhere, even if it couldn't be from his tongue.

The speckled flakes of icy blue that floated in Aaron's eyes could tempt even the holiest of men to shed his skin, soften his resolve, and wade into their waters. No one else had eyes like that—a watercolor palette of frost, cobalt, and aquamarine, dense with pain and wild enough to look animated.

Behind them was a person so complex and beautiful that Daniel could spend a lifetime just learning more.

He crawled into Aaron's lap, threading his arms around his shoulders. "Put the ring back on."

The watercolor palette sparkled with fire, and Aaron's whole being suddenly buzzed, like a million blinking fireflies.

"Put it back on." Daniel nodded. "I won't take it off again."

"Daniel Alexander Greene." Aaron's fingertips shook as he unlooped Daniel's arms from around his shoulders to squeeze his hands. "Will you marry me?"

"Yes." He wrinkled his nose and wiped at one merry little tear as Aaron slid the ring on his finger. "God, duh."

Aaron chuckled. "Can I kiss you?"

"Mr. Silva, do not go losin' your bite. You didn't even ask permission before you knew my name." He lowered his voice and whispered into Aaron's mouth, "Don't start now."

They ignited where their lips met, hyped and hungry with exploration like they'd never tasted something so stirring. Like they couldn't wait. Like it wasn't blocks and blocks of running to get home where the institution of an apartment had transformed back into a home. The lights softer, hued in yellows, welcoming them into their bed where they undressed. Where they unraveled, the skin of Aaron's bare chest hot beneath his fingertips.

"Can you say it?" Daniel fanned a sheet over them.

Aaron nodded. "I. I. L-l-love you."

"You sure can," he whispered, through a silly attempt to buffer some of the tears with his brow tensed and smile uncontrollable. He combed his hands through Aaron's hair and kissed him over and over. "Can you say it again?"

Aaron cleared his throat. "I. L-love you, Daniel."

"Say it again."

"I l-love you."

"Again."

"I love you."

He asked and asked, and Aaron repeated until it poured from his lips through a proud and effortless smile. Tears wet his beautiful eyes and both of their faces—oh, who knew whose tears they were as the sheets cocooned around them, as comforting as the words they spoke.

Promises of hope in austerity, faith in disorder, and humor during chaos.

Promises of a bold creed: No. More. Mistakes. Then, okay, maybe patience for mistakes. Then, dammit, maybe grace for those mistakes made on purpose.

Promises of fully there and forever-with-you. "That you'll have your *space*, that I'll be so *present*."

Promises of carnal pleasure and take-what-you-need. "What's mine is yours, every inch of me, have it. Own my body, my mouth, my inside, my out."

Promises all made just in time for the amber rays of a new day to coax them from the tangle of each other's arms, from the tender little contracts spoken in a twilight of sleep and dreamlike kisses.

Promises all made in earnest, raw with imperfections. All real. All unified by three simple words.

"Say it again."

Epilogue

"FIFTEEN MINUTES," Daniel said. "Are you ready?"

Aaron glanced up from the eucalyptus leaves he'd been arranging around a vase on his consultation desk just in time to see his fiancé's giddy little shoulder shimmy while he blew up balloon number... sixteen? Seventeen? Whatever number he was on, it was too many. They didn't need that many balloons, just like they didn't need the chocolate "scones" Daniel had gotten up early to "bake." The ones that resembled something one might find in a clogged drain.

"Are you ready for the big grand soft opening of Silva Interiors?" Daniel squealed as he tied off the balloon. "I just like saying it. Silva Interiors. So fucking *licensed*."

"We've been over this." Aaron smirked as he twisted the vase around to inspect it from all sides. "Saying 'grand soft' is contradictory. It's just soft; the soft opening. It's literally only people we know."

"Aaron, I need you to look at me." Daniel leaned his palms onto the desk. "Look into my eyeballs."

He peered up, grinning as he met Daniel's gaze. "Yes, sweetheart?"

"Just because something occasionally has to be *soft* does not mean it's not still grand."

"Ahh." Aaron nodded. "Reference to my dick, then?"

"Grand." Daniel inhaled, fanning himself, as embellished as ever. "God, *so* grand, Aaron-nuh. Even when it's soft."

Aaron chuckled as the front door cracked open and Olivia stepped through, cradling a magnum bottle of champagne in her arms and toting a huge balloon shaped like the same magnum bottle of champagne.

"Good golly, Miss Salvador Dali. Look at this!" She popped her sunglasses to her head, her wide eyes drifting around the little four-hundred-square-foot space in wonder. "I haven't seen it since you finished it. You guys. This is incredible."

Aaron pursed his lips, but he couldn't hide his smile, and he sure as hell couldn't fake humility. With the walls draped in an Oxford blue Lincrusta, boldly veined houseplants poised on every surface, and the furniture *just right*, it did look incredible. It looked goddamn spectacular.

"Isn't he brilliant?" Daniel skipped over and pushed up to his toes to peck Aaron's cheek. "He's been working nonstop for months. He deserves this."

Aaron locked eyes with Daniel just in time to see the admiration in them, but the credit was hardly all his. They'd *both* worked nonstop for months. It'd been a journey to get here. Well, *journey* implied an arduous road. It was a road marked with a lot of changes—mostly simple budgeting but some major downsizing. They moved out of Aaron's plush apartment and into a more affordable bungalow on the south side of the city, which had—deep breaths—carpeting in the bathroom. (Carpeting. In the fucking bathroom.) But none of it was painful like he expected. In fact, it was sort of… magical.

It was all the extra time he got to pour into his sweet little troublemaker, holed up but hopeful inside their teeny home, where they ate leftovers in bed, made love next to a wood-burning fireplace (because Daniel insisted, not because it functioned), and planned their wedding—now only two months away. Daniel had supported him in every possible way as he finished design school—both practically and emotionally, picking up last-minute posterboard and letting Aaron spiral about what-ifs. But shockingly, he'd also supported them financially.

It was mind-blowing watching his nervy little fiancé transform into such a boss. They both assumed he'd succeed, but nothing could've prepared them for how well. For how dramatically he was going to kill it.

Daniel was fucking *killing it*.

Not only had he increased his class sizes by 24 percent since he took over, but he'd upgraded the online booking system and hired four new instructors. He also extended his reach into two senior centers, which were both tickled pink that someone wanted to come teach sexy tap numbers set to cabaret songs. He even managed his team well, ruling with intuition, grace, and this empathetic yet firm hand that had people eager to learn from him, to be around him, to please him.

Aaron was no different. It was hot banging the boss.

He covertly smacked Daniel's ass, making him yelp as he scurried back to his balloon station, twisting over his shoulder to offer a pretty little pout. *Dazzling.*

"Is your mom coming?" Olivia asked as she unwrapped the foil from the champagne.

Daniel snorted. "Silly, silly girl. You think *my mother* would miss Aaron's big grand soft opening?"

"You just need to say soft, baby," Aaron said as he angled the settee a few inches to the left. "It doesn't need the *grand*."

"She wouldn't miss it in a million years." Daniel began blowing up a pearly pink balloon, which didn't work with the aesthetic, but who had the heart to tell him? "She said she bought matching pantsuits for her and Butchie, which—not gonna lie—is a little concerning." He puffed the balloon bigger. "And what's worse is she mentioned a pantsuit *theme*." Even bigger. "Like, what the hell does that mean? I'm a tad worried it'll involve way too much blended polyester for one middle-aged couple."

Aaron had crouched down to snag an errant rubber band from behind the sofa as Daniel trailed off. When he stood back up, Daniel and Olivia were both staring with their mouths hanging open at the young man poking his head through the front door.

"Hello," the guy said, a wide smile splitting his face as he ripped off his sunglasses. "I need a new toilet-paper holder. Is this place open?"

Aaron's heart thumped in his chest as he blinked a few times to ensure it was real. His little brother was here. Andrew. Was *here*.

"Andrew!" Aaron rushed to him, barreling into his body to grip him into a hug. "Holy shit—*what*? What are you doing here?"

"That's the thing about airplanes," Andrew grunted as Aaron squeezed him tighter. "They can go anywhere."

Aaron released the hug to hold his shoulders and study him. With Andrew's flight schedule and Aaron's schooling, it'd been over a year since they'd had a chance to see each other. Andrew had filled out a bit more—biceps for days—and his style had gotten snappier. He wore selvedge jeans, a crisp blue blazer, and tobacco leather boots. Long gone were the days of the skinny little boy with the unkempt hair and Jolly Ranchers stuffed into his pockets. He was all grown up.

"God, it's good to see you," Aaron said, scanning him to make sure he was indeed unmarred. "You doing okay? You need anything? What do you need?"

"I don't need anything, man," Andrew said, his smile so pure. "Life is good. Just came to see you."

They both had their dad's eyes, although Andrew's had never gotten jaded. *He* had never gotten jaded. All Aaron had ever wanted was for him to be safe, but he was better than safe. With every year that passed, he was thriving more and more. Happy.

"I've been in cahoots with your fiancé to surprise you. Come on now." Andrew slapped his arm. "I wouldn't miss your big grand opening."

"It's the soft—" Aaron shook his head, too grateful to argue. "So glad you're here."

"Geez, look at this place." Andrew drew a long inhale as he gazed around. "You've always been talented, but this. *This* is next-level."

Yeah, there was a big chance Aaron's entire career would be next-level. Who would've thought having all those connections with all those wealthy men would jumpstart his business the way it had? He and Daniel liked to call it the *ultimate repurposing*. Old clients got an updated kind of service.

"Dude, I'm just—" Andrew whirled around to grip him into another hug. He whispered, "I'm *so* proud of you."

Aaron had to breathe as he folded his arms around his brother. In a lifetime spent trying to keep him safe, he'd never expected that one day he might also make him proud. *Proud* hit deeply enough for his eyes to prickle. "Thank you."

"And this must be Daniel." Andrew grinned as he stepped around Aaron to extend his arms toward Daniel. "I feel like I already know you, but it's so nice to finally meet you in person."

Daniel blinked, his whole body still as a long, lumbering silence ensued.

"Um." Andrew flashed a glance back at Aaron, then outstretched his arms again. "Really, *really* nice. Bring it in."

Aaron tilted his head at his frozen fiancé. "Ahh, so he probably needs a minute. Yep, give him a sec. This is how he was when I first met him."

Daniel's lips parted like he might finally say something when the balloon stole his glory. It slipped from his fingers and farted about the room in little loop-de-loops until it flumped onto the desk. Aaron snorted a chuckle while Daniel blinked double-time like he was orienting himself back to this earthly plane.

"Oh. S-sorry about that, everyone." Daniel cleared his throat and smoothed the fabric of his shirt. "Apologies for my, uh... stuckness. I don't think I was expecting the two of you to look so—what's the word?—fraternal. Fraternal as fuck."

Aaron chuckled harder as he smeared a hand over his face.

"And you're both right in front of my face, aren't you? Practically twins." Daniel blew out his breath as he perched his hands on his hips. "Sure is a lot! S'a lot for me."

"Hug the man, Daniel," Aaron said, nodding gently. "He's trying to give you a hug."

"Right! Yes, of course. Here I go." Daniel shuffled forward and lightly hugged Andrew, then swiftly pulled away. "Nice to meet you, Andrew. But I am happily engaged to your brother."

Andrew opened his mouth to speak, then closed it, his face scrunching in confusion.

"And I'm Olivia," Olivia announced in a voice about four octaves too low, suddenly wedged between Andrew and Daniel in the stealthiest, most hare-footed maneuvering possible. "Might I interest you in some champagne, Andrew?"

"Oh." Andrew blinked at her. "Hi. Olivia, was it?"

"Indeed." Still too low. And her eyes had this feral bird-of-prey look. "Champagne?"

Andrew's brow line lifted as his gaze darted around between the three of them. He eventually shrugged. "Sure, I guess I could go for some."

Olivia's smile was saccharine as she slid her arm under Andrew's elbow. "Right this way, then."

Daniel coughed under his breath, "Please behave."

She whipped around to hiss in a harsh whisper, "You shut your bitch-bag mouth, Daniel!"

Daniel flinched as she thrust a finger toward Aaron.

"You go home to *that* every night! So, a pilot, hmm?" she asked, twisting back to Andrew and adopting a syrupy tone as she guided him toward the booze. "So airy. Speaking of, how would you like to get some later? Air, that is?"

"Oh dear," Daniel whispered once they meandered away, wincing as he tapped his fingertips together. "He'll be okay, right? My fear is that she's in heat. It could get kind of dicey for him—"

"Come here." Aaron nabbed Daniel's wrist and led him toward the back room, a cross between an office and a storage closet, where he shut the curtain behind them and cupped Daniel's face in his palms. "I needed a minute alone with you before everyone got here."

One of Daniel's eyebrows arched. "To...?"

"Tell you how much I love you."

Daniel smiled as he tossed his gaze upward, his teeth scraping over his lower lip. "See, this is what no one sees. Everyone thinks I'm the squishy one, but *you're* the squishy one." He poked Aaron in the stomach. "Underneath all this muscley business, you're just a big ol' squish, Aaron Silva—"

He whirled Daniel around and wrapped him in a hug from behind. He'd gotten efficient at that move, and plus, with his face buried in the crook of Daniel's neck, he could properly huff the orange sherbet. Like a weirdo. "It's true," he said, his words muffled as he inhaled Daniel's skin. "I'm a closeted squish."

Daniel giggled while they swayed side to side, while they beheld the view of Silva Interiors through a slit in the curtain. Yes, there were far too many balloons scattered and Olivia was currently hitting on Aaron's brother, but it was also where their friends and family would soon gather to warmly honor him. To honor *them*.

The picture before him was a real-life vision board, and the creature in his arms had been responsible for gluing down all the pieces.

"Thank you, kid," Aaron whispered, his lips grazing Daniel's ear. "God, thank you, thank you, thank you."

Daniel shook his head, amusement waxing in his tone. "Stop thanking me. You've done all the work."

"But you've been the thing." He rested his cheek against Daniel's, clutching him tighter. "The precious thing that's made all the work worth it."

Daniel hummed, so low and satisfied it was almost a moan as he rubbed Aaron's arm.

"I don't deserve the most precious thing in the world." Aaron rocked them in a sweet, anchoring rhythm as he smiled at his vision board of a life. "But here you are in my arms."

Side to side, they rocked. Back and forth. To and fro. Over and over. Daniel welded into his lead beautifully. Or maybe he'd been the leader all along. Either way, they swished and swayed until it was time to end the final dance to the last chapter.

"I love you too, mister." To seal the last chapter with a kiss. "I love you too."

Right before they started the next.

Keep reading for an excerpt from
Cross My Heart
By Darcy Archer.

Chapter One

TYLER FANTANA slammed into the dirt, and a meteor hit his chest with scalding force. His heart had stopped beating. Sixty-nine thousand fans shouting, the smell of sweat and grass. Blinding lights, all the cameras.

Groggy, Tyler blinked and shook his head slowly, trying to situate himself.

He flinched. This had happened before, he felt certain. Why did he feel so disoriented?

Right. NFL game at the top of the season, the pinnacle of his career with the San Diego Swells. A pile of guys on top of him.

Suddenly he was back on the ground, blood in his mouth, skull echoing with the impact of the tackle that had brought him down, an entire linebacker landing on his sternum and the sudden crushing pain in his chest as he hit the thirty-yard line sideways and knew in his bones that he'd never get up again in this life.

Team gone. Light gone. Not breathing. Just that jagged, grinding agony like a fist squeezing him into paste.

I already did this. Oh God, please, I already did this.

The world had winked out, only fading back into focus as he woke up in the back of an ambulance, his heart pounding erratically as he gasped for breath and grabbed at the EMTs.

"Tyler?"

Dr. Reynolds's question yanked him back to the present. The older woman's voice was firm, professional, and had a no-nonsense edge to it. "Talk to me. Slow breaths. What happened just then?"

He tried to take deep, slow gulps of oxygen. Counted heartbeats. Visualized. All that holistic new age crap. His stupid, screwed-up heart wouldn't slow down. Where was he? He couldn't get enough breath to answer her. Why couldn't he talk? His eyes stung, and he blinked rapidly. "Bad."

Dr. Reynolds's office smelled of lemony antiseptic. It was autumn. November. Tuesday? This was another checkup with his cardiologist. His sister had driven him. He still wasn't allowed behind the wheel. Right. Was Nadia here?

"Stay with me now." Reynolds stood back, giving him space. "Are you all right? Can you describe the pain? Look at me." She leaned back and ran a penlight over his pupils, frowning at something. "Your heart rate was— Does that happen often?"

"Maybe." He shook his head, then nodded. Did she want the truth or the lie? "I don't know."

"I was taking your vitals," Dr. Reynolds said briskly. "Use your three-three-three and breathe for me. Take a moment. Three objects. Three sounds. Three body parts."

Tyler nodded and tried to focus. He found the objects as he inhaled slowly and shifted his eyes around the bright room, consciously counting each one: Clock. Pen. Shoe. This was so embarrassing.

"I'm going to remove this, if that's okay." She leaned in to unwrap the blood pressure cuff from his thick bicep with practiced efficiency.

Velcro rip. Hum of the AC. Paper rustling under him. He held the breath inside himself, and his galloping heart slowed to a trot.

As the cuff loosened, she unthreaded it and stepped back again, presumably to give him space. She glanced over his chart, and her brow furrowed in obvious disapproval.

His muscle mass was way off, whittled down by two months of sitting on his butt.

As she paused to make a note, he made his body parts move: open hand, lick lips, blink eyes. He let the breath out. "Better."

"Excellent. You see?" Reynolds checked his eyes, waiting until he nodded to continue. She pressed a chilly stethoscope between his pecs and looked at the ceiling, listening for something inside him before she spoke. "Just a panic attack, yes? That's common. Nasty but normal."

"It felt like—" He shook his head, wiped his wet mouth. "How do I tell the difference?"

"You ask someone qualified." Dr. Reynolds crossed her arms. "But anecdotally, cardiac arrest feels like crushing and panic attacks sharper stabs. With arrest, the pain spreads outward from the chest, but the pain of a panic attack stays in one spot. Neither one is pleasant." Her stethoscope shifted to his back, and the slight pressure made him flinch like an idiot. "Try to distinguish between the memory of pain and your current level of discomfort. It's not easy."

"No." Tyler took a few more deep breaths and let the air out slowly. "These were short and sharp. Memory, I guess." He pressed a hand to his side. "Jesus."

"Talk to yourself. Listen to yourself." She pressed her lips together, regarding him as though through glass. "Blood pressure is still higher than I'd like," she noted. "And you've lost almost four pounds of muscle since our last visit. Potassium levels far lower than they should be. Iron too. Your recovery seems to have plateaued."

"Sorry, Doc." Tyler sat awkwardly, perched on the exam table, cringing as the paper liner crinkled beneath him.

"This isn't blame." She shook her head. "Your heart has been pushed past breaking, Mr. Fantana. Commotio cordis can cause severe trauma to the valve and surrounding tissues. It needs to heal. Just a time-out is all. A reasonable recovery window. You're better, but not better enough."

He nodded and waited for further scolding.

"The heart is a powerful muscle. You had significant bruising and other injuries besides. It's barely been two months. One moment." Dr. Reynolds picked up the phone and pressed a button. "Can you have Ms. Fantana come back to exam room five?"

Great. Now Nadia was going to get scolded too.

"Tyler, your sister needs to be aware. Team effort, right? Hang on. I'll be right back."

With a smiling nod, Reynolds left him sitting there feeling like a jerk. The door closed behind her with a hiss and clunk. The memory of his primetime collapse still swirled around him, almost visible, tangible around him, the exam room like a double exposure he could touch and taste. He stared at the speckled linoleum floor.

A tap on the door. "Hey, big bro. Everything okay?"

He turned to look and raised his voice so she'd hear. "Panic attack. Stupid."

Nadia poked her head in. "Okay if I come in?"

"Doctor's orders." Tyler shrugged. "I think she wants to do more scolding than one dummy can handle, so you get some too."

"Stop worrying, Ty," she said, reaching out to place a hand on his knee, stilling the judder. "It's just a checkup."

"I guess." Tyler sighed, running a hand through his shaggy hair. He couldn't help but feel vulnerable, stripped of his armor. He'd been an MVP his whole life, and now… this. "I think she went to pull the labs."

Tyler sat hunched, foot tapping an anxious beat. With each passing second, his eyes darted between the ticking clock and the closed door to the hall. The sterile peach walls and vague watercolor prints did nothing to soothe his nerves. Beside him, Nadia fidgeted with the strap of her purse, watching him less like a little sister and more like an anxious mom.

As they waited, Nadia tried to distract him with a silly story about Mr. Poops, a lazy marmalade cat that had wandered into her garage last year and decided her home was his, but Tyler's mind was back on a stadium field a thousand miles away with his teammates.

Grass. Mud. Tackle. Agony. A stadium full of strangers and millions of screens across the country, all roaring for blood.

"Thank you," Dr. Reynolds said to someone, then stepped back inside, flicking through a sheaf of pages. "Mr. Fantana?"

"Guilty." Tyler straightened, shooting his sister a tense smile.

"Sorry about that. I asked your sister to join us because we all want the same thing."

"Absolutely." Nadia squinted, brave-facing it.

"You aren't getting better." Reynolds crossed her arms over her white coat and squinted at him kindly. "Trouble is, you know everything that I'm going to say to you. They punched you in the heart. You're still a world-class athlete inside there, but your body and your mind need to heal."

"I understand, ma'am." He nodded, but the thought of doing anything more than what he was already managing seemed impossible. Hell, he had a worthless degree in sports medicine, and he still couldn't get his ass in gear.

She wasn't done. "I've told you before: you need to eat healthier, exercise more, and for heaven's sake, do something about your stress levels. The memories will prey upon you if you don't process them."

Tyler swallowed hard, feeling the weight of her words press down on him. How could he make her understand the nightmares and the panic attacks? It sounded stupid and melodramatic to him, and he saw them up close and personal every day of his life since the accident.

Nadia watched him take the scolding, her eyes full of awful pity.

"I've been trying, Dr. Reynolds," he protested weakly. "But it's not easy. Not when I'm… like this." He looked down at his boxer briefs, his grayish skin, his infamous muscle mass now tasked with hauling him from the bed to the couch and back. He felt like a wrecked car on cinder blocks.

"Mr. Fantana, this isn't the end, just a change. Six months ago, you were one of the fittest athletes in the world, but you are not twenty anymore. Or even thirty," she admitted. Her fierce scrutiny made him feel raw and scalded. "Your heart may have taken a hit, but it's not irreparable. You need to take responsibility for your own well-being."

"Responsibility? You think I don't—" Tyler began, anger bubbling up inside him before he caught himself, clamping down. He couldn't afford to let his rage get the best of him. Not now, when everything was so precarious.

"We can get you whatever you need, Mr. Fantana." Dr. Reynolds didn't look away. "Give yourself time."

"Time." He gave an ugly laugh as her words sent him spiraling back into that mud and pain and the game that had stopped his entire career stone-cold.

"I say the same thing, Doc." Nadia squeezed his hand, reminding him where he was. "But he's so much better than he was. Every day, he's better."

"Tyler," Dr. Reynolds said, her tone cautious, "we both want the same thing: for you to heal. But I can only do so much. The rest is up to you." She tapped his chart and raised her brows. "Your muscle tone, your blood pressure, even your oxygen levels are still way beyond normal levels for an average man your age, and the whole country knows that you are much more than average."

He bobbed his head but couldn't look her in the eye. "Yes, ma'am." He did know better.

"Your diet is critical. Lay off the starches and dairy fat. Start incorporating lean proteins and fresh produce. No soda, no snacking. Stretch!" She raised both hands in exasperation. "Again, you know all this. And you must, and I mean today if at all possible, start exercising regularly. Even just walking twenty minutes a day will make a big difference. Looking good is not enough. Get yourself moving again. Blood flow. You still have your drive, your competitive oomph."

He tried to focus on Dr. Reynolds's words as she scolded him, shamed him, but he wanted to run.

"All right," he muttered, his voice barely audible. "If it kills me, I'll try harder." Tyler clenched his fists, his clammy legs sticking to the paper under him.

"Not harder. Smarter," she emphasized, tapping a pen against her clipboard. "No killing. And light exercise. All of you. Not just your body, but your mind too. Therapy. To talk through this process. You need both to heal."

"He will. He is," Nadia said.

"Uh, yeah," he replied, rubbing the back of his neck, feeling the heaviness of stagnation and regret like a lead weight in his chest. He'd never seen a therapist in his life. "Therapy and exercise. Got it."

"Good." Dr. Reynolds gave him a stern look, her eyes drilling into him. "You need to take this seriously, Tyler. Your life depends on it."

"Understood." He swallowed hard, feeling her words more than he heard them. It wasn't like he didn't understand the severity of his situation. But it was harder than he'd anticipated to come to terms with the fact that his body, which had once been a well-oiled tackle machine, had betrayed him so completely. And now he needed to confront that reality, to face the fact that he couldn't outrun his own mortality.

"Okay," he said finally, meeting her gaze. Even the suggestion of therapy was a hard pill to swallow. "I'll do it. I'll take responsibility for my health."

Nadia nodded. "We got this, Ty."

"Excellent," Reynolds repeated as she looked back up. "We have faith in you, Tyler. And I know you can do this."

"Thank you," he whispered, his voice thick with misery.

"Good," she replied, giving him a curt nod. "Your team doctors will receive my report by Thursday. The Swells care a lot about you."

He didn't answer that. The team docs were nice enough, but he knew who paid their bills and why. He was already past his prime, and plenty knew it. The coaches had more complaints each year. The owners ragged him about his endorsements and his rowdy rep. The San Diego Swells cared about his cost and his stats. Keeping him healthy was money to them. Boris Jarlson wanted to squeeze as many seasons out of him as possible before tossing him on the heap.

Dr. Reynolds looked him over again, making him feel like a rump roast. "I know you can get back to top form, Tyler. You can play again, win again. But you need to put in the hard work. If you'll—excuse the expression—tackle this problem before it flanks you. Just take the steps. You'll get where you're going."

Tyler nodded, still avoiding her eyes. The weight of stagnation and regret settled upon his shoulders like a heavy cloak, threatening to smother him.

Dr. Reynolds opened the door and patted him on the back as he stepped through it. Nadia lingered behind to mutter something with the doctor. He didn't even have the energy to feel angry or sad, but maybe feeling stubborn would be enough.

He stepped back into the hall, and the door closed behind him. Knowing they had another long drive back to Cinnamar, he swung by the bathroom to pee and splash his face.

The real work was just beginning. He was staring down a long road to recovery, but maybe he was finally ready to tackle it head-on, fueled by the same determination and grit that had once propelled him to football stardom.

Back in the waiting room, he stood shifting his weight, anxious to escape.

Finally Nadia emerged, looking anxious, linking her arm through his in wordless support. With his sister's help, perhaps he could regain control.

"You good?" she whispered, her gentle touch a balm against the harsh reality of his prognosis.

The lingering scent of disinfectant filled Tyler's nostrils as he pushed through the glass door of Dr. Reynolds's building, the warm sunlight outside a stark contrast to the sterile environment behind him. He squinted against the brightness.

"That was fun, huh? Good ol' Dr. Reynolds," Nadia called out softly, her deep-set brown eyes searching his face with concern. She leaned against their car, arms crossed over her chest. "You look like you just went ten rounds with a grizzly."

Tyler snorted, despite the turmoil brewing inside him. His sister always had a way of lightening even the darkest moments without getting maudlin. "More like two rounds with a cardiologist who doesn't believe in sugarcoating."

"You can take it," she replied, a smirk tugging at the corner of her mouth, though her eyes remained worried. "She's tough, but she knows her stuff. Come on, let's get you home."

Nadia held the passenger door open for him, waiting until he eased himself into the seat before shutting it gently. She kept up a steady stream of chatter during the drive, clearly trying to distract him from spiraling into despair. He was grateful for her snarky optimism, even if he couldn't muster a response.

Instead Tyler stared out the passenger side window, watching the familiar scenery pass by without really seeing it: long stretches of late wildflowers over the valley slope. Cinnamar was about fifty miles northeast of Reynolds's office in San Diego, so the drive both ways ate up a lot of his sister's time. IT work was flexible, but she had her own life.

His mind kept drifting back to that fateful third quarter, the crowd's exhilaration, the lightning pumping through his veins, the satisfying smack of helmets, pads, and hard muscle colliding as he dodged tackles, in the zone.

Until suddenly, a blindside hit took his legs out from under him. Then muddy grass, staring at people's shins. He remembered the referee's whistles shrilly blaring as he clutched his chest, his vision spotting, fading, failing. Then waking up in the ambulance, an oxygen mask strapped to his face.

"Heart attack," he heard the EMT say, a hand touching his head gently. "Tyler Fantana, dude. Would you believe? We need to get him to the hospital stat before he codes."

Just like that, at the peak of his career, his whole life yanked from under him. Now here he was, trapped in his hometown, lying awake every night in his childhood bedroom, adrift and unsure how to climb back to the fancy life he'd wanted way back when.

Tyler snorted awake and realized he'd dozed off in the rocking car.

"Feel better?" Nadia glanced over at him, her expression sympathetic.

"Maybe." A late fall rain had covered the low hills with California poppies, asters, and purple lupine that would die fast once December hit. He shrugged.

She turned to consider him. "It's not a race, huh? You can do this. I know you can."

"Exercise. Therapy," Tyler muttered, staring out the window at the sloped landscape. He could feel the weight of his sister's vigilance, knew she was searching for any signs of weakness or self-pity.

Nadia glanced at the rearview before responding. "She's putting you on notice. This has as much to do with your mental state as your heart. And she wanted me as a witness. It's going to be okay."

"Therapy? I know I got to take responsibility for my health, Nadia. But it's... hard. My whole life I've been this invincible meathead, and now—"

"Hey," she cut him off gently, reaching over to place a comforting hand on his bulky forearm. "You're not a meathead. And you don't have to be invincible, Ty. You just have to be the best version of yourself that you can be right now—bum heart and all. You've faced worse than therapy."

"Thanks," he said, his voice barely audible over the hum of the car engine. He turned to look at her in a moment of raw vulnerability. "I just... I don't want to disappoint anyone, you know?"

"Wow. Okay... Tyler Fantana, NFL superstar, America's Tightest End, reduced to seeking validation from his little sister?" Nadia teased, though her voice was warm with old affection. "Who would've thought?"

"Hey, now," Tyler huffed, trying to muster a playful glare but ultimately failing. "Don't go getting a big head about it. Last thing I need is an even more insufferable sibling."

"Too late," she laughed, reaching over to ruffle his hair affectionately. "But seriously, Ty, you can't ever disappoint me. Or anyone who truly cares about you. We just want you to be happy and healthy, okay?"

"Okay," he agreed, his throat tight with emotion. He tried to smile, but it felt false.

As they drove through their small hometown, familiar streets and businesses whizzing past them, Tyler felt the first glimmers of determination blooming within him. The road to recovery might suck, but with Nadia by his side, he knew he had a fighting chance. And maybe, just maybe, he could find a little happiness in the process. Though the doctor's words still stung, Tyler felt a faint flicker of stubborn hope.

"Promise me something." Nadia took the exit that led to their childhood home. "Promise me you'll do whatever it takes to get better. No excuses, no half-assing it. No ditching me. Just... promise me you'll try."

"I promise," he whispered, meaning it for once. It was time to take control of his life again, to face his demons head-on and reclaim the future that had been snatched away from him on the thirty-yard line. "Full-ass only."

"Good," she said, her lips curving into a small, proud smile. "Now let's get you home and start planning your Super Bowl comeback."

"Easy for you to say," he muttered, crossing his arms over his broad chest.

The car turned on the block and then bumped onto the drive as Nadia slowed to a stop and glanced his way again.

"Stop. I'm fine. Reynolds is still a tightass, though," Tyler grumbled as he climbed out and slammed the car door with a huff. "Like I'm not trying hard enough. The panic attack rattled me, is all." He headed toward the porch. Nadia had renovated the place twice since their mom passed.

"Uhh. Yeah." Nadia caught up with him, keys jangling. "She's just worried. We all are. You've been through a lot, and it's time to get back on track. Baby steps."

"Mom always said I was a big baby. Like, the biggest ever in this town, twenty-two inches or something and eleven-plus pounds. A mutant." He grinned, but she didn't.

"Ty, listen," Nadia said, her voice gentle yet firm as she unlocked the door. "You need to take this seriously. Therapy and exercise will help you get better, on all fronts."

"Fine," he conceded. "But what if it's not enough? What if that's the last game I play? The last yardage. My legacy for all time. Eating mud on the thirty."

"Glory ain't everything, you know." Nadia knocked their shoulders together, giving him a small smile. "Mom wanted us to love our lives. That's all."

Tyler sighed, running a hand through his messy hair as he thought about their mom, gone almost nine years now. It felt like forever since he'd last truly loved his life.

A high-pitched meow as Mr. Poops trotted up and headbutted Nadia's leg. "See? Poops agrees." She scooped up the fat feline and draped him across her shoulder. "Hello. Yes, I know…. Hey, mister." Poops kept pushing his face against her ear and hair.

"All right," Tyler said, determination in his voice. "I'll do it. I'll go to therapy, I'll exercise, and I'll work on getting better—for myself, for Mom, and for the people who matter."

"Good," Nadia replied, squeezing his knee before unlocking the door and pushing inside. "I'm proud of you, Ty. You're stronger than you give yourself credit for. And I don't mean your biceps or your butt."

"Thanks, sis," he murmured, a small smile playing on his lips. Deep down, he knew she was right—he could face all this crap and come out stronger on the other side.

He left her checking the mail.

Tyler pushed open the door to his childhood bedroom, the creaking hinge a familiar sound that turned him thirteen again. The walls needed repainting, still hidden under faded posters of his favorite football players and bands, smothering him in memories of his early gridiron glory. Big fish, small pond. Old banners from childhood championships and postcards from people he didn't remember. He ran his fingers along the dusty trophies lining the shelves, reminders of a time when he was unstoppable on the field, when football was the only way he could save his life and his family.

Nadia wouldn't take his money, but at least he'd paid off the mortgage on this house. The rest of his savings was more than enough to tide him over if they killed his contract.

"Wow," Nadia said, leaning against the doorframe, cradling the cat again. "Hello, time capsule. Now I know why you've been keeping me out."

"Yeah," Tyler murmured, his hazel eyes lingering on a photo of their mother. "Feels like a lifetime ago. I've been tossing stuff, but then I lost interest." Tyler had been about twelve when their dad had finally pissed off. From that moment, his poor mom had put everything into keeping the house note paid and keeping them safe.

"Get some rest," Nadia advised softly. "We can talk more tomorrow." She left, closing the door behind her.

Alone with his thoughts, Tyler sat down on the edge of his twin bed, the springs groaning beneath his beefy frame. His glamorous NFL career now felt like a mirage.

Guilt gnawed at him as he remembered every well-wisher, every teammate, every fan he'd let down. He clenched his fists as he laid back, the frustration building inside him like a bonfire. But beneath it all, he still felt that dim glimmer of hope—the chance to rebuild himself, maybe even find happiness again.

"Mom only wanted us to care about stuff," he whispered to himself. "I've got to try, for her sake."

But sleep eluded him as he lay in the dark, his mind racing with thoughts of his past and the uncertain future that awaited him.

Restless and agitated, he finally threw off the covers and padded to the window. The night sky beckoned, stars sparkling like distant promises.

"Maybe some fresh air," he muttered. He slipped quietly out the back door and into the cool night. He knew staying with Nadia was only enabling his inertia.

Baby steps for the biggest baby.

The soft grass whispered beneath his feet as he walked, the familiar scents of the small backyard calming him: mowed grass, his mom's beloved gardenias, the tangled passionflowers covering the back fence. He gazed up at the stars, feeling small but maybe connected to something bigger than himself.

"All right, universe," Tyler whispered, his breath visible in the chilly air. "I'm going to take control of this healing crap. I'll work out, I'll eat organic broccoli, I'll even get counseling—whatever it takes to get back to the stuff I know how to do better than anyone."

His decision made, determination surged through him like an electric current. He knew the road ahead would suck, but with Nadia's support and their mother's memory just out of sight, he was ready to get in the game.

"Here's to getting better," Tyler murmured, raising his gaze to the heavens once more before turning back toward the house, a newfound sense of purpose propelling him forward.

A couple minutes later, the dim glow of Tyler's laptop lit his rough knuckles as he sat at the kitchen table, surrounded by the quiet darkness of the house. He could hear the faint ticking of an old clock on the wall, a gentle reminder that time was still moving forward, even when he felt stuck in place.

Even without having a panic attack, he used Dr. Reynolds's three-three-three trick to anchor himself where he was. Raising his eyes, he saw three things: juice, flowers, cat. He heard three things: the hum of the fridge, the hall clock, Poops purring on the sill. He moved three things: opened the laptop, patted his chest, sat down.

"All right," he whispered to himself, inhaling deeply. "Let's do this."

His oversized fingers skittered across the keyboard as he tapped out an email to a local therapist he'd found through a quick search. His hands always seemed clumsy using any kind of technology. The weight of admitting he needed help was heavy, but with each word he typed, he felt a little bit lighter.

Hi, Dr. Bailey, Tyler wrote, swallowing his pride. *My name is Tyler Fantana, and I'm interested in scheduling an appointment to discuss my current issues. I don't know if you follow football, but I've experienced a major health setback at the start of the season, and I'm not coping so great with the necessary adjustments.*

He hesitated for a moment before adding, *I want to get better, but to be honest, I don't know how to do that without some professional help.*

Before he could start messing or second-guessing, he clicked to send the email on its way. First step toward regaining some balance. His stupid heart pounded in his chest, a mixture of anxiety and hope swirling within him. He allowed himself a slight smile, proud of taking the initiative to confront his depression head-on.

Next, Tyler turned his attention to finding a place where he could begin his physical rehabilitation. He browsed through various gym websites, but he quickly realized that he couldn't just walk into any random workout studio without drawing all the wrong kinds of attention. The locals would get weird, and once the word got loose, the paparazzi would be relentless.

"Damn," he muttered under his breath. "Going out in public will just make things worse."

A small head butted his leg. Mr. Poops obviously thought a human in the kitchen meant mealtime and mandatory massage.

Tyler bent to scritch the purring cat's ears and give him one long stroke to smooth his back and up his extravagant tail. "No way, Poops. I feed you now, I'm toast come morning." Mr. Poops had been a feisty stray that just kept being cute until Nadia gave up and offered him room and board in exchange for being loud and adorable.

Though skeptical at first, Tyler had become a big fan. Poops spent a lot of nights curled up on the foot of his bed, for which he was deeply grateful. Some nights, just having another heartbeat close made all the difference.

Lost in thought, Tyler chewed on his lip as he tried to come up with a solution. He knew how badly he needed to regain his strength, but the thought of being hounded by photographers, their cameras capturing his every hiccup and falter, was unbearable.

"Maybe there's a private gym somewhere," he mused, fingers tapping restlessly on the table. "Or a trainer who can come to the house." Mr. Poops hopped into his lap, stalked in a circle, then settled down to nap while Tyler googled and growled at the screen.

Money was no problem, but privacy was something else entirely. He continued his search for someplace close enough to use often, growing more frustrated by the minute as he scrolled through endless listings that wouldn't suit his odd situation.

"Come on, there has to be something," Tyler whispered to himself, determination refusing to let him give up. As he browsed, he absentmindedly stroked the dozing cat.

To be fair, he'd started his physical rehab and occupational therapy in San Diego five weeks ago, until the team's primary PT had leaked a story and pictures of his big naked butt to TMZ for fifty grand. The pictures didn't bug him all that much, but the "insider" gossip made him sound like a grouchy basket case with a sex addiction. The team had clamped down swiftly, but the press proceeded to lose their minds with theories and predictions based on nothing.

The Swells owners had apologized and groveled, but Tyler wasn't having it. He'd put his foot down: no more NFL leeches, no more leaks, no more Mr. Nice Patient. Apart from cardiac oversight from Reynolds, he'd do his recovering in Cinnamar. With that much egg on their face, the Swells didn't have much choice.

Trouble was, organizing discreet treatment and physical rehab out here in Never-Heard-of-It, California, was almost impossible.

As the first hint of dawn filtered through the curtains, Tyler's eyes remained glued to his laptop, his fingers clattering on the keyboard to suss out a solution. He rubbed his weary eyes, but he refused to give up.

The soft creak of the kitchen door caught his attention, and Nadia shuffled in wearing her favorite fuzzy socks and yawning behind a hand. The cat hopped down to greet her with a hopeful yowl. Nadia's gaze fell on Tyler, and she made a grim face.

"Tyler, tell me you have not been up all night flipping out," she said, her voice tinged with worry. "You should have woken me."

"Couldn't rest, stay still," he admitted, running a hand through his unkempt hair. "I been trying to figure out this workout situation. Sounds dumb, but I'm not just some guy when I go to a gym, so I need a PT clinic or a club where there's no cameras allowed."

"Oh. Oh shit. Yeah. I didn't even consider—" Nadia leaned against the counter, studying him for a moment before completing the thought. "You know, there might be another option," she said, her words slow and thoughtful. "What if you went back to our old high school and asked if you could use their gym and track after hours? It'd be private, and if paparazzi hassle the kids, the sheriff will throw 'em in jail."

"Hey. Hey!" A wide grin spread across Tyler's face. He closed the laptop, pushed it aside, and stood up from the table, his eyes wide. "Nadia, you're a genius!" He swept her up in a bear hug that lifted her off her feet and shook her until she giggled.

"Hey, easy there, mister!" she laughed, playfully swatting at his arm. "I'm just trying to help."

"So you did," he assured her, setting her down gently. "This may be exactly what I need. Thank you." For the first time in months, he felt right about something. Confident. Baby steps.

"Hey, no problem." Nadia smiled wide. Mr. Poops made a plaintive, pitiful sound at her shins. "Now, how about some breakfast, huh? You look like you could use some fuel."

"Deal," Tyler agreed. "As a reward for your brilliant idea, I'm making you a huge spread. Flapjacks, eggs, bacon, the works!" Even that felt like a step. Getting off his ass. Participating in the world.

Nadia laughed. "You don't have to do that."

"I want to," Tyler insisted, already gathering necessaries from the fridge, pantry, and cabinets. "It's the least I can do. And I'll even clean up when we're done!"

"Wow, and next thing pigs fly," Nadia teased, her laughter filling the kitchen. "I need to feed Mr. Poops."

As Tyler bumped around the kitchen, he couldn't help but feel grateful for his sister's unwavering support. Her offhanded suggestion had given him something to strive for, a concrete goal that could help him take back control of his life.

"How about this?" Nadia broke through Tyler's thoughts by rattling the canister of cat food like a maraca. "Maybe you should stop by the school this morning and see if it's possible. No time like the present, right?"

"Right." Tyler nodded, flipping pancakes with a casual dexterity that surprised even him. For the first time in a long while, he felt motivated. "I will. Right after breakfast."

"Mom would be really happy to see you being so brave, getting back up," Nadia said gently, as if reading his mind. "She only wanted you to be happy, Ty. However you make that happen."

"First, though," he added with a grin, "I got to get my ass back to high school."

TESSA HATFIELD, a metro-St. Louis native, discovered her love of writing on a whim that has never ebbed. She writes gushing yet playful romantic comedy with lovingly flawed characters, pulling inspiration from her former life as a professional dancer, her years spent as a wild Mizzou Tiger, and her love for creating art grounded in imperfect human reality. She is the recent winner of the Best Banter Contest for the Michigan Romance Writers, as banter is the crème fraîche of life and her personal love language.

When she isn't crying over her laptop in a coffee shop (which is totally healthy) or smothering her sweet baby boys in kisses (which is always), she can be found working out aggression in Latin dance classes in majestic Colorado, where she lives with her husband and three children.

Website: tessamhatfield.com

Twitter: x.com/TessaMHatfield

Instagram: instagram.com/tessamhatfieldwrites

Follow me on BookBub

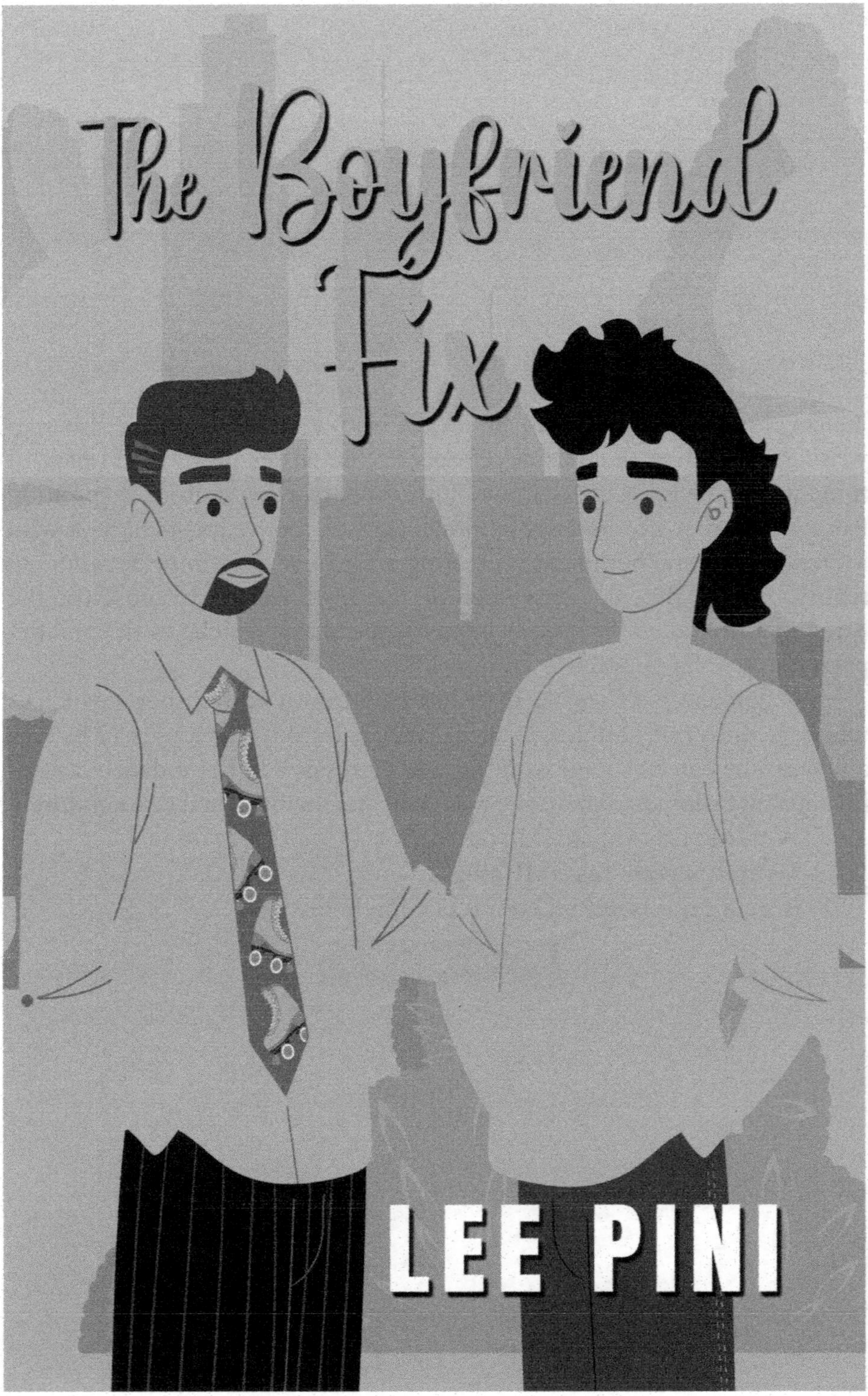
The Boyfriend Fix
LEE PINI

Renowned surgeon Ben McNatt is up for the job of his dreams, and when he gets it, he'll be the youngest chief of neurosurgery in his hospital's history. His success rate is flawless, but his perceived lack of compassion is hurting his chances. He's always viewed relationships as a distraction, but a loving partner might change his colleagues' ideas about his heartlessness. He'll do whatever it takes for this promotion—even pretend to date. The natural choice for his fake boyfriend is the cute guy at the coffee shop.

Jamie Anderson is in student loan debt up to his eyeballs. He has three roommates, and not in a quirky found-family way. He works sixty hours a week as a barista, and his boss won't stop hitting on him. He's even given up on love. He makes do with fantasies about the hot doctor that comes in for coffee every day like clockwork.

A fake relationship might solve Jamie's handsy boss problem too. And there's no way it will lead to real feelings when that's the last thing either of them wants.

So why are they having so much trouble convincing themselves they aren't falling for each other?

SCAN THE QR CODE
BELOW TO ORDER!

Treading Water

*WHAT HAPPENS
WHEN LOVE IS SINK
OR SWIM?*

ALEX WINTERS

Actor Tucker Crawford is having the worst summer ever. Thanks to a viral video of him trying to swim, he's the laughingstock of Hollywood and his role in a hit TV series is in jeopardy. The only bright spot is Tucker's sexy new swim coach, Reed Oliver, but even that has its problems—because Tucker is deep in the closet and has never been with a guy.

Reed Oliver is having the best summer ever. He's just scored a high-paying freelance gig teaching a Hollywood actor how to swim. The two of them have the run of a deserted summer camp, complete with an Olympic-size swimming pool. But when cocky playboy Reed meets shy, virgin Tucker, sparks fly and Reed's walk-in-the-park coaching job becomes a minefield of temptation. Once they kiss for the first time, there's no way to overcome their mutual passion and no looking back. But after two weeks of secluded intimacy, can they keep their romance alive in the real world?

SCAN THE QR CODE
BELOW TO ORDER!

ONLY
THE
BRIGHTEST
STARS

ANDREW
GREY

The problem with being an actor on top of the world is that you have a long way to fall.

Logan Steele is miserable. Hollywood life is dragging him down. Drugs, men, and booze are all too easy. Pulling himself out of his self-destructive spiral, not so much.

Brit Stimple does whatever he can to pay the bills. Right now that means editing porn. But Brit knows he has the talent to make it big, and he gets his break one night when Logan sees him perform on stage.

When Logan arranges for an opportunity for Brit to prove his talent, Brit's whole life turns around. Brit's talent shines brightly for all to see, and he brings joy and love to Logan's life and stability to his out-of-control lifestyle. Unfortunately, not everyone is happy for Logan, and as Brit's star rises, Logan's demons marshal forces to try to tear the new lovers apart.

SCAN THE QR CODE
BELOW TO ORDER!

DESTINED

JAMIE FESSENDEN

When Jay and Wallace first meet at an LGBTQ group, they have no idea they'll be dating six years later. In fact, they quickly forget each other's names. But although fate continues to throw them together, the timing is never quite right. Finally they're both single and realize they want to be together... but now they can't find each other!

With determination and the help of mutual friends, Jay and Wallace can finally pursue the relationship they've both wanted for so long. It's only the beginning of the battles they'll face to build a life together. From disapproving family members all the way to the state legislature, Jay and Wallace's road to happily ever after is littered with obstacles. But they've come too far to give up the fight.

SCAN THE QR CODE
BELOW TO ORDER!

A Second-Chance Romance from Best-Selling Author

BRU BAKER

ONE NIGHT
IN DALLAS

"Likable characters and offbeat humor." — Publishers Weekly

Over a decade ago, Avery Laniston fell in love with his brother Bran's best friend but walked out on him and married his career instead. He's regretted it ever since. After twelve years abroad, he returns for Bran's wedding, hoping to make amends—only to get stranded in an airport with the man he left behind.

When Paul Gladwell finds himself stuck in Dallas with Avery on the way to Bran's wedding, he decides a one-night stand might be the ticket to closure. Instead it rekindles a spark that threatens to burn him a second time. The romantic atmosphere at the wedding venue doesn't help, nor does scheming from their friends and family. But the worst culprit is Paul's heart, which refuses to listen to his head's warning that Avery hasn't changed.

Avery knows he hurt Paul before, and he's determined to make it right. But he doesn't know where his next job might take him, and Paul is hesitant to trust him again. Can Avery prove he'll be the partner Paul deserves—that he can balance his career and his personal life? Or will he add one night in Dallas to his years of regrets?

SCAN THE QR CODE
BELOW TO ORDER!